A Prisoner
in Malta

ALSO BY PHILLIP DePOY

THE CHRISTOPHER MARLOWE SERIES

A Prisoner in Malta

THE FEVER DEVILIN SERIES

The Devil's Hearth

The Witch's Grave

A Minister's Ghost

A Widow's Curse

The Drifter's Wheel

A Corpse's Nightmare

December's Thorn

THE FLAP TUCKER SERIES

Easy

Too Easy

Easy as One-Two-Three

Dancing Made Easy

Dead Easy

The King James Conspiracy

A Prisoner in Malta

Phillip DePoy

MINOTAUR BOOKS
NEW YORK

A PRISONER IN MALTA. Copyright © 2016 by Phillip DePoy. All rights reserved. Printed in the United States of America. For information, address St. Martin's Press, 175 Fifth Avenue, New York, N.Y. 10010.

www.minotaurbooks.com

The Library of Congress Cataloging-in-Publication Data is available upon request.

ISBN 978-1-250-05842-3 (hardcover)
ISBN 978-1-4668-6258-6 (e-book)

Our books may be purchased in bulk for promotional, educational, or business use. Please contact your local bookseller or the Macmillan Corporate and Premium Sales Department at (800) 221-7945, extension 5442, or by e-mail at MacmillanSpecialMarkets@macmillan.com.

First Edition: January 2016

10 9 8 7 6 5 4 3 2 1

ACKNOWLEDGMENTS

Acknowledgment should be made to decades of theatre work with institutions including the Actors and Writers Workshop, the Academy Theatre, Theatrical Outfit, and the Alliance Theatre for continually reminding me that the difference between theatre and life is entirely negligible. Also I acknowledge Lee Nowell's contributions as first reader, best friend, constant companion, great artist, and spiritual cohort. Finally, acknowledgment is made to Keith Kahla and Janet Reid for cooking this up.

Then let some holy trance convey my thoughts
Up to the palace of the imperial heaven
—*"Lament for Zenocrate,"*
CHRISTOPHER MARLOWE

A Prisoner
in Malta

†

PROLOGUE

1583, LONDON

IN THE PRIVATE CHAMBERS OF LORD WALSINGHAM,

PRINCIPAL SECRETARY TO QUEEN ELIZABETH,

AND HER SPYMASTER

"Get Marlowe." Walsingham stood behind a small wooden table. His heavy burgundy coat made him larger than he was; the meticulously trimmed beard betrayed a ruthless attention to detail. "Get him and bring him to me. Today."

"Today? It's too soon." The man in red stood in a darkened corner. Even in Walsingham's private rooms, he was cautious. "He's not ready."

"I know," Walsingham agreed impatiently, "but it's time, nevertheless. This plot to murder our Queen is verified: her life is in peril. And I don't have all the facts I need to prevent it!"

Walsingham's gloved fist pounded the table.

"And I'm telling you that Marlowe's not your man!" The man in red took a step out of the shadows. "Not yet. I won't do it."

"Listen," Walsingham hissed, eyes narrow, "it's not too late for Her Majesty to retract her generous offer of making you her chief physician. And *never* too late to expose your family in Portugal."

The man in red reached for his dagger. It was an instinctive reaction that he instantly halted. He had never once met with Walsingham without wanting to kill him, but he knew that the spymaster's death would mean the end of his wife and children.

Walsingham saw those thoughts play across the man's face and ignored them.

"I wouldn't send Marlowe out without testing him first,"

Walsingham said, his voice calmer. "I want him to be ready as much as you do."

"I know," the man conceded. "You're right. What did you have in mind? To make him ready, I mean."

"Before we send him up against the vermin Throckmorton, and God knows what other conspirators," Walsingham explained, an uncharacteristic fear edging his voice, "I would set him a task that will be as instructive as it is vital to our cause. It will prove his mettle. But it must be done quickly. I have it on perfect authority that the Throckmorton plot is weeks from fruition. Our Queen is in dire peril."

"Sir, a task is never instructive. Only a teacher."

Walsingham smiled. "Which is why you will be with him. You may observe, firsthand, his readiness for the road ahead."

The man in red sighed. "I see." There was no use trying to stay ahead of Walsingham. He always won because he thought of everything.

"You must leave for Cambridge now," Walsingham concluded. "It's nearly dawn. You could be there by midmorning. You'll be taking one of Her Majesty's coaches."

The man in red didn't move. "And what is your task?"

"The coachman has a packet for you, it contains details. Don't reveal them to Marlowe, yet, but the core of it is this: one of our most valued agents has information vital to destroying the plot—information that must be given to me in person. You must take Marlowe and fetch the agent."

"Why can't this agent come to you?"

"Because this agent is a prisoner on the island of Malta," Walsingham answered tensely, "guarded by the Order of Saint John."

"Guarded by the Knights of Malta?" The man in red took a deep breath. "That won't test Marlowe. It will kill him."

Walsingham shook his head. "He can't die. Neither can you. This prisoner is too important. Without the three of you, our nation— I do not exaggerate when I say that our nation may be lost."

The man in red lifted his chin suddenly, realizing a feint within this scheme. "The Island of Malta is filled with Jews."

"Which is the other reason you were chosen." Walsingham rapped three times, hard, on his desk.

The door to the chamber opened.

"Hurry, Doctor," Walsingham said, looking down again.

The man in red stared at the top of Walsingham's head for a moment, and then turned, silently leaving the room.

The door closed.

And as it did, the wall tapestry behind Walsingham rustled, and the person who had been hiding there stepped into the flickering candlelight.

ONE

Christopher Marlowe stared at the newly mown lawn, and the tower of St. Benet's Church reaching sweetly toward God in morning's light. In the old graveyard, roses were blooming, even though March was cold. The tower was the oldest building in Cambridge, and Marlowe did his best to appreciate the ethos of grandeur and nobility. But the beauty of the day overtook him, and all his thoughts were light. He was nineteen, standing in Cambridge, about to go to class. He could scarcely believe his good fortune. A boot-maker's son was a rarity at any college.

Everywhere students rushed; professors glided in stately manner. The grass, greener than a linnet's wing, collected sunlight against the advent of late frost: "nature's rarest alchemy, the golden bell of heaven's fire."

All in black, Marlowe was nearly invisible in the shade, though his smile was brighter than sunlight. He wore his hair deliberately shorter than the fashion; it was a great source of aggravation for his tutors. Most of that ire was obviated by the fact that Marlowe's mind was the best in his class. His bright demeanor had endeared him to most of his fellow students as well; his eyes existed only to beguile.

Suddenly those eyes were distracted by the flair of a familiar crimson cloak.

"Doctor," Marlowe called out, stepping into the light to greet his old friend.

But just at that moment a voice behind him shouted, "Whoreson!" It was followed by the sound of running footsteps.

Marlowe spun around, and there was Walter Pygott, dagger in hand, face red with ignorant rage. Marlowe had been expecting this encounter for weeks. Pygott had battered or threatened nearly everyone else in the new class at Cambridge, and was widely regarded as a grotesque waste of skin. Worst of all, he behaved with impunity because his father had donated money to restore a window in St. Benet's Church. This had been done not by a doting parent, but by a man who sought to rid himself of his son's revolting company.

Unable to achieve any other sort of notoriety, Pygott quickly turned to picking fights and insulting his fellows. Easily seventeen stone, the bully used his weight more than his wits in every skirmish. He was a ridiculous figure in his ill-fitting green tunic and bright red codpiece, hair slicked down with butter.

"Christopher Marlowe," Pygott sneered, "I've been looking for you, you contemptuous base-born *callet*!"

"Callet?" Marlowe turned only slightly toward the cur.

Pygott planted his feet. "You heard me."

Marlowe smiled.

"The Scots use the word *callet* to mean a prostitute," Marlowe explained. "I will tell you plainly: that is not true of me. I never accept money for my favors—though I often deserve it. If, on the other hand, you meant the original French definition—that I am a frivolous person—I will assure you that I am among the more serious persons you will ever meet. Keep your dagger pointed at me and find that out. Or you could ask my friend, the man in the red cape just to your right. Am I correct in saying that I am a serious person, Dr. Lopez?"

"Hello, Chris." Lopez shoved back his cape and smiled.

Lopez had come from the street beyond the library. Black hair, dressed in red, he did not look old enough to be a royal physician, though he was nearly twice Chris's age.

"Dr. Lopez?" Pygott jeered, recognizing the famous name. "The Portuguese Jew bastard what made poisons for Robert Dudley?"

"You've read a pamphlet on the subject," Marlowe said disdainfully. "Surprising. Wouldn't have taken you for a reader."

"That pamphlet?" Lopez added. "Pure libel, I assure you. I was entirely exonerated of any wrongdoing."

Without warning Pygott jumped, crashing into Marlowe with the dull force of a falling boulder. It took Marlowe by surprise, and both men tumbled to the ground. Rolling, Marlowe kicked, but Pygott came out on top, and put his dagger in Marlowe's face.

The point of Pygott's blade was so close that it nicked Marlowe's eyelid when he blinked. Still, Marlowe was smiling.

"What have you got to smile about, cobbler-son? I'm about to stick this knife in your eye!"

Marlowe flicked his own dagger and Pygott flinched, feeling a sharp pain under his codpiece.

"That's why I'm smiling," Marlowe explained amiably.

The full measure of his predicament settled slowly over Pygott's face as he realized exactly where Marlowe's blade was resting. Pygott tried very hard not to move.

"I could live quite cheerfully with an eye patch," Marlowe went on, still smiling. "It would make me dashing. But what's your life going to be without this?"

To emphasize his point, Marlowe pressed his blade slightly forward and drew a single drop of blood from the larger man's flesh.

Pygott tossed his dagger away instantly, eyes wide, lower lip trembling. His pale green tunic began to show signs of sweat.

"Now apologize," Marlowe insisted.

Pygott swallowed and began in a weak vapor of a voice, "I am heartily sorry, Mr. Marlowe, for calling you a contemptuous base-born callet and a—"

"Not to me, you idiot," Marlowe said. "Get off me and apologize to my friend before I lose all my patience."

Pygott lumbered to one side, careful not to lose his balance and fall onto Marlowe's knife. He managed to stumble to a standing posture.

Marlowe leapt up. His blade stood out in the slant of late-afternoon sunlight. Pygott stared at it and began his speech.

"I—I am heartily sorry, Dr. Lopez," he stammered, "for calling you a Jew bastard, and for insulting your island and the entire Portuguese race."

Marlowe looked at Lopez.

"There's a Cambridge education for you," he said, shaking his head, "an equal ignorance of everything. You'll go far, Pygott. You're headed for Parliament; anyone can see that."

"Parliament?" Pygott gaped, not moving.

"Codpieces are going out of fashion, by the way," Marlowe continued. "They're ridiculous."

"Let him go, Marlowe," Dr. Lopez said softly.

"The college is pretty this time of day," Marlowe said absently. "Especially when the weather's soft like this."

Pygott stayed, uncertain what to do. His lip began to tremble more violently, and blood was beginning to spot the unfashionable bit of haberdashery.

"Please, young man," Dr. Lopez encouraged Pygott, "take your leave."

"Yes," Marlowe concurred. "Be gone. But avoid the church. There is no sin but ignorance and you, I fear, will surely burn there."

Without a word, Pygott wandered off, slightly dazed, in the direction of the church.

"That wasn't necessary," Lopez chided.

"He insulted you," Marlowe disagreed, "and he jumped on me. It was quite necessary."

"You draw too much attention to yourself," Lopez went on. "That dagger you wear, its filigreed hilt is too elaborate."

"It was a gift from my father," Marlowe protested, "and it serves a purpose."

"It attracts too many eyes! You've only been at Cambridge since January and everyone on the campus knows your name."

"I do it on purpose," Marlowe said, grinning. "It's my theatrical nature."

"The last thing a man in this world wants to be is unusual," Lopez said. "And you, my friend, are unique."

"I'm late for my last session," Marlowe said. "Will you walk with me?"

Lopez pulled his red cloak around his neck. His long black hair seemed to be cut from midnight, out of place in the daytime.

"You give your thoughts too much tongue," Lopez began as they walked in the direction of Old Court. "You give every man your voice when you should lend your ear."

"You came here to tell me that I talk too much?" Marlowe threw his arm around Lopez.

"You've drawn too much attention to yourself," Lopez said in a very confidential voice. "The way you dress, for example."

"What's wrong with the way I dress?" Marlowe asked, not quite aware of his old friend's strange behavior.

"All black. It's too somber for a young man," Lopez insisted.

"This from a man in a flame-red cape." Marlowe shook his head.

"You lend your money too freely," Lopez went on, "and you quarrel entirely too much."

"But I always win," Marlowe answered impatiently. "And I'm always good-natured about it. Rodrigo, what are you doing here?"

Marlowe stopped walking. They were nearly to the Parker Library. All of the students were gone; classes had started. The relative silence made it easier to hear noise from the street, beyond the church, where some minor commotion arose.

"You haven't yet become your true self," Lopez explained. "A man's only genuine occupation in this life is to discover who and what he truly is, and then do his best to become that. Most never manage it."

"This is quite a lot of advice," he said, "from a Portuguese Jew who's pretending to be a Protestant in England."

"Chris," Lopez said quietly. "I am to become Her Majesty's physician-in-chief."

Marlowe took Lopez by both arms.

"What? At last! My God!" Marlowe's voice boomed. "*That's* why you've come to Cambridge, I understand now: to tell me this wonderful news."

"Please lower your voice," Lopez said. "That is not the reason for my visit."

"Look, honestly," Marlowe suggested, ignoring the older man's comment, "just wait here until my session in poetics is concluded, and then you and I will go to the best pub in Cambridge."

"No, I'm sorry." Lopez looked around as if to make certain no one was looking at them. "You're not going to your class."

Marlowe blinked. "What?"

"You're coming with me to London. Now."

Lopez flicked his cloak and a coach appeared out of nowhere at the other end of the yard, headed toward them slowly. It was an ornate closed cab with a spring suspension, four wheels, and two muscled horses. It had been the source of the commotion out in the street. Marlowe recognized it as a very new Boonen construction—the kind built exclusively for the Queen.

Marlowe eyed the conveyance with suspicion.

"I'm not getting into that thing," he said.

"You have to," Lopez said simply.

"I might ride a horse to London," Marlowe ventured.

"Get in the carriage, please." Lopez held out his hand politely.

"That thing? No. It'll rattle my brains out."

"But it will keep us from being seen as we travel," Lopez whispered. "And, I insist. You are riding at the request of the Privy Council, and we are expected before midnight."

"The Privy Council." Marlowe's mood sobered. "Well. I've had the strangest notion that something odd was going to happen. Just as I concluded it was my encounter with Pygott, here comes a very expensive coach."

The coach pulled up beside them. Lopez opened the door. Marlowe peered inside.

"Do I really have to?" he asked.

But he knew the answer. The Privy Council had summoned. Not a living soul in England could deny such an order.

"Go on," Lopez insisted.

As soon as they were inside, the driver took off. Lopez closed the shutters. Light leaked in through the spy holes, but the cab was still very dark. The seats were covered in black leather, worn and softened. The wooden doors were scratched a bit, as was the floor. This was not a ceremonial vehicle, it was a workhorse.

"We're headed west," Marlowe said cautiously. "London is south."

"We're bound for the River Cam," Lopez explained. "We'll turn there and follow the water awhile."

Marlowe grasped the idea immediately. "If we're being followed, we'll see it when we turn south at the river."

"Exactly."

"I don't suppose you'll tell me why I've been summoned?"

"No."

They rode in silence for a distance.

In Cambridge, Walter Pygott was peeing on roses in the graveyard near the great tower of St. Benet's when he heard a noise behind him. Thinking it was one of the priests come to scold him, he tied his codpiece loosely and spun around.

"I wasn't doing anything," he began.

But he froze; fell silent when he saw the knife so close to his heart.

"You're a bastard idiot," the whispered voice told him, "with pudding for a dick and maggots in your brain."

"I—I—do I know you?" Pygott stammered. "I expect you're one of the little weasels I put to the ground here lately, thinking to get revenge while I'm indisposed. Look. Let's have an understanding. The rules of this place is: I'm on top."

"Not today. Not anymore. Not ever again."

"All right," Pygott said, smiling.

With that he drew out his rapier and thrust it forward, directly at his attacker's heart. It missed because the attacker moved to one side and slashed Pygott's sword arm. The cut was deep and Pygott howled.

Turning in a circle, a dance move, the attacker was suddenly behind Pygott, and slashed the back of the idiot boy's thigh—slashed it to the bone. Pygott went to his knees.

"Wait!" he cried. "Wait! You're not doing this right!"

The attacker turned again, a blur, a gray shadow, and kicked Pygott in the head with the hard heel of a boot.

Pygott grunted and fell flat on his back. Blood soiled his buttered hair.

"No," Pygott managed to say, but his voice was a dream, a distant memory. "You're not a student here."

Pygott reached up and grabbed his assailant's coat, but his hand was met with the blade, and blood dribbled down Pygott's arm.

The assailant stooped then, hovering over Pygott like a carnivorous animal.

"Your useless life is over now," came the whispered taunt. "Despised by everyone, a traitor to your country, who will mourn your passing?"

With that the dagger plunged into Pygott's heart. Blood gushed from the wound. Pygott's killer stood, rolled the body over with the heel of a boot, and was gone.

The Queen's coach was out of town and into the countryside before Marlowe spoke again.

"Can you tell me, at least, if I'm in some sort of trouble?" Marlowe leaned forward. "Should I try to leap out of this carriage before we get too far?"

"Don't jump, you'd only hurt yourself," Lopez said, "and I'd recapture you."

Marlowe looked into his friend's eyes.

"Have you captured me now, Rodrigo?" Marlowe's voice could barely be heard.

"I am required to bring you to London," Lopez answered without blinking, "whether you will or no."

Marlowe nodded amiably, but surreptitiously reached for his dagger.

Without warning, Marlowe found a rapier point tickling him just underneath his jaw. Lopez wore a cold mask of indifference, and held his rapier with a casual disdain. He seemed calm, but there was menace in the way his chin jutted forward.

"This is unexpected," Marlowe drawled easily.

"I have survived the destruction of my home," Lopez whispered violently, "the brutalization of my family, and the torture of the Inquisition. You think you always win, Chris, but you would not prevail against me. Let's be clear."

"You saved my father's life," Marlowe said, not moving, "and for that I am in your debt. Have I been mistaken in our friendship?"

Lopez sighed and closed his eyes.

"You have not," he said. "I have not slept in several days, and the urgency that compels me to fetch you so unceremoniously to London is . . . not inconsequential."

"You're not yourself," Marlowe went on. "I can see that, but would you mind very much taking your rapier from my throat? It's making me uncomfortable."

Lopez stared at his weapon as if he'd forgotten it was there, then put it away immediately.

"Now let me ask again," Marlowe continued. "Am I in danger?"

"No." Lopez closed his eyes. "You are in no danger from the council. In fact, the opposite is probably true."

"What? The council is in danger from me?"

"Likely, but that is not what I meant either. I—there was a great deal of persuasion brought to bear on this enterprise. I tried, in fact, to save you from it altogether. But now, it's my family, you see. They always threaten my family."

Marlowe sat back, his hand well away from his blade.

"I have no idea what you're talking about," he said, "but I can see that you're in great distress. And I think I speak for both of us when I say that no good would come from testing each other. One of us would lose a friend, and the other, a life. I'd rather not do either. Today."

"Agreed." Lopez sighed, and appeared to relax a bit. "And I'm sorry. Sorry that my wits are raw, and that I dare not tell you what the council has in mind. I can say that they require our assistance—yours and mine—and that they mean you no harm. Other than that, I am sworn to silence."

"Secrecy," Marlowe snorted. "If there is one thing I cannot abide, it's a secret."

"Spoken," Lopez offered wearily, "like a very young man."

Marlowe was about to object when Lopez suddenly raised a finger to his lips. A second later Marlowe realized that the coach was slowing down. Ear to the window, he could make out the sound of several voices whispering low: men on horseback.

Lopez silently drew out his rapier again, and turned to Marlowe, who produced his dagger. Lopez slid quietly to the floor, preparing to leap from the coach. He motioned for Marlowe to do the same.

But before Marlowe could move, the coach came to a complete stop, an arrow shattered the shutter, and the shaft plunged into the leather seat, narrowly missing Lopez's head. Outside the coach driver screamed; the horses complained loudly.

Marlowe reached out and snatched the arrow from where it had lodged. He jabbed it through the black fabric of his doublet and fell back onto the seat, concealing his blade.

A moment later the coach door opened.

Lopez sprang out, snarling and cursing in Portuguese. He scattered the men outside, taking them on all at once.

Marlowe lay stone-still, waiting for his opportunity. He knew that Lopez wouldn't need help.

A rude shadow appeared in the open doorway of the coach. Marlowe could see the man through half-closed eyes.

"You two take care of that Portuguese grease spot, boys," he growled. "I think this one in the cab is already dead."

The man leaned in, and Marlowe's senses were assaulted by the smell of sweat and garlic.

"Here he is," the odiferous voice said tauntingly. "Dead before he's old enough to whisker."

Without a word, Marlowe plunged his blade into the man's belly.

"Christ!" the man howled.

Marlowe kicked with both feet and the man flew backward out of the coach. Marlowe leapt after him.

Lopez was acquitting himself perfectly against two men near the horses. The man that Marlowe had stabbed was lying on his back, groaning. Marlowe charged. The man made an attempt to roll up, but was unable to do anything except bleed profusely.

"I'm cut dead," he wailed.

Marlowe bent over the man.

"You're not doing well," he agreed, "but you're not dying either. Excuse me."

Marlowe stood up straight and turned toward Lopez.

Lopez was still handling the matter at hand, but Marlowe spied a fourth man on horseback, mostly hidden by a nearby gathering of apple trees. That man had a pistol. The pistol was aimed at Lopez's back.

"Damn," Marlowe whispered.

He sipped a breath and began to run. Cocking his arm and steadying his eye, he used the forward motion of his body to give force to his knife. The blade flew through the air and caught the man on horseback in the forearm. The pistol jerked wildly and went off. The man fell from his horse and the horse shivered. It ran away squealing in an eerie high pitch.

The noise momentarily distracted the men attacking Lopez, who used the distraction to his advantage, stabbing one of the men in the chest, his rapier plunging deep into the man's rib cage.

The other man, shortest of the lot, suddenly realizing that he was alone, surveyed the scene, smiled, turned, and began to run as fast as he could in the same direction as the squealing horse.

Only then did Marlowe look around, get his bearings, and take in the landscape.

The coach had stopped in a deserted field close to a grove of crab-apple trees heavy with early fruit. In the distance the River Cam could be seen, with its lush fringe of ferns. There were wheeling clouds in the sky, high and white as milk. The day was ending, but the sun was gold, still an hour before setting.

"It's a lovely spot for an ambush," Marlowe observed, nearly to himself.

"Were you playing dead in the coach?" Lopez asked, trying to catch his breath.

"Yes."

"Why?" Lopez put away his rapier.

"I'm not sure," Marlowe answered. "Maybe I hesitated because I felt badly about how I treated Pygott. Or maybe it was just a game. I don't know. Where's the coachman?"

"Dead, over there, other side," Lopez said, breathing hard. "Come here for a moment, would you?"

Marlowe strode toward Lopez, but stopped a few feet short.

"That man," Marlowe gasped, staring at the one Lopez had stabbed in the chest. "I know that man!"

"Yes," said Lopez, his rapier still out.

"He came to see me earlier this very week." Marlowe stared down at the unmoving figure. "He wanted me to work for the Catholic Church."

"I know." Lopez finally put away his weapon. "These are the Pope's men. They wanted you to spy for the Vatican."

"No," Marlowe said, "it was clerical, they only wanted me to—that man, he works for my father, in Canterbury. Or so he said; I'd never met him. He only wanted me to find something of importance to my father and then . . ."

But Marlowe's voice trailed off as he realized that he had been duped.

"Yes, it was a test," Lopez said. "That would have been the beginning of your—our Papal espionage."

"But I turned them down," Marlowe said uncertainly.

"Yes, well, the Pope is the sort of person who never accepts anything but agreement with his dicta. Which is why he sent these men after our coach."

"What did they want?"

Lopez stared at them. "They wanted the money that the Pope would pay them to stop our coach."

"No, I mean what was their object in stopping us?"

"Oh, to kill us," Lopez answered quickly.

"Kill us? Why? Just because I said *no*?"

"Perhaps because the Pope has an inkling—or information—concerning the importance of—concerning why you have been summoned by the Privy Council. And why we are riding in Her Majesty's second-best coach."

Marlowe glared at the bleeding ruffians. "But, these men—they're idiots. I mean to say: they don't seem like spies or agents or—Christ, Lopez, look at them! This is the best the Pope can do?"

"These are hired roisters, men happy to make a farthing to kill a cat. They are only the first wave. There will be more, many more—and better—before we're done."

TWO

The coachman was not dead. When he'd seen the highwaymen coming at him, he'd screamed and fainted. He was, it seemed, unused to ruffians—or passengers, for that matter. His primary work for the Queen was squiring the royal furniture from one place to another.

Marlowe and Lopez resumed their journey after a cursory attendance to the wounded. Lopez was of the firm opinion that they should all be dispatched at that moment, but Marlowe's gentler sensibilities won out in the end. The Pope's men were left bleeding, groggy, and alive under the crabapple trees.

The coach followed the River Cam; it was rough going. Lopez kept the shutters open, unwilling to be surprised by any further attack. So while the ride was difficult for the backside, it was pleasing to the eye. The Cam roiled sweetly, grouse and quail abounded; here and there a deer looked up.

"How long will this trip take?" Marlowe asked, staring out the window.

"Another two hours, possibly three."

"It'll be after dark by then. How long if we ask the driver to speed the horses?"

"Five hours."

Marlowe turned his attention to Lopez, whose eyes were closed.

"How is it longer," Marlowe asked, "if we go faster?"

Lopez sighed.

"If your eye is fixed on a destination in the distance," he said, "it's impossible to watch the road in front of you."

Marlowe shook his head. "I disagree. The eye should always be on the horizon. The faster you get there, the better."

"I'm going to sleep now," Lopez murmured.

Lopez began, almost immediately, to snore. If Marlowe had his doubts as to whether or not the sound was theatre or reality, he kept those doubts to himself.

Instead he chose to review certain odd events of the preceding days, trying to make some sense of his present predicament. He thought of his naive meeting with the Pope's men, only two days earlier.

Professor Bartholomew's long lecture on the origin, development, and uses of the letter *J* in the English language had dulled Marlowe's senses beyond rescue.

"The letter *Y*, you see," Bartholomew droned, "was thought less masculine than the letter *J* when, in 1066, with the Norman invasion of England, the letter *J*, which had not existed in our language before that time, was introduced. It replaced all male names that began with *I* or *Y*. For example, *Yames* became *James*. And so forth."

Student after student fell victim to the deadly torpor induced by the lecture, until Marlowe was one of the few left awake. As the session ended, bleary-eyed young men staggered from the dark hall. As they did, a strange trio of rough men fell in with the throng.

Once out in the morning sunlight, the students began to disperse, some to study, others to class. Marlowe bid a good morning to several of his fellows, among them Richard Boyle, a childhood acquaintance, and Benjamin Carier, an older student, a quiet bookworm.

When they were gone and Marlowe walked alone, the three strange men came quickly from behind to surround Marlowe. They were all in dark brown cloaks with hoods, giving them a monkish appearance.

"Are you Christopher Marlowe?" one man asked in a rasping voice.

Marlowe quickly assessed the situation and decided on a reasonable course of action.

"I am not." Marlowe smiled.

"Are you the Christopher Marlowe what was born in Canterbury? Whose father is John Marlowe, shoemaker, and mother Catherine?" the man pressed.

"No, that's him, just up there," Marlowe said, pointing in the direction of several students who were just walking into the chapel.

"You don't remember me," another man said, "but we was at the King's School in Canterbury together, you and I."

"No," Marlowe said politely, "we weren't. You've never been to school, and I'm not from Canterbury. Sorry. That's Chris Marlowe, just up there. See?"

The first man smiled. He had only three teeth, his stubble seemed made of splinters, and his eyes were dead. "Look, mate. I work for your father, and he's in a bit of a stew."

"You know," the second man spoke in a whisper, "it's tough times for a Catholic in this man's country. Some of the talk, well, let's say it's not going in favor of your old Da."

"My father's not Catholic," Marlowe began.

In point of fact, Marlowe's father had been born just after King Henry VIII's Act of Supremacy, the law that established the English King, and not a foreign pope, as head of the church. The Anglican Communion was in all other ways indistinguishable from the Catholic—confusing times for the religious in England. But by the time Henry's daughter Elizabeth was on the throne, that confusion had been removed: it was illegal to be a Catholic in England. The Pope's subterranean war to pull England back into the fold was met by Elizabeth's iron determination to uphold her father's law, provoking the most savage plots and heartbreaking betrayals in the history of the country. So Marlowe was absolutely unwilling to admit any religious affiliation, especially to such rude strangers.

"The Anglicans, they've got a certain item what says he *is* Catholic," the first man continued.

"It won't go well for your father," the second man insisted, "if this *item* is brought to light."

"If you worked for my father," Marlowe said, his fears mounting, "you would have known that he favors the gamache over the buskin, and I see that two of you wear calf-length boots. Not his style. And the third, your silent partner, wears boots that were made in Spain."

"That's a nice bit of testing," the second man said, grinning. His face was round and pockmarked, and his nose had been broken several times. "But your father makes both, as you well know, the calf-length and the high boot. If you would care to peek inside one of mine, you'll find his seal."

"I wouldn't do it," the first man said, chuckling. "Once that boot's off, none of us would survive the stench."

Marlowe stared down at the boots for a moment. Two pair actually had been made by his father. The workmanship was unmistakable.

"All right," he said.

"You are Christopher Marlowe," the second man said.

"What is it that you want, exactly?" Marlowe asked.

"I told you," the second man said to no one in particular.

"In that church resides the item in question." The first man pointed to the high tower of St. Benet's Church, adjacent to the college. "It's nestled in a box on someone's desk. It's locked, the box is. You just bring that box to us. We'll see that it's opened, and the evidence against your father is destroyed."

"That's all a bit vague," Marlowe said cautiously.

"We'll give more details," the second man said, "when you agree to do the job."

"The job is," Marlowe said slowly, "that I break into a church office, steal a locked box, and give that box to you without seeing what's inside."

"Yes." The first man nodded once. "For your father."

"I see."

"So what's it to be?" the second man asked.

Marlowe looked at the silent third man, the shortest of the lot, barely over five feet tall. "Doesn't he ever speak?"

"Swallow my bollocks," the third man grunted, but his voice betrayed a Spanish accent, or something like it.

"I wouldn't do that either," the first man warned, chastising the Spaniard with a gaze.

"Well." Marlowe took in the trio at a glance and smiled, his hand on his dagger. "This bit of burglary you've suggested? I thank you, gentlemen, but no. I will not steal a box from a church."

Marlowe prepared himself for what seemed a certain and unpleasant battle, when from behind he heard the grating whine of Professor Bartholomew's voice.

"Mr. Marlowe!"

Marlowe looked over his shoulder, and there stood the old man, his black robes dripping off him like night's water.

"Professor," Marlowe said.

"Tell your classmates to disperse," Bartholomew commanded. "I wish to speak with you privately."

His manner was so imposing, so imperious, that the three men backed away a step or two.

"We'll talk again," the first man warned.

Then, as one, they turned and walked away with a deliberately casual air.

"Mr. Marlowe," the professor said in a lowered voice, "I wish to speak with you about a disgraceful bit of pen scratching of which, I am told, you are the author."

"Sir?" Marlowe kept one eye on the retreating trio as he tried to understand what Bartholomew was saying.

"This!" Bartholomew held out a crumpled page and thrust it into Marlowe's face.

Barely readable in its disheveled condition, Marlowe was able to make out the first line on the torn and wrinkled page.

" 'Come live with me, and be my love,' " he said out loud. "Yes. That's mine."

"Unacceptable, Marlowe!" the old man snorted. "Shameful!"

"I'm still working on it," Marlowe hedged. "It's not finished."

"Oh, yes it is," Bartholomew snapped. "You're to write no more in this vein. Not one word, do you hear me? I'll have no student of mine engaging in *enticement*!"

"It's a poem, sir," Marlowe began, "not a description of actual events. I have not, as yet, attempted to seduce a shepherdess."

"Ghastly," the professor concluded.

"You know," Marlowe said, smiling, "I'm the only one who doesn't fall asleep in your classes."

"Yes, yes," Professor Bartholomew sighed, "I know. Why else would I be speaking to you in such a friendly manner?"

Without waiting for an answer, the old scholar turned on his heel and lumbered away, back toward the relative sanity of his offices.

Marlowe was awakened by a sudden thumping.

"London Bridge," Lopez announced.

Well over three hundred years old, not quite a thousand feet long, the bridge's stone construction was wide enough to accommodate the coach they were riding in, and another to pass it. Supported by nineteen arches—coincidentally the same number as members of the Privy Council—the bridge felt as solid as a mountain. Still, Marlowe, roused from his sleep, had an uncomfortable, queasy feeling as the carriage jolted over the black water of the Thames.

Lopez noticed. "Are you ill, my friend?"

Marlowe sat up. "Not exactly. It's just—I don't like water. Where, exactly, are we going? I mean, when you say 'the Privy Council'—"

"I see that you are in some distress," Lopez said sympathetically, "so I will speak plainly. Her Majesty enjoys traveling from place to place, hence this coach for—what shall I say?—furniture moving. But she currently resides in the Palace of Whitehall, and that is where we are going."

"We're *furniture*?" Marlowe swallowed. "I'm to see the Queen?"

"No, no," Lopez said quickly. "You are meeting with Walsingham."

Sir Francis Walsingham, principal secretary to Queen Elizabeth, was the man in charge of Her Majesty's foreign, domestic, and religious policy. His reputation was towering, and Marlowe found himself in reluctant awe. A rabid Protestant, he had, almost single-handedly, enabled exploration of foreign lands, established English colonies across the globe, and created the greatest navy in the world. He was also the man for whom the word *spymaster* had been invented.

"God's bleeding skin," Marlowe whispered.

Lopez raised his eyebrows.

"If I were you," he told his young friend, "I'd be very careful about how I used my words from now on. You're in London. Every ear can hear; every tongue can lie."

"Yes." Marlowe tried to make sense of everything, but failed.

"And let me remind you that London thoroughfares are made almost entirely of street brawls, quarreling, and knife-play."

"I don't know how that's any different from every street in England," Marlowe said. "Besides, I've just realized that I might get the chance to see Penelope. If Her Majesty is staying at the Palace of Whitehall, so, surely, are her ladies-in-waiting."

"They are," Lopez affirmed warily. "But do you mean Penelope Rich?"

"I mean Penelope Devereux," Marlowe corrected. "I know she's married to Robert Rich, that bastard, but she's not his. She belongs to me. I loved her the moment I saw her. Her hair is better than gold, and her eyes—"

"Don't be ridiculous. She's in love with Philip Sidney, Chris. Always has been."

Marlowe nodded. "I know. She hates Rich, loves Sidney, and occasionally wants me."

"What are you saying?" Lopez asked.

"I'm trying to take my mind off what's to come," Marlowe railed. "I'm trying to think of this as one of my *occasions* with Penelope. Christ! You never said I'd be meeting with bleeding Walsingham!"

"I didn't want to frighten you unduly, Chris," Lopez answered. "But if I were you, at this point, I would be very much afraid."

THREE

Side streets became back alleys under a moonless sky. The coach was taking a deliberately confusing route to get to Whitehall. Although he had been in London many times before, nothing looked familiar; everything had a dreamlike unreality. He might as well have been traversing streets in an imaginary kingdom. Few people were abroad, and those who were eschewed so obvious a royal conveyance.

At last the coach passed through a small archway, and the air seemed suddenly calmer, quieter. A lawn stretched out around the narrow road they traveled, and the way was less jolting.

There were no lights, no torches anywhere, so that when a building suddenly loomed beside the coach, its towering stone walls were startling.

"Out," Lopez grunted before the coach had come to a halt.

Marlowe leaned forward and took the door handle.

"You'll introduce me," Marlowe said hesitantly, "or, present me, or—"

"No," Lopez interrupted. "Go on."

"What? Alone?"

Before Marlowe could protest further, Lopez all but shoved him out of the coach. Marlowe tumbled onto the gravel path, nearly fell, and turned to demand an explanation. But the coach was already rumbling out of sight.

A sudden sound startled him, and he spun around, grabbing for his dagger, but his sheath was empty. He realized, just as he saw two men storming his way, that Lopez had relieved him of the weapon before tossing him out the door.

"Come along," one of the men said calmly. "You're a bit behind your time."

As the two men drew closer, Marlowe could see that they were guards of some sort, an elite corps. Both wore pistols; one had withdrawn his sword, but it seemed more ceremonial than a weapon. Both were dressed in a dark blue uniform that bore a patch, a flourish of red above a helmet and a solid red horizontal bar. It looked to be a family crest, possibly Walsingham's, though why the state secretary would have his own family guard and not the Queen's was a puzzle.

Marlowe did not speak, suddenly aware of Lopez's advice to be careful with his words.

The two men strode quickly along the wall to a dark wooden door. The man with the sword suddenly became more vigilant, scanning the night for any sound, any sign of movement. The other man produced a large skeleton key and unlocked the door, then drew out his pistol.

"In you go, sir," he said to Marlowe.

Marlowe peered in. The room was dimly lit. A single taper burned on a small table. Otherwise the room appeared empty.

"Quickly, if you don't mind, sir," the man with the sword whispered.

Marlowe stepped into the room. The door closed and locked behind him. There was a moment of profound silence.

Then, out of the shadows, a man emerged. He was tall. His black skullcap and starched white ruff accentuated his face, especially the eyes: sad, penetrating, brilliant. His beard and mustache were so coiffed that he appeared more a character in a play than a ruler of the country. A long burgundy robe concealed the rest of his body.

"Marlowe," he said.

His voice was unexpectedly melodious, like the low notes of a viola da gamba.

Marlowe nodded once and, with some effort, held his tongue.

"We require your services."

Marlowe swallowed.

"The Queen and I," Walsingham continued.

"I—I'm not certain—sir," Marlowe stammered.

"My men have been watching you for two years," Walsingham interrupted, "in Canterbury and in Cambridge. You are a remarkable young person. We believe that you have certain talents which will serve your country well."

"Talents?" His voice sounded strange in that room.

"You are unsurpassed in your ability at using words to persuade," Walsingham began, "and if your words fail, you are likewise adept with a dagger and a rapier. You rarely exhibit fear. You never avoid confrontation. Your theatrical talents make you a man able to play many parts. Your amorous exploits are legendary among your companions. And you are a spectacularly convincing liar."

Marlowe smiled, regaining a bit of his usual flair.

"I believe, sir," he said confidently, "that you have just described your perfect agent."

"Indeed." And while Walsingham did not smile, his eyes brightened noticeably.

"I assume I have little choice in this matter."

Walsingham tilted his head ever so slightly. "If you did, would you refuse the adventure I am about to propose?"

"It would be unduly coy, sir, for me to say that it depends on the proposal," Marlowe admitted, "but I am already flattered beyond measure."

"I have not flattered you," Walsingham said curtly. "You have the arrogance of youth. That alone provides you with all the flattery you need. I merely catalogue your abilities."

"My amorous exploits? What have they to do with—anything?"

Walsingham looked down. "Many a secret whispered in bed eventually topples a nation."

"I see, sir."

"You do not," Walsingham countered. "But now we arrive at a

delicate moment in our conversation. I am loath to tell you more than I want you to know, but if I do not, you will not understand the immeasurable gravity of the situation which brings you here. How to proceed?"

Marlowe took a breath. Against his friend's advice and the instincts of his better angels, he spoke his mind.

"I am, sir, all of the things you have enumerated. I am a playwright, a musician, a steadfast friend, and a mortal enemy; bold, pleasant, and resolute. Now and then, when occasion requires, I will stab. I am my father's son, but I have rejected his church, as I rejected the Pope's men, as I believe you know, when they desired that I betray the law. This above all: there is nothing I would not do for my country, for my Queen, and for my honor. Nothing."

Walsingham allowed Marlowe's words to hang in the air a moment.

"A brave speech," Walsingham said at length, "and spoken with the fervor one might expect from a Cambridge man. But I must not forget that you have admitted, in that very speech, that you are a liar."

"*A spectacular liar,*" Marlowe responded instantly, "is what you said."

"Dear me," Walsingham said without the slightest distress in his voice, "however will I know when you are telling the truth?"

Marlowe shrugged. "I don't even know myself most of the time. But my heart is good, I always mean well, and in the end I never fail to be honest with a true friend."

"That may present a problem, in that I have neither the time nor the patience to cultivate a mutual friendship with someone possessed of so much youthful exuberance."

"I would never presume to achieve so lofty a friendship as yours. I was referring to—that is, I had in my mind a bond which already exists, one that ties me to this enterprise, no matter what it is."

"Dr. Lopez."

"Dr. Lopez," Marlowe confirmed. "I would do anything for him."

"Good. We had hoped to hear you say that." Walsingham turned to the shadows at the far side of the room. "Had we not?"

Lopez stepped into the dim circle of the candle's light.

"Yes."

Marlowe jumped, but only slightly.

"Then," Walsingham sighed, "we shall have chairs."

Without warning several men appeared out of the darkness bearing chairs. Walsingham sat immediately at the table, then Lopez.

"This is why you sent Dr. Lopez," Marlowe realized aloud. "You knew that I would trust him; you suspected that I could not lie to him."

"Yes, yes, yes," Walsingham mumbled impatiently. "Sit. I must tell you quickly what needs to be done. We have little time to save our country from deceit of the highest magnitude; disaster and destruction."

Still partially stunned, Marlowe sat. Walsingham had a sheaf of papers in his hand.

"These hideous pages are the result of dangerous work by certain members of my staff," he began, sotto voce. "What I am about to reveal, the content of these statements, must never be discussed outside this room. Do you swear it?"

Marlowe nodded quickly.

"These vile papers were discovered in May of last year," Walsingham continued, "and are from the Spanish ambassador himself."

"Mendoza," Lopez whispered, in case Marlowe was unfamiliar with the diplomatic roll call.

"Yes, Bernardino de Mendoza," Walsingham sneered. "They were addressed to certain persons in Scotland, and tell of a Papist plot to invade England, to displace our true Queen, and to thrust onto the throne of our country the Scots Catholic, Mary."

While it was certainly no secret that Mary had tried for a decade and a half to claim the throne of England, Marlowe could scarcely believe that she would be so bold as to take control by force.

"Surely Her Majesty Queen Mary would realize that she could never rule England," Marlowe blurted out.

Walsingham rubbed his temple. "She has supporters in our

country. The plot calls for an invasion from without coinciding with insurrection from within."

"Surely you—surely the Privy Council would not take such a threat seriously. Who could possibly think that such a mad plan would work?"

"Francis Throckmorton," Walsingham said solemnly.

Marlowe did not believe his ears. Sir Francis was a nephew of Sir Nicholas Throckmorton, one of Her Majesty's diplomats and a close friend of Walsingham's, so such an accusation would not have been an easy one for the old man to make.

"Francis has been traveling abroad these three years past," Walsingham continued, his voice a bit less spry, "meeting in secret with Catholic malefactors. We know he saw Paget and Morgan in Paris. Now we believe that he was the intermediary for these vile communications."

"I do beg your pardon," Marlowe interjected, "but the names *Paget* and *Morgan* are unknown to me."

"Charles Paget is a Catholic conspirator," Lopez intervened. "A Cambridge man himself, some twenty years ago. This summer he traveled in secret from Rouen to England, under the name of Mope. He is somewhere in the country now, arranging for this Spanish invasion."

"Thomas Morgan," Walsingham continued, "is an out-and-out spy, a secretary to the Scots Queen."

"I can see that you take these papers and their threat in deadly earnest." Marlowe bowed his head. "It's just that I am struggling to believe it all."

"I assure you, young man," Walsingham said, "that I take these issues more seriously than you can possibly imagine. I must. Alas, these are only hints. Allegations. Innuendo."

"Has Francis Throckmorton been arrested; questioned?" he asked at length.

Walsingham sighed and sat back.

"We are on the brink of that action, yes," he answered, "but it requires the utmost delicacy. Francis is the nephew of a member of the Queen's diplomatic corps."

"And you have a friendship with his uncle," Marlowe said absently.

"Marlowe," Lopez snapped. "You may *not* speak in such a familiar tone!"

Before Marlowe could rouse himself to apologize, Walsingham raised his hand slightly.

"Peace, Rodrigo," he said softly. "Our friend is young, and distracted in his thoughts. I would be, too, were I in his place. And he has not yet heard the task for which he has been summoned."

Marlowe composed himself, seeing that a final bomb had not been exploded. His eyes flashed between the other two men at the table.

"There is a prisoner in Malta," Walsingham intoned at length, "one of our most important spies. He is the key to arresting Throckmorton, but more important, he has in his head certain facts, information that exists nowhere else in the world. Without him, and the knowledge locked in his brain, these letters are useless. They are too vague. Our man in Malta has details, names, dates. He is, therefore, the key to preventing the possible ruination of our county."

"Right, then," Marlowe announced suddenly. "You wish me to fetch him back to London. Done."

In spite of himself, and the situation, Walsingham could not stifle a smile.

"That island is a Catholic stronghold, Chris," Lopez warned, "ruled by the Knights of Malta, ruthless, devious, brilliant men. They withstood the entire Ottoman Empire and have built the most secure prison in the world. Our man is in the bottom of that prison."

Marlowe smiled. "I like a challenge."

"You have not fully considered the consequences of your decision here tonight," Lopez said, his voice almost desperate. "You can still say no."

"If you love England, you can scarcely say no," Walsingham objected, glaring at Lopez. "If you cannot rescue our spy, we may well be lost; very likely find ourselves in a Catholic nation with a Scots Queen on the throne. And, make no mistake, Mary is a woman utterly controlled by Spain. England, the England that we love, would cease to exist were she queen."

For an instant there was no sound in the room, as if hearts and lungs had ceased their labors, and the air itself refused to move.

Then Marlowe smiled and stood.

"When do I leave?"

Walsingham surrendered to the merest show of relief before nodding curtly. "Immediately."

Without hesitation, Marlowe turned to go, seized by a sudden thrill of excitement.

"Ah," Walsingham sighed, examining several notes on his desk, "one thing more, alas."

Marlowe turned, but not completely.

"Are you aware of someone called Walter Pygott?" Walsingham asked softly.

"Pygott?" Marlowe turned fully to face Walsingham. "Of course. He's a student at Cambridge. Odd that you should mention him. He and I had an amusing encounter."

"Yes." Walsingham's face was ice. "He's dead. Murdered."

"Dead?" Marlowe looked at Lopez. "No. He was alive this afternoon."

"My messenger's horse was much faster than your coach," Walsingham explained. "You are named. There is a warrant for your arrest."

"A warrant for me?" Marlowe's head twitched a bit. "But that's ridiculous."

"His body, the body of this Pygott, was found in your rooms at Cambridge. Stabbed dozens of times, with a dagger very much like the one you are wearing now. Did you kill him?"

"Of course not." Marlowe glanced at Lopez. "I did roust him a bit, but the doctor was there. He saw the whole thing. Pygott was alive and well when we left. He stumbled off, and then Dr. Lopez got me into the coach that brought us here. The doctor is my complete defense against this bizarre allegation."

Walsingham turned his gaze to Dr. Lopez.

"It's true," Lopez said calmly. "Marlowe could not possibly have murdered the boy. I will attest to that in any inquiry."

"There we have it, then," Walsingham said, looking down. "I am certain you have nothing to worry about. The Cambridge constabulary is nearly nonexistent and of no consequence, of course, but you must sort it out as soon as you return from Malta. For now, be on your way with all haste. I believe, Dr. Lopez, that you know a Portuguese captain by the name of de Ferro."

Lopez nodded slowly.

"He will provide your swift passage." Walsingham stood. "Time is of the absolute essence."

With that, the door to the room opened, several men appeared, and, without a word, escorted Marlowe and Lopez out of Walsingham's chamber and back into the coach.

"Seems I won't be seeing Penelope after all," Marlowe lamented as the coach took off. "Alas."

The door closed. Walsingham remained standing.

From behind him, a woman's voice, deep with strain, asked a single question.

"Will it work?"

"This is only one of several plans, Your Majesty," Walsingham said without turning around.

"But will it work?"

"I've had an eye on Marlowe for some time now."

"Yes, we know," the Queen said from the shadows.

"He could prove a formidable agent."

"Or a spectacular disaster."

"Quite right," Walsingham agreed. "But the damnable Jew swears to the boy's abilities."

Her Majesty took a single step into the flickering candlelight.

"Have a care how you speak of our royal physician," she said without emotion. "He has saved our life, as you well know."

"He'll be your first physician if he comes back, Majesty. The greater concern is for the young poet."

"Wanted for murder," the Queen mused. "Do we know who killed the Pygott boy?"

"We do not," Walsingham confessed, "but his death serves our purpose. The father, Robert Pygott, is one of Throckmorton's conspirators. He'll come after Marlowe, and Marlowe will expose him."

"Or he'll kill Marlowe. You're using Marlowe as bait."

"Yes, Majesty." Walsingham sighed. "But as I say, he's very capable. And it might be useful to know who killed the younger Pygott."

"Have you read any of Marlowe's pages? He's one of Kyd's protégés."

"Is that all there is to the relationship?" Walsingham said, gathering up the papers from the desk in front of him.

"Are you suspicious of everyone?" she asked.

"Yes," Walsingham answered, and there was no hiding the weariness in his response.

"When will they return, my doctor and your newest agent?"

"*If* they return, Majesty, it will be within the month."

The Queen's voice softened. "I know you are concerned, Francis."

"Yes. God." Walsingham's face, at last, betrayed his deepest anxieties, though they remained unspoken.

"They will return—all three." And without another word, the Queen was gone.

"I wish I had the same confidence," Walsingham said to himself, blowing out the candle.

FOUR

Just after dawn that morning, an unnamed Portuguese ship slid almost silently out of its dock in Hastings, bound for the Channel Islands and beyond. The ship was a spectacular carrack. It was large enough to be stable in the heaviest sea, and the hold was unexpectedly capacious. Its high, rounded stern sported a larger-than-usual aftcastle, and the spar protruding from the prow was unusually long. Ships like it had sailed around the world.

As Marlowe leaned over the rail, rubbing his eyes and watching the land fade away in the dim light, he cleared his throat.

"We would cut our journey by a week if we went over land instead of sailing to Catania," he told Lopez.

"Did you know that my people invented this kind of vessel?"

Lopez stared down at the high, rounded stern of the ship.

"Really? I don't think of Jews as a great seagoing people."

"The Portuguese." Lopez sighed. "The Portuguese have used what we call the *nau* for a hundred years or more—to map the world."

"This insane ocean voyage will take too long!" Marlowe insisted. "Why are we on a ship at all?"

Irritated, exhausted, and impatient, Lopez barked back, "You don't consider the danger of traveling over land through France. Have you already forgotten that we were attacked in the coach from Cambridge to London? You don't think of how often we would be stopped, or have to change horses, or pause to eat and sleep. On this ship you are as safe as you would be in your own home, and it never has to stop for food or rest. Do you understand that dozens of brilliant men, the Privy Council included, have constructed this plan to the letter? I love you, my friend, but you don't know everything! We travel by sea for your own safety: you are wanted for murder!"

"That's not a genuine concern," Marlowe scoffed. "You're my defense against that charge! You know I didn't do it, and any judge in England would be forced to believe you."

Lopez shook his head impatiently. "There are other reasons. It will take awhile to set the rest of Walsingham's plan in motion: Italy, at Catania, and on the Island of Malta itself. When the time comes, we'll enter the port of Valletta under assumed identities, as Jewish merchants. That's essential to the plan, and, of course, the reason I was chosen for this task."

"I don't understand that."

"There were, at one time, over five hundred Jews on the island. When the Knights of Saint John took control of Malta, many Jews left. Since the Great Siege of the Ottomans was repulsed by the knights, most Jews on the island are little more than slaves."

Marlowe shook his head. "Then why are we masquerading as Jews?"

"Three reasons," Lopez answered. "First, free Jews may visit the country through the port in Valletta, which is where our objective, the prisoner, is hidden. Thus our visit to that city will avoid suspicion. Second, no one in his right mind would pretend to be a Jew on Malta, so our identities and our true purpose will be protected. Finally, I can tell you from experience that oppression creates a bond between like-minded people more reliable than religion, heritage, or blood. The network of anti-Catholic resistance on Malta is stronger and more secretive than any in Europe. They are allies made of iron."

Marlowe nodded.

"I see the wisdom of this," he admitted, "even though the overall plain is utterly mad."

"Yes," Lopez agreed curtly, "and I haven't told you about the prison itself. It's impenetrable, under constant guard by over a hundred men; there are several levels and our prize languishes in the bottom-most one."

"So, the task is impossible." Marlowe shrugged. "We'll manage."

Lopez pursed his lips. "There is a final problem: we cannot be certain that our man is still alive."

"What?" Marlowe's eyes widened.

"I withstood the torture of the Inquisition for a week," Lopez said quietly, "and nearly perished. I will never be the person I was before that horror. The man we seek to rescue has been a prisoner for nearly three months."

"I think of the Inquisition as a thing of the past," Marlowe mused. "The height of their power was over fifty years ago."

Lopez looked away. "For me, the height of their power was three years ago, when they had me in their secret chambers."

"So—this man, this prisoner we're after," Marlowe said softly, "he might be dead."

"And even if he is still alive, it's very likely that his mind is gone."

"And his mind," Marlowe said, nearly to himself, "is primarily what we need."

Lopez nodded.

"With every new fact or element revealed to me," Marlowe said, "this enterprise seems increasingly fatal."

"Agreed."

"Then why are we doing it?"

"The desperate have no other remedy but hope."

"Hope," Marlowe countered, "is no shield against a sword or an arrow. But there is something else that concerns you, I can see it in your eyes."

Lopez looked out to sea. "Has it occurred to you, Chris, to ask why *you* have been chosen to do this impossible task?"

Marlowe smiled. "You mean that there are reasons other than my many talents enumerated by Sir Francis Walsingham."

"Yes."

Marlowe's mind was set spinning. A hundred answers, and then as many more questions, whirled in his brain. He didn't speak, but a slow fear began to boil at the back of his neck.

"Why would they pick me?" he finally said aloud.

"What would the Privy Council lose," Lopez said deliberately, "by sacrificing a rash young poet without peerage?"

Marlowe's breathing increased. "But you—you're about to become the Queen's physician."

"I'm a Portuguese Jew," Lopez answered, exasperated. "I have absolutely no illusions about my real place in the grander scheme of things."

"They think we won't be able to accomplish this task," Marlowe surmised.

"Yes, but go on. There's more to it than even that."

"They expect us to be caught and tortured in Malta as spies."

"Most likely. And what does that tell you?"

"They want us to give up what we know," Marlowe whispered, "because what we know is not true. We're being deliberately set up as—as decoys; sacrificial pawns."

Lopez looked away.

"If Walsingham fed us false information," he rasped, "and we give up that information under torture, it would mislead the enemy; give England an advantage."

Then the most desperate element of the Privy plan fell into place in Marlowe's mind.

"You realize what this *could* mean," Marlowe whispered.

"Go on," Lopez encouraged, knowing what Marlowe was thinking. "Lay it all out on the table. Say it out loud."

"This mysterious prisoner we are to rescue?"

"Yes?" Lopez encouraged.

"He may not even exist."

"There." Lopez sat. "That's the worst of it."

Both men sat in silence, each lost in desperate thought, for the span of a quarter of an hour.

"Well." Marlowe finally roused himself. "Objectively speaking, it's not a bad plan on Walsingham's part. Sacrifice pawns to a knight in order to save the Queen."

"Yes," Lopez answered absently. "Good plan."

"Right, then," Marlowe said, his energy returning. "Give me one good reason we should go on, if it's true what we've just said."

Lopez looked up.

"That's easy," he said to Marlowe. "What if everything we've just said is wrong?"

"Then we'd have to go to Malta," Marlowe agreed, "and gamble that Walsingham told us the truth. Because if he has, we must certainly rescue this prisoner."

"Exactly."

"What odds would you take?"

"Half against half," Lopez said.

Marlowe smiled. "Well, then. I've won with worse odds. Everything's going to be fine. Let's get some sleep."

Lopez nodded, but neither man moved toward his bed.

FIVE

The Channel turned into the Bay of Biscay and then the Atlantic. The ocean at night, black even under a full moon, was calm for the season. Marlowe and Lopez stood on deck, staring silently at the water, each lost in thought. Everyone else on board, save the pilot, was asleep.

An icy wind cut across the deck, rattled the ropes, and thundered the sails. Lopez drew his crimson cloak around him; Marlowe shivered.

"If there's even a chance that our prisoner exists," Marlowe said for the third time, as much to convince himself as to encourage Lopez, "we have to go through with the plan."

Lopez did not respond.

"I have put myself in his position," Marlowe went on. "Even if my mind were gone, I would not like to die from Catholic torture in a land so far from home. Just bringing this man back home in any condition would be a worthwhile endeavor."

"And of course," Lopez sighed, "there is always the possibility of a miracle."

"Sorry, what?"

"Despite what most of these Christians in England seem to think," Lopez told Marlowe, "I am a man of deep faith. I believe in the possibility of miracles. We might survive. This man, this prisoner, he might actually be real, and have information in his head that will save England."

"I see." Marlowe rubbed his arms to get warm. "Well, it's going to take more than the Maccabees' lamp oil to save us from this folly."

Lopez turned to his friend, smiling. "Do you mock my religion?"

"Of course not." Marlowe did his best to seem serious. "Your miracle is lamp oil that lasted for a week, our miracle is a man who came back from the dead, for eternity. Why would I make sport of that?"

"You don't see that the metaphor is the same?"

"What metaphor?" Marlowe scoffed.

"Light," Lopez said softly, "in time of darkness."

Marlowe smiled at last.

"So," he sighed, "we go to Malta; see if we can find some poor bastard that's got himself stuck in a hole."

Lopez returned his gaze to the rolling sea. "I suppose we do."

They passed another quarter of an hour in silence, each once more in the prison of his own thoughts, when Marlowe roused himself.

"Lopez," he whispered. "Look."

He pointed northward, to the stern of the ship.

Lopez scanned the sea but was unable to discern whatever it was that Marlowe thought he saw.

"What is it?" he finally asked Marlowe.

"Just watch," Marlowe said slowly, eyes locked on a certain quadrant of the sea, "and in a moment you'll see one or two of the stars, just at the horizon, blink out and then return, ever so quickly."

"A ship?" Lopez answered quickly.

Another moment of surveillance, and Lopez saw what Marlowe had seen, the merest of moments: stars on the horizon disappeared and came back. There was a ship following them, running without lights.

"I'll wake the captain," Lopez said softly.

"Should we extinguish some of our lamps?" Marlowe asked.

"Not yet," Lopez advised. "We'll let them think that they're invisible to us for a moment longer."

Lopez moved quickly to the pilot and whispered some short instructions, and then went below. Marlowe stayed on deck, trying to hold the phantom ship's position in his gaze. It seemed to be gaining on them, but it was impossible to know that for certain.

A few moments later half the crew emerged from the hold almost silently. The captain stood with Lopez and the pilot, staring in the direction of the pursuing vessel. The rest of the men deployed themselves on deck, hiding. After a moment the captain and Lopez came to Marlowe, on the leeward side. The captain whispered in Portuguese; Lopez translated a second later.

"Captain de Ferro is afraid that the vessel behind us is the *São Martinho*," Lopez told Marlowe, "the flagship of Don Alonso."

Marlowe's throat tightened. "The Duke of Medina Sedonia."

"Yes."

"The greatest commander of all the Spanish naval forces."

"He's not certain," Lopez hedged. "It *could* be the *São Martinho*. He says."

"It has forty-eight heavy guns," Marlowe said, unable to keep the concern from his voice. "It's a Portuguese ship like the ones you were bragging about. Only *much better*!"

"*Não se preocupe*," said the captain.

"He's telling you not to worry," Lopez translated.

"I disagree!" Marlowe raged. "We should be very, *very* worried. We have a giant Spanish warship up our backside!"

"*Tenho que ir agora*," the captain announced, and departed.

"He said he had to go," Lopez explained.

"To jump overboard?" Marlowe ranted. "Because that's what I'm thinking about doing."

"He has a trick." Lopez shrugged.

"A trick?"

"He's done this before, Chris," Lopez said in soothing tones, trying to calm his friend. "Captain de Ferro, he's never been caught."

"He's never been chased by a ship like this!"

"It's just one ship."

"It's not *just* one ship. It's the best ship in the Spanish navy! The greatest fleet in the world!"

Lopez put his arm around Marlowe's shoulder.

"Come with me," he told Marlowe calmly, "and watch what happens."

Marlowe allowed himself to be taken to the stern of the boat where several men were lowering something into the water. It took a moment for Marlowe to see that several large barrels had been placed in the ocean and were drifting away, more or less in the direction of the pursuing Spanish ship.

"Our captain has explained to me that he has, on several occasions in the past, employed this stratagem." Lopez patted Marlowe's shoulder. "It's worked almost every time."

"Almost?"

"Well," Lopez admitted, "it's not a science."

"What, exactly, is he doing?"

"Ah, well," Lopez answered, "I think, as a budding playwright, you'll appreciate that showing you is better than telling you."

"But—" Marlowe protested.

"Watch."

Marlowe, barely able to contain himself, tried to focus on the retreating barrels. He counted to three. After a moment they were impossible to see in the swirl of night and wave.

Beside them stood a short man with a long, ornate snaphance rifle, the very latest in handheld firearms. The man rested the rifle on the ship's rail, whispered something in Portuguese, opened his eyes wide, held his breath, and fired the gun.

A second later the ocean behind them turned to flame. A swath of fire at least fifty feet wide and twenty deep appeared in an instant between the Spanish ship and Captain de Ferro's unnamed vessel.

At that moment, the lamps all around Marlowe, every light on the ship, went out.

The short man with the rifle looked up at Marlowe.

"See?" he said in a heavy accent. "Nothing to worry about."

"It's very confusing for the other ship, you understand," Lopez said, unable to hide his pleasure at the event. "They are thinking,

'Has the other ship caught fire? Was it sabotaged? Is that the ship at all?' By the time they realize that we've ignited three large barrels of olive oil spread out over thirty feet, we'll be long gone."

"Easy," the short man agreed.

"If it was easy," Marlowe said, his composure returning, "then why do I have the suspicion that just before you fired, you whispered a prayer?"

"I can see perfectly at night and I'm an excellent marksman," the man replied, taking his gun from the rail, "but I'm not an idiot: only God could make a shot like that."

Marlowe watched the flames for a moment, unable to see the other ship behind them.

"Is this part of your miracle?" Marlowe asked Lopez. "Do you expect these flames to last eight days?"

Lopez looked out to sea. "Again he mocks my faith."

"That's a Spanish warship back there somewhere," Marlowe responded quietly. "Someone already knows what Walsingham has put us up to."

"Yes." Lopez turned and went below without another word.

Later that night, in his cabin, Marlowe lay awake, staring at the low ceiling by the light of a short candle. In his mind he watched as scene after scene played itself out. In one, he and Lopez were captured by the Inquisition. In another, the prisoner they sought was dead. In a third, the Spanish monster destroyed Marlowe's ship, taking no prisoners, leaving no survivors.

The tossing of the waves told him that the ship was speeding forward, but in his tiny room everything seemed so still. A bed, four walls, a basin, a candle, a chamber pot—these were hardly the companions he'd wanted by his side when Death came.

After several hours he gave up the notion of sleeping. He threw off his covers and went back on deck. The pilot nodded once as Marlowe emerged from the hold, and then, without a word, glanced backward urgently.

Marlowe came up to the wheel and looked in the direction the pilot had indicated. There, in the first red sky of morning, not more than a league away, was the Spanish ship.

Marlowe turned to the pilot.

"Sometimes the trick works," the pilot said in perfect English, "and sometimes it doesn't."

Marlowe took a moment to assess the man. He was made of leather and salt. His eyes were permanently rimmed in red, and his hands were more like talons than any human appendage. He was a man who had spent his life at sea.

"What are we going to do?" Marlowe asked, trying to keep a rising panic at bay.

"Ask the captain." The man shrugged.

Only then did Marlowe notice that Captain de Ferro was sitting on the rail in the last shadows of the night, staring down at a book. He was dressed in a purple velvet mandilion, the short, fashionable coat that some nobles wore, and black silk breeches. His boots were expensive calf-length buskins made of Spanish leather.

Marlowe approached the captain as calmly as he could manage.

"Pardon, Captain de Ferro," he said deferentially.

The captain looked up.

"Ah. Marlowe." He closed his book. "You're on deck early."

"Your English seems to have improved greatly since last night," Marlowe observed.

"I don't like to speak English in front of the men when there is a danger at sea," he explained. "That makes them nervous. They want to know what's being said by their captain at all times, you understand."

"I do."

Marlowe also understood that a man who pretended not to speak English might also pretend other things.

"As you can see," de Ferro continued, "our ploy last night did not, alas, have the desired effect."

"In that we are still being pursued by that ship," Marlowe allowed, "yes, it does appear that your trick did not work."

"No need for worry." The captain held up his book. "I have this."

"And that is?"

"A book of tides," de Ferro answered. "I have compiled information about these waters for twenty years. I know that if we go *here* we find currents that will slow a ship, if we go *there* we risk being torn apart by mad waves. I know this part of the ocean better than any man alive."

"Better than the Duke of Medina Sidonia?"

"He knows the wide ocean. I know the coastal waters."

"Possibly," Marlowe allowed, "but the duke is unbeaten, and almost singularly responsible for the success of Spain's navy."

"Yes, but also," the captain insisted, "I am Portuguese. We invented these ships. He is Spanish. They invented the guitar. If you want music, speak with him. If you want to sail *this* part of the ocean, speak with me."

"You're saying that you're going to sail into waters where he can't follow."

The captain tapped his book. "Yes."

Marlowe smiled. "I see."

"But we have something worse to worry about," the captain complained.

"Spies," Marlowe said.

Captain de Ferro nodded. "Why else would that Spanish ship be following us?"

Marlowe nodded and lowered his voice. "I can think of a dozen reasons, but it does appear that there may be a traitor among your crew."

The captain's face lost a bit of its sunny disposition.

"You serve a Queen," the captain answered grimly, "and you are under the protection of a man I greatly admire. Otherwise, I might be forced to see you answer for such a personal accusation."

Marlowe bristled, partly in defense, partly owing to lack of sleep.

"I have never met a Queen," he responded to the captain, "I need no man's protection, and I would gladly answer to you in any manner that you see fit."

The smile returned to de Ferro's face.

"Ah!" he boomed. "A fine speech! I see that my friend Rodrigo is true when he tells me that you are a brave man, as well as something of a poet. Good."

A voice behind them startled Marlowe.

"I believe the word I used was *foolhardy*," Lopez said, "not *brave*."

"It comes to the same thing," the captain insisted, "in an enterprise such as this."

Marlowe turned to see that Lopez, too, had not slept. The doctor's eyes seemed circled with charcoal, and his body was tense.

"But my friend Marlowe has a point, you see," Lopez continued, speaking to de Ferro. "He would like to know why such an impressive ship would be following us if everyone in your crew is trustworthy."

"*Someone* knows your mission," the captain said plainly, "but not my men. They have no idea what you're doing."

"Possibly." Lopez glanced in the direction of the Spanish ship. "Although I am forced to ask: who else would give us away? Not our master, not you, not Marlowe or me. What other possibilities?"

Marlowe sniffed. "Endless. Someone at Cambridge, the coachman, the men who attacked us—"

"Yes," Lopez interrupted, "we should have killed them."

"I'll kill a man if necessary," Marlowe snapped, "but not for mere convenience."

"But if they were the ones who set this ship after us . . ." Lopez protested.

"It could have been any one of a hundred shadows at Whitehall, hundreds more at the Hastings docks and, lastly, as I was saying, it could be one of the men on this ship." Marlowe turned to the captain. "How did it come to pass that Captain de Ferro's ship was waiting for us?"

"My ship has been at the ready for two days," the captain answered.

"By royal order," Marlowe asked, "or some other commission?"

"I'll show you." The captain strode toward the steps. "The document is in my cabin."

With a slight glance at Marlowe, Lopez followed immediately. Marlowe took a moment to study the Spanish ship once again, and then sped after it.

The captain's cabin was so grand that Marlowe was momentarily taken aback. It was really three rooms: an office of sorts, sleeping quarters, and a large closet for a chamber pot, stool, and wash-basin. All were fastidiously tidy. The back wall was taken primarily by shuttered windows, and all the shutters were open, so that a view of the Spanish ship was amply displayed.

Captain de Ferro, his face stern, went to his desk and picked up a small golden cylinder. He uncapped it, withdrew a single page, and handed the page to Lopez.

Lopez unrolled the document. Marlowe stood close enough to see what was written there.

"Make ready your ship immediately," it read. "Two passengers, a doctor and a student."

There was nothing else on the page.

"Nothing more?" Lopez asked. "No money, no explanation?"

The captain shook his head.

Marlowe's eyes narrowed.

"Our captain has done this sort of work before," Marlowe announced, taking a single step backward. "He has received other letters like this one. He recognized the handwriting. Or, possibly, that golden tube. No further words were necessary."

All eyes fell on the tube. It was plain, a foot or so long, with caps at each end.

"May I?" Marlowe asked.

He moved toward the captain's desk without waiting for permission.

Captain de Ferro took a single step, blocking Marlowe's progress, and smiled.

"You may not," he told Marlowe.

Marlowe nodded. "And that tells me as much as I need to know."

"I've told you nothing," the captain insisted, but his voice betrayed a small doubt.

"You won't allow me to examine that case," Marlowe said pointedly, "I therefore conclude two possibilities. One: the container offers some evidence of Spain. Two: there is, somewhere about it, our Queen's royal signet."

"I wonder which it could be," de Ferro said without moving.

"If it is Spanish," Marlowe went on, "he won't let me see it because he knows we are on Her Majesty's Secret Service. But if he thinks we're counteragents of the Pope, he won't let me see it because it belongs to the Queen."

"Why would he think we're agents for the Pope?" Lopez asked.

"The three men who visited me in Cambridge," Marlowe answered. "If Walsingham could know about them, others could too. The situation would be easy to misinterpret, don't you think?"

"It's a puzzle," de Ferro said slyly.

"Wait!" Marlowe barked. "I have realized the obvious. Doctor, may I see the note again?"

Lopez handed over the document. Marlowe took only a moment to scrutinize it.

"Yes." Marlowe looked up. "This was written by Walsingham. The captain is not a Catholic agent. He may be a spy, but he works with us, with Her Majesty."

"Written by Walsingham?" Lopez asked. "Are you certain?"

"On Walsingham's desk I happened to see certain papers to which his signature was affixed, and made note of his handwriting. It's quite distinctive. Look at the capital letters M and L on this page."

He handed the paper back to Lopez, who studied it for a moment.

"They are the same as you saw in the pages on Walsingham's desk?"

"Yes." Marlowe stared at de Ferro.

The captain smiled. "Rodrigo, I trust you completely, but I do not know this boy. He's aboard my ship for an hour or so, and suddenly there is a Spanish war vessel following me. I know my crew, I know my friend—there was only one variable."

"I." Marlowe nodded. "You made the right decision. I would have suspected me too."

"I still do," de Ferro said.

"Yes," Marlowe admitted. "Just because I recognize Walsingham's handwriting doesn't mean I'm not a Catholic spy. But my mind is at ease. I no longer suspect you, and, of course, I do not suspect myself."

"You're very quick," de Ferro said cautiously.

"But to the point," Marlowe countered, "what do we do about that ship, the one that is following us?"

All eyes gazed out the windows at the Spanish vessel. It was clearly drawing closer.

"I plan to do what any smuggler would do with dangerous cargo aboard," de Ferro said, his voice turned cold. "Get it off my ship."

SIX

Half an hour later, with the Spanish ship close enough to make out men on its deck arming themselves and loading cannons, de Ferro stood at the wheel, along with the pilot.

All hands were on deck, all four masts were rigged, and all the sails were pregnant. The ship was careening wildly with the wind, and the coastline was visible on the leeward side. No one spoke. Most, including a sheet-white Marlowe, hugged a mast or a rail for dear life.

As they drew closer to land, the waves began to rise, and the ship became airborne, rising high and then crashing down with bone-crushing intensity onto the cold, marble ocean.

Lopez was steady, but he had wrapped his arms around the same rail that Marlowe clutched.

"You told me," Lopez shouted over the raging chaos, "in the coach, on the bridge, that you did not care to be over water. I see now it's more serious than that."

Marlowe nodded, soaking wet, eyes stinging from the salt. "I nearly drowned when I was a boy. In Canterbury we have the Great Stour River. It runs through the center of the city. I fell in. When I was dragged out, I was dead. A man sat on my stomach and pushed out the water. I awoke from my own death."

"So it's not the water that you fear," Lopez shouted. "It's death."

"Oh, no," Marlowe disagreed. "I'm fine with dying. It's absolutely the water that I hate. Let me die in a knife fight, not on the water. Not aboard a Portuguese ship."

At that moment a wall of water washed the deck, and Marlowe's grip was tested as he sank to his knees, but terror was a strong glue. His mouth was filled with salt water, his eyes burned, his hands were numb, and he was certain that he felt his soul rising toward the morning sky.

The ship continued its battle with tides for another half hour. Then, slowly at first but with increasing relief, the sea turned calm once again. The ship had steered away from the coast, and the open water was, by comparison to the coastal madness, as still as the grave.

Soaked to the bone, shivering, and glad just to be alive, Marlowe and Lopez helped each other to stand.

The captain appeared before them, out of the sea spray.

"We've lost the Spanish ship, at least for the moment," he barked. "The longboat is prepared: two men and supplies. You make for shore. Stow the boat out of sight, wait for dark, and sail the coast to Bilbao, as we discussed. The longboat has a folding mast and sail."

"I hate this plan!" Marlowe howled.

"It's not ideal," de Ferro agreed, "but we have friends there. One of the men I'm assigning to you, he is a Basque. . . ."

"No!" Marlowe bellowed, turning to Lopez. "I'm for abandoning the captain's plan and striking out on our own."

"On our own?" Lopez coughed. "How?"

"Take the longboat by ourselves, set the sail and manage."

"Can you sail a boat like that?"

"No," said Marlowe. "*You're* the one from the proud race of circumnavigating sea folk!"

"I'm a doctor!"

"I'm a student!"

"Gentlemen." Captain de Ferro's voice boomed. "I understand your concern, but you need Gaspar. He's from my own hometown, and I trust him with my life. In the second place, you need Argi Zabala. He's a Basque, as I've said. He'll get you out of Spain in secret, with his countrymen."

Without waiting for a response, de Ferro hauled himself along the rail to help his men lower the longboat.

A second later a small dark man dressed all in blue tugged at Marlowe's arm. The man was the marksman who had set the barrels of oil aflame.

"We go now," he said. "I am Argi, the Basque."

With that he turned and strode away. Marlowe and Lopez followed him to the longboat. The captain stood by, head down.

"You'll make it to Malta," the captain assured them. "You may even be early. Walsingham should like that."

"Walsingham," Lopez said. "I don't trust him."

The captain looked away. "Beware of him, Rodrigo. With that man, nothing is as it seems."

"I know," Lopez answered.

"Go," de Ferro said, still not looking at Lopez or Marlowe.

In the next second Marlowe and Lopez were over the side and the longboat was dropped into the sea. It hit the water before Marlowe turned to look at the other man in their quartet, Gaspar. He was older than Argi, wrapped in a thick brown blanket. His hair was long and disheveled; his eyes displayed a keen intelligence. And he was smiling.

The waves were high but rounded. Argi took one oar and Gaspar the other. They pulled with their entire bodies, and the longboat flew over the water. Before long they could hear crashing waves: the shore was fast approaching. There was no sign of either ship at sea.

As the longboat hit the sand, Marlowe jolted forward.

"Welcome to Spain," Lopez whispered.

On board the Portuguese ship, Captain de Ferro stood at the rail with the pilot.

"I've had enough of this," de Ferro said to the pilot in Portuguese. "Let's go. I did as I was told. I got them off my ship—exactly as Walsingham directed me to do."

"Why did he put them on this ship," the pilot asked, shaking his head, "only to take them off again?"

The captain could only shrug.

"What about your friend, the doctor?" the pilot asked.

"I gave him Gaspar and the Basque," de Ferro shot back defensively, "what more do you expect? Now take the wheel, come full about, hug the coast, and put as much water between us and these damned English spies as you can before sunset."

The pilot nodded once. "The Basque will get them through, and you'll see your friend soon enough."

"Take the wheel!"

The pilot stood for a moment, staring at the captain, then moved up the stairs to the aftcastle and turned the wheel gently but steadily until the ship was headed north.

Captain de Ferro felt the wind shift. He glanced once toward shore, where the longboat might have landed. Then he turned his face into the wind, and his mind toward other matters.

SEVEN

The merchant ship *Ascension,* belonging to the English gentleman Mr. Cordal, moored at the port of Valletta early on October 9, a Sunday. Men were already throwing bags of grain at a pallet on the dock by the time the ship was tied up.

The plank was lowered, and five Jewish men of business descended slowly, with a cold air of great dignity. All were dressed in black save for a white prayer shawl around the neck tucked into a buttoned cloak. Their heads were covered and the shawls obscured their faces. Their hands were out of sight, their eyes stern and cold. They moved as one, close together, and caught the eye of the Customs and Revenue Officer of the Knights of Malta almost instantly. He was a tall man, almost skeletal, dressed in a red tunic emblazoned with the white cross of the Knights.

He approached them with two armed men at his side, but the businessmen did not stop, nor did they even acknowledge the officer's presence when he began to speak.

"Gentlemen," he announced sternly, "there is a matter of—gentlemen. Every ship in from Marseilles must pay the extra—stop!"

Only one man stopped. The rest kept moving. The man who had stopped handed the officer a heavy leather pouch, opened it, and glared at the officer. Without waiting for another word, the man turned and rejoined his companions.

The officer was left staring down into the pouch. He had never seen so many gold coins. By the time he finally looked up, the Jews were gone.

Ten minutes later, in a lovely courtyard a mile or so from the dock, Marlowe took off his black cloak, grinning. The courtyard, twenty feet square, was filled with golden light, and planted with a stunning variety of flowers and Mediterranean spices. They filled the senses, creating an air of peace.

"That was absolutely remarkable," he said to no one in particular, "the way you bypassed the authorities. Brilliant."

Marlowe glanced around at his companions. They had kept to themselves on the voyage from Marseilles, and Marlowe had been a bit unwell in the rough seas. Lopez explained that these men were wealthy Jewish merchants from Malta, in league with the grander plan, and that had been enough for Marlowe at the time, seasick as he was.

A young man said something in a language Marlowe didn't recognize.

Lopez nodded. "My friend says that money is a universal language, and one they've spoken to the harbor master many times."

"Yes, I see that. Pardon my asking, but what language was he speaking just now, your friend? It's like nothing I've ever heard before."

"Not surprising," Lopez told him. "It's Judeo-Portuguese, better than any code. It's at least five hundred years old, and yet only we speak it."

An older man with a gray beard and deep-set eyes threw the cowl of his cloak back from his face and scowled at Marlowe.

"We have no time for idle discussion," he rumbled in English. "If you are found here with us, we'll all be killed. Get your business concluded today. My son has the plan."

The old man turned to leave.

"Today?" Marlowe shot back before thinking. "No. We need more time. Much more. We've been tossed off a Portuguese ship, smuggled through Spain and the Basque territories under barrels, jostled in carts around France until our bones are loose. If it hadn't been for our friend Argi we'd already be dead—five times over. And may I remind you that I was sick for half the sail from Marseilles to here on that burnt cork of a ship. I don't think I could conclude my bowels today, let alone an impossible rescue operation. Lopez. Tell them."

"He needs food and drink, and a few hours of sleep," Lopez explained reasonably. "He'll be ready then. Why don't we all reconvene at, say, the second hour after midday?"

Marlowe cried out a wordless objection. The old man closed his eyes and said something that sounded very much like a curse in the arcane language.

Lopez turned to Marlowe, smiling. "He says he'll bring you a nice breakfast."

"That's not what he said," Marlowe disagreed, "but I could murder a nice breakfast."

Lopez nodded. "And then a pleasant nap here in this courtyard."

The old man looked up to the sky for a moment, as if asking a question, then, reluctantly, gave orders. Moments later a large meal, a cask of wine, and several blankets were proffered. Everyone save Lopez and Marlowe went inside. Marlowe sat on a wide wooden bench, admiring the garden that surrounded the courtyard. Lopez stood.

"They don't want me in the house," Marlowe concluded. "I'm unclean."

"Yes." Lopez avoided looking at his friend.

Marlowe gnawed on a dried date. "I notice they don't use names. They won't tell us their names."

"Better that way," Lopez said, still not catching Marlowe's eye. "Safer."

"Yet you seem to trust these men. Why?"

Lopez glanced toward the house. "Because we have to, so it's really pointless to debate. But the Jews on this island have good reason to hate the Knights of Malta."

"I've heard stories," Marlowe acknowledged, "and I understand. A mutual hatred makes good allies, you said."

"It does, if these men are who they say they are."

Marlowe tore off a joint of chicken. "I suppose we'll see soon enough."

Marlowe was asleep on the bench, under a blanket, within the next five minutes.

Afternoon sunlight slanted into the courtyard before Marlowe awoke. Momentarily blinded, he heard voices close by, murmuring.

"Ah," Lopez said, "he's awake."

Marlowe sat up.

"You know," he said to Lopez sleepily, "I've had a thought. Is it possible that Pygott was killed by those same men who attacked us on the road to London, do you think? Several of my classmates saw those men on the campus—Boyle and—the other one—Carier. I was with them when I—"

"Not now," Lopez interrupted impatiently.

Lopez and another man were standing over a table that had not been in evidence before Marlowe had fallen asleep.

"Come," the man said to Marlowe. "Look."

Marlowe stretched, cracked his neck, and stumbled over to the table. He couldn't be certain, but it appeared that the other man at the table was among the cloaked companions from the ship. The table was completely covered by a map.

"This," the man was saying as he pointed, "is the entrance to the prison where they are holding your English spy."

Marlowe opened his eyes wider. He hadn't expected so blunt a description of their prize. He studied the man for a moment. He was still dressed in the black cloak, his face was dark, his beard thick, and his eyes lacked all emotion.

"Once in," the man continued, "there is a long corridor that descends to an open room. The open room has three doors. We can't be certain which door leads to the hole. We're told it's the one on the left. Do you understand me?"

"Right," Marlowe yawned, "I'm awake. Take the left door and hope for the best."

"At the end of that hall," the man continued, impatiently, "there would be a sharp drop to a stinking hole. The only way into it or out of it is a ladder mounted on the wall beside it, too big for one man to move."

"Our man is down there?" Marlowe asked. "In that hole?"

"As far as we know," the man answered. "With seven others."

"Who are they," Marlowe asked, "the others?"

"No idea," the man answered.

"Do you mind my asking how you got this intelligence?" Marlowe ventured.

"I do mind," the man answered plainly.

"They have their own man on the inside," Lopez announced. "That man won't reveal himself, not even to us when we're there. He won't help us. But he's there."

Marlowe thought for a moment.

"He's a Jew who's managed to acquire a position as a guard," Marlowe concluded. "Brave."

"Foolish," the man at the table snapped.

"It's his younger brother," Lopez explained.

"No!" the man shouted. "Wrong!"

"He doesn't want you to know it because he doesn't trust you."

"Because I'm a Christian or because I'm an Englishman?" Marlowe asked the man.

The man gritted his teeth and hissed his answer. "Because I'm a Jew who has lived life on the edge of a dagger. I trust no one."

"Good philosophy," Marlowe answered amiably, "but I'm afraid I can't completely agree with it. I trust Dr. Lopez, for example, and he trusts you. So, by proxy, I trust you. I realize it's foolish. But I seem to have been born without a fear of death. And once death is removed from your list of fears, almost everything else is . . . fun."

The man's jaw relaxed and he gaped at Marlowe, uncertain how to respond. At last he murmured a single syllable.

"Fun?"

Marlowe smiled. "Yes, but why are we rushing? Why does it have to be today?"

There was a moment of silence.

"Partly because our home and our family are in danger," the man continued at last, "but mostly because today is October 9, the Feast of Saint Denis. There will be fewer guards in the prison. They seem to take any excuse, these Christians here on Malta, to get drunk."

"Saint Denis," Marlowe mumbled. "Patron saint of the *possessed,* as it happens."

"Auspicious," Lopez answered wryly.

"How do we get past the first door, into the damned place?" Marlowe asked.

"We'll have a letter allowing us to visit my 'father,'" Lopez interrupted, "who owes a heavy tax to the Knights. I'm visiting to tell him that the money has been raised and he'll soon be free."

"They've picked out a man in that situation who occupies a cell in the same building as the hellhole where our man languishes," Marlowe deduced. "Clever. But who am I in this play?"

Lopez grinned. "You're my Christian bodyguard."

The man at the table laughed.

"He's laughing," Lopez explained, "because the first thought they had was to put you in a dress and say you were my daughter."

"A girl who prepared proper food for her grandfather," the man at the table explained, smiling with his mouth, but not his eyes.

"I assured them that you would prove a formidable bodyguard," Lopez went on, "as long as you weren't wearing a dress."

"This man couldn't protect his codpiece in a whorehouse," the man at the table mumbled.

Marlowe tilted his head. "What an odd thing to say. I don't wear a codpiece, as you can plainly see, and why would I want to protect it in a whorehouse? Your insult makes no sense. Maybe you'd care to put my abilities to the test."

"Oh." The man lost his smile. "I would like that very much. I would quite enjoy proving to my father that this plan will not work."

"We don't have time for a quarrel," Lopez objected, mostly to the man at the table.

The man ignored Lopez, planted his feet, and leaned forward onto the table, preparing to lunge.

"Fine, then, we won't quarrel," Marlowe began reasonably. "Let's just leave it at this."

In a blur, Marlowe's dagger was in his hand and he kicked the table just enough to hit his opponent in the midsection. In the next breath Marlowe leaned forward, thrust his hand into the man's cloak, and grabbed the dagger hidden there. Then Marlowe stabbed down his blade, hard. It stuck deep in the table between the man's second and third fingers.

The man hadn't had time to draw a single breath.

"Now," Marlowe explained softly, showing the man his own dagger, "if you weren't my friend's friend, that blade would be in your hand, nailing you to the table, instead of between your fingers. And I'd kill you with your own dagger. If Jewish girls can do that, then put me in a dress. Otherwise, tell me the rest of your plan so I can get off this scab of an island and back to my drinking in England."

The man worked hard to control his rage. His chest rose and fell like a bellows, and his eyes were coals.

"That's what a bodyguard does, you see," Lopez explained after a moment. "That sort of thing."

The man moved his hand away from Marlowe's dagger at last. He nodded, calming.

"Maybe this will work after all," he said finally. "Maybe."

EIGHT

Once fully explained, the plan was not remotely to Marlowe's liking.

After he and Lopez pulled their man out of the hole, they were to dress him as a guard, leave the prison as quickly as possible, and head for the docks where the *Ascension* would be waiting. Marlowe pointed out the many flaws in the scheme, but had been assured that the strategy was a product of older, wiser heads.

The same group of men who had been onboard the *Ascension* escorted Marlowe and Lopez to the prison. Marlowe alone eschewed his previous rabbinical disguise, following the rest of the enclave in his own clothes through the streets and narrow alleys.

The sun was low in the sky over the port of Valletta, but the stones in the plaza outside the prison complex of the Knights of Malta retained the day's heat and made everyone sweat.

A gate opened into an arena with a tiled floor surrounded by twenty-foot walls. It was a plain, undecorated space, perhaps forty feet square. This complex had always been a prison. There were no guards at the gate, but at least ten were milling around in the arena as Marlowe and the rest made their way across the tiles and arrived at a tall wooden door.

Four guards stood on either side of that door, all staring at the visitors. A fifth man took the papers Lopez offered. He shook his head, looked at the men, and read the papers once more.

"Well, I don't know how you managed this," he said at last, in a clearly English accent, "but it appears you have the required sum in safekeeping, and permission to visit the prisoner. What I don't understand is why you lot want inside now? You've paid the fees. The old man's out in a day or two."

"As it says there, the old man is my father," Lopez explained, feigning deference. "I worry about his health. If he knew that he was soon to be released, it would do him a world of good. Please, at least let me speak with him, if only for a moment."

The man in charge sighed. "Just you, then."

"And my bodyguard," Lopez added.

"Bodyguard?" the man boomed.

Marlowe stepped forward. It was decidedly not a part of the plan.

"That's right, mate," he said in a deliberately vulgar, heavy accent. "He's got Hebrew superstition: thinks it's unlucky to go in a Maltese prison without a Christian token. And that's me."

"You're not a Jew." The man was clearly surprised.

"Do I look like a Jew to you?" Marlowe fired back, just at the point of being offended.

"I don't know what you look like, *mate*," the knight snapped, "but you're not coming in here."

Marlowe took a step back and smiled.

"I judge you to be a Kettering man, by your speech," Marlowe said, a bit more confidentially, giving his own rough accent free rein. "Me, I'm from Corby."

"Corby?" The knight's demeanor softened considerably. "What the hell are you doing here playing shield man to this Jew?"

"I might ask you," Marlowe answered amiably, "what in God's name you're doing on this godforsaken rock. We've all got to work, ain't we?"

The man shook his head, even smiled a little. "Well, we're both a long way from home, and that's the truth."

Marlowe leaned closer to the knight. "Look, my employer—I mean to say, that's his old dad in prison. And they love their dads, these Jews do. But then, don't we all?"

The knight leaned in further and whispered, "Truth be told, I have no idea who mine was."

"That being the case," Marlowe said, patting the knight on the arm, "you and I could very well be brothers. I never saw much of my sire, but they say he raked it in all over the county. And you and me being from the same region—I mean, imagine if he knew your mum!"

The other man stared for a second, and looked as if he might draw his weapon. Then he burst into laughter.

"God," he said to Marlowe, "it's good to hear a familiar-sounding voice."

"Amen to that."

"I suppose you ought to go on in then," he said to Marlowe. He turned to the others and barked, "Let these two pass!"

The huge door opened, and Lopez stepped in, followed immediately by Marlowe. Before they had taken two steps, the door closed and was bolted, oddly from the inside, by another guard.

Lopez showed that guard his papers without speaking a word. The guard nodded and pointed down the torchlit stone hallway. It sloped, ever so slightly, downward.

When he felt certain no one could hear, Lopez whispered to Marlowe, "What the hell was that you did back there at the door?" he asked.

"Theater," Marlowe answered, smiling. "I could tell instantly, from his accent, that he was from Kettering. I improvised."

"But—" Lopez began.

"I relied on the camaraderie of the lonely," Marlowe said simply. "And there is no one so lonely as an Englishman far from home."

"God in heaven," Lopez replied, exasperated.

"It got me inside," Marlowe bristled. "Let's get on with it."

"Fine. Do you remember the code that Walsingham gave us? The words you are to say to our man to let him know that you are his salvation?"

"I do," Marlowe said, demonstrating indignation with a rude hand gesture.

The downward slope of the hallway emptied into a small, rounded room. There were no guards. Marlowe began to see the wisdom of staging the event on the Feast of Saint Denis.

The room had three doors, as predicted. Lopez pointed to the one on the left. Marlowe took a single step in that direction before the door in the center opened wide. He froze. Another guard appeared, this one, too, in the white-cross tunic. He seemed only mildly surprised to see Lopez and Marlowe.

"Papers," was all he said, in a voice that betrayed boredom beyond endurance.

Lopez handed over the false documents and waited in silence for what seemed a very long time.

"All right," the guard grunted. "He's in here, your father. Come on."

Lopez didn't move, uncertain what to do.

"I'll wait here, sir," Marlowe said instantly, assuming his arch accent. "Just you sing out if you need me."

Lopez hesitated, and then headed toward the center door. The guard looked down, stood back so as not to touch Lopez as he entered. Then, oddly, looked up at Marlowe, nodded once, and closed the door.

Marlowe waited several seconds, looking back up the hallway, and then plunged ahead, grabbing the door on the left with both hands and pulling hard. The door made too much noise, but it opened. The hallway past it was black. Marlowe took several steps before deciding that his eyes would never adjust to the darkness. He backed up quickly to the round room, took a torch from the wall, and was on his way once more.

The dark hall was fetid and cold. There was moss on the walls, and unidentifiable insects skittered away from the torch. Marlowe trod carefully, wary of falling into the very room from which he hoped to rescue his prize. Beyond the sphere of torchlight, he may as well have been at the bottom of the ocean. After a moment he fancied he could hear sounds. Ten more silent steps and he realized that he was hearing the hopeless noises of men breathing, moaning—some, praying.

The smell was overwhelming.

Another five steps and the torch revealed a hole some twenty feet in diameter. As promised there was a ladder mounted on the wall, as well as a nearby sconce in which to place the torch. How he would manage the ladder by himself was a momentary puzzle. Nearly twenty feet in length and a good four feet wide, it would weigh as much as several men.

He secured the torch and considered his dilemma. After a second he realized that gravity was his ally. The primary challenge would be drawing the ladder upward, not lowering it down.

He set his shoulder to one of the ends of the ladder and boosted it from its wall braces. It was heavy, but when he was about to drop it he simply jumped away and let it fall. It made quite a clatter. He shot to the other side and did the same thing, and the entire ladder crashed to the stone floor.

The men below began to call out. Most of them were speaking in strange tongues. None spoke in English.

Down on all fours, Marlowe shoved the ladder with all his might until it inched along toward the hole.

"Look out," he said softly to the men below. "*Cuidado. Fais attention!*"

He moved the ladder until it teetered precariously on the edge of the hole for a moment, and then slid, more slowly than he expected, downward into the hole, scraping along the stones as it fell.

He shot to the torch, grabbed it, and peered over the side. There were, perhaps, a dozen men crammed into the hole. All of them seemed dead. No one was standing. One was covered in blood.

Marlowe stood on the precipice, momentarily unwilling to descend.

"If you are an Englishman," Marlowe ventured, "then answer me this: what manner of martin is this, whose wings we should clip?"

There was a long moment of chaotic babbling, but no answer to the coded phrase. Marlowe held the torch closer to his face.

"Can you see me?" he asked more urgently. "I am asking you what manner of *martin*?"

Some of the men fell silent, looking up. Some may even have realized that Marlowe was not one of the guards.

After a few desperate heartbeats, just as Marlowe began to

consider that his prize was not there, a young man's voice—a boy's, really—called out hoarsely.

"House martin."

The first part of the countersign was perfect. Marlowe could not make out the speaker. He stared into the hole.

"And how is that pronounced in the Border Lands?" Marlowe asked.

After a moment, barely above a whisper, the final countersign was given.

"Throckmorton," the voice rasped.

"Can you raise your hand?" Marlowe asked. "I can't see you."

A pile of rags in the corner stirred, tried to sit up, raising both hands.

"Can you get up the ladder?"

The limp puppet staggered over to the ladder and tried, three times, to hold it, to lift a foot to the first rung.

Marlowe realized that it would take a century for the man to crawl out of the hole on his own.

"Wait." Marlowe laid the torch on the floor beside the ladder. "I'm coming."

Against his better judgment, Marlowe began a speedy, spiderlike descent. Several other prisoners in the hole mustered a bit of energy, seeing some vague, nameless hope of escape.

One foot, three—with each step Marlowe felt his heart insisting strongly that it wanted out of his chest. Two seconds that lasted a year brought him to the lowest rung he needed in order to grab his man's hand.

"Reach," Marlowe commanded.

A pale, almost skeletal hand shot up like a drowning man's. Marlowe took hold of the wrist and pulled, already climbing back up the ladder. The man groaned.

"Put your feet on the ladder," he urged. "Climb!"

Marlowe glanced up at the torch and did his best to listen for any approaching footsteps. He knew he'd made noise with the ladder, but he had no way of knowing whether or not it could be heard past the thick wooden door.

He held tight to his prize's hand, and climbed as quickly as he thought he dared. One rung, two, six—it seemed to take another century to reach the top. The man below was doing his best to struggle upward on the ladder with one hand, but his feet faltered and he slipped more than once.

Marlowe glanced down at him.

"I'm going to let go of your hand," he said. "Take firm hold on the ladder."

"No," the man whimpered.

"Take hold," Marlowe commanded.

With clear reluctance the man let go of Marlowe's hand and flailed for a moment before grabbing the next rung of the ladder.

Marlowe leapt upward onto the floor and grabbed the torch in one hand, taking out his dagger with the other.

"Come on, then," Marlowe insisted frantically.

The man pulled himself slowly over the rim of the hole, into the torchlight. He was truly little more than a boy, face smudged with dirt and blood, clothes like sheets wrapped around him, hair a rat's nest.

"Take my arm if you need to," Marlowe whispered, holding out the elbow of his torch arm.

The man heaved himself upward, swung his body around, and came to a precarious halt on the floor. His quavering body threatened to tilt sideways and fall back into the hole. He lunged and grabbed Marlowe's elbow, scattering ash and sparks from the torch.

Some of the other prisoners began coming up the ladder. Marlowe could hear them. It was clear that his man was in no condition to help him pull up the ladder, and he knew he couldn't do it himself. He also found that he didn't have the heart to leave men in such horror. If they could get up the ladder, Marlowe was willing to let them.

How that would play out when it was discovered by the prison guards, or how it would affect the Jewish allies, Marlowe chose not to consider. He only knew he had to get out of the prison with the man on his arm.

He rushed to the door, dragging the man along. He stood a moment, listening. He could hear nothing from the other side of the door.

He looked his man in the eye and whispered, "Stand against the wall, behind the door."

The man did.

Marlowe grasped the door handle with his dagger hand and leaned hard with all his weight. The door scraped open. The round room was empty.

He looked behind the door.

"Come on," he whispered to the man. "And stand behind me."

The man obeyed. Marlowe stepped out into the room, pushed the door closed, and, moving sideways, eye on the center door, replaced the torch whence he had gotten it.

The man was rasping when he breathed. Marlowe turned to him.

"Sh," he whispered, finger to his lips.

The man nodded and did his best to be silent.

Marlowe found it nearly impossible to simply stand still, staring at the center door, willing Lopez to appear so that they could run. The blood was racing through his veins and thoughts scattered like lightning in his brain.

An eternity passed, and then the center door began to inch open. Marlowe planted himself, grasped his dagger, and held his breath.

The guard he had seen before stepped out, saw Marlowe, and nodded. Lopez appeared behind him.

The guard drew a pistol. Marlowe drew his rapier.

"This is for you," the guard said to Lopez. "You'll need it."

Momentarily trying to make sense of the gesture, Marlowe stared at the guard.

"Thank you," Lopez murmured, taking the gun.

"You're the little brother," Marlowe concluded.

The man made no response.

Then, without warning, another guard, the one who had been

manning the front door of the prison, could be heard clattering down the long hallway.

"What's all that racket down there?" he shouted.

The guard next to Lopez whispered, "Stab me. Here!" The man pulled his tunic up and pointed to a place in his side.

"I'm not certain it's necessary," Lopez began.

"If you leave me like this," the guard insisted desperately, "they'll suspect. If you stab me, they'll send me to the hospital, where my brother can get me. Do you understand?"

Lopez nodded and stabbed the man in the proper spot. The man fell back against the wall and slumped to the floor, bleeding profusely, and closed his eyes.

Marlowe could hear the other prisoners from the hole, some of them at least, shuffling up the hall toward the door on the left.

"Why don't you go and take care of the other guard," Lopez urged. "The one up there in the hallway."

"Yes," Marlowe answered, rousing himself. "Look after our man. He's not well."

With that Marlowe launched himself up the hall. Within ten feet he encountered the guard.

The man was taken by surprise, but training or instinct did not fail him. He drew his sword.

"Stop," the man warned menacingly.

"Ah, good," Marlowe said to the man, "military sword against rapier and dagger. The former is a clumsy man's failing; the latter is a clever man's grace. As luck would have it, I am quite graceful. You're about to die."

That was a lesson from Lopez: taunt an opponent with the idea that he's already lost, even before the fighting has begun.

The guard hesitated and Marlowe thrust his rapier directly into the man's midsection. Blood spotted his tunic.

But the man did not go down. In fact, the wound only seemed to anger him. He raised his sword high above his head and brought it down in a flash.

Marlowe barely dodged it, turning sideways. Then he kicked the sword, hoping to dislodge it from the man's hand. As he did, he nicked the man's fighting arm with his dagger.

The man retained his weapon. He roared and whirled, this time aiming the edge of the blade Marlowe's way.

Marlowe twisted and managed to deflect the cutting edge with the hilt of his rapier, but the force of the blow was so powerful that it kicked him backward against the stone wall.

The man cocked his blade straight back, ready to thrust the point directly into Marlowe.

Dazed, the breath knocked out of him, Marlowe saw the point firing toward his heart. Instantly he dropped onto the floor. The point of the sword struck stone. A spark crackled there.

Marlowe rolled toward the man, reached, and stabbed his dagger into the man's boot, through the foot.

The man howled and raised his leg reflexively. Marlowe sprang to his feet and kicked the man backward. Already off his balance, the man fell against the opposite wall and then onto the stone floor, moaning.

Marlowe stood on the man's sword and placed the point of his rapier at the man's gullet.

"Be still!" Marlowe commanded.

The man did his best to dampen his complaint.

Marlowe reached down to retrieve his dagger.

As he did, the man drew a pistol from some concealed place underneath his tunic and cocked the hammer.

Just in time Marlowe swatted the gun from the man's hand, but it went off. The sound echoed in the stone hallway like thunder.

"Help!" the man began to yell. "Help me!"

"Marlowe!" Lopez shouted. "Silence that man. Now!"

Marlowe looked down.

"God forgive me," he said.

Then he thrust the rapier into the man's heart. The man stopped yelling and more blood stained his tunic.

Lopez appeared in the next second, dragging the nearly dead prisoner behind him.

"Our man's not going to make it to the ship," Marlowe said, pulling his dagger from the guard's foot.

"Oh, yes, he will." Lopez reached into the pouch on his belt.

He produced a vial of water and a small leather pouch.

"Drink this," he commanded.

The prisoner drank.

"Now," Lopez continued, holding the small pouch to the man's face, "breathe deeply, several times."

The man did as he was told. A split second later the man's head snapped backward.

"Holy hell," he snorted in a high-pitched voice. His eyes opened wide.

"What was in that?" Marlowe asked.

"I'll tell you later," Lopez said. "Get that tunic off the dead man. And the helmet. We'll need the helmet too."

Marlowe immediately got the guard out of his white-cross tunic. Slipping it over the thin prisoner, he tied it around the narrow waist with the guard's belt. Setting the guard's helmet onto the prisoner's head, Marlowe stood back.

"It looks like an ill-fitting costume in a cheap play," Marlowe whispered.

Suddenly they could both hear other prisoners from the hole moving slowly toward them, up the hall behind the door on the left.

"It'll have to do," Lopez snapped. "Come on."

He took off up the hall to the exit, dragging the prisoner along.

They came to the front door; it was still bolted from the inside. Lopez grabbed the lock.

"Wait," Marlowe said suddenly.

He stepped forward, took a deep breath, and jerked the door open.

"Look out, mate!" he yelled in his ruffian accent, hoping that the Kettering man was still in evidence. "They're getting away! Something's happened. We were overcome. I think the guard down there is dead. I've got another one here. Wounded!"

As his eyes adjusted to the hot light of the arena, he could see that the Kettering man was, indeed, still there.

"The—the prisoners are trying to escape?" he said, not believing it.

"Yes! Down there!" Marlowe pointed.

Lopez stepped out, holding up the disguised prisoner.

"I don't know how many there are," Lopez gasped, "or how they got out. But they're coming. That guard, at the center door—there is a lot of blood. And this one is dying."

"Get help," Marlowe urged. "Get your men. Now!"

The Kettering man, a growing look of panic on his face, turned and shouted to his men.

"We've got trouble!" he announced.

"I'm a doctor," Lopez said with great authority. "I'll take care of this wounded man. You just get in there. I'm worried about my father! God knows what those other prisoners will do!"

It was a very plausible improvisation.

"Christ," Marlowe complained loudly to everyone in earshot. "This is a mess!"

The other guards came running.

"Get in there," the Kettering shouted, "we've got men escaping!"

The guards shoved Lopez aside and rushed in. The Kettering man paused at the door.

"I don't understand what's going on," he said to Marlowe. "Maybe you ought to wait here a moment."

"No, thank you, mate," Marlowe sang out. "You can't keep your prisoners inside. And, see, that's really the purpose of a prison, ain't it? Keeping prisoners inside? So, no, I'm not staying here, not with them vermin about."

"And I've got to tend to your guard here," Lopez said urgently. "He's badly wounded."

"I don't—I don't know," the Kettering man stammered.

Suddenly there was much shouting from within the prison hallway.

"We've got one dead, one wounded," someone was shouting, "and all—all of the men in the hole—they're out!"

"Out?" the Kettering man exploded. "Bleeding Christ! How the hell did they get the ladder down?"

He turned and ran into the prison stronghold.

Marlowe and Lopez stood frozen for a stunned moment, looking around, both unable to quite believe that the plan had, for the most part, succeeded.

"Let's go, then," Marlowe urged softly.

"Immediately," Lopez agreed.

With that they both strode quickly toward the gate, and their waiting comrades, dragging their prize between them.

The *Ascension* had already cast off most of her lines by the time Marlowe and company appeared on the docks. The prisoner was unconscious by then, still being dragged between Marlowe and Lopez, who were attempting to make the man appear drunk.

Two anxious sailing men stood on the deck of the ship by the gangplank, ready to haul it up. One of them was rocking back and forth impatiently; the other kept his eyes on the long street leading to the docks.

"Come on, then," the impatient man yelled when the group drew closer.

Lopez turned to the old man at whose house they had been guests. The man's hood was pulled forward so far that his face could not be seen.

"I fear that they will come for you," Lopez said to the old man. "I pray that your son is safe."

"Nothing in this world is certain," the bass voice rumbled.

"What can we do to help?" Lopez asked.

"Pray," the old man said.

"That I will," Lopez vowed.

Then the old man turned to Marlowe.

"And you," he said softly. "Would you pray for a Jew, Christopher Marlowe?"

"God, of course I would. Do you mistake me for a Spaniard?" Marlowe scowled. "I've prayed for Dr. Lopez daily—in both Latin and English. I'd pray for you in your own language, if I knew it."

The old man nodded. "Then learn this word first, and let us speak it together: *shalom*."

"*Shalom*." Marlowe nodded. "I know that one. It means *peace*."

"Yes," the old man said. "It also means that something is complete: you've found your man, your work is done."

"It also means, if my education does not fail me," Marlowe answered, "the absence of discord. That meaning seems, perhaps, best of all."

The old man turned to Lopez and said, softly, "You were right about him."

With that the old man and his family turned, moving, again, as one, and seemed to float across the docks and back into the town.

"Come on!" the sailor at the top of the gangplank shouted again. "We're away with this tide!"

Marlowe and Lopez muscled their man up the plank and onto the deck in short order. The plank was drawn, the last lines cast off, and the *Ascension* lurched away from the dock as if it had been shoved toward the open ocean by some giant, unseen hand.

The sudden jolt startled the prisoner into semiconsciousness.

"Where am I?" he piped, slightly panicked.

"It's all right, my friend," Marlowe assured him. "Walsingham sent us. You're on an English ship with the Queen's men. You're safe and you're going home."

The man raised his head, looked at Marlowe, and began to cry. "Home?"

"That's right," Marlowe assured him. "Now, what do you need?"

"Water, food, bath," the prisoner managed to gasp.

"Which first?" Lopez asked.

"At the same time," the man said, "if possible."

And then he collapsed again.

"I'll get him into a tub," Marlowe volunteered, "if you can manage the food and drinking water."

"Done," Lopez agreed. "His room is the first on the right down below."

The *Ascension* was a clean ship. The crew was all professional men, sailing men, and clearly better paid than most. They wore a sort of uniform dress: black boots, loose pants, blue shirts. Marlowe considered the crisp air of order and confidence and came to the conclusion that Mr. Cordal, the ship's owner, was probably also in Walsingham's employ. Good business and the Queen's government were certainly affable bedfellows, but Marlowe was also suddenly wary of every man onboard.

He all but carried the prisoner down the steps to the appointed room below. There was a large bed, a writing desk, a hooked rug, and an ornate brass tub already filled with steaming water. On a small table close to the bed there was a pitcher surrounded by several mugs.

Marlowe eased the prisoner down onto the bed and then checked the pitcher. It was filled with fresh water and orange slices. He filled a mug, sat on the bed, roused the prisoner, and helped him to drink the mug dry.

The prisoner nodded, gasping a little.

"Food's on the way," Marlowe assured him.

"I—I should tell you," the man began, and then lapsed, once more, into unconsciousness.

Marlowe laid him down and began to pull off the oversized boots. Next he wrestled with the tunic. The prisoner's half-opened eyes displayed a degree of alarm that Marlowe didn't quite understand.

"It's all right," Marlowe said soothingly. "The bath's drawn, we'll just get you into it. Come on."

The prisoner's eyes opened wider, and the voice squeaked, but didn't seem to form proper words. At the same time, Marlowe dragged the prisoner's foul undershirt off and stood back, prepared to help the prisoner up, out of the grimy trousers, and into the tub.

He was not prepared, however, for what he saw next.

The prisoner was, in fact, a woman.

At that moment in Valletta, in the lovely courtyard, the merchant Abraham Abulafia, descendent of the great Hebrew mystic of the same name, threw back his hood and sat down at the table next to his son, Mikha'el.

"What now?" Mikha'el asked, picking a date from the tray on the table.

"Now? We wait," his father said.

"Wait for the knights to realize that we helped set free their prized English prisoner, you mean. Why did we do this, father? Why did we help these English?"

The old man sat back, feeling the setting sun on his face.

"Rodrigo Lopez," he told Mikha'el, as if it were the complete answer.

"Your friendship with him has always troubled me," the younger man said, shaking his head. "He's a *convert*, a traitor to his faith."

The old man shook his head and smiled. "If I told you that I was a camel, would you believe me?"

"What?"

"Just saying the words, 'I'm a Christian' scarcely makes a man a convert. Lopez pretends, yes. But do you really imagine that Walsingham and the English Queen believe him? They know. They know a camel when they see one."

"But, if they know—" Mikha'el began.

"They don't care," his father interrupted.

"Why?" It was a question with several meanings.

"It doesn't matter to the Queen because Dr. Lopez is, perhaps, the greatest healer in the world, and has twice saved her life. Walsingham doesn't care because he sees Lopez as the perfect instrument: both spectacularly worthwhile and supremely expendable. But why does Lopez do it? That should be your question."

"Yes," Mikha'el demanded, "why does he do it?"

"He does it to be the Queen's personal physician." The old man's eyes narrowed. "He will soon be the only man in the world who can hold a knife to the heart of England's monarch."

Just as Mikha'el realized what his father was saying, a thin gray cloud passed overhead, and seemed to cut the sun in half.

NINE

Marlowe stood speechless, unable to avert his eyes despite a desperate attempt to do so. The prisoner from Malta was a woman. There was clearly no denying that. There was also not the slightest hope of explaining it.

Marlowe tried to speak, but found he had lost the faculty.

When Lopez plunged through the cabin door, food in hand, the same malady instantly struck him.

Barely able to drag herself from the bed, the young woman slowly made her way to the steaming tub.

"After what I've been through," she croaked, "I don't mind being stared at, but this silence is making me uncomfortable. Is that my food?"

Lopez nodded dumbly.

The woman tore off the rest of her clothing and lowered herself into the tub, splashing water everywhere.

"God's pig-pissing kingdom," the woman said, sighing and sinking down into the hot water. "Now. Food?"

Lopez stood motionless. Out of the corner of his mouth he whispered, "Marlowe! What have you done?"

"What do you mean what have I done?" Marlowe shot back.

"I mean," Lopez demanded with a fuller voice, "who is this woman and what have you done with the prisoner?"

"That woman *is* the prisoner," Marlowe answered, as if he were explaining some holy miracle.

Lopez allowed his eyes to drift toward the tub. "No."

"I'm afraid he's right," the woman said languidly. "But I won't make it back to England if I don't eat something soon."

Marlowe took two steps, grabbed the wooden bowl of food from Lopez, and strode toward the tub. The woman rose slightly out of the water and stretched out a long pale arm.

"What do we have?" She grabbed the bowl and sat back into the water. "Beef, biscuit, lentils—is that honey?"

"It is," Lopez confirmed hesitantly. "You're—how did you—who are you?"

As if she hadn't heard Lopez, the young woman attacked her food, apparently attempting to put the entire contents of the bowl into her mouth in one gulp. Crumbs and bits of meat fell into the water, but she retrieved them and popped them into her mouth as well. The bowl was empty in seconds.

"More," she gasped, her mouth still full.

She held out the bowl, eyes closed.

Marlowe only hesitated for a second before taking it from her and returning to Lopez.

"You heard her," he told the doctor. "More."

"I—yes—well." And with that, Lopez was off.

Marlowe turned about.

"I believe we have a few things to discuss," Marlowe said, straining to remain calm, sitting down on the bed.

"I'm really not going to talk about anything until we're back on English soil," she answered. "I don't know who you are."

"I'm the man who pulled you out of that stinking hole in Malta," Marlowe responded softly. "I'm the man who killed someone to save your life. I'm the man whom Sir Francis Walsingham, the Queen's spymaster, sent to rescue you."

She turned to look at him. "I don't remember much about the last few days."

"Will you tell me your name?"

"Will you tell me yours?" she countered.

"I am Christopher Marlowe," he answered immediately.

"You're Kit Marlowe?"

"What? *Kit?* Why would you call me that? My name is Christopher. And why do you say it as if you've heard the name before?"

"Because I have," she answered simply, sinking low into the water.

"No. But, I mean—Oh, God! It just occurred to me: we've rescued the wrong man!"

"What?" she asked languidly.

"I pulled the wrong person out of that prison!" His voice sounded hollow.

The woman remained in a state of water-borne well-being. "Not from my point of view. And you should probably remember that I knew the countersign."

"That's right. But how did you know it? Walsingham's countersign?"

"House martin? Because that's what he told me to say. It makes sense, too. You can see how he would get from Throckmorton to house martin."

"What?" Marlowe swallowed.

"For one thing, they sound alike. But I refer to the legend that a house martin will capture a house sparrow by closing the entrance of the nest. And house martins will gather *en masse* to kill a sparrow. And the sparrow, as you surely know, was, to the Greeks, Aphrodite's kindred. Aphrodite is the queen of love, is she not?"

"What are you talking about?"

"Throckmorton's plot is an attempt to trap our Queen in her own nest, and amass an army to kill her. I have the details of his plan. If I can manage to return to England alive, the Queen will be saved."

She glanced his way. Marlowe held his breath.

"Set your mind to rest," she continued persuasively, if somewhat giddily. "You have plucked the proper posy."

"This is no time for easy alliteration," Marlowe warned her. "And how do you know to call me *Kit?*"

"It's a nickname your father gave you when you were little," she said softly. "It was told to me so that you would believe what I say."

"Told to you by whom?" Marlowe stammered.

"Let me revive myself," she sighed, "and I will tell you everything. But rest assured that you have done as you were told to do. You have rescued Her Majesty's spy."

With that she slipped further into the water until her head was entirely under.

Lopez chose that moment to return with another bowl of food. He was breathing heavily. He'd run.

After taking the briefest of moments to survey the room, holding out the bowl in his left hand, Lopez glared at Marlowe.

"Now what have you done with her?" he demanded, setting the bowl on the bed. "Where is she?"

"Under the water," Marlowe whispered.

"What a blunder!"

"No, we—apparently we've done exactly as we were told." Marlowe stepped closer to Lopez. "She knew the countersign. She says she has Walsingham's information, enough to hang Throckmorton and save the Queen."

"But—" Lopez squeezed his eyes shut. "She's a woman. Not even a woman. A girl."

Marlowe gazed at the tub. "She's a girl who withstood the tortures of the Inquisition and the hell of that prison. She may be the bravest person I have ever met."

At that her head popped up from the surface of the steaming water and she shouted, "God in *Heaven*, is there anything better in life than a hot bath?"

Lopez nodded. "So. Brave, then, but still a girl."

Marlowe could only stare at her profile.

"I wouldn't stay in that water any longer," Lopez called out. "Bathing is very unhealthy."

"Right," she said, not looking at them, "I'm going to get out of the tub now and eat more, and drink more, so I hope that there are clothes for me somewhere."

Marlowe took a step in her direction.

"Clothes for a man," he said. "The informal uniform of the crew, a pair of black boots, these loose-fitting pants, and a blue shirt. Laid out on the bed, beside your next bowl of food."

"I feel it would be better for all concerned if everyone, most especially the crew, were to continue thinking of me as a man," she said firmly. "Agreed?"

"Most assuredly," Lopez assented quickly.

"Then, gentlemen, if you would avert your eyes for but a moment, I shall quickly repair to my former identity: a frail boy named Richard."

Lopez instantly turned his back. Marlowe only lowered his eyes.

The spy slowly climbed out of the tub. Marlowe did his best not to look, but his best proved none too good. While she turned to dress, Marlowe could not help but observe that this spy might, like the sparrow, also be kin to Aphrodite.

When she was dressed, her hair tied up in a kerchief, her body concealed by ill-fitting clothing, she cleared her throat.

"Quickly now," she admonished. "We have much to discuss. I want to know what ship I'm on, how you got me out, what day and month it is—so many things."

She sat on the bed, scooped up the bowl, and began, once more, to eat like a sailor.

Lopez and Marlowe stood as her brief tale unfolded through mouthfuls of food.

Disguised as Richard, the sickly son of a lower courtier, she gained an invitation to the Throckmorton country estate under a pretense of health. London's continuing troubles with plague enjoined many a wealthier citizen to retreat to the countryside.

Once there, "Richard" charmed the lady of the house, and the servants, sufficiently to be privy to all gossip. The gossip led to discoveries, discoveries led to schemes. Richard was returning to London with a head full of information when someone alerted Throckmorton: *Richard* was a spy.

Alone on horseback and bound for London, Richard was taken by highwaymen, drugged, shipped, and fed to the Catholic forces on Malta, the Pope's most secure prison stronghold.

"But," an astonished Lopez gasped, "how did you survive?"

She was lying back on the bed, the empty bowl resting on her belly.

"The character I played was devised by my superiors just so," she answered. "Already sickly, pale, and a bit dull-witted, Richard frequently babbled, passed out, pissed himself, cried, and generally acquiesced to any question long before any severe torture was proffered. I was lucky in that my inquisitor was only after information, not entertainment, as so many of those pigs are. When it became obvious to him that Richard would tell all if it were but suggested that he might be slapped, very little else was done to persuade him to give out his secrets."

"But you didn't actually give out your secrets," Marlowe said.

"That, also, was the brilliance of my tutors," she admitted. "I had memorized an entire script of parallel information, some of it even true, though harmless, that I could spout under duress. It all sounded entirely plausible, and, when bits of it were verified, the inquisitor was convinced that he was teasing out the truth. But lack of food and water, and the general hellish conditions of the prison, were beginning to take a toll. If you had been delayed by two weeks, I would have been dead."

With that she sat up, placed the bowl on the floor, and looked both men up and down.

"Yes," she went on, speaking directly to Marlowe, "I can see why you were sent on this foolhardy mission."

"Why would you know the reason I was sent on this mission?" Marlowe snapped.

"But"—she turned her attention to the other man—"are you not Dr. Lopez?"

Lopez did his best not to register surprise. "How on earth would you know that? Who are you?"

"Will you tell us your name, at least?" Marlowe asked, only a little more gently.

She smiled.

"You'll know soon enough, so I may as well tell you."

She stood and held out her hand.

"Gentlemen, I am Frances Walsingham, only daughter of Sir Francis, lady-in-waiting to Queen Elizabeth, and her finest spy. But please, for the time being, call me Richard. Oh, and by the by, thank you both for saving my life."

TEN

Before Marlowe or Lopez could even comprehend what they'd just been told, let alone respond, the door to the cabin burst open and the captain of the vessel filled the doorframe.

He was a large man, all in blue. Even his beard had a slightly azure tint. His eyes were ablaze and there was a pistol in his right hand.

"Which one of you is Christopher Marlowe?" he boomed.

Before Marlowe could answer, Lopez stepped quickly to the captain, looked up at him, and murmured calmly, "Why do you ask?"

"I've just been given to understand," the captain seethed, "that this Marlowe is wanted for murder! I'll have no such man on my ship when we're about the Queen's business."

Marlowe reached out and took Lopez by the elbow, locking eyes with the captain.

"I am that man," he said, "but I am no murderer. I have been falsely accused. The doctor here is my witness, and his testimony is unimpeachable, as is his character. As soon as we're back in London, he'll testify and that will be an end to it. Also, Captain, I have been about the Queen's business saving this young man, who is Lord Walsingham's prize possession at the moment. I have done more of the Queen's work in the past seven days than you have in a lifetime as a ferry boatman. So use that pistol or put it away, but I'll not desert this post."

"I should point out that if you decide to use the pistol," Lopez added, "it will, most assuredly, be the last thing you do in this life."

To make his point, Lopez glanced down at the dagger in his hand. It was lodged against the captain's gut.

The captain only hesitated for an instant, but it was enough for Marlowe.

"Now," Marlowe said reasonably, "how is it that you've come into this sordid and completely false bit of information about me?"

"What do you mean?" the captain asked, clearly muddled.

"Seeing how you feel, you wouldn't have let me on board if you'd known this information before we set sail," Marlowe reasoned, "so I must assume that someone onboard has just told you about me. Is that correct?"

"Yes."

"Someone is using this ridiculous murder accusation," Marlowe went on, "to disrupt my duties for the Queen."

"Please lower your pistol, Captain," Sir Walsingham's daughter entreated in a deliberately low voice. "It's a bumpy sea, and I fear an accident."

Marlowe could not prevent a brief smile.

The captain, as if he had just remembered that there was a gun in his hand, lowered the offending weapon.

"Who told you?" Lopez insisted. "Who gave you this information?"

"New crewman," the captain grunted. "Picked him up in Malta. Just in from Lisbon, he said. A Basque. I should have thought about this."

"A Basque?" Marlowe snapped.

"Why did you take on a new crewman," Lopez asked, "knowing that this was a secret mission?"

"Lost three on the voyage here," the captain answered gravely. "Had a run-in with a warship. Brief, but it cost three lives and all the spare timber we had aboard."

"But this mission—" Lopez began.

"Do you know anything about the Basque people?" the captain growled. "They hate the Spanish. They hate the Portuguese. They hate the French. They've been living in those mountains for thousands of years, speaking their own language, and they don't ever complain. I calls that a perfect crewman: no affiliation, don't talk, and this one's a great marksman."

Lopez and Marlowe looked at each other.

"Argi," they said at the same time.

"Where is he now?" Lopez demanded. "We have to speak with him."

"On deck."

Marlowe lowered his head. "Doctor, would you please stay with our guest? I'm going to speak to my accuser."

The captain hesitated, but after a moment stepped aside. Marlowe stormed out.

Topside, in the day's final light, the sea was rough. The men secured everything on deck, and running lamps were lit. Marlowe caught sight of Argi tying a barrel to the rail, intent on his work. Marlowe moved silently and unnoticed, knife out. Once he reached the man's side, Marlowe took Argi by the hair and held the point of his blade just under the shorter man's jaw.

"Hello, Argi," he said pleasantly.

"I didn't expect you so quickly," Argi said calmly.

"I'd imagine not."

"But I'm glad you got my message," Argi went on. "We've got to get off this ship."

"Your message."

"Dead earnest, my friend," Argi assured him. "Get the other two up here any way you can, and we're away. I have a longboat ready."

"Again? Why are you always so interested in getting me off the water?"

"I heard that you hated the water," Argi suggested.

"We're not going anywhere with you."

Marlowe cast his gaze about the deck. Several other crew members had already taken notice of his knife; more were certain to follow.

Argi also saw that the deckhands were about to become a problem. He broke free from Marlowe's grasp, spitting in what appeared to be terror rather than rage, and shouted, "Yes! I stole your money! Here!"

With that he took out several coins and tossed them onto the deck.

"What the hell?" one of the older men said, coming toward them both. His uniform was a bit more kempt than most, and he had the air of someone in command.

"When he was helping us with the prisoner downstairs," Marlowe snapped, "this man stole money from my pocket."

"True?" the older man asked coldly.

Argi nodded.

"I'll fetch the captain," the man said.

"He's down in the cabin," Marlowe grumbled. "I'll take this man to him myself."

Before the older man could respond, Marlowe took Argi by the arm and dragged him below.

Once down the stairs, Marlowe let go and whispered, "What in God's name are you doing?"

"I'm trying to get you off this bilge scow," Argi said urgently. "You're wanted for murder!"

"I *know*," Marlowe answered, more amused than concerned. "I'm really going to have to do something about that. But at the moment I have more important matters."

"You don't realize that your 'more important matters' have everything to do with your murder."

"My murder?"

"The one you did. The man you killed."

"I didn't kill anybody, Christ." Marlowe rolled his head, snapping bones in his neck.

Without warning the captain of the *Ascension* swept into the corridor.

"Now we'll sort this out, by God!" he boomed.

Lopez and Richard appeared, flanking the captain.

"It's true," Argi railed immediately. "This man, this Christopher Marlowe, he killed a fellow student in Cambridge."

"No—" Marlowe began.

"He tried to hide it," Argi went on, "but they found the body in Marlowe's room, stuffed into a mattress!"

"Stuffed into a—what manner of idiot would I have to be to hide a dead body in my own room?" Marlowe asked of no one in particular.

"Ask the crew." Argi lowered his voice. "Some of them have heard this too! Or send out one of your birds. You know what I mean."

The captain's scowl was a mask of rage and indecision.

"Like Cyrus in Persia," Argi went on, winking.

"Do you mean that there are messenger birds on board this ship?" Lopez asked slowly.

The captain took a moment to decide exactly how he wanted to answer, and then said, grudgingly, "Only one left."

"You sent out one to tell Walsingham that we had rescued the prisoner," Marlowe assumed.

That seemed to surprise the captain. "How did you know?"

"How did I—Lopez, does everyone think that I'm feebleminded?"

"Not *everyone,* surely." Lopez glared at the captain.

"The solution seems simple," Richard suggested. "Send out your last bird. Find out if my rescuer is, indeed, a monster."

"It's the only way, really," Argi confirmed.

"Blast!" the captain bellowed.

Without further ado, he shoved Marlowe to one side, Argi to the other, and lumbered up the stairs, cursing.

"What are you doing on this ship?" Lopez asked Argi. "And why are you trying to get Marlowe thrown off it?"

"I was on my way back to my own ship, to meet with Captain de Ferro, when I heard the news." He suddenly looked around. "Maybe we should go into the cabin."

Without waiting for agreement, Argi slipped into the small room. The others, unable to determine any other course of action, followed him.

Once inside, his voice lowered even more than it had been, Argi went on.

"There is a warrant for your arrest," he said to Marlowe, "and more than usual effort is being employed to secure your capture. We believe that it is an effort to destroy this rescue mission; prevent you from getting your man back to London."

Marlowe tried his best to see Argi in a new light. The intimation that he was a part of some larger scheme, one of which Marlowe was unaware, was startling.

"You said, 'We believe,'" Marlowe exhaled slowly.

"Do you think you're the only one in Walsingham's employ?"

Marlowe looked around. "I'm beginning to feel that I was, until a few days ago, the only one who *wasn't*."

"There is great concern that the warrant will result in your capture and the detention of our man here, the prisoner. And he is vital. Do you understand that?"

"I understand that better than you do," Marlowe said quickly, "but do you mean to say that if I'm to be arrested, he might also be detained?"

"Yes. The doctor, of course, won't be held long, but you and this man, God knows what could happen to you."

After a moment of consideration, Lopez nodded.

"There's a point in this," he said softly.

"No." Marlowe stepped back in the crowded room. "I have no confidence in this whatsoever. How are we to know that *this* isn't some ploy from the Pope's men? Take us off this ship, sent by Walsingham himself, and we're lost."

"If you stay on this ship," Argi said firmly, "you will be arrested the moment we land in England. There are men waiting. There will be no discussion. You three will be taken. What do you think was in the bird-message that this captain sent?"

"On the one hand," Richard mumbled, "we stay on the ship, we arrive in England, we're arrested, I'm killed before I can relate my information."

"Yes," Marlowe agreed, "because the men waiting to arrest me in London are most certainly *not* Walsingham's."

"On the other hand," Richard went on, "we get off the ship, it's a trap, probably from the Pope's men, and I'm killed before I can relate my information."

"And impossible to be certain which of your observations is true," Lopez observed solemnly.

"Hang on a moment," Marlowe said slowly.

He took three steps backward, as far as he could until the corner of the cabin stopped him. His eyes watched some vision of the mind, but they darted as if the vision were alive.

"If this were a play," he began, nearly to himself, "I would know what to do."

"What?" Lopez moaned incredulously. "Stop that immediately! This is no time for—this isn't a play, it's life and death!"

Marlowe shook his head. "No, Doctor. Theatre is the truest metaphor of life we human beings have yet invented. Better: this life *is* a play, you understand?"

"No, Marlowe!" Lopez exploded. "This isn't theatre!"

"Yes, it is. It has an author who has devised a plot, and characters, and dialogue—all to a purpose. And it's simple. What would I do if I ran up against a dilemma like this in writing a scene? How would I get the characters out of the quandary, in this case, off the boat? I only need to decide the author of this particular story, and I'll know what to do."

Argi turned to Lopez. "Is it possible that he has lost his mind?"

"Entirely," Lopez snapped.

But Richard seemed more willing to consider Marlowe's perspective.

"Walsingham knew what to do," Richard said, "as soon as he found out that Throckmorton was the traitor, an author of the plot against our Queen."

"Exactly." Marlowe nodded once.

"I'm not certain I understand what's being said here," Argi confessed quietly.

"Are you a character by Walsingham," Marlowe asked pleasantly, "or were you created by the Pope?"

Before Argi answered, Richard began to pace the cabin, speaking quickly. "While you were on deck just now, Lopez told me that this man, this Basque, was a member of the crew that brought you part of the way to Malta."

"And we were set off the ship because a Spanish war vessel was after us," Marlowe said, falling into Richard's rhythm. "But that was suspicious to me at the time."

"However," Lopez said, wading into the rapid fire, "he smuggled us through Spain, no mean feat, almost single-handedly."

"He could have killed us at any time," Marlowe said.

"But you hadn't yet retrieved your prisoner," Richard answered. "He had to wait until you'd accomplished your task."

"Why?" Marlowe fired. "If the point was to keep you from giving Walsingham your information, why risk having you rescued and then trying to kill you? Why not just leave you in prison and let you be taken care of there, in Malta?"

"Which is nearly what happened," Richard agreed.

"Which means that Argi wanted us to succeed in rescuing you," Marlowe went on. "He was instructed to help us do it."

"I was!" Argi insisted.

"If Argi were a Catholic agent," Marlowe concluded, "he would have killed us in Spain, or turned us in to Catholic authorities there. That would have been easy. And either way we'd be dead now."

"And when I heard of the danger for you, as I was making my way back to my own ship," Argi interrupted vehemently, "I got to this boat, got on, and now I'm trying to save your lives! Again!"

Marlowe nodded. Richard stopped pacing. Lopez smiled.

"I believe you," Marlowe said simply. "Let's get off this rotten log."

Without another word, Marlowe headed for the door.

"I don't know what just happened," Argi said a little helplessly.

"We're leaving this ship," Richard said.

"Ah." Argi turned at once. "Good. This is good."

Seconds later the odd quartet appeared on deck only to be confronted by the captain of the *Ascension* and several of his more formidable men.

"Where do you think you're going?" the captain demanded.

"You can't be serious," Marlowe railed. "Not five minutes ago you told me to get off your ship. That's what I'm doing."

"No," the captain grunted. "The Basque was right. I sent out a pigeon. We'll wait for an answer."

"You've got to make up your mind, Captain," Marlowe said, deliberately setting his voice at an irritating pitch. "Do you want me on or off? This indecision ill befits a captain."

The captain was at a momentary loss for a response.

"Let's go," Marlowe said to his compatriots.

"Wait. Wait." The captain appeared to be using every bit of his brain power to reason out a proper handling of the situation. "You can go. You're the wanted man, the murderer. The rest? They stay. Especially the prisoner. Sir Francis has been most specific on that account."

"I'm not staying on this ship without my chief protector," Richard said firmly.

"Oh, yes, you are."

"And I'm not leaving without Richard," Marlowe added.

The captain turned to his left and spoke to a very large man. "Throw the man in black over the side, Albert. Put the rest back down in the cabin."

Albert was nearly seven feet tall, bursting from his uniform, eyes like an insensate bull. When he received the captain's order, he groaned with what sounded like pleasure.

But before he could move an inch, Marlowe had drawn his dagger and rapier.

Lopez took two steps backward and drew out his rapier. He was smiling in a way that could freeze blood.

Argi instantly sat down, folded his arms behind him, and skittered away toward the rail like a crab.

Richard lunged forward and grabbed two pistols from the captain's belt, cocked them, and pointed them both directly at the captain's face.

"Please don't throw me over the side, Albert," Marlowe said plainly to the man on the captain's left. "I could probably swim back to Malta, but I've already said a proper good-bye to my new friends there, and if I show up again so soon, you understand—it would be rude."

No one moved for a moment.

Then, from the railing, a small voice all but whispered.

"The longboat is ready," Argi called out softly. "Let's go."

Eyes locked on their targets, the unlikely trio—Marlowe, Lopez, and the Maltese prisoner—backed slowly toward the sound of that voice.

"Blast," the captain muttered under his breath, seething.

Without warning, the captain dropped, drew another pistol from his boot, and fired it.

A ball nicked the side of Marlowe's thigh.

Without hesitation, Richard fired both guns, and two of the captain's men fell to the deck, groaning.

The crewman Albert dove toward Marlowe. Marlowe easily stepped aside, but found he lost his balance on his wounded leg, and toppled to the deck. Lopez leapt to his side, standing over him.

Marlowe rolled and got to his feet just as Albert got his bearings and flew forward again. Marlowe thrust, and the rapier found flesh, but Albert was already in motion, and his sheer size carried him on. He landed on top of Marlowe, nearly crushing him.

Marlowe stabbed with his dagger three times into Albert's side. Albert snorted, but barely moved.

Lopez appeared over them and kicked Albert in the side where the stab wounds bled.

Meanwhile Richard had taken out the government-issued cutting sword that had come with the uniform and was fending off three attackers, one of them the captain.

"Go to Richard," Marlowe groaned to Lopez. "I'll take care of the behemoth."

"Now!" Argi was calling. "We should leave now!"

Lopez raced to Richard's side, stabbed the captain twice in the arm, allowing Richard to slice into the side of one of the other attackers.

Unfortunately, more crewmen were gathering, slowly realizing what was happening. It would only be seconds more before the entire crew overwhelmed the escaping quartet.

"Get to the boat!" Lopez commanded Richard.

"Not without both of you!" Richard shouted back, losing the deep voice.

Hearing that timbre, Marlowe managed to free one arm from underneath the barely conscious Albert, and sliced off one of Albert's fingers.

That did the trick. Albert howled, and partially revived.

"All right, Albert," Marlowe gasped. "You win. Throw me overboard. I surrender."

Hearing this, focused on nothing else, Albert grinned, made it to his feet, picked Marlowe up with one hand, and staggered toward the rail.

"Come on, then," Marlowe called to his comrades. "Time to go."

Richard sliced into another crewman, kicked him backward, and tossed the nearly worthless blade at the captain.

"You should arm your men with better weapons," Richard said between breaths. "These swords are toys."

Then Richard kicked the captain under the chin, kicked him so hard that he lifted off the deck a little before he fell backward.

"That's for being an idiot!"

Lopez grabbed Richard by the elbow. "Marlowe is in earnest. It's time for us to leave."

The rest of the crew had massed, weapons at the ready, and were on the verge of overtaking the moment.

"Now!" Marlowe called from high above Albert's head.

In the next second Marlowe was flying through the air, over the side, toward the choppy ocean. He registered an instant of exhilaration, a thrill of flight, before the dark water rose to greet him and that joy was replaced by a terror of the deep.

Argi stood in the longboat, knife in hand, ready to cut the rope that held the boat in place.

Lopez ran, dragging Richard along. They leapt into the longboat and Argi chopped the tether. The boat plummeted into the drink.

Marlowe struggled in the icy water; it soaked him to the bone almost instantly. He swam, but his sodden clothes threatened to drag him down. He swallowed first one, then several gulps of salt water, and his eyes were caked with it, making it nearly impossible to see as the waves rose around him. He could hear voices calling his name, but there were many, too many. His father, a childhood friend, Thomas Kyd—they were all beckoning him.

Then he felt his head whack against something hard, and several hands grabbed him; pulled him upward.

He landed, belly down and floundering, in the longboat. He belched salt water from his stomach and lungs, and sat up immediately, dagger drawn.

"That was your plan?" Richard howled angrily. "To get thrown into the ocean?"

"I hate the water," Marlowe mumbled.

"It worked, though," Argi suggested.

As his eyes cleared, Marlowe could see the sailors on the *Ascension* standing at the railing, some with firearms.

"They won't shoot," Argi went on. "They can't risk losing the prisoner. I don't know why, but this person is very important."

Marlowe regained himself. "You hear that?" he asked Richard. "You're very important."

Lopez glared at the ship. "That was a very strange turn of events," he mused.

Marlowe studied the side of Lopez's face for a moment.

"You mean that the captain was quite willing to have me removed from the ship on such flimsy evidence as gossip from a new crewman."

Lopez turned. "I hadn't even thought of that," he said. "I was only thinking how violent the confrontation grew, and how quickly. That captain and his crew are dressed to look fairly disciplined, under some sort of royal control, but that chaos was the behavior of—I'm sorry, Argi, my friend, but it was more like the men on your ship."

"They were like privateers," Richard realized. "Did we get on the wrong ship?"

"Or is Mr. Cordal less Walsingham's man than we thought?" Lopez added.

"Or did someone offer this captain enough money to subvert his more loyal intentions?" Marlowe concluded.

Marlowe turned to Argi.

"Tell me again how you came to be on that ship?"

Argi busied himself with the mast and sail. "Help me with this, will you? With this kind of wind, we'll manage ten knots. We'll be aground in Sicily in four hours. From there—"

"Argi," Lopez insisted. "What are we doing?"

"We're taking this prisoner to the proper authorities," the Basque said, still avoiding eye contact.

"I hope you won't mind if I ask," Marlowe interjected, "which authorities might you recognize as proper?"

Argi looked up at last. "Lord Walsingham has plans within plans, you must see that. The information that the prisoner has is too much for a single, straight line. You and the doctor, you are only a part of the larger map of things."

Then Argi continued his work, readying the sail.

"He's saying," Lopez said to Marlowe, "that it isn't as simple as just rescuing the prisoner and bringing that person back to London."

"There's something else going on," Marlowe agreed.

"Before anyone's imagination ranges out of hand," Richard said, "I would like to insist that I know Sir Francis very well, and one of his tricks is to make people think too much."

Lopez and Marlowe turned as one toward Richard.

"If he can make an enemy believe that there are ten possible answers to every question," Richard continued, "then he has succeeded in making confusion reign, has he not?"

"In which case, simplicity becomes a ploy." Lopez nodded.

"And honesty a diversion," Marlowe added.

The ship rose high on a great black wave, and came crashing down, nearly filling the longboat with dark water.

"You can talk some more if you want to," Argi suggested, "but could you bail while you do it?"

Silently agreeing, everyone took up something and hastily went to work emptying the longboat of water.

By the time the sun had set, a violent wind threw the tiny vessel forward. A nearly full moon was on the rise. The stars came out.

Before midnight the boat had landed on the shores of Sicily, near the tower Cabrera in Pozzallo.

As they dragged the boat onto the sand, Marlowe could not help noticing Richard's exhaustion.

"I fear this part of our adventure has weakened you again," he whispered.

"I confess"—Richard nodded, gulping air—"that I am not fully recovered from my ordeal in Malta."

Marlowe took Richard by the arm.

"We should rest for a while," he announced to the others.

"No," Argi insisted. "No rest. We have horses in Pozzallo. We ride to Messina. We cross to Italy. We ride in stations."

"Ride in stations?" Lopez asked.

"Stations, stations," Argi ranted. "We ride from one station to the next, where we change horses, sometimes eat, ride on—it's very fast. I have a map."

He held up a crude square of leather. There were, in fact, locations, instructions, and even several passwords carved into it. And everything was in English.

"This is from Walsingham?" Marlowe asked, staring at the map in Argi's hand.

The Basque nodded once.

"All right." Richard smiled. "Let's go."

Marlowe turned to Lopez. "I wish there were a word or phrase," he began, "that could describe the eerie feeling I'm having: that this has all happened before."

"You mean the feeling of being put off a ship and landing in a foreign land?" Lopez responded.

"Well."

"I understand," Lopez told his friend, "this is all too familiar."

The moon illuminated the beach with silver light, and gave everything there the aura of a dream. So it was less shocking than it ought to have been when Argi produced two double-barreled pistols from somewhere in his part of the longboat.

"I am afraid, my friends, that there are only two horses. One for me. One for the prisoner. You two wait here. Someone from Captain de Ferro's ship will be along shortly to pick you up. We made better time from the *Ascension* to here than I thought we would, so it may be a few hours. But it's a nice beach, and there's rum in the longboat."

With that he stepped forward, holding one gun to Richard's head and the other aimed at Marlowe. Both guns were cocked.

Marlowe took the slightest step and Argi smiled.

"You have seen what kind of a shot I am," he said to Marlowe. "And at this distance? Be reasonable. Don't be a dead man."

Marlowe kept his eyes locked on Argi, but spoke to Lopez.

"You and Richard can find your way back to London even if I'm a dead man, can't you, Doctor?" he asked.

"Of course," Lopez said calmly.

"Or—" Richard began.

In a blur, Richard wrapped an arm around Argi's neck, kicked the man's feet out from under him, and dragged him backward.

The guns went off but the shots were wild.

Marlowe leapt forward and instantly relieved Argi of his pistols.

Argi's face was purple, and he was flailing so violently that he kicked off one of his boots before he passed out.

"Not bad," Marlowe said to Richard, tossing the guns aside.

Argi thudded into the sand next to the boat.

"I'd rather not go back to London without you, Kit," Richard said lightly. "Is your leg all right to ride?"

"My leg?"

"You were shot."

"I'd forgotten. It's nothing. And why do you keep calling me *Kit*? That's only for my father."

"If I may point out," Lopez interjected, "there are still only two horses. And unless we want to kill Argi, which I am loath to do since he's probably only following orders, possibly Walsingham's orders, someone ought to wait here with him. We don't want him following after us, making a nuisance. And who knows, he may even have told the truth when he said that Captain de Ferro's ship is on the way."

"But—" Marlowe began.

"I should be the one to wait behind," Lopez interrupted, rummaging around in the longboat for the promised rum. "I speak Portuguese, you do not. I know de Ferro, you do not. Also, I cannot be killed. I think you'd agree."

"I think it would be very difficult to do it," Marlowe said, looking down to stifle a grin.

"Well, then."

Lopez sat on the gunwale of the longboat, pulled up a bottle of rum, leaned forward, and retrieved the leather map from the sand beside the unconscious Argi. He tossed it to Marlowe.

As if on cue, a horse whinnied from somewhere close by.

Lopez removed a woolen scarf from his neck. "Place this around your wounded leg. Let the wound breathe."

Marlowe hesitated, then touched the scarf. "You'll get it back in London."

"Go on," Lopez urged. "With any luck at all, I'll see you in London in three weeks' time."

"I'm afraid he's right," Richard said softly. "We should go."

Marlowe nodded.

"Three weeks, then," he said, not looking at Lopez.

Richard took Marlowe's arm and, without another word, they headed off.

The moon was high. Lopez watched the two silvery figures rise up into the air as they mounted their horses. He watched as they disappeared over the next dune.

Only then did Lopez hoist the bottle of rum over his head for a moment.

☩

"Good-bye, my friend," he whispered, and then drank very deeply from the bottle.

From behind him a groggy voice called out, "Save a little of the rum for me."

Lopez did not look back, but he did hold out the bottle. Argi hobbled over and took it.

"That went well," he said to Lopez, taking a healthy drink.

"I hate this plan," Lopez growled.

"You're not the one who was beaten by a girl." Argi handed the rum back to the doctor. "The captain's ship is just over there, in a small cove. Let's go."

Lopez stood, took the rum from Argi, and finished half the bottle. "I suppose so." He sighed.

Without warning, a shot rang out. A plank in the longboat splintered. Lopez leapt forward. Argi dropped.

An instant later six or seven men appeared over the top of the nearest dune.

"Maltese knights!" Argi cried.

"No," Lopez countered, pulling out his rapier and dagger. "Look at them!"

All of the approaching men were dressed in azure uniforms with thick black gloves, crowned with Arabic headdresses.

Argi rolled in the sand, scooping up his guns as he went. With a single motion he laid the weapons in his lap and began to reload first one, then the other.

Lopez advanced. Two men in the lead were carrying Bedouin swords, thick steel but less wieldy than the rapier. One ran directly for Lopez while the other moved to the side, outflanking him.

Two more steps, and Lopez dropped to one knee. He sucked in a deep breath and threw his dagger at the man coming at him. It hit the attacker in the belly, and the man howled. Lopez had his red cloak off in the next instant. He charged the other man to his side, whirling the cloak above his head. When he was close enough, the cloak descended, covering the man. Lopez thrust his rapier and pierced that man's heart.

Argi was up, double-barreled pistols loaded. One blast took down one of the agents, but his second gun would not fire, soiled by sand.

Argi was in peril; three men were coming his way. He withdrew a small knife from his boot and roared an incoherent threat.

Lopez saw, let go of his cloak, and rushed to Argi's side.

As he did, another shot rang out, and Lopez felt a white-hot explosion in his side. As he fell he saw a silver blade cut Argi from shoulder to waist. Argi fell backward into the sand. Lopez struggled to rise but a second bullet bit his arm.

Lopez watched as several agents swarmed around Argi.

Then the flash of a dagger caught his eye as it flew directly toward his head.

ELEVEN

LONDON

It was a small room, but it was in the Palace of Whitehall. Marlowe stood, paced, and even dared to sit down once or twice. Hours passed. He'd studied every inch of the room. It was ten foot square. Only one wall was given a tapestry, the other three were bare, gray stone. There was a table with two chairs, a desk with another chair, a small washbasin and a chamber pot, which seemed odd. There was no cot or bed. It was impossible to determine what manner of room this was supposed to be.

A sizeable bunch of gillyflowers and musk roses lay on the table. They made the air very sweet, and brought to Marlowe's mind, once again, the journey he and Frances had shared, returning to London.

The sky was dark and Frances was sleeping, still dressed as Richard. The shelter she and Marlowe had found barely kept out the rain, and she was shivering in her sleep. Marlowe saw it, and covered her with his riding cloak.

He watched her face, glancing every now and again across the moonlit fields somewhere in the south of France. They'd already endured nearly a week's hard riding, with another long week ahead. There was little time for talk, but when they managed a word or two, every syllable imprinted itself on Marlowe's brain, like a cattle brand, or Inquisition torture.

Marlowe found that he could not sleep well lying next to her. Everything about her was distracting, fascinating. Even as she slept, sighing slightly, dressed convincingly as a man, her body was a flame, fluttering, blinking; living in a circle of light.

At first he did his best to tell her how he felt, but she hadn't taken him seriously. So he hid his true feelings, instead discussing his theories, idle supposition, concerning the murder of Walter Pygott.

Lying in that field in France, he knew he was in love with her. He also knew that she had feelings for him, but would never acknowledge them, not even to herself. The daughter of the most powerful man in England was unlikely to glance more than once at the son of a cobbler.

In the end he began to compose lines of poetry in his head.

"It lies not in our power to love or hate," he thought. "For will, in us, is overruled by fate."

A sudden flurry of approaching footsteps roused Marlowe from his contemplation. His heart jumped a bit. There was no telling who was about to come into that room.

The door swung wide and Sir Francis Walsingham strode in, dressed in deep burgundy, skullcap atop his head. Behind him there were two guards and a remarkably beautiful young woman. She was adorned in blue satin and lace. Her hair was pulled back and decorated with violets the exact color of her dress.

Marlowe gasped and held his breath.

Walsingham moved briskly to the desk and sat. The young woman took a chair at the table, eyes down. Marlowe watched as the guards drew weapons, stepped into the hall, and closed the door behind them.

It took the entirely of Marlowe's strength to remain silent.

His fortitude was rewarded, at last, when Walsingham looked up and Marlowe saw that the old man's eyes were red—from sleeplessness or tears, it was impossible to tell.

"As you know," Walsingham began, his voice hoarse, "my—my daughter, Frances, was able to obtain a great deal of information this past Christmastide while she was ensconced at Coughton Court, the Throckmorton home in Warwickshire. She posed there in the guise of the sickly *Richard,* whom you have met. Unfortunately, someone in that household, we do not yet know who, alerted

Throckmorton to the possibility that *Richard* might be a spy. As my daughter was bound for London, she was taken prisoner and held on Malta.

"That might have been the end of the story but for the fact that," Walsingham paused and consulted several papers in front of him on the desk, and then said, "a certain person by the name of *Tin*, a serving girl smitten with—with Richard, happened to overhear that something had happened to Richard on the way back to London. Tin, the rare girl herself, able to both read and write, penned a letter to the courtier she supposed to be Richard's father. The missive came to me, and your recent adventure was set in motion. What you do not know—"

"Oh, for God's sake, Father," the girl at the table sighed impatiently, "Marlowe isn't one of your idiot underlings. He's a genius: a poet possessed of a remarkable mind, and a swordsman second to none. Please don't give him speeches, especially about facts of which he is largely aware already. Just *speak*."

Marlowe realized then that the lovely young woman seated at the table was Frances Walsingham. He would not have recognized her at all but for the fact that she'd called the old man "father." He studied her perfect oval face, the blush in her cheeks, the dark green eyes—he should know that face anywhere, but he found himself searching for any other sign of the ragged girl in men's clothing. There were golden hoops in this woman's ears, and a starched white collar held her neck stiffly. The dress was ornate, though not overdone, and revealed less of her figure than had the ill-fitting uniform from the *Ascension*. Her hands were white as snow, not at all the hands that had held swords and battled men. Primarily it was her demeanor that made this woman a different person from the girl he'd come to know. This woman was not a gallant spy. She was a lady-in-waiting at the court of Queen Elizabeth.

He realized then that he was staring, and felt a fool for not having recognized her as soon as she had entered the room.

"I—I," Marlowe stammered, staring at Frances.

She stood. "This is all a bit too awkward for everyone. Let me speak plainly, then, if my father will not."

Marlowe nodded. Out of the corner of his eye he could see that Walsingham, too, was nodding.

"Christopher Marlowe," she continued, extending her hand, "you saved my life, and, more important, you may have saved our Queen. I am in your debt, as is your country."

Marlowe stared at the white hand, so close to his body.

"I am uncertain," he managed to say, forcing the merest smile, "whether I am to kiss this hand, or clasp it."

He turned to Walsingham.

"You see, my lord," he went on, "I have come to know this individual, a little, during our travels, and found her to be the bravest person I have ever met. My admiration for her is boundless, as is my respect. On our arduous journey from the banks of Italy to the streets of London, we—I was constantly astonished by her ability to—"

"Marlowe means to say," she interrupted, coming to stand by his side.

But her father would not let her finish.

"I began to train my daughter in the art of spy craft when she was nine years old," Walsingham snorted, not looking at either of the other two. "She has so far exceeded my wildest hopes, that I, too, Mr. Marlowe, find myself constantly amazed by her. She is sufficient unto herself. She needs nothing and no one. She is a more formidable child than any man's *son* on this planet."

"The point is," Frances interjected, obviously encouraging her father to proceed with his business, "that I stand here as a result of Mr. Marlowe's efforts, and you wish to thank him for his service."

"Ah," the old man said, and sniffed. "Yes. Well. Christopher Marlowe, you are as of this moment in my direct employ. A small fee will be paid into a secret account for your benefit only. Of course, none of what we're saying in this room can be known by anyone else. To the rest of the world, you are still a student, a poet."

"I don't understand what it means," Marlowe began, "to be in your *employ*."

"Your immediate task is to address the murder charge against you," Walsingham answered gravely. "That circumstance is most severe."

"But the solution is immediately at hand," Marlowe insisted. "Dr. Lopez will testify that we left Pygott very much alive in Cambridge. Lopez will be in London any day, and there's an end to the ridiculous charges."

"You misunderstand," Frances said softly.

Walsingham looked away. "We have received word."

"Rodrigo Lopez," Frances explained, barely above a whisper, "is dead."

Marlowe was certain that his exhaustion and the rigors of travel had affected his hearing, or his comprehension.

"Dead? No." He shook his head. "That can't be. He was fine when we left him on the beach. And—and he is a man who cannot *be* killed. He's not dead. You've been misinformed."

"We received a missive from Captain de Ferro," Walsingham confided. "He found the doctor and another man beside a longboat on the shores of Sicily, near Pozzallo. Each had been shot at least a dozen times, stabbed repeatedly. Both men were dead."

"It wasn't Lopez," Marlowe insisted, but his voice had weakened.

"I'm afraid it was, my boy," Walsingham said, almost warmly. "It's a great loss to the nation, and to our Queen. He twice saved her life. He was to be the royal physician."

"He told me." Marlowe's head was swimming. "I'll—I'll return to Sicily. I'll find the men who killed him."

"No," Walsingham said simply. "You will return, under some disguise, to Cambridge. You will find the murderer of this boy Pygott. That is your only mission!"

"What?"

"Listen to me." Walsingham stood up, his voice gaining strength once more. "I have plans for you. Her Majesty has plans for you. You've been tested and found to be superior in every way. You saved the life of my daughter, England's finest spy. There are great things in store for you. Things you cannot accomplish from the end of a hangman's rope."

Marlowe opened his mouth to further protest, and then his mind cleared, and he saw something on Walsingham's face.

"There's more to Pygott's death than the revenge killing of a bully," Marlowe concluded. "This has something to do with his father, a man with wealth and connections. Sir John Pygott is one of Throckmorton's conspirators."

Frances turned to her father, a faint smile on her face.

"I told you he was quick."

Walsingham nodded. "This is a paltry man with middling means, unhampered by learning or wit."

"Well," Marlowe agreed, "that's Walter Pygott, certainly."

"Was," Frances corrected. "That *was* Walter Pygott. You must ask yourself who might wish to see him dead."

Marlowe shook his head.

"I must ask myself who would *not* wish it," he mused. "That would be a smaller number. Everyone at the campus hated him, and with good cause. He was a bully and a braggart and he had bad hair. But knowing that his father is a traitor to our Queen, I begin to suspect that the son might have had some small part in the treachery, and *that* is what got him killed."

Walsingham smiled. "There you are, Marlowe! There is the man England needs, who can digest tragic news and still turn his mind to the pressing task at hand. Yes, we believe that Walter Pygott's death is the result of chicanery and plotting. The attempt to blame you for the murder is a part of a larger ploy to eliminate you as our agent."

Marlowe stared into space. "Solve Pygott's murder and I pull a thread that may unravel the larger tapestry."

Walsingham let go a sigh. "Exactly."

Frances came close and touched Marlowe's arm. There was a palpable spark, but everyone in the room ignored it.

"Come, then," she said. "Let us see to your disguise, and plan your next few moves."

"Resolve this business with all haste," Walsingham admonished. "The plot against the life of our Queen is at hand, perhaps not even days away. Go now."

With that the door swung open and guards entered.

Frances tugged on Marlowe's arm, leading him from the room.

When they were gone, Walsingham sat down once more, shuffled the papers on his desk, and then smiled.

TWELVE

CAMBRIDGE

It was a small room, but close to the college. Marlowe stood in the doorway staring at the wreckage of his former home away from home. He studied every inch of the place. It was eight foot square with a small window and two narrow closets, one for personal items and the other for a basin and chamber pot. The desk had been overturned, and black ink was everywhere. Torn scraps of paper were strewn wildly. The worst of it was the bed. It had been torn apart. All four posts had been broken, and the mattress, or what was left of it, was revolting. It appeared to have exploded from the inside, and there was evidence of blood and viscera. A bizarre odor of decay and citrus hung in the air, despite the open window. Someone had attempted to obviate the smell of a dead body by rubbing lemons on everything.

Marlowe was uncomfortable in his disguise. The skullcap was tied too tightly under his chin, and glue from the theatrical ginger beard itched. The odd cassock he'd been forced to wear was constructed so that he had to stoop a bit, as if his back were slightly twisted. He had only seen himself for a second in a looking glass, but he was certain that even his own father would not know him.

As he stepped into the room at last, he heard a slight rustling behind him. Stepping quickly behind the door, he drew out his dagger.

"It's a fine room," an ancient female voice called out, "if you don't look at the shape it's in at the moment."

Marlowe stepped from behind the door, knife in hand. The woman was Nell Whatley, the owner of the Pickerel Inn and, therefore, also the owner of the room. The bar below was a bit on the rough side, but Nell was well known for keeping things in hand. She was as short as she was wide, covered in a stained green apron, and she carried a well-used wooden bat in her right hand.

"The only thing there is to see here," he said pointedly, "is disaster. What happened?"

"What happened?" She shrugged. "You know college boys. Bit of fun is all."

"No." Marlowe deliberately stared her down, daring her to recognize him. "There was a dead body found in this room. It's the gossip of the town."

"Ah." Her shoulders sagged, but only a little. "Well, yes, as it happens, the boy who lived here, a new student from the countryside and a bit of a wild one, killed another student and tried to hide the body in that mattress."

"That seems unlikely," Marlowe said. "You can't hide a body in a mattress that thin."

"I thought so too when I opened up the door," she agreed, "but that's what the law says, and I never disagrees with the law. Especially when they're wrong. You calls it out when they're wrong and it only makes for trouble."

"So you were here when the constabulary found the body."

"I had to open the door for them, didn't I?" She took a good look around. "God, they made a mess, worse than what was here to begin with."

"And you've left it as it was? Were you asked to do that?"

"Well." She shrugged. "What was the point? I mean, if someone was to take the room, of course, I'd have it cleaned."

"Here's my offer, then," Marlowe said coldly. "Cut your rate in half, I'll clean up the room myself, pay for at least a month in advance, and keep mostly to myself about it."

"Half?" She coughed. "I don't think so."

"All right." Marlowe put away his knife and headed for the door. "I'll just go downstairs, have an ale, and begin describing the look of this room, and the smell, to everyone there. In a very loud voice. I speak loudly when I've had ale."

"Half it is," Nell said quickly, holding out her hand.

Marlowe moved just as swiftly, placing the exact amount in her hand, and ushering her, unceremoniously, backward out the door.

"What made the law come to you in the first place?" he asked as she stepped out into the hall. "Did someone put them up to it?"

"Doubtless," she agreed. "But everyone in the place was complaining about the stench, weren't they? Thought it was something dead in the Cam at first, but the smell was inside, not outside. So."

"The smell made people complain, you're saying?"

She nodded.

"What sort of people? Other students who live here?"

"Not just them," she told him. "It was customers down in the bar as well."

"Any customer in particular?" Marlowe asked, his hand on the door. "I mean a regular or a stranger?"

"Let me think." She held out her hand.

Marlowe sighed and placed a coin in the outstretched palm.

"Now you mention it," she said, not looking at him, "it was a rude tough that's been in several times before and since what complained at first."

"Before anyone else noticed the smell."

"Well"—she turned to leave—"before I noticed it, anyway."

"When I come downstairs later," Marlowe called, "you'll point that man out to me, if he's there."

"If he's there," she answered, taking the stairs, "and if my memory don't fail me, you see what I mean."

"You'll make full price on this room yet," Marlowe said.

"And you'll ask one too many questions after a while," she told Marlowe, not looking back. "That room may have another tenant all too soon."

Ignoring her, Marlowe turned and surveyed the room again with a more objective eye. It was clear that only an idiot could believe the so-called evidence. No one would murder a man in his own room and then try to stuff the dead body into his mattress. And yet the indictment, shown to him by Frances, was clear:

> Christopher Marley indicted for manslaughter in that he did, on or about March the twenty-fifth kill and murder one Walter Pygott, son of John Pygott, Esq., the proof upon investigation being the discovery of a body identified as Walter Pygott in the room of this Christopher Marley found above the Pickerel Inn. Said Marley having fled and no other evidence being presented, the indictment stands.

Marlowe moved about the room slowly, examining the mattress, the overturned desk, and the papers on the floor. It was lucky that the old woman hadn't cleaned. The first thing that struck him was that there was not enough blood in the mattress. If the body had been stabbed on the bed, or in the room, for that matter, there would have been much more blood. Next he noticed spilt ink that covered a portion of the floor in one corner. Someone had stepped in that ink and left a bootprint. The heel and sole of that print were very distinctive: the heel tapered backward, and was smaller than most English heels. The sole came to a sharper point than most English boots. The print had been made by Spanish footwear. A closer examination of the floor revealed that the print had been stamped several times in ink about the room. It was small and the strides were short. The man who wore those boots was barely five feet tall. Marlowe silently thanked God that his father was a boot-maker. The prints could have been produced by the Spaniard in the group of men who attacked the coach on the way to London. Marlowe realized the wisdom of Lopez's opinion: those men should have been killed.

After searching about on the floor around the desk, he found a piece of paper that had been imprinted with a nearly complete Spanish bootprint. The ink had dried. He carefully folded the page and tucked it into his robe.

Thus encouraged, he scoured the room for more clues. No other footprints were proffered, but he found a torn bit of cloth on one of the bedposts. The cloth was clearly not from Pygott's foppish haberdashery; it was a ruder fabric. He pocketed the rag.

The wool stuffing inside the foul mattress was clotted with blood and smelled like decaying rats. Marlowe donned his gloves, held his breath, and combed through the wool. He was rewarded with a farthing and a sixpence, both dirty. It was impossible to say, of course, that they'd belonged to Pygott, but Marlowe reasoned that they wouldn't have gotten into his mattress any other way. And there was a satisfying bit of irony in imagining that he would buy several pints of ale with dead Pygott's sixpence.

It occurred to Marlowe then to examine the door. It had never been broken, not battered, not forced in any way. That said to him that Nell Whatley may have known more about the murder than she let on, because she had unlocked the door for the murderers as well as the law. It was possible, of course, that they had stolen the key. But Marlowe had seen her take the key from a chain around her neck, a chain that hung low and sank into her bosom. It was more likely that she'd been paid, or coerced.

Marlowe spent the next hour crawling around on his hands and knees, sneezing, then breathing through his mouth so as not to smell the room. He discovered several other threads of cloth, a silver earring, and most significantly: a smudge of blood on the outside of the door, and another in the hall. Pygott had been killed elsewhere and then carried into the room. That explained the relative lack of blood in the mattress. The body had been loaded into it and left as clumsy, heavy-handed, ridiculous evidence of Marlowe's guilt. It might have been laughable under other circumstances.

After that Marlowe began to straighten up the room. He set the furniture aright, repaired the bed, and collected his papers, most of which had been destroyed beyond use. He stacked the books in one corner, checked the chamber pot, found it and the washbasin empty, and then sat down at the desk to consider what to do about the mattress.

Clearly he couldn't sleep on it; even the idea of keeping it in the room any longer was out of the question. He was, however, loath to destroy it away. It might be found to contain other clues upon further examination.

Another five minutes' consideration gave him a decision: take the mattress out of the room, down the stairs, and into the alleyway behind the Pickerel. There it could hang on a line and air out with impunity: no one who came within three feet of it would ever consider stealing it.

That settled, he wrestled the offending lump outside, largely unheeded, and threw it over a line by the back wall of the public house. The alley was barely three feet wide, cluttered with refuse and bird droppings. An empty barrel collected moss and mold. It appeared to be seldom used. Still, Marlowe moved the mattress so that it would not entirely block the way. Then, adjusting his robe, checking his beard, and securing his cap, he strode back through the door and into the bar.

The Pickerel was said to have been a brothel as well as an inn, partially owing to its riverside location, but inn or whorehouse, it was all the same to Marlowe. The place was cozy, the ceiling was low, the light was dim, and the ale was flavored with rosemary, Marlowe's favorite.

The pub was crowded and loud early in the afternoon, filled with every imaginable sort of person. A riot of color seized the eye with exactly the same violence that noise ravaged the ear.

The fireplace was in the wall opposite the door. A pot of stew churned lazily, as well as a joint of beef, unattended. The fire was low, the coals orange like sunset's horizon, a color that said, "Welcome in."

At the bar, an oaken barricade against the onslaught of students and laborers, stood the woman of the house. Standing beside her was the famous husband, Pinch, who had fought in many Spanish campaigns. The popularity of the Pickerel was based, at least in part, on Pinch's reputation as a great liar. The rumor was that Pinch had acquired such a name by stealing, but Nell swore his name was to be attributed to the gesture that first brought them together. Pinch was a vague, towering skeleton, nearly six feet tall. Standing next to his wife, it was impossible to understand how they had managed to have children, but they had. The three young serving maids at the Pickerel were their handsome daughters. They weaved through the glut of men with the grace of dancers. They set a cup here, got a plate there, cheerfully enduring the occasional rude suggestion, lewd gaze, or unholy proposition.

Marlowe nudged his way up to the bar and placed himself immediately in front of Nell. She glared at him, but did not speak.

He smiled. "I've cleaned the room a bit," he said, pitching his voice so that only she could hear. "I found some interesting items."

Nell's face hardened. "How's that?"

"I say I've found things in the room," he said, his voice filled with menace, "things that tell me you have not been completely honest with the authorities."

"I've worked it out, you know," she said, leaning close to his face. "You haven't fooled me with your disguise and your fancy talk."

"What?" he asked, drawing back from her.

"You ain't never a college student." She laughed. "You're a spy."

Marlowe straightened up. "No—" he began.

"Listen here," she whispered back violently. "I goes to the theatre at least once a month; stands right up front. I ken an actor's beard when I sees one. I'm not just anybody."

"I don't take you for just anyone," Marlowe countered viciously. "I take you for an aide to murder."

Nell twitched and the look in her eyes changed significantly. Suspicion had been replaced by fear.

"I understand it now," she muttered, head down. "You are in the employ of Mr. John Pygott. But you ain't like the others."

That was unexpected.

Marlowe leaned forward.

"What others?" he demanded through clenched teeth, obviously threatening her.

Without warning a bony hand clutched Marlowe's throat and

began to lift him off the floor. Pinch was seeking to intervene on his wife's behalf.

Marlowe's dagger was in his hand immediately and it sliced a small bit of skin from Pinch's forearm, just enough to make Pinch gasp and loosen his grip.

"Husband!" Nell shrieked.

For an instant the noise of the place abated, and several eyes turned toward the commotion, but everyone in the Pickerel knew better than to intrude on petty squabbles, especially if they involved a blade.

"I mean your dame no harm, Pinch," Marlowe insisted, "and I am not in the employ of John Pygott. But I know this: someone brought his son's body here. And Nell, you helped them load it into that room upstairs. I assume they paid you well to do it, and to keep silent, but I believe I have proof, as I was saying, that it happened. I found things in the room just now. Shall I speak with the bailiffs about it?"

It was a good bluff because it frightened Nell.

"Wait," Nell said immediately. "There's more to it."

"Yes, I thought so." Marlowe nodded. "I will not submit you to the authorities if you will simply tell me who these other men are."

Pinch held the wound on his arm, and nodded gravely. Nell's eyes betrayed uncertainty, but a glance or two at Marlowe's dagger seemed to urge her to reply.

"I don't know who they are, not by name," she said, and it sounded true, "but they comes in here almost every evening now, like they're looking for something or waiting for someone. Take a table. Just you wait. One or the other will pop in soon enough."

"There were only two?"

"Aye."

"Was one, by any chance, a Spaniard?"

"Could be," she mused. "He was a bit dark-faced, and he ain't say nary a word. The other's rough. Rude."

"Makes advances," Pinch tossed in solemnly. "At the girls. I don't like it."

Marlowe smiled. "Please forgive my cutting you, Pinch. It was a thoughtless response."

Marlowe's dagger disappeared.

Pinch's head jerked sideways. "Well, then. I don't believe I've heard an apology in this place for ten years or more. After all, I took you by the throat."

"You were only doing what any loving husband would do," Marlowe assured him. "Nell, you are the most fortunate of women."

At that Nell's entire demeanor softened. "Well, he's tall, I will say that. Good for reaching at things in high places."

Pinch leaned down a bit and winked at Marlowe. "And not so bad at reaching a few of the lower places too, if you catch my meaning."

Nell slapped Pinch's bicep and even blushed a little. Pinch displayed a largely toothless grin. Marlowe did his best not to be distracted by evidence of marital harmony in so base a couple. He paused only a second before daring the next question.

"One more thing," he said, gazing boldly into Nell's eyes. "What about that room's previous tenant? Marlowe, I believe, was his name."

Nell nodded. "Nice boy. Good manners. It's a shame that someone's got it out for him, but there you are."

"Any idea what's happened to him?"

She shrugged. "If you believe the rabble, he's fled on account of murdering Pygott. But if you ask me, the same men what killed the fat boy killed poor Marlowe. Too bad."

"Nice boy," Pinch repeated, shaking his head.

"Well." Marlowe straightened up. "I'll just have a seat by the fire, then."

Without further comment, Pinch went back to work, and Nell caught the eye of one of her daughters. There was work to be done.

The rest of the bar's population had already resumed their previous behaviors: drinking, laughing, cursing, eating, and falling asleep in their food.

THIRTEEN

Marlowe strode to a table near the fire, settled back, and watched the crowd. Before long one of the daughters glided up to the table, winked, and rested her weight on one leg. Her skin was alabaster with a blush of pink. Her hair was plaited gold silk.

"Food or ale?"

"Why not both," Marlowe said above the din.

"Indeed," she agreed. "You've taken a room, have you?"

"I have. Not the most felicitous of chambers."

"What with the dead body they found there, you mean."

"Yes." Marlowe smiled.

"I spot you for new in town," she said, "so I'm taking care of you. I'll bring you the stew because it's fresh, if I skim the top away, whereas the joint of beef is older than me. We flavors our ale with rosemary and ivy, so as to make it go with stew, and it's only a halfpenny a tankard. There's manchet comes with it."

"Manchet. Lovely," Marlowe said enthusiastically. "I could murder a slice of bread."

Without another word, she turned and slid away. Marlowe watched her go. She moved like a skater over frozen water, and he wondered why he had never noticed her before. Only then did he allow himself to consider how fortunate he had been that no one at the inn recognized him. Still, he renewed his determination not to engage too deeply with anyone, lest he be detected. His entire investigation of Pygott's death depended on anonymity.

Marlowe stared into the fire then, and could not prevent his thoughts from rushing to Frances Walsingham, her face, her hands—her ability with a rapier. He saw, in his mind's eye, the contour of her cheek, and thought of several exhausted conversations beside fires in the South of France. The sound that her blue dress had made as she took his hand in London, leading him out of the tiny chamber where her father sat, filled his ears, obliterating any other noise.

So it was that he did not notice when the girl brought his stew and ale.

"Here we go," she said, breaking his reverie.

"Ah." He rubbed his eyes. "Very nice. Thank you."

"Manners," she said almost mockingly. "I don't get much in the way of 'thank you' around here. You've just won a bit of extra ale."

She was off once more.

Marlowe devoured his stew, and the bread was gone with it before five minutes had passed. He sat back, oddly contented, only to be startled when a man grabbed the skirt of his serving girl and nearly sent her tumbling. The noise of the room abated, but only slightly.

"Come on, sweet." The man began to bunch up her skirt. "Just a peek at the old bird's nest!"

The girl slapped his hand with a mummer's grace.

"No, Ingram," was all she said.

She turned from him and continued on her way, but Marlowe saw that Pinch had taken notice, and Nell tapped her nose with her index finger, then nodded in the offender's direction.

Marlowe squinted in the direction of the man. Difficult to see in the lamplight, but that could have been one of the men who accosted him on campus, and on the road. He turned back to Nell; she affirmed his silent query with another nod.

Meanwhile, the man stood unsteadily and wobbled after the girl. She was almost to the bar by the time he caught up.

"No?" The misbegotten man she'd called Ingram roared.

He jerked her arm so suddenly that she dropped the handful of cups she was carrying. The clatter was like a cymbal's clash against the tables. What was left of the human noise of the place receded like water. Every eye was on the scene composed by Ingram and the proprietors' daughter. Menace radiated from Pinch, and Nell was already rounding the bar.

"Now, then," Ingram went on.

Oblivious of the danger around him, or the crowd that watched his every move, he reached his hand up under the girl's skirt. The next thing Marlowe knew, old-man Pinch appeared beside Ingram, roaring. He had Ingram's arms pinned in the blink of an eye. There was no question of a struggle. Pinch was twice the size of Ingram, and only half as drunk.

At last Marlowe recognized the man. He was indeed one of the three that had asked him to steal from the church, and then, not much later, attacked the coach to London. This was the man that Marlowe had stabbed and left bleeding on the roadside.

"What was you saying to my daughter?" Pinch roared.

Nell stood by, bat in hand, eyes all flame.

"Pardon!" Ingram croaked, unable to move. "Drink takes a man out of himself. I see that now!"

"Out!" Nell bellowed. "And never come back here again, or my husband will snap you like a stick. Do you hear me?"

Pinch grunted and shoved the man toward the door.

"Ingram Frizer shall not return to this place!" He sounded more like a terrified schoolboy than a murderous villain. Frizer looked about, eyes unable to focus, and the steam of human noise rose up again, entirely filling the room.

The serving girl breezed close to Marlowe. "Mum says he's all yours now."

Frizer managed to stagger out the doorway.

Marlowe laid money on the table, stood, and left calmly, with only a slight nod to Nell. Once outside, he followed the careening drunkard down the narrow street.

Noise from the river, and the smell of fish, filled the air. Frizer was easy to follow. He lumbered into people, hit walls; fell down twice. No one took much notice. Just another ale-soaked brawler.

After a few twists and turns, Frizer fell into a baker's shop.

Marlowe quickened his step and arrived at the door just in time to see Frizer wave off the baker with a rude gesture and crash into the back room.

The baker cursed, shook his head, and went back to work arranging brown loaves of bread on a board.

Marlowe paused, trying to determine if Frizer would return. After a few moments, Marlowe entered the shop.

"Ah," the baker said, acknowledging Marlowe's presence.

"I'm told you have an almond-and-ginger cake," Marlowe announced softly.

Marlowe knew about that particular cake. He'd had one his first week in Cambridge. The bakery was well-known for it.

"Best in England," the man asserted seriously. "I take a little gum dragon and keep it in rosewater all night, that's what gives it the character, you see. Then in goes almonds and sugar and ginger and cinnamon, beat into a paste. I dry it in the oven. Just dry it, mind. Makes my mouth water just talking about it."

"I'll take one." Marlowe reached for his purse.

"Sorry," the baker said, eyes narrowed. "Haven't made any today."

Marlowe looked up. "No? Are you certain? Perhaps your man in back could find one."

"My man in back?" the baker asked in a loud voice. "You're quite mistaken. And I'm afraid you've caught us at a bad time, alas. We're closing."

"Closing? It's three in the afternoon."

"Nevertheless."

"I see." Marlowe secured his purse. "Another day."

"Well," the baker hedged, "the almond-ginger's more a winter cake. And spring's coming on. Don't know that we'll have it again until November, you understand."

"Yes, I think I understand," Marlowe answered, glancing toward the back room. "But tell Ingram Frizer that I came to see him."

Before the baker could gather his wits or respond, Marlowe was out the door.

FOURTEEN

Marlowe turned his attention to the next possible source of information: Professor Bartholomew. As he passed St. Benet's Church,
he was suddenly seized by a very bad idea. What if he allied himself
with this Ingram Frizer and agreed to steal the documents from
this church? That way he would be privy to the Catholic plans, at
least to some extent. He might even make a confidante of Frizer,
which could lead to more intelligence, though the word *intelligence*
scarcely seemed applicable to Frizer at all.

He pocketed the idea, and hurried past the church, around the
corner, and into the campus yard. There he was struck by a scene
at once familiar and foreign. Students were rushing to class, but it
seemed a decade ago that Marlowe had been one of those boys. A
wave of intense sadness took hold of him as he stared at the spot
where he and Lopez had stood, Lopez enjoining him to leave the
college for a wider world. The man who saved his father's life was
gone, and Marlowe was not the same person who had stood on that
spot only a few weeks earlier.

Realizing that such thoughts might capsize him, he shoved them
out of his mind, quickened his step, and hurried toward Bartholomew's offices. Into the stone building, up the stairs, and down
the silent hall, Marlowe tried not to think of what he'd say to his
old professor. Spontaneity was best for lying.

To knock on the door or to simply barge in? He chose the latter.

"I do beg your pardon, Professor Bartholomew," he began as he
opened the door.

The sight of the president of the college stopped him. William

Cole was reviled among so many of the more conservative faculty because he was a Puritan and a married clergyman. He glared at Marlowe.

Cole was standing in front of Bartholomew's desk with a fistful of papers. Bartholomew was seated.

"Yes, I beg *your* pardon, young man," Bartholomew said quickly, "I am past my time for our appointment. Do come in. President Cole was just leaving."

Cole's face reddened and his hand crushed the papers he was holding. He clambered past Marlowe, utterly ignoring him.

"If I had known that the president—" Marlowe began again.

"Close the door, young man," Bartholomew admonished harshly, "and lower your voice!"

Marlowe stepped inside and shut the door behind him. The offices were comprised of two large working rooms, a smaller private water closet, and a curtained alcove that Marlowe took to be a sleeping cubicle. The stone walls were high, and there was a tapestry on the one beside the entrance door, but the rest were obscured by floor-to-ceiling bookshelves overflowing with volume after volume. A slight haze of dust hung in the air, and the silver motes floated in the sunlight from a large arching window. There was a desk with a chair where the professor sat, and only one other chair beside the window.

Bartholomew looked Marlowe up and down, then shook his head. Easily, in a single movement, he produced a cocked pistol from a drawer and laid the gun on his desk directly in front of him. He kept his right hand near it.

"What is the meaning of this ridiculous costume you are wearing, Mr. Marlowe?"

Taken aback, Marlowe was momentarily struck dumb.

"I suppose it has something to do with the assertion that you've murdered that idiot Pygott, yes?" Bartholomew went on.

Marlowe could only nod.

"Sit," the old man commanded. "I'm afraid our time must be short for the moment. I have a class and I think it best not to be seen with you."

✝

Marlowe sat. "You recognized me right away: bad news for my disguise."

"I've been expecting you," Bartholomew told him. "I know you've been away, to London at the very least. And it was easy to deduce that a stranger barging into my offices might be Christopher Marlowe since that stranger spoke in a voice I knew and wore boots I recognized, though a face that I did not. There is also the matter of your dagger, which is quite distinctive, that filigreed hilt."

Marlowe glanced down. "Yes. Someone else pointed that out."

"You ought to conceal it better under that cassock," Bartholomew concluded.

"I should." Marlowe nodded. "How on earth would you know I've been to London?"

"I happened to see your little imbroglio with Pygott," Bartholomew said with a wave of his hand. "I saw him leave. I saw you get into a coach. And then you were not in classes after that. Not only does it stand to reason that you were not in Cambridge when Pygott was killed, but I surmised that you went to London on royal business. I know the Queen's conveyance when I see it. But, to the point: I have been expecting you, as I say. I have learned information that may prove quite startling to you."

"You—you have already given me several surprises," Marlowe stammered. "Would you be willing to swear to what you've just told me—about seeing Pygott alive, as I left for London—in a court of law?"

At that Bartholomew put his hand on the gun.

"I cannot do that," the old man said, "for reasons of my own. But I can offer you this insight: John Pygott, the father of the unfortunate corpse, is a close friend to a certain family called Throckmorton. The boy, Walter, was a frequent guest at certain so-called hunting parties held on the grounds of Coughton Court, the Throckmorton home in Warwickshire. The gatherings are, in fact, secret meetings. Walter Pygott was there at Christmastide."

"Go on." Marlowe held his breath.

"At Coughton Court," Bartholomew continued, "Walter Pygott

met the sickly son of a London courtier. Said pale young person had quit London for reasons of his health, or so it was told. This person, called Richard, was, in actuality, a spy."

Was Bartholomew in league with the conspirators? How else would he know these things? Marlowe's hand crept closer to his dagger. Bartholomew noticed and picked up his pistol, aiming it at Marlowe's head.

"A spy?" Marlowe asked disingenuously.

Inexplicably, Bartholomew raised the index finger of his free hand to his lips and nodded once in the direction of the door.

Marlowe hesitated, then turned silently. He could see a moving shadow through the space underneath the door. Someone was just outside, listening. The professor was aiming his gun at the door, not at Marlowe's head. Marlowe moved slowly and deliberately, rising out of the chair, soundlessly inching toward the door. Dagger bared, he reached for the handle.

Glancing at Bartholomew, who stood stony, pistol at the ready, Marlowe threw open the door.

A familiar figure filled the doorframe.

Bartholomew smiled instantly, and lowered his weapon. Marlowe could only gape.

"Frances," Bartholomew said softly but warmly. "Welcome to Cambridge."

She was dressed in travel clothing, a simple pale dress and a thick brown cape. She had tied up her hair and wore a cap. Her eyes were the color of emeralds.

She stepped into the room and closed the door.

"You were about to tell my friend what happened to poor Richard," she said, gliding toward the chair in front of Bartholomew's desk.

"Yes," Bartholomew said, setting down his pistol.

Marlowe allowed a dozen or so questions to race through his mind before he put away his dagger.

"Walter was angry with me—with *Richard*," Frances explained, "because I had bested him at cards. He drew his rapier. I disarmed him. I should not have done it, but my anger or pride got the better of me, I suppose. He could see quite clearly that I was not as help-less as I pretended to be. It made him suspicious. That suspicion, coupled with his shame at being disarmed, set him running to Throckmorton; I'm almost certain of it. With only a modest bit of investigation and bribery, Throckmorton discovered that the court-ier who was supposed to have been my father was childless. I was on my way back to London by the time he'd discovered that fact. I thought it best to deliver what intelligence I had gleaned as quickly as possible. It was considerable. That's when I was taken on the road and, eventually, buried in a hole in Malta."

Marlowe marveled at her brevity, as he had on so many other occasions.

"Why are you here in Cambridge?" he asked.

"A fair question," she admitted. "I've come to visit Professor Bartholomew, though I also hoped to see you."

"How does Professor Bartholomew fit into our little drama of intrigue and mayhem?" Marlowe asked.

The old man lifted his shoulders. "Lord Walsingham and I are acquainted."

Frances smiled. "Slightly more than that, I believe, sir."

Bartholomew looked away, but said nothing.

"At any rate," Frances continued, "the professor is—how shall I put it?—woven into the fabric of our play."

"You knew what you were doing when you interrupted those men," Marlowe said to the professor, "the men who were Catholic agents, out on the quadrangle. You were interceding."

Bartholomew shook his head. "I was merely—"

"You were also investigating me," Marlowe went on, "making certain of my loyalties."

"Well." The old man glanced at Frances.

Marlowe sat in silence for a full minute.

"Incidentally," Marlowe told them both at length, "I solved Pygott's murder. The assassin is a coarse brute called Frizer. Ingram Frizer, one of the Catholic ruffians. I will shortly have enough evidence to prove that assertion, and then I can get on with saving the Queen."

"Ingram Frizer?" was all Frances could say.

"Yes."

"Oh, dear," she said.

Marlowe examined her face. She was genuinely concerned, or confused, or confounded.

"Is this name familiar to you?" he asked.

She glanced at the professor. "Will you be late for your class? We shall have our visit a bit later this afternoon, I think."

He seemed to understand. "My offices are at your disposal."

He stood, gathered several books, and headed toward the door.

Marlowe watched, biting his tongue. He had so many more questions.

"Oh," Bartholomew said as his hand touched the door handle, "do remind me to tell you what's happening with Cole. The president of this institution has some peculiar notions. And he is, I fear, quite angry with me at the moment. It's important."

He looked as if he might say more, then turned abruptly and left, pulling the door shut.

"You know Ingram Frizer," Marlowe whispered.

"I didn't want Professor Bartholomew to carry any more knowledge than he had to," she began, "but, yes, I do know that man. Frizer is a double agent. He was at Coughton Court when I was there. He works for the Pope in order to spy for my father."

"Frizer?" Marlowe asked a little louder. "I don't think we're talking about the same man. The person I mean is scarcely bright enough to put on his pants."

"Yes," she agreed, "that is his gift. No one would ever suspect him of counterintelligence."

"No, they would not," Marlowe asserted.

"You must believe me when I say that he is not the man who murdered Walter Pygott."

"I find that difficult," Marlowe muttered. "He must at least know who did it. Possibly his compatriot, a Spaniard."

✝

Frances exhaled, folded her hands in her lap, and said, with an obvious effort at patience, "You will have to realize, Kit, that these phenomena are very much more complicated than that."

"Than *what*, exactly?" he snapped.

"You are irritated," she answered calmly.

"I am." He leaned closer to her, lowering his voice. "I hardly need tell you how difficult it was for me to leave you in London."

"Difficult for me, too," she admitted, "but we have a larger task before us."

"You are everywhere in my mind," he whispered harshly. "All my faith has been replaced by a single belief: that you could make me immortal with a single kiss."

"No," she said sweetly. "I cannot be your religion."

"A clever deflection," he said, sitting back. "You are as quick with words as you are with a rapier—and twice as deadly."

"Are you quite finished?" She shook her head. "You have a murder to solve, England to save, and no time to waste."

Marlowe stood. "In the solving of the murder there is something to be gained in the thwarting of the plot."

"Yes, we're all agreed on that." She stood and stepped close to him. "Walter Pygott is key to both, in some way. What do you know of Ingram Frizer, by the way?"

"He was one of the men who accosted me here in Cambridge, and who subsequently tried to kill Lopez and me on the road to London. Earlier today I followed him out of a bar and into a baker's shop. I knew he was up to something."

"Would that bar be at the Pickling Inn?"

"Pickerel," he corrected, "where I've procured my old room, the room where Pygott was found."

"You're certain you weren't recognized?"

He had momentarily forgotten his disguise, a good sign: it was becoming more natural to him, which would make it more believable.

"I had complete confidence in this costume," he admitted, "until Professor Bartholomew saw through it."

"Well," she said, touching his arm, "there are few minds in this world the equal of his."

"Yes," Marlowe agreed, "but you seemed to know me right away as well."

"Even if you dressed as a woman with a veil across your face," she said softly, "I would know you. I could feel your heart beating the moment I stepped into this building."

"There," he said, his head tilted slightly. "There's the kind of talk I want."

"And there will be words aplenty," she answered, "as soon as you solve the murder and save the Queen."

"Yes. To that end, you must tell me what your father did not, when last we met."

"What?"

"The details of the plot," he insisted, "the information for which I went to Malta, and Lopez died. I have a right to know what was in your brain, what was so important."

"Yes," she said at once. "In short, Throckmorton's effort is straightforward. Catholic agents in England and Spain are collaborating to murder our Queen."

"Yes, replace Elizabeth with the cousin Mary," Marlowe said impatiently, "and make England a Catholic country again. I know that."

"But the murder of the Queen alone would not achieve that end," she went on. "There must also be an invasion exactly coincident with the day of the assassination."

"Ah," Marlowe mused, "and that means there would also be support from within our own country, a secret organization of English Catholics."

"We think so."

"Because while the Pope may have very spiritual reasons for wishing to reclaim our souls," Marlowe said, "Spain makes use of religion to acquire our land."

"As cynical an observation as it is accurate," she asserted.

Marlowe began to pace.

"Do we know," he wondered, "who will lead this attack from within? Were you able to learn that at Coughton?"

"No. And we have no suspects for the leader of the invasion from without. I was, however, able to discover several of the invasion sites so that we may have armies ready in those places."

"Well, it doesn't really matter who actually leads the invasion armies, does it?" Marlowe began pacing faster. "Mendoza is the one behind them."

"Yes," she agreed, "the Spanish ambassador is coordinating the efforts. You suspected this?"

"Your father told me." Marlowe stopped moving. "And Lopez."

He found it difficult to say his friend's name out loud. It conjured a ghost, and the ghost filled Marlowe with a keen sense of loss.

Frances seemed to read those thoughts. "We will stop this monstrous plot," she said softly, "and in so doing, avenge the death of your friend."

She smiled, and in that smile there was a spark. Marlowe saw it, but could not interpret its meaning. Instead he made a deliberate effort to ignore it.

"How will it be done, this assassination of the Queen," Marlowe asked, "do we know?"

"Ah," she answered, moving toward the door. "That is why I have come to Cambridge. I am here to meet with Ingram Frizer. He may know the method and means of the attempt on Her Majesty's life."

"Frizer." Marlowe shook his head. "I can't believe he's on our side."

She pulled open the door and, for an instant, stared into his eyes.

Marlowe was momentarily overcome with a desire to taste her lips.

FIFTEEN

The bakery was closed when Frances and Marlowe came to its front door.

"You saw Frizer go into a back room?" she whispered.

Marlowe nodded, already headed for the alleyway between the bakery and a small butcher shop. The way was narrow and filled with refuse, but there was a door in the side wall of the bakery, and Marlowe hurried to it.

Frances had tied up the hem of her dress. She was wearing leather pants and low-heeled boots underneath her cloak. The hood was pulled up and forward, obscuring her face.

Marlowe had taken out his dagger and pulled a part of his cassock to one side, exposing the rapier's scabbard.

With a single glance between them, Marlowe threw open the door. He jumped in, Frances beside him, her rapier already drawn.

The room was empty, and small enough to assure them both that no one was hiding behind the confusing array of bread tables and flour sacks and stacks of wood.

It was stifling; the oven was still very hot.

Frances lowered her weapon.

Marlowe took one more look around and was about to sheath his dagger when he suddenly realized that the geometry was off. Judging from the outer room, this back chamber ought to have been nearly twice as large as it was.

A cursory examination of the wall opposite the oven revealed what appeared to be a loose panel. Marlowe pointed at it and stood to one side. Frances nodded and hid herself behind the flour sacks.

Slowly Marlowe wedged his fingers behind the panel and took in a deep breath. Then, without warning, he threw it open.

Ingram Frizer and the baker leapt from their hidden place roaring. Frizer had a pistol in each hand, and the baker held a heavy wooden hammer.

Marlowe immediately kicked one of the guns from Frizer's hand and had his blade against Frizer's gullet.

At the same time Frances battered the baker's hand with the hilt of her sword, forcing him to drop his mallet. She tilted backward and held the point of her rapier directly in front of the man's left eye.

For an instant, silence was everything.

Then, with forced nonchalance, Frizer said, "Hello, Richard."

"Ingram," she responded, her eyes locked on the baker.

Frizer attempted to laugh.

"And I suppose you'd be Marlowe, then," he said, not moving. "I should have recognized you when you followed me."

"Agreed," said Marlowe, keeping his knife at Frizer's throat. "You should always recognize men you've tried to kill."

"Out on the highway?" Frizer shrugged. "I doubt I would have killed you. But I was in a bit of a spot. You have to appreciate that. I had to go along with what was transpiring, didn't I? How would I have explained myself otherwise?"

"You're lucky Lopez didn't kill you." Marlowe at last withdrew his blade. "He wanted to. I prevented him, and later regretted it."

"Marlowe," Frances admonished, "put up your dagger. Frizer has news for us."

With a great show of reluctance, Marlowe relinquished his hold on Frizer and returned his knife to its sheath.

The baker moved quickly, first to look into the front room, and then to the side door. When he was certain no one was listening, he came to stand beside Frizer.

"Right, then." Frizer lowered his voice and stepped closer to Marlowe and Frances. "I've had a communication with a slip called Tin. She tells me, and I believes her, that someone at court, someone close to the Queen, will, within the month, seek to poison Her Majesty in the innermost royal chambers."

"Inner chambers," Frances said. "That would have to be one of the ladies-in-waiting."

"Like you," Marlowe said before he thought better of it.

"And Elizabeth Throckmorton," she said, "whose father is the uncle of the conspirator in charge of this plot. But she cannot be the one. She is true, and her passion for our Queen is beyond question. How did you hear this information?"

"I told you: from Tin. Tin what's in love with you. She done it for your sake."

"I mean," Frances said impatiently, "did you speak with her in person?"

"Well," Frizer said, "no. I got a message. She can read and write. Did you know that?"

"Let me see the message," Frances demanded. "I know her hand; I can tell if your message is a forgery."

"Ah," Frizer said, a sudden light in his eyes, "an excellent point. I don't have it on me. Shall we repair to the Pickerel?"

Marlowe shook his head. "We shall not. Your welcome at that establishment has, you may recall, vanished."

"In the public house, yes," he admitted, "but we could take ourselves up the alley right to your room."

"My room? You've hidden the letter from Tin in my room?"

"I've hidden several items of importance there. Once the beadles was done with the place, I deemed it the safest cell in Cambridge what to hide certain things. And then there's the smell of the place. That alone is enough—"

"What else did you hide there?" Marlowe demanded.

"I'm afraid I'm not at liberty to answer that completely, Mr. Marlowe."

The baker folded his arms. "And I'm afraid I shall have to ask you all to leave my establishment. This kind of talk is bad for my business."

"I can say, however," Frizer went on, ignoring the baker, "that

I have secreted away, under a certain floorboard, a newly printed version of the Rheims-Douai Bible, so-called."

"The new Catholic Bible?" Marlowe snapped.

"Why do you have that?" Frances wanted to know.

"Out!" the baker bellowed. "I cannot have talk of illegal books in my kitchen!"

Marlowe glanced at Frances. "Maybe we should go."

"The Pickerel it is," Frizer agreed, and headed for the door.

SIXTEEN

Marlowe was relieved to find that the combined effect of removing the foul mattress and leaving the window wide open had, to a great degree, relieved his room of the stench of death.

They were an odd trio: careless Frizer, bearded Marlowe, and the hooded specter of a man who was a woman who was a spy. Even inside the room, Frances kept her hood up.

Frizer went right to work prying up a floorboard. Frances sat at the desk. Marlowe felt compelled, for reasons not completely clear to himself, to watch at the door. Within minutes Frizer had unearthed the letter from Tin and the volume he had mentioned.

"I received this letter," Frizer said, holding them out for display, "inside a sack of barley sent from Coughton. You see, while Richard was living in luxury in the estate there, I was working in the stables, mostly mucking but also tending, and I got to be friends with the stable master, who, as it happens, is Tin's father, and a man as loyal to the Queen as you or me. As for the Bible, I reckon it incriminates Pygott as a Catholic agent."

Frances came to him and took the letter, holding it to the light from the window. Marlowe seized the Bible.

"This handwriting is the same as in the letter that came to Lord Walsingham," Frances said slowly. "It does indeed say that someone at court will poison Her Majesty in the royal chambers."

"It's from Tin," Frizer said.

"This New Testament is—unusual," Marlowe rejoined, almost to himself. "There are great long passages in Latin. Incorrect Latin."

✝

"A bad copy," Frizer surmised.

"No," Marlowe mused. "The Rheims–Douai Bible is a Catholic device. It translates the New Testament from the Latin Vulgate into English. It was printed under the order of William Allen, the man in charge of the College of Douai at Rheim. It's all supposed to be in English. And this is very bad Latin."

"What does it mean?" Frances squinted.

"Not certain." Marlowe sat on the bare bed ropes. "Let me see. This section says something about Calais. Here's *Dover*. And Folkestone."

"Stop." Frances froze. "Those are invasion instructions. The attack is to leave from Calais and land near Dover and Folkestone. That's what I overheard at the Throckmorton estate."

"Then is Allen the man coordinating the attack from within?" Marlowe stood.

"And his protector, the Duke of Guise," Frances suggested, "is the one in charge of the invasion from without."

Marlowe turned to Frizer. "You said that you got the letter in a bag of barley, but where did you get this Bible?"

"That," Frizer answered, eyebrows raised high, "was found on the person of one Walter Pygott, which is why I say that it proves him a Catholic bastard."

Marlowe glared at him. "So you did have something to do with Pygott's death after all."

"I did not," Frizer said instantly, though with a smile. "We found his body in the garden beside the church. Lovely roses there, for this time of year."

"*We?*" Marlowe asked.

"Me and my companion, the Spaniard."

"But you did bring the body here," Marlowe said steadily.

"We did. The thought was to get you arrested, keep you out of the way."

"But why?" Marlowe asked.

Frizer stiffened. "Can't say. But it was orders."

Marlowe stared at him, but realized after a moment that Frizer wasn't to be trusted. Trying to pry the truth out of him would be a waste of time. So he chose a different tack.

"This was—when? Recently?"

"No," Frizer answered. "Same day as our encounter with you and the doctor. Or that night, rather. The body was just lying there. Smelled of piss."

"What can you tell me about this Spaniard?" Marlowe asked.

"He's an addled egg. Lost part of his brains, is my guess. But he's Philip's man for certain adventures."

"He works for the King of Spain," Frances said suspiciously, "and cavorts with you."

"The Spaniard is a perfect assassin. He's killed more than a hundred men, and that's just in England. He allows as how big plans is afoot, but he don't say what. Not yet."

"But you still stick with him?" Marlowe's suspicions were making him sweat.

"Orders."

"And who has issued you those orders, I wonder," Frances mused.

Frizer dropped his devil-may-care attitude. "Lord Walsingham, of course."

"Right." Marlowe thought for a moment before he sighed. "Which means, I suppose, that you did not kill Pygott. Walsingham wouldn't have me chasing after his own man. But I can still suspect the Spaniard."

Frances nodded. "Do you know his name?" she asked Frizer.

"I do. But not because he told it to me. I had to find it out for myself, which means it may be a false name. A *nom de guerre,* as they say. He is called Aldano Zigor."

Marlowe blinked.

Frances was the first to speak. "That is not Spanish, you understand."

"I believe that it is a Basque name," Marlowe agreed.

"Is it?" Frizer asked, but the lilt in his voice made it evident that he already knew what Frances had guessed. "Well, as I say, it could be a contrivance."

"Are you certain that he's one of the Pope's men?" Marlowe demanded.

"Certain?" Frizer smiled. "What, in this life, is certain? I only go by what I've been told. By Walsingham."

"And *he* told you," Frances insisted, "that this man was a Catholic spy."

"He implied it."

Marlowe's mind was racing. He considered and discarded several far-fetched notions before he decided upon a plausible story.

"Suppose that Pygott was given this Bible to deliver to someone here in Cambridge," Marlowe began slowly. "His reputation as an idiot and a bully rendered him something of a risk, however, so this man, this Aldano Zigor, was dispatched to get the Bible and kill the boy."

"Which he did," Frances continued, "and then he pretended to come upon the body with Frizer as a witness."

"And then they both dragged the body to this room to incriminate me," Marlowe went on, "because the Pope's men knew that I had been summoned to London."

"Because they saw you and Lopez in the Queen's coach," Frances added.

Marlowe nodded. "Kill the messenger, retrieve his communiqué, and frame your enemy, all with a single murder. You have to admit it was nicely done."

"An admirable bit of deductive reasoning," Frizer complimented, "but for a single, insignificant pebble in the road."

Frances and Marlowe turned to Frizer.

"The Spaniard and I have been inseparable for nearly a year, until two nights ago. He's never left my side, nor I his—not before we found Pygott's body and brought it here. He could not possibly have killed Pygott."

Marlowe paused a moment, trying to decide if he should believe Frizer or not. Every instinct told him not to. Then he spoke.

"And what has separated the two of you now?" he chose to ask Frizer.

"I woke up and he was gone. That's what I was doing here at the Pickerel when I got drunk, looking for him."

"But the point is: this so-called Spaniard could not have killed Pygott," Frances said.

"Maybe not," Marlowe answered, "but I find the coincidence of his probable heritage to be a bit disconcerting."

"What?" Frizer complained.

"Mr. Marlowe and I have recently encountered another Basque," Frances answered, "a man who may well be responsible for the death of Dr. Lopez."

"The man in red?" Frizer sputtered. "He's gone?"

"I'm afraid he is," Frances said softly.

"Well, someone's a better man than I am. I tried to kill Lopez on three different occasions. The most recent time was in your presence, as you well know."

"No, but you tried to kill him before that?" Marlowe's hand moved nearer to his dagger.

Frizer saw the hand move. "You've not been told?"

"Told what?" Marlowe demanded.

"Lopez," Frizer said quietly, "was a double agent."

Marlowe laughed a little too loudly. "You think Lopez is working for the Pope?"

"The Pope?" Frizer shot back, astonished by the question. "No. He's a double agent for the Jews."

"Working for the Jews?" an astonished Marlowe barked. "What Jews?"

"I have it on the greatest authority," Frizer assured him.

"I don't care if Jesus sat on top of you and shouted it into your ear," Marlowe declared, "it's not true! You've been tricked."

Frances took Marlowe's forearm in her gloved hand.

"Kit," she said gently, "what does it matter now?"

Marlowe glared at Frizer. "It matters."

"I mean," she went on, "wouldn't we rather ask ourselves about this Bible?"

"What about it?" Marlowe snapped.

"Is it genuine or is it a ruse?"

"Why would it be a ruse?" he asked her, his ire receding.

"Well," she suggested, "not to denigrate your education in the least, but aren't there at least a thousand people in this town alone who could spot bad Latin and translate it?"

He started to speak, then exhaled and nodded.

"You mean this message," Frizer began, "the one he just translated, is a fake?"

Marlowe sighed once more. "Probably. A decoy. She's right, it's too obvious."

"That's right, but more important," she went on, "I'd like to know a little more about the Spaniard with the Basque name."

"Yes," Marlowe agreed, "it's too much of a coincidence."

"Why is that?" Frizer wanted to know.

"A Basque named Argi," Frances said softly.

"The one you think has killed Lopez," Frizer said.

"There's likely to be some connection," Frances went on. "How many Basque patriots does one run into in England?"

"Personally," Marlowe said, "I'd like to know a little more about this baker with whom you seem so friendly. What's his role in all this?"

"Oh, he's nothing," Frizer said, nodding. "I thought you was after something more immediately consequential."

"Such as?" Marlowe asked.

"Such as, my lad, who murdered Pygott? Because it ain't me and it ain't the Spaniard. And if you don't find out who *did* do it, you're cooked. How much good would it do Walsingham, or the Queen, to have you in prison?"

"I'm afraid he's right, Kit," Frances said. "This is all a tangled knot. We ought to follow one thread at a time."

"I can't agree," Marlowe said firmly. "All of these events, Pygott's murder, the death of Lopez, the information you gleaned at the Throckmorton estate—it's all one. It's all of a piece."

"It's all of a knot, she said," Frizer insisted, "and she's got it right."

Marlowe took a step closer to Frizer. "What, exactly, did she get right?"

An uneasy silence filled the air, but try as he might, Marlowe could not discern why.

"Kit," Frances said at length, "sit down."

Marlowe sat back down on the frame of the bed while Frances spent the better part of ten minutes telling him a story.

Frances Walsingham stood in the private courtyard between her father's offices and the outer orchard at Whitehall. Dressed in leather breeches, knee-high boots, a padded doublet, and a kerchief to tie up her hair, she waited, rapier in hand.

With no warning, a shadow flew from the darkness behind a thick column next to her. She collapsed, as if unconscious, then rolled, came to her feet, kicked dirt into the air in front of her, and thrust her rapier.

"Christ," a voice in the dust coughed. "Who taught you that?"

"No one." She grinned. "It's not something that most men would ever think of: surrender in order to achieve a goal."

"That fainting trick, you mean," Lopez said, stepping into the clearer air beside her. "It's good. But for a moment you were on the ground. That's bad."

"I was never still." She sheathed her rapier. "I rolled and was on my feet in one single move. I kicked up a screen, as you taught me. And I stabbed you. You, finest swordsman in the world."

Lopez had spent several years with the girl, and had told her many times that she was his finest student.

Her father stepped from the darkness next to his door. His face was grave.

"She's ready," Lopez said.

"No, she's not," Walsingham sniffed.

"Yes, I am," she insisted. "I bested *Lopez*. No one can do that."

"You did not draw blood," Walsingham said, "and he is not at his best."

Lopez nodded. "Your thrust but touched my leg. A bee sting."

"And he's not at his best," Walsingham went on, "because of this Marlowe boy."

Lopez smiled. "He's a remarkable young man."

"He's a boy," she complained.

"He's older than you by three years," her father growled.

Lopez looked away.

"The point is," Walsingham continued, determined to make his point, "Marlowe is our next objective. You and Dr. Lopez will encounter him, engage him, and observe him. Then you will both report back to me to say if he will do or not."

"Do what, exactly?" she asked, but she was smiling. She knew what her father meant. She only wanted him to say it out loud.

"To see if he will be our man," Walsingham snapped impatiently. "To see if he is as good as Lopez tells me that he is. To see, in short, if we may use him to our greater ends, if he will serve his country and his Queen."

"And just how do you propose that I *encounter* him?" Frances asked.

"Lopez is a friend to the Marlowe family," Walsingham went on, "as you well know. This is how we knew about the boy at all. Lopez is already hatching a plan that will introduce him to you."

Frances smiled. "You just called him a boy."

"When will you start taking this business seriously?" her father demanded nearly at the top of his lungs.

"Just as soon," she said, kissing him on the cheek, "as it ceases to be so very amusing."

Marlowe stared at Frances.

"You don't mean to say that your imprisonment on Malta was only a ruse to test me, to observe me?" he stammered.

"Of course not," she answered immediately. "You were to be assigned as my protection once I came back from the Throckmorton estate. That would have happened at the end of your first term here at Corpus Christi College. But my capture accelerated the plan, and gave it more importance."

"But Lopez was *observing* me," Marlowe said to himself, stunned. "He was watching me, testing me—without telling me about it."

"I'm afraid so, to some extent," she confirmed.

Marlowe began to wonder if it was possible, just possible, that Frizer's observation about Lopez might be worth examination: that Lopez was a double agent. Clearly he would not work for the Pope, but would he have other loyalties, other motives?

Lost in thought, he was the last to hear the door handle turn. Frizer had already produced an ugly knife from his boot, and Frances had drawn her rapier. They all watched as the door handle moved slowly, as if in a dream, and the door cracked open.

In the next second a demon exploded into the room, a rapier in each hand, dressed in gray costume from head to foot—including the boots—with a headpiece that obscured all but the eyes.

At once, with a single winglike move, the figure disarmed Frizer and then kicked his legs out from under him. Frizer's knife went flying, and he landed hard on his back with a thud and a grunt.

In two more strides the figure was in the center of the room, arms wide. One rapier point was drawing a thin trickle of blood from Marlowe's throat, and the other was pressed against Frances's bosom, between two ribs, aimed at the heart.

All four stayed frozen in that tableau until the figure spoke.

"Hello, Ingram," the girl's voice said.

"What?" Frizer managed to growl, still flat on his back.

"And Richard," the girl continued, staring at Frances.

Another single heartbeat of silence ticked by in motionless stupor.

Then, in a blur, Marlowe's gloved hand grabbed the rapier at his throat and pushed it back toward its owner.

The girl in gray lost her balance and Marlowe took advantage of her twisted posture. He slid off the bed, raking his back on the frame, and kicked the girl's shin as hard as he could.

She let out a yelp and her rapier came away in Marlowe's hand. He rolled over Frizer and was on his feet with the girl's own weapon in his hand. Without another thought, he thrust, and stabbed the fleshy part of the girl's forearm, the arm that held the other rapier at Frances's breast. That rapier clattered to the floor at once.

Frances produced her dagger and leapt. She held the point of it against the girl's cheek, just under her eye.

"Don't move," Frances said, "or the eye is gone."

"Wait," Frizer called out, doing his best to sit up. "Hang on. Don't go sticking that girl no more, the two of you."

He grabbed on to the bed and hoisted himself up. He brushed the rapier in Marlowe's hand aside, and elbowed Frances backward. He examined the girl's wounded forearm. Blood had already soaked her sleeve. Then he pushed back her headpiece, exposing dirty blond hair and a fearless face. He kissed her on the cheek.

"Hello, Tin," he said lovingly. "What brings you to Cambridge?"

"Tin?" Marlowe gasped. "This is the girl who's been sending the messages?"

Frances pulled back her cowl and gazed into Tin's eyes.

"You are responsible for saving my life," she said to Tin. "If not for you, no one would have known I was in Malta. I'm sorry I did not recognize you. I am in your debt."

"Richard," was all the poor girl said.

"Yes." Frances looked down. "I am heartily sorry for that particular deception, but you must understand—"

"I understand," Tin said quickly. "I may understand this better than you do."

"Tin?" Marlowe repeated, only a heartbeat behind the rest in his thinking.

"What are you doing in Cambridge, girl?" Frizer insisted.

"I've been following you for a day and a half," she answered boldly. "I watched you at the baker's, and came here with you, only a dozen steps behind. And as to my reasons for doing it, here are three."

Tin reached into a pouch attached to her belt and produced a packet of letters.

"More letters from Mendoza?" Frances guessed.

Tin nodded.

"But why bring them here?" Frizer snapped.

Tin looked at Marlowe.

"I know these other two, sir," she said to him softly, "but yours is not a face I recognize."

"My name is Robert Greene," he answered at once, "late of Corpus Christi College here in Cambridge, now of London, returned for the purposes of researching my latest play, *Friar Bacon and Friar Bungay.*"

"Friar Bungay?" she asked.

"It is a comedy."

"Then what, may I ask, are you doing in a room where a student was found murdered," Tin went on, "the room of one Christopher Marley, who killed that student?"

"That's *Marlowe*," he corrected before he thought better of it. "And Mr. Marlowe is, himself, a budding playwright. He was helping me with my play. I came calling, found these two miscreants in his room, and was about to summon the beadles when you made your overly dramatic entrance. Just stand there, and I'll have all three of you arrested."

It was a bold performance, and Frances stifled a smile.

Frizer nodded.

"True enough," he said to Tin, "this gentleman found us here. But we was just about to explain to him the nature of our business."

"Something," Marlowe sniffed, "about saving the Queen. A fantastical elaboration."

"Oh, but it's nonetheless true, sir," Tin reported enthusiastically. "Our Queen is in danger from the Catholic devils, and these two, most especially this girl—they're working for Lord Walsingham. Lord Walsingham *himself.*"

"Is this true?" Marlowe demanded in mock surprise.

"It is," Frances said, straining to keep a straight face.

"Let me see those letters, then, girl," Marlowe demanded.

Tin looked to Frances. Frances nodded. Tin handed over the pages.

Marlowe sat back down on the bare frame of the bed and read the letters quickly. They confirmed what he and Frances had discovered or guessed.

"These are indeed from Mendoza," he said absently as he finished the second letter. "And the Duke of Guise is to lead an invading army, supported by Spain, to attack our nation within the month."

"What?" Tin exploded. "It doesn't say that!"

"Ah." Marlowe looked up. "You've read these, have you?"

She nodded.

"But you've only read the surface of the letters," Marlowe went on, "the words as they are written. You've failed to discern the Spanish code."

"Spanish code?" Tin asked, a bit more subdued.

"It's simple, really," Marlowe said lazily. "Spanish is very much closer to Latin than is English. The code takes advantage of the relatively few Latinate words in our language, uses them to say things in Spanish when the letter, on its surface, seems to be in English, and fairly straightforward. This sentence here, for example, says, 'I am anxious that you should try our newest liqueur, my friend, so I will send you a keg of Eudisse, which comes from Bilbao but is like the port which is popular in your own city of Portsmouth.' Do you see it?"

"See what?" Tin said weakly, blushing.

"Our word *anxious* is derived from the Latin *angrere,* which means 'to cause pain' or 'to choke,' and *keg of Eudisse* is an all-too-obvious anagram of the words 'Duke of Guise.' Taken together with the syntax of the sentence, we arrive at the very certain message that the Duke of Guise intends to sail from Bilbao to Portsmouth, choke off all other port activity there, and ascend toward London, to cause our country the greatest pain."

Tin looked to Frances. "Does it really say that?"

Frances nodded. "If he says it does. He's very clever."

"We've got to get this information to Walsingham at once," Frizer said urgently.

"Agreed," said Marlowe, jumping up. "You must take these letters to him."

"Me?" Frizer said. "Not likely."

"Has to be you, Ingram," Frances admonished.

"Just tell him what I've said here," Marlowe added, "and that these letters are in the *first* Spanish code."

"Why don't you do it?" Frizer asked. "I hate London and I have continuing business here."

"No," Frances explained, "he has to stay here to find Pygott's murderer."

"Shouldn't be too difficult," Marlowe added, "now that I know who did it."

"What?" Tin looked about wildly. "Do you mean Walter Pygott?"

"It's all right, he can't harm you now," Frances said soothingly. "He was murdered here. But thanks to you we know that Pygott was the one who betrayed me to the Pope's men."

"And thanks to my brief investigation here in this room," Marlowe continued, "I surmise that the murderer was a Spanish or Basque man called Aldano Zigor. I have only to find him."

"Who?" Tin asked.

"A compatriot of mine," Frizer confessed. "But I've already told you he did not do the killing."

"I disagree," Marlowe said simply.

"You believe that he is the murderer because of something you found in this room?" Tin continued.

"Several things," Marlowe answered. "A bloody bootprint and a bit of cloth encouraged me to believe that Frizer and his crew were responsible."

"Bit of cloth?" Frizer asked.

Marlowe produced the torn bit of fabric he'd found in the room. It was an exact match for the missing patch from Frizer's dirty brown overshirt.

"But when I learned," Marlowe went on, "that Frizer is, in fact—wait, how much should I tell her?"

He glanced between Frances and Frizer.

"I would say that you could tell her everything. She's probably guessed most of it anyway."

"Do you mean the bit about Ingram's being a double agent?" Tin piped up. "I knew that."

"How could you—" Marlowe began, then shot a look to Frances. "And by the way, *Richard*: I am the one who saved your life. This girl sent a letter to London. I sent myself to Malta, killed a man, dragged you out of a hole, *and* undressed you onboard a ship."

"I see your point," Frances said softly. "I really do. But I think you have no idea what it takes to produce valor of a similar sort in a woman."

"And although I am a woman, sir," Tin said firmly, "I will not be slack playing my part in Fortune's pageant."

"No doubt," Marlowe agreed, "and I have seen the power of a woman's will in these past weeks."

"But that is something I've known for a lifetime," Frances said gently, "not just a few weeks."

Frances turned to Tin then.

"I am heartily sorry for deceiving you when I was at Coughton," Frances said. "I had no intention of encouraging your affections, you know that. You have taken great pain to help a person who does not exist. You cared for a shadow. Richard was an insubstantial thing, a player on a stage. He is not here."

Tin lowered her head, then took a single step closer to Frances and spoke in a voice so soft that it was barely audible.

"Do you really think," she began, not looking up, "that I did not know what you were? I loved you on the first day I saw you, because I knew you to be the bravest woman I would ever meet. Who ever loved that loved not at first sight?"

Silence overtook the room for the span of several heartbeats before Marlowe's sigh blasted the air.

"God, Tin," he whispered, "that's the same thing that happened to me."

Tin looked to Marlowe then. Her eyes were filled with tears.

"I know," she said, her voice still barely making a sound. "I could see it in you the moment I walked into this room. I recognized a fellow sufferer. We are doomed, you and I, Mr. Greene, to love this shadow."

And although Marlowe did not quite understand what the girl meant, he nevertheless felt a stone sink in the pit of his stomach, and knew that she was right.

SEVENTEEN

Downstairs in the public house not five minutes later, the strange trio took a table by the door, Tin disguised in gray, Marlowe claiming to be Greene, and Frances with her hood pulled so far over her head that she appeared to have no face at all.

Frizer slipped out the back with the letters from Mendoza, and was on his way to purchase a horse with money Frances gave him. Walsingham would have the information before dawn.

After a moment, one of Pinch's daughters wafted her way to the table and winked. She was the one who had attended him before.

"Look at this," she said to Marlowe. "You've already made friends here in town. And mysterious ones at that: a lady hiding her face and a young boy spitting-ready to kill someone. Better have some ale, eh?"

"Three, please," Marlowe said, smiling.

"By the way," she said more confidentially, "I'm sorry about the fuss before."

"Your mother was right to protect you."

"You're a gentle soul," she said, nodding.

With that she was off.

"Frizer attacked that girl," he explained under his breath, "in sight of everyone here."

"He was drunk," Tin surmised. "He does that when he's drunk. Tried it with me. Once."

"And I'm certain that he learned his lesson there," Frances said quietly.

Tin nodded.

"Do you really think that this Basque/Spaniard will show his face?" Frances continued.

"I do. I think he may have heard what happened to Frizer. That kind of news travels fast. And he'll want to know if Frizer gave anything away in his stupor. He'll be here, and he'll be asking questions."

"Possibly," Frances agreed.

"It's what I'd do," Marlowe explained.

They sat watching. As he often did, Marlowe saw the public house as a stage, the men and women making their exits and entrances. How many parts had he played in the past weeks: a schoolboy, a soldier, and now a bearded leopard, waiting to pounce?

Then, out of the corner of his eye, Marlowe saw Aldano Zigor, the Pope's assassin; he was obvious. Zigor slipped into the relatively crowded room through the side entrance and stepped into the shadows next to the door. He wore a woolen hat and a short leather cape, as if to call attention to the fact that he was a foreigner. He was searching the room as if his life depended on it.

Frances cleared her throat softly. Marlowe nodded once.

Just then the serving girl returned with three tankards and momentarily blocked the man from their view.

"Let's make it a penny for all three," she said, winking, "and call it a reward for a gentle soul."

Marlowe smiled at her and handed her a coin. "Let's make it a shilling," he said softly, "and call it an apology from Ingram Frizer. Not all men behave that way."

"What in God's name?" she began, staring at the coin.

Before she could finish, Tin stood and strode with great speed toward Zigor. Zigor saw her coming and stepped back through the side door to the alleyway.

Marlowe was up instantly, brushing past the girl and flying to Tin's side.

Frances stood more slowly.

"We'll be back at the table in just a moment," she promised warmly.

✝

Bursting into the alleyway, Marlowe thrust his dagger just in time to stop Zigor's small knife from slicing Tin's hand off. Tin had that hand around Zigor's throat.

Zigor took three quick steps backward and produced a *cinque-dea*. It was short, more than five times thicker than a rapier, with a ribbed double blade as well as its deadly point. It was an odd weapon for a Basque mercenary, a bit antiquated, and almost certainly Italian in origin.

Tin drew her rapier, as did Marlowe.

Zigor licked his lips, then spoke.

"My English is not good," he began, his eyes darting quickly between his adversaries. "I wish to be finding Ingram Frizer. He is my friend. I have see you with him."

To make certain they understood his point, he pointed in Marlowe's direction with his little knife.

"He's gone," Marlowe said simply.

"Dead?" Zigor asked.

"No, I mean gone away. Not in Cambridge."

Zigor appeared to take the news badly.

"Where?"

"Where did he go?" Marlowe asked. "I have no idea. But since he accosted the daughter of this establishment, his reputation isn't worth much in Cambridge."

"I see. Yes."

From behind Marlowe, Frances, standing in the doorway, spoke quickly and in Portuguese.

"*Assassino,*" she whispered, "*o que é que vos levou a fazê-lo?*"

"Do *what*?" he asked, but his eyes were cold.

"Pygott," Marlowe said simply.

"You think I kill that boy?" Zigor laughed.

"That's what Argi told us," Frances continued.

"Argi?" he asked, his face affectless. "Who is Argi?"

"You know very well who he is," Frances pressed. "He sails with Captain de Ferro, and he murdered Rodrigo Lopez."

That took Zigor by surprise. He lowered his formidable sword an inch or two, and blinked.

"Lopez is dead?"

He seemed genuinely weakened by the news.

"You knew him?" Frances asked.

"No. But he is—a great man, no?"

"He was," Marlowe said softly.

"But about Pygott?" Zigor asked, deliberately changing the subject.

Marlowe started to speak, then stopped, reached down into his boot, keeping his eyes locked on Zigor's, and produced the silver earring that had been secreted there.

"I think this is yours," Marlowe said to Zigor, holding it out for him to see.

Zigor glanced down at it. "It might be. I lost one like it."

Marlowe examined the man's ears, then. The twin to the object Marlowe had in his hand was resting in Zigor's right ear.

"It does seem to be a match for the one you have there," Marlowe said. "I found it in the room where they say Pygott was murdered."

"No—wait." Zigor was obviously trying to collect his thoughts.

"Maybe you ought to tell us everything," Marlowe said grimly.

Then, taking a gamble of his own, Marlowe put away his weapons and took a step closer to Zigor.

Zigor took in a single breath and sheathed his blade as well.

"Where I should begin?" he asked.

"Maybe we should go back inside?" Tin suggested.

"Better out here for the moment," Marlowe answered absently, staring at Zigor. "Too many ears inside—one way or another."

"Tell us about killing Pygott," Frances said. "That's what's pressing most."

She moved her cloak then, only briefly, but long enough to reveal that she was holding a pistol in each hand. After a second, they were gone and she stepped into the alleyway beside Marlowe.

Zigor sighed. "We find him—*como uma rosa no jardim*."

"Like a rose in the garden?" Marlowe snapped. "Where?"

"*A Igreja.*"

"The church. St. Benet's, do you mean?" Marlowe asked.

Zigor nodded.

"That's what Frizer said," Frances noted.

"Yes," Zigor went on. "Ingram too. We find him—Pygott. Already dead."

"You're claiming that you didn't kill him?" Marlowe pressed.

"*Ouve-me*," he insisted, "I follow Ingram. We go to the church to steal."

"Wait just a moment," Marlowe said. "You mean you went to St. Benet's to steal something that you wanted another student to steal? The man you attacked, along with Lopez, on the road to London a month ago?"

"Yes. A student who is called Marlowe. But he is not willing to do the work. So, we try to kill him. That also did not go well. So Ingram makes another plan: get this Pygott to steal. Ingram has a plan to meet Pygott at the church."

"But you found Pygott's body in the garden. This is what you want us to believe."

"Yes. Also: Pygott, he already have the—it's a Bible. We find it on his body."

"That doesn't make sense." Marlowe shook his head emphatically. "It was supposed to be something that would incriminate a man named John Marlowe, the student's father. Why would Pygott care about that?"

Zigor started to speak, then gave up.

"*Desculpa.* You talk too fast. I cannot understand. I need Ingram to tell you."

"That's convenient," Tin muttered suspiciously.

"But I must to go," Zigor concluded, looking around. "*Existem inimigos à minha procura por todo o lado.*"

"'Enemies looking for you everywhere?'" Marlowe snorted. "You have your share of enemies standing before you."

"You? No," he disagreed. "No enemy. For me? Is business. *Católico, Protestantes, Judeu*—it's matter not to me."

"But you are in the employ of the Catholic Church," Frances pressed.

"But, like Ingram," he admitted, "only for the money."

"What about the item you say you found on Pygott?" Tin wanted to know.

"Ingram."

"You did help Frizer to carry the dead boy's body to a room upstairs here at the Pickerel, is that correct?" Frances confirmed.

But before Zigor could answer, a grating voice from just inside the doorway startled them all.

"What the hell are you ruffians about out here, then?" Pinch growled, stepping out of the shadows with his large wooden club in one hand and a butcher knife in the other.

Everyone turned his way.

"This is Ingram Frizer's friend," Marlowe said quickly. "We were just telling him what happened here."

"Telling him to clear out," Frances added.

"Oh." Pinch nodded. "Well, that's done then."

Marlowe turned back around to see that it was true.

Zigor was gone.

"Incidentally, Mr. Greene," Pinch went on, "there was gentlemen of the constabulary in your room earlier today, when you was out. They say that this Marley, the murderer, is suspected of being back in Cambridge, and might approach the digs what's rented to you. So watch out for yourself. Of course, they're watching the place now, these beadles, so you're not alone. Thought you should know."

And away he lumbered.

"Christ!" Marlowe whispered. "Now the law is watching my room!"

"Steady, Mr. Greene," Frances answered. "They're only trying to help."

Marlowe shook his head and stepped toward the door to the bar.

Back inside, at their table once more, the odd trio sat in silence, trying to make sense of everything.

Marlowe's mind raged. Every thought that rose up was met with a warring opposite. Lopez was gone, and that caused Marlowe pain, but Lopez had been watching him, observing him. It was even possible that Lopez had purchased the murder of Pygott. Why would he do it? To test Marlowe? Or worse: to get Marlowe out of the way? Every thought of Lopez as a friend and hero was matched by a suspicion of Lopez as a spy and a traitor.

Then there was the notion that the law was watching his room. It would only be a matter of time before someone discovered that the real Robert Greene was in his grotesque digs in London, suffering illness and regret, working on his newest theatre piece.

He ended his tormented introspection by staring at Tin's profile. She was an odd rival, enamored with Frances as much as he was.

Even more apparent was the cool way Frances held herself: assured, capable—complete. Her father had trained her well. She needed no one. Marlowe feared that Tin's pronouncement was accurate: he and Tin were doomed to love someone who would not love them in return.

Half an hour and three more ales later, decisions were made.

First, Ingram was not to be trusted. Second, Zigor had to be found. Third, Frances and Tin were to return to Coughton.

That was a risk, but Frances would go as herself this time, a lady-in-waiting to the Queen. Even if Throckmorton was certain of her dual identity as Richard, he would hardly be so bold as to threaten Lord Walsingham's daughter. Frances would say that she had need to speak with her acquaintance Elizabeth Throckmorton about some fabricated, slight matters of court. Tin would resume her place as her father's daughter. Their goal would be to discover further details about the plan to murder the Queen in her own chambers; even, if possible, to uncover the identity of the Queen's killer.

Marlowe would remain in Cambridge. The Pope's assassin close at hand and the local law out to arrest him, it was clear that his freedom, and his life, depended on finding Pygott's killer.

EIGHTEEN

The streets of Cambridge looked foreign to Marlowe in the dark of the moon. Every shadow was a lie, every sound a threat. Ominous figures moved just at the edge of his sight. Men were after him, for reward or for the law. The riverside shambles that passed for homes all seemed animated with menace, and nothing could completely eradicate the premonition that he would die that night.

What surprised him was how comforting he found the prospect of death. Dying was only a chance to sleep, and he was mortally tired. His discomfort lay more in the dread of what might happen if he were arrested or killed before he could succeed in his task. Harm could come to Frances. The Queen might be killed. The country would be overtaken by Spain. And he would be remembered as a murderer, not a poet.

So staying alive, finding Zigor, and forcing him to admit that he murdered Pygott was, for the moment, the only task in the world.

Thanks to Pinch, whose hulking manner and slack-jawed mien belied a keen mind and a great wealth of information, Marlowe had learned that an enclave of Basque sailors and criminals infested an encampment somewhere in the Coe Fen south of the city.

As he drew nearer the fen, the unmistakable smell of *marmitako*, the Basque fish stew with potatoes, onions, tomatoes, and peppers, filled the air. In the distance he could hear the faint singing of *bertsos*, Basque improvised melodies. In short, Pinch's information was accurate.

Marlowe had already doffed his cumbersome cassock in favor of the sleeker black pants and tunic that had been hidden underneath. The ginger beard was still in place, and still just as irritating.

He walked along the edges of the path, keeping clear of sucking mud, noisy stones, and, as was sometimes the case in these more unsavory environs, small steel traps.

As he drew closer to the singing, he could see several open fires. Men were gathered around them, mostly eating, some sleeping. The seated singer was extemporizing with equal fervor and concentration, and the men closest to him were rapt, oblivious to anything else.

How to proceed? Marlowe wondered.

Stealth seemed the most sensible bet, but to what end? He could approach the men silently, but he would have to confront Zigor at some point, and any furtive behavior would be seen as a threat by the rest of the men. Better to be bold.

Just as he made that decision, he recognized the singer in the flickering firelight. His pulse quickened. His blood heated and made his face red. His hands began to shake ever so slightly.

He took a deep breath and then several quick, loud strides toward the encampment. His voice booming a deliberately joyous greeting.

"Argi! You're in England!"

Argi stopped singing, leapt to his feet, a dagger in his hand.

The rest of the men turned toward Marlowe. Most of them were armed as well. One of them was Zigor, who tried to hide his face in the shadows.

Argi twisted his neck several times, squinting, trying to recognize the man coming toward him.

Marlowe rushed to Argi's side, brushed the knife to one side, and embraced the smaller man.

Argi was momentarily taken aback, until he felt the point of a blade at his spine.

"If you move or cry out an alarm, you're dead," Marlowe whispered in his ear.

"So are you," Argi answered. "These men will kill you."

"The difference is," Marlowe snapped fervently, "I don't care, but you do. A man who sings the way you just did? He loves life."

Argi recognized something in that voice.

"Marlowe?" Argi exhaled. "Is it you underneath this ridiculous beard?"

"Yes."

"What do you want?"

"I came here for Zigor." It was only half the truth.

There was a moment of stillness, followed by great mock joy on Argi's part.

"My friend!" he bellowed.

The men around the fire relaxed; most of the weapons were put away. Marlowe stood back from Argi and beamed.

"Let me look at you," he said.

As he did, he saw Zigor out of the corner of his eye. He wheeled around.

"And Zigor!" he shouted. "I thought I might find you here."

Zigor stood, uncertain of what was happening.

"One word from me," Argi warned softly, "and these men will kill you and cook you for stew."

Marlowe grinned, turned madly about to address all those men.

"Men of the Pyrenees," he began, "you whose ancestors protected your homeland from Visigoths of Iberia and Muslims to the south, Franks from the advancing north, and Satan from hell itself, you would know my struggle! You whose forefathers survived the bloody partisan War of the Bands and resisted the rule of any tyrant, you must hear me. I come to you now because my home is threatened by those same forces that have plagued your families for a thousand years. I need your help. You must come to my aid!"

His impassioned speech was met with stunned silence.

Argi leaned close to Marlowe's ear.

"They told me you like to write plays," he whispered enthusiastically. "I think you would be very good at it."

Marlowe nodded, keeping his eyes on the audience.

"I thought it was worth a try." He shrugged. "They don't seem particularly impressed."

"Well," Argi allowed, "it would have had great success if any of these men spoke English."

"They don't speak English?"

"Not a one of them," Argi grunted. "Just Zigor and me. That's all."

"But it was good speech," Zigor said.

Marlowe turned his attention to Zigor alone. "You know why I'm here."

"No." Zigor seemed completely at sea.

"Pygott," Marlowe snapped.

"What?" Zigor squinted.

"*Tu não sabes?*" Argi said to Zigor. "*Este é o homem—*"

"Say no more," Marlowe interrupted. "Not here, and not in Portuguese. I would prefer that the rest of these men did not know my name, or my predicament."

"I know who you are now," Zigor finally understood. "I see that you are not this *Greene*."

"We should take a walk," Argi said.

Without another word, Argi headed out of the circle of men. Marlowe and Zigor followed.

Back on the path that skirted the fen, away from the fires, Marlowe once again found it difficult to see anything but vague shapes in the darkness.

After a few moments of silence, when they were far enough from the camp, Argi spoke up.

"It really was a good speech," he said. "Of course, it would have been much more effective in Portuguese. How do you know so much about my people?"

"You killed my friend, Rodrigo Lopez," Marlowe rasped.

Darkness prevented Marlowe from seeing what Zigor did, but the sound of a pistol cocking was unmistakable. In the next heartbeat, the point of Marlowe's dagger was pressed into the back of Argi's neck, just below the skull.

"If you don't throw your pistol into the water," Marlowe said to Zigor, "I'll kill Argi now, instead of asking him why he murdered Dr. Lopez."

"My friend, my friend," Argi gasped quickly. "What are you saying? I did not kill Lopez!"

"You may not have done it alone," Marlowe snapped bitterly, "no single man could have. Captain de Ferro was a part of it, I'm certain of that."

"No," Argi pleaded, "you have it wrong."

Marlowe heard Zigor's shuffling steps move to his left side. The man's leather cape made a distinctive sound.

Marlowe countered, keeping Argi's body between himself and the shadow form.

"Shoot if you want to," Marlowe warned, "but you'll just be killing your cousin, here."

Argi stopped struggling a little, and Zigor stood completely still.

"How did you know we are cousins?" Argi asked.

"I know everything."

A guess, a bluff, a brag—Marlowe acknowledged these as the best tools of any good actor, and every great spy.

"So then why is it that you don't know about Lopez?" Argi asked, almost argumentatively.

Unfortunately, Marlowe spoke again before he thought.

"What about him?"

"Ah, there, you see." Argi's voice was genial. "You do not know everything. Let us talk, yes?"

Marlowe let Argi go. A second later he heard the sound of the pistol uncocking.

"Let's walk this way, toward town," Marlowe suggested, heading toward the outer streets of Cambridge, and torchlight. "I want to see your faces."

The cousins exchanged a few words in a language that Marlowe did not understand.

"What is that?" he asked. "What are you saying?"

"Oh," Zigor answered, "we are trying to say if we kill you or no."

"I see." Marlowe took a few more steps. "What's the decision?"

"For the moment," Zigor said calmly, "we talk."

Only a few minutes later they were near a small dock where lamps were lit. No one seemed to be there at the moment, but the lamps meant someone would be returning soon.

The trio stood in the street, near enough to see one another, far enough away to avoid being too well seen by others.

Softly, and in English that was occasionally impossible to follow, Zigor related a brief portion of his story.

"In July of last year," Zigor began, his English strangely improved, "I am fighting with my cousin, Argi, in the Battle of Ponta Delgada."

"This is to keep Portugal out of the Spanish Empire, you understand," Argi added.

"We sailed on an English mercenary galleon captained by de Ferro," Zigor went on. "In the ocean near the Azores, off São Miguel Island, we were severely defeated; taken prisoner by Spanish forces."

"I manage to escape with Captain de Ferro," Argi said solemnly, "but Zigor is not so lucky."

"They take me to Spain." Zigor looked about suspiciously, making certain he was not being overheard. "The Inquisition, they make me their spy."

"Zigor is a well-known assassin," Argi interjected, a strange pride in his voice.

"I am to go to England, meet Ingram Frizer, a Catholic spy, and enlist him in the cause: to rid England of a Protestant Queen."

"Zigor had to agree," Argi insisted. "The pay was good and the alternative was death."

"I make my way to Cambridge and meet Frizer at the Pickerel Inn, as they tell me to do. He has found two other men to help. One is a brute whose skull is thicker than armor; the other is an excellent man with a knife."

"Both local," Argi added.

"But what was your assignment, you and Frizer?" Marlowe asked, certain he did not believe Zigor's story.

"A Bible," he answered. "An illegal book, hidden in St. Benet's

Church. I don't know why it's important. Frizer says that strangers and foreigners breaking into a church would be suspected. So we find a student at the college to get it."

"And Frizer picked me." Marlowe took in a deep breath. "He suspected that my father might be amenable to the Catholic cause, and he had no idea that I would soon be working for—"

Marlowe stopped short of saying Walsingham's name, though he was certain that Argi knew it.

"One of the others, the knife man Frizer hired, he insist that we should not let you go, so we set out to kill you, but that was the day Lopez came to visit. No one wants to fight that man in an open yard. So. We follow the carriage and attack it. But Lopez, he kill the thick-skull, Marlowe stab Frizer and then throw a knife at me."

Zigor pulled back his sleeve, revealing a significant wound. Marlowe smiled.

"Are we ever going to get to Walter Pygott?" Marlowe asked.

"Oh. Yes. I know that Pygott is the one who brings the Bible to the church in the first place," Zigor went on, "so we go back to Cambridge and get him."

"How did you know he was the one who delivered it?" Marlowe asked.

"It doesn't matter," Zigor said quickly, "but when we find him, he says that he delivered the Bible to someone in the church. Frizer told Pygott that he was to go back into the church; get them back."

"You realize that most of this doesn't make sense," Marlowe objected. "Why deliver something to the church just to steal it back?"

"Because someone in the church has hide this Bible," Zigor explained. "And will not give them to anyone."

"And you thought *Pygott* could find it?"

"Pygott knows the man who has hide it," Zigor said, "and would offer him money, which was all the man in the church wanted. So. It is arrange that we meet him in the garden behind the church. But when we get there, we find Pygott dead, but the Bible is tuck into his pants."

Zigor paused, as if it were the end of his story.

✝

"But you didn't leave the body there," Marlowe prompted.

"No," Zigor admitted. "Since we are not able to corrupt you *or* kill you, we cause you trouble. We take the body in your room."

"But the landlady saw you."

"Yes. We give her money."

"And whose idea was it to hide the Bible in the room?" Marlowe asked.

"Oh." Zigor looked into Marlowe's eyes. "You know this?"

"Whose idea?"

"Frizer. We don't want to get caught with illegal book. I don't like it, but he says leave the Bible for a while, let things cool off. He also has another piece of paper in his dirty shirt—a letter from a friend, he says. That goes under the floor beside the Bible."

In conclusion, Marlowe thought, Zigor did not kill Pygott either. If Zigor was to be believed.

A fishing boat drew up to the dock near the place where the three men were standing. They stepped a bit farther into the shadows.

"I don't believe most of what you've just told me," Marlowe whispered, "because it sounds sane and plausible, and nothing about this entire affair has been half so coherent. Ergo, I must assume that you are applying spy tactics of some sort for a reason as yet undisclosed."

"You don't believe him?" Argi asked indignantly.

"I mean no personal offense," Marlowe answered politely. "I don't believe you either. I think that you and de Ferro killed Lopez, and eventually you will have to answer for that."

"Why don't you do something about it now?" Argi asked.

It was as much a threat as a question.

"Because I could be wrong," Marlowe admitted. "I was half convinced that the prisoner in Malta, the person Lopez and I were sent to rescue, did not exist."

"But he did."

"He did," Marlowe confirmed.

"Then," Argi began hesitantly, "what now?"

"Now I try to put my thoughts about Lopez out of my head for the moment. Why don't you tell me what in the name of hell you're doing in Cambridge *now,* because I sense it has nothing to do with my business here."

"Ah, you are correct." Argi looked away. "But I cannot tell you more. I am working, still working, for Captain de Ferro. And you know who is his master."

Marlowe was again seized by the icy notion that everyone in England worked for Walsingham.

"If I set that, too, aside for the moment," Marlowe insisted, "will you tell me what you meant about Lopez a moment ago, in the camp?"

"Dr. Lopez was not the man you thought he was," Argi explained. "His entire life was a secret, a lie."

"No," Marlowe began.

"Then believe this," Argi interrupted. "We were overtaken on the beach not long after you left us. The men who attacked us were not with Captain de Ferro, they were something I have never seen before: men in uniform with a cloth on the head."

Marlowe shook his head.

"If you're going to lie," he said calmly, "you have to do it with more conviction. You have to make me believe it. Have you ever been to London?"

"What?"

"In London," Marlowe went on, "there is an actor named Richard Tarlton, an original member of the Queen's Men, an extraordinary actor and clown. His talent for impromptu street poems on any subject is nothing short of miraculous. I *know* he's an actor and yet I believe him more than I believe you."

Argi shook his head, as if saddened by Marlowe's lack of belief.

"So," he said, shrugging, "what then shall we do?"

"Now?" Marlowe heaved a very heavy sigh. "I would like to ask for your help."

Argi tilted his head sideways and stared at Marlowe. His face betrayed the very firm conviction that Marlowe had lost his mind.

"Even though you think I killed your friend Lopez?" he asked.

"If you and Zigor are telling me the truth, you see," Marlowe reasoned, "you won't mind helping me discover who actually did kill Pygott—if it wasn't Zigor, I mean."

"It's a test?" Argi suggested.

Zigor nodded. "Makes sense. And it's not interfere with our—with the other work."

"Exactly," Marlowe agreed. "There is no larger political affiliation involved. I just want to find Pygott's murderer. And who better than you to help me?"

"Of course." Zigor nodded.

"Right, then." Marlowe clapped his hands together softly, once. "Let's begin by going to the garden where you say you found Pygott's body."

"Now?" Argi balked. "I can't see my own hand."

"Good point," Marlowe conceded. "Meet me there at dawn."

"Yes," Zigor said readily.

"And if you don't," Marlowe retorted softly, "I shall know what to do."

NINETEEN

It was nearing daylight in the churchyard. Marlowe had hidden himself in the chilly shadows of a doorway, waiting. He had rid himself of the itching beard, and wore a black cape with a cowl to cover his head and face. He still hadn't slept, and his nerves were jangled beyond all reason.

Just as he was about to concede that the other two were not coming, there they were, rapiers drawn, side by side, striding into the little garden.

They looked about, scowling. Argi said something in the Basque tongue, and Zigor laughed once.

Marlowe drew his dagger silently and prepared to throw it. Zigor was the more serious threat, he thought. Argi was a marksman, not so adept at swordplay.

Then, for no reason Marlowe could discern, Zigor fell to his knees, his face close to the ground.

"Hah!" he said softly.

His hand shot forward and grabbed something. He sprang to his feet and showed Argi what he'd found: a small bright red tie.

"What's that?" Marlowe announced loudly, stepping from the shadows ready to throw his knife.

Both men whirled to face him. When they saw who he was, Zigor smiled. It was an oddly friendly expression, Marlowe realized.

"It's a piece of cloth!" Argi said.

"Come see," Zigor added enthusiastically.

Curiosity overcame caution, and Marlowe stepped rather quickly,

✝ squinting at the small object that Zigor held between his thumb and first finger.

"Christ in Canaan," Marlowe whispered, "do you know what that is?"

"It's a piece of cloth!" Argi said again.

Marlowe took it and examined it carefully.

"I believe this ribbon is a tie from Pygott's codpiece," he said slowly.

"What?" Argi stared at it. "How do you know that?"

"We had a bit of a tussle, Pygott and I," Marlowe began.

"You fight!" Zigor suddenly realized. "I know this. He was on top of you, and you nearly cut off his barnacles! I saw. Ingram too."

Marlowe casually dropped the red tie into a small pocket in his right boot.

"It was a very garish codpiece," Marlowe went on. "It looked ridiculous and appeared to be half-empty."

The other two laughed.

"I'm certain that red tie was on his costume," Marlowe went on, "which means that he passed this way."

"At least," Argi agreed. "It could also mean—"

But Marlowe was already on his knees examining the grass. There he found a dull brass button, pressed almost flat into the ground, which he picked up and slipped into his boot before the other two saw it.

No sense in showing them everything, he reasoned to himself. The button might be as significant a clue as the codpiece tie—if he could discover whence it came.

"You say it's been several weeks since you found the body here?" he asked, staring at the ground.

"Yes," Zigor answered. "More."

"The same day you saw me fight with Pygott."

"Still—weeks ago."

"If I believe you, there is knowledge to be gleaned from this scene," Marlowe said, almost to himself. "For one thing, we have his tie that may be from Pygott's costume. But also look here: the grass is different in this patch than anywhere else around it."

Argi leaned over to examine the grass.

"I don't see it," he said after a moment.

"No," Zigor told him, "look. This grass is grow more."

"The difference is not readily discernable," Marlowe continued, "but you will see that many of these blades, just here, are growing differently."

"Maybe," Argi said, turning his face sideways. "But what would make them do it?"

"If they'd been fed by blood," Marlowe concluded.

"Yes, now you believe me!" Zigor snapped. "We find the body right here! Pygott's blood!"

Marlowe looked up at him.

"I'll agree that your story has a syllable of veracity," he allowed, "but this doesn't mean that you didn't kill him. You could have done it, and left him for someone else to find."

"No," Zigor insisted. "Why I would do it?"

"For the Bible."

"No." Zigor lowered his voice. "It's only Catholic Bible, Ingram says. Not important, just enough to get your father in trouble."

Marlowe realized then that Zigor had no idea what was in the Rheims-Douai Bible. And since the Bible had been on Pygott's body, Pygott had gone into the church to get it, after which someone had met him and killed him, but not for the Bible.

Still, Zigor and Argi were not to be believed.

Marlowe stood. "So let me see what you would have me believe. Pygott was visiting Coughton when Throckmorton gave him certain information. He delivered it here, to someone in the church. Then he came back to retrieve it, and when he did, someone was waiting here to kill him, but *not* for the information. For some other reason."

"Yes," Zigor said.

Marlowe nodded. "So let me ask you this question: why, if

169

Pygott delivered his information to someone in this church, why was it necessary for anyone—me *or* Pygott—to go in there and steal it back?"

Zigor nodded. "This I wonder myself. It is Frizer's idea, is all I know. And my job is to help him, so."

Frizer was a double agent. Pygott had delivered the information into the hands of Catholic conspirators. Frizer wanted the information back in order to give it to Walsingham. That much seemed possible.

And if Pygott had not been killed for the Bible, for the secret information, Marlowe was forced to return to the idea that any one of dozens of Pygott's classmates might have killed him. He was certainly a boy who wanted killing.

"Why are you two here, again?" Marlowe asked, mostly to check the consistency of their story.

"As I say, I am here to work for the Spanish." Zigor shrugged. "Or they kill me."

Argi folded his arms. "And I was sent here by Captain de Ferro."

"But you want me to think that you're really working for London." Marlowe's eyes darted to Zigor.

"Yes," Argi insisted.

"No." Marlowe lips thinned. "You and your cousin are not working at odds. One of you is lying. Or both."

"No one can tell me I lie." Zigor smiled. "How many men I have kill? Do you know?"

"I do not." Marlowe returned the smile. "But before you add my name to that list, let me tell you what I think. I think that you two are working for another cause altogether. Neither of you is concerned with the battle between England and Spain, Catholic and Protestant. I believe that you have another war on your hands."

Zigor and Argi exchanged glances.

"You reject the French King Henry of Navarre, and all Spanish authority. Or really, any outside rule of your homeland. You are Basque patriots. You believe that the land in the western Pyrenees belongs to you alone. I agree. Therefore we have no quarrel, as long as your efforts toward your cause do not hamper my endeavor to solve this murder."

Argi shook his head.

"You really are good at speeches," he said. "You *should* write a play."

"I'll consider it. Do we have an accord?"

Zigor took a tiny step toward Marlowe. Marlowe's hand instinctively flew to his dagger.

"No," Zigor said, glancing toward Marlowe's scabbard, "I only want to say: I am not truly work for Spain, you must know this."

Marlowe looked deeply into the man's eyes for the first time.

"I know that if I had an Inquisitor's hot poker close to my face," Marlowe answered, "I might agree to almost anything."

"Face?" Zigor laughed. "This I can do. But where they take this hot poker? I kill my mother to make it stop."

"Then do we have an agreement?" Marlowe pressed.

"You want us to help you?" Argi asked. "Help to find who murdered Pygott?"

Marlowe turned a kindly eye toward Argi. "Are you going to tell me any more about Lopez?"

"Other than what I have said?" He shook his head. "I cannot. But I will still offer to help you."

"Right, then." Marlowe sighed. "I'll be in touch if I need you."

He turned and headed away.

"Where are you going?" Argi called out.

Marlowe stopped, turned around, and lowered his voice. "I have to put on that damned beard again, and go back to college."

TWENTY

Several hours later Marlowe sat in Professor Bartholomew's class encased once more in his lumpy brown cassock and transformed by the itchy beard.

Bartholomew was wheezing on about Aristotle, dressed in the typical black academic robes. He was standing behind a tall table strewn with papers and books. There was a small inkwell built into the table, from which a short quill extended.

"I find that students these days," he said disdainfully, "often mistake Aristotle's first principle. When the master uses the word *plot* he does not mean to say *story*, but rather he refers to an arrangement of the moments of action, the way these moments are presented to an audience. He is discussing structure, you see. Structure."

The class was past its time, and, as usual, half the students were asleep. Everyone else shifted and sighed in an effort to make the professor understand that the class was over.

After several more sentences, the professor ground to a halt in the middle of a phrase. He was staring directly at Marlowe, as if he had just noticed the new presence in his class. He looked around then at his comatose audience and sighed.

"Very well," he grumbled. "Dismissed!"

Many a man jumped to his feet. Others forced themselves awake and stumbled out of the room. When Marlowe was alone with Bartholomew, he strode boldly toward the professor.

Before he could speak, he saw Bartholomew's eyes dart suddenly to the left, in the direction of a side door. It was suspiciously ajar. They had an audience. Bartholomew spoke in a deliberately theatrical manner because of it.

"So you have decided to apply yourself to this class, have you?" he demanded before Marlowe could speak.

"I—yes."

"You look familiar, but I cannot place the name."

"It's Greene, sir," Marlowe offered. "Robert Greene."

"We had a student by that name only a few years ago," Bartholomew said slowly.

"I am that man, sir," Marlowe answered formally.

"I thought you were in London," Bartholomew said, "writing plays."

"Yes," Marlowe said quickly, "but I have come to Cambridge on a matter of financial importance to me. You have a student in this class, I believe, by the name of Walter Pygott. He is the reason I visit your classroom today. I had hoped to see him here, but he was not in evidence. Could you tell me where he might be?"

"Yes, well," Bartholomew stammered in his usual manner. "You see, the fellow—why is it you wish to see him?"

"As I say," Marlowe continued, his eyes flashing toward the open door, "my motive is a simple one: he owes me a great deal of money. Upon several visits to London, he required of me large sums for gambling and whoring, sums which he has yet to repay and which I have come to collect."

"Ah." Bartholomew nodded. "That does sound like our Master Pygott. Alas, I fear your journey has been in vain and your debt must be forever unrequited: Walter Pygott is dead."

"Dead?" Marlowe grumbled.

"Murdered, it is said, by another student."

"Well. I must say I am not surprised. He was a foul boy."

"Just so," Bartholomew agreed.

"I suppose I shall have to pursue his father, Sir John Pygott."

"I suppose."

✝

"By the by," Marlowe drawled, "who killed him, do we know?"

"A man by the name of Marlowe," Bartholomew said. "One of our better students."

"Marlowe, yes," Marlowe answered, "I've heard the name. Remarkable poet, unbeatable swordsman."

"His poetry was lacking in dignity," Bartholomew said stiffly. "But I do believe there are few in England who might best him at swordplay."

"And where is Mr. Marlowe now?"

"Fled," Bartholomew answered. "On a Portuguese ship, some say."

"And it is certain that he is the murderer?"

"Certain?" Bartholomew said lightly. "Pygott's body was found in Marlowe's room. Stuffed inside the mattress."

"Stuffed inside the—surely not. Unless it was a monstrous huge bed. Pygott was not a small man."

"Still, I have told you the fact of the matter."

"But this is insane. This Marlowe, his reputation is not that of an idiot. He would never have done such a thing."

"I may be inclined to agree." Bartholomew began to pack up his papers. "I have another class."

"Yes."

Marlowe took one last look at the open door. The gap was wider, and there was a visible shadow of two figures.

"Are there other students who might have wanted to kill Pygott?" he asked Bartholomew. "Aside from Marlowe, I mean."

"Dozens," the old man answered instantly. "But why would that interest you?"

"If I can present the true murderer to Pygott's father," Marlowe said a little too loudly, "that could get me my money."

"You catch his son's killer," Bartholomew concluded, "and he might pay the son's debt."

"Yes."

"It's the right idea," Bartholomew agreed, eyes shifting once more to the open door, "but I cannot help you. And I am late for my next class. I am leaving now, through those doors there."

Without another word, the professor was off in the direction of the open door. There was an all-too-obvious scuffling of feet beyond the doorway, and the figures who had been listening disappeared seconds before Bartholomew pulled the door wide and shambled into the room beyond.

Marlowe folded his arms. Bartholomew was a riddle. Did he know more than he would say?

He seemed unwilling to help at all, at least with spies listening in the shadows. Marlowe turned his mind to the students most affected by Pygott's bullying.

He knew Richard Boyle had been especially troubled. Marlowe had gone to the King's School with him in Canterbury. Then there was Benjamin Carier, a shy, introspective man from Kent known to have Catholic leanings. They seemed a good place to start.

Hearing the noise of approaching students behind him, Marlowe realized that another class was about to begin. He hurried out of the room through the same door that the professor had used, partly hoping to catch a glimpse of the shadows that had hidden there. The room was, however, little more than a hallway, and it opened onto a narrow path between buildings.

Marlowe paused before leaving the small preparatory room, wondering who had hidden there, and why. But the more pressing issue, questioning his old school chum Boyle, and the Catholic sympathizer Carier, hastened him outside and onto the path.

There were no students about in the narrow passageway. Marlowe took a small gate between two other buildings and moved quickly into the larger common yard. The sun was out, and late students were hurrying to classes. Several flew by Marlowe before he was able to stop an older one, an upperclassman, dressed in burgundy red.

"Pardon," he said without ceremony, "but I must find my friend Richard Boyle. It is a matter of grave urgency. Do you know where he is, what class he's in now?"

"Boyle?" the man asked, affronted that he'd been delayed in his forward progress. "Never heard of him."

With that, the man broke away and hastened toward the nearest building.

"Boyle's sick," someone else called out.

Marlowe turned to see a small man, a boy, really, with his arms filled with books, too many to carry happily.

"Sick?" Marlowe asked.

The overwhelmed boy lowered his voice. "With drink. He's in his room."

The boy rushed away, dropping and retrieving several books as he went.

Boyle had enough money to live on campus, in one of the finer rooms, having descended from an ancient landed family. Marlowe had been to the rooms several times, but he'd been tremendously drunk. He had to concentrate to remember a window looking out toward St. Benet's. His back to the church's general direction, gauging which of several windows might be Boyle's, he took a guess and hurried into that building.

Up a narrow set of stairs, only one flight, he was presented with several doors.

"Boyle?" he called out softly.

No answer.

"Boyle!" he shouted.

"Christ!" came the answer. "What is it?"

Marlowe judged that the sound had come from behind the second door on his left. He stepped quickly, grabbed the handle, and thrust the door inward.

"You are not in class," he said plainly, before his eyes adjusted to the sight of Boyle's room.

The deranged disarray of the place was alarming. Marlowe feared, for a moment, that fiends had destroyed all of Boyle's belongings. And there lay Boyle himself, sprawled out as if someone had dumped a pile of dirty laundry on his bed.

The pile of laundry groaned, and tried to sit up.

"What *is* it?" the pained voice demanded.

"I say that you are not in class," Marlowe repeated. "You do not take your education seriously."

Instantly Boyle was up, dagger in hand, eyes focused, his stance firm on the floor. His hair was a wiry halo, his face smeared with grease, and his blue-and-white-striped tunic was made almost entirely of spilt food.

"Is this serious enough for you?" he hissed.

Marlowe merely shook his head. "Put that away."

Boyle blinked. He tilted his head, trying to get a better look at the face behind the beard.

"Do I know you?" he asked.

"Will you sit down?" Marlowe responded.

Boyle held his dagger steady, and scratched his backside with the other hand.

"No," he said slowly. "I do not believe that I will sit down. What's your business, then? Because it's not to hasten me to class. I'll get my paper whether or not I go to a single lecture. And let me tell you why."

"No need," Marlowe said, edging his words with boredom. "Your father's family has land in Herefordshire and your mother gave you the diamond ring that you never remove from your hand. I know that you can purchase your degree. But you won't, because you fear that a boyhood compatriot of yours, one Christopher Marlowe, might best you among the regions of knowledge. That is a thing you cannot abide. Ergo, you languish here, in this filth, because you must, and not because you prefer it."

Boyle hesitated, then lowered his dagger.

"There is only one person I know," he said, trying not to smile, "who uses ten words when two would do, and who thinks so highly of himself as to speak his own name in the third person: a whoreson bastard called Marlowe."

Marlowe nodded. "I see no reason to impugn my parents just because I've caught you drunk in the middle of the day."

"Drunk!" Boyle roared. "I'm not drunk. It's much worse than

that, I'm waking up from being drunk. I've a dead rat taste in my mouth, a bed full of piss, and a head so stony I can barely stand to stand."

"Then, as I was saying, why don't you sit down?" Marlowe said again.

"Right."

Boyle fell back on his bed. The bed nearly collapsed.

"Where have you been?" he managed to ask Marlowe, "and what are you doing in that ridiculous getup?"

"I have been abroad, finding a wider education than I ever could here in this place," Marlowe began, "and I'm disguised as you see me to avoid being arrested for a murder that you committed."

Eyes closed, dagger across his chest as if it were a flower on a corpse, Boyle managed to mumble, "Which murder is that?"

"Walter Pygott's," Marlowe answered loudly, "you know very well."

"Pygott?" Boyle opened his eyes. "Hang on a moment. You're the one who killed *him*."

"No, in fact, I am not."

Boyle struggled to sit up once more.

"And that is why," he said, shaking his head to clear his brain, "you visit me here?"

Marlowe stood very still.

"You think *I* killed Walter Pygott?" Boyle growled.

"Well," Marlowe confessed, "you're not my only choice. I think Carier got the worst beating of anyone on campus. I suspect him too, if that makes you feel any better."

"It was Carier, then," Boyle yawned. "Pygott was caught cheating on an examination. Carier saw it. He went to Professor Bartholomew on that account, but nothing was done about it. And after that, Pygott nearly killed Carier, as you know."

"So you didn't kill Pygott?"

Boyle sighed. "I wish I had done. I hated him. What a worthless lump of flesh he was, always bullying the younger boys, picking fights and then running to his father, or worse: to Bartholomew."

Marlowe's head snapped back.

"What? Bartholomew?"

"They were thick," Boyle said, then belched.

"How do you mean?"

"Pygott was in Bartholomew's rooms quite often," Boyle yawned. "Crying."

"This is—this is very puzzling." Marlowe stared down at the list.

Boyle sheathed his dagger, shook his head violently for a moment, and then stood.

"Give me a moment," he growled. "I've got to wash my face. Then we'll go to St. Benet's."

"What? To church?"

"Wait!" Boyle lumbered forward and nearly toppled his washbasin. He spent what seemed to Marlowe an eternity splashing his face with cold water and fixing his clothing.

"Now," Boyle said at last. "Shall we?"

"Why on earth are we going to St. Benet's?" Marlowe asked, irritated.

"Carier is a devout man," Boyle mumbled, heading for the door. "He prays every morning about this time. Likes to make a show of it. We'll look for him there first because I'm certain that's where he is."

Marlowe followed Boyle out into the hall and down the stairs. The building was fairly quiet and their boots clattered on the stone steps.

In no time at all they were out of the building and across the lawn, headed toward St. Benet's. The tower of the church loomed above the yard. The Saxon archway that connected that tower to the rest of the church seemed cold.

Marlowe had a strange sense of foreboding as they drew nearer the spot where Pygott had been killed. As they came to the front door of the chapel, a sense of impending danger provoked him to pull his dagger from its sheath and keep it discreetly by his side.

Boyle led the way. He pushed through the heavy wooden door. It creaked, the hinges complaining. The oddly darkened chapel was

✝ illuminated only by the light through the high, clear windows; no candles were lit. There was a single figure, on his knees, close to the stone slab altar near the spiral staircase, apparently praying.

"Carier?" Boyle whispered loudly.

The man did not move.

"It's Boyle. And Marlowe."

Instantly Marlowe wished he could retrieve his name from the air, silence it from being heard.

A second later the praying man stood. He was dressed in some sort of an azure uniform and thick black gloves, crowned with an Arabic headdress. He drew his rapier. In that same second, three men in similar dress charged down the spiral staircase.

Marlowe's rapier was out and his dagger in hand and held high as he looked about wildly for the best defensive position.

Boyle, too, had a blade in each hand, and he was turning, trying to keep his eyes on everything at once.

Two more men rushed into the chapel from the tower entrance. Marlowe and Boyle found themselves surrounded.

"Were these men lying in wait for us?" Marlowe whispered.

"How could they have known we were coming?" Boyle muttered, mostly to himself.

Marlowe suddenly realized the answer.

"They saw me talking to Bartholomew in his classroom," Marlowe muttered. "They were hiding in the side room. They followed me to your place, overheard what we said. I've been an idiot."

"Who are they?" Boyle asked.

"I believe they're agents of the Pope."

Boyle seemed to wake up at that suggestion.

"Ah," he said, and then he smiled. "Well. Only five."

"Yes," Marlowe said. "Shouldn't take us long to dispatch them."

"Agreed," Boyle boomed. "Listen, would you mind very much if we had breakfast after we've killed these men? I really need something to eat."

"I know just the place."

As they had been talking, they'd backed toward the corner opposite the spiral stairs. The uniformed men were positioning themselves, moving slowly, without speaking a word. Each had a rapier and a dagger.

As they began to close in, Marlowe saw that their eyes were dim, rimmed in red. These men were under the spell of hashish.

Marlowe's heart beat faster. The attackers would be unpredictable, fearless, and largely insensate. They would be much harder to fight than ordinary opponents.

"Their eyes," he whispered to Boyle.

"I see," Boyle responded nervously.

Without warning, Marlowe began to sing very loudly.

"Oh, western wind, when will thou blow that the small rain down can rain?"

Boyle seemed to understand immediately, and joined in.

"Christ that my love were in my arms, and I in my bed again!"

Boyle spread his arms wide, as if he were entertaining on the stage.

The odd gambit worked. The uniformed men, momentarily confused, had stopped advancing.

Marlowe used that moment to fly forward, his rapier leading the way. He jumped high, his cassock roiling around him, and thrust the point of his sword directly into the nearest man's midsection. The man blinked, trying to comprehend what had just happened, looked down, saw blood, and roared. Marlowe landed hard on the stone floor.

The assassin grabbed Marlowe's rapier with a gloved hand, pulled the point out from its target, and swiped at Marlowe with his dagger, still clutching Marlowe's sword.

At that same moment, another of the uniformed men appeared near Marlowe's right shoulder. He loomed ominously, rapier and dagger in hand.

Marlowe thrust his blade again. It slipped through the first man's grip and drove deeper into the man's stomach, this time nearly going through to the other side, out the man's back just below his rib cage.

The man grunted, but seemed otherwise unmoved as Marlowe withdrew his sword.

The second man, the one to Marlowe's right, attacked with a sudden ferocity. Marlowe barely had time to pivot and deflect the second man's dagger with his forearm. The dagger cut into the cloth of the cassock but did little other damage.

Marlowe leapt backward, sucked in a breath, and attempted to disarm the second man, thrusting and then swirling his own rapier. The second man parried and took a step forward. Marlowe twisted, stabbed the first man again. That man had not moved, and was bleeding profusely.

The second man took advantage of Marlowe's momentary distraction to thrust his rapier at Marlowe's chest. Fortune and ill-fitting clothing saved Marlow again: the second man's rapier pierced the garment but not the man.

Without thinking, Marlowe dove to the floor, hit on his side, and rolled like a log toward the first man, toppling him in the direction of the second. Before either of the assassins could recover, Marlowe was on his feet again. He stabbed the bleeding man a fourth time, and, at last, that man went down. The second man ignored his compatriot and cocked his arm, suddenly sending his knife hurtling toward Marlowe's face.

Marlowe fended off the point of the missile by crossing his sword and knife in front of his face. The flying dagger hit Marlowe's hand, nicked it, but did little other damage.

Instantly Marlowe spread his arms, dagger and rapier out, and snarled, smiling.

Just as he was about to leap again, a gun went off.

Glancing over his shoulder he saw that Boyle had shot one of the assassins in the face. Another lay close by, stabbed through the heart, his breast a fountain of blood.

Unfortunately the effort had taken its toll on Boyle. He was red-faced, winded, and nearly done in. And there was a third man headed his way.

Marlowe returned his attention to the man closest to him just as that man thrust his blade, with the force of his entire body, directly toward Marlowe's heart. Marlowe only had time to squirm sideways, but his attacker had so expected to make contact that he was thrown off balance. Marlowe saw that and used it. He kicked the man's shin as hard as he could, then brought the hilt of his rapier down onto the back of the man's neck.

The man went sprawling, belly down, onto the hard gray floor of the church.

Instantly pouncing, Marlowe planted his boot in the small of the downed man's back, knocking the wind out of him, and flew to Boyle's side.

Boyle was gasping for breath, trying to speak.

"It's all right," Marlowe began.

"My pistol," Boyle whispered. "It has a second barrel. If the ball has not fallen out . . ."

Marlowe saw the weapon on the floor, glanced toward the last standing assassin, and nodded.

With a single motion he feigned forward with his rapier in the direction of the assassin, but dipped the point of his blade low at the last possible minute, managing to snare the pistol by its trigger grip. Flipping it high, the gun soared into the air. The assassin glanced up at it. When he did, Marlowe threw his dagger. The dagger caught the man in his throat, and stayed there. The man gurgled a vague complaint, and then dropped to the floor just as Marlowe caught the pistol and whirled in the direction of the fallen man, the one whose back Marlowe had stepped on. That man was rallying, had gotten to his knees. Marlowe cocked the pistol, aimed, and fired. Alas, the flint did not ignite, and there was no telling if the ball was still in the barrel.

The assassin was on his feet in the next second, vacant-eyed and hulking.

Boyle sucked in a deep breath.

"Right," he said to Marlowe. "Shall we?"

As one they both exploded forward, rapiers ahead of them, and before the last assassin knew what was happening, Boyle and

Marlowe had both stabbed him in the heart. He fell backward, dead before his head cracked on the floor.

Boyle was doubled in half and dripping with sweat.

Marlowe leaned heavily on one foot.

"This *bleeding* cassock," he growled. "It's like fighting in swaddling clothes."

"I hate my pistol," Boyle managed to say, still unable to straighten up.

"Yes," Marlowe agreed. "So do I. Now. Breakfast, did you say?"

TWENTY-ONE

Marlowe and Boyle sat in the public room at the Pickerel, backs to the wall. Boyle looked sick. Marlowe was angry.

"Those men weren't sent by the Pope," Marlowe muttered, his eyes darting everywhere.

"Obviously," Boyle groaned. "The Pope doesn't hire hashish-mad Arabs to do his work."

The public room was quiet. A few men were dozing, dead drunk, at tables. Several other men were drinking quietly. Jen the barmaid offered ale, and Boyle argued with her for a full five minutes about breakfast. It was late for breakfast, Jen pointed out. Boyle insisted he would be dead without it. In the end, a handsome bribe won the day, and breakfast was on: boiled eggs, last night's beef, oat muddle, black bread and butter, and more ale.

That settled, Boyle closed his eyes and slumped in his chair, breathing heavily.

Marlowe seethed.

"I suspect Bartholomew," Marlowe whispered.

"Hm?" Boyle muttered.

In his mind's eye Marlowe was standing in front of the professor, in the classroom, knowing that several shadows were lurking in the room just beyond, listening. Bartholomew had known they were there.

"Suppose Professor Bartholomew is not the man he seems to be," Marlowe said, barely out loud.

"What man does he seem to be?" Boyle's eyes were still closed.

†

"He seems to be a doddering college professor, but let us suppose that he is, in fact, a spy."

"What?" Boyle said loudly, his eyes flying open and lighting up. "A spy?"

"Sh," Marlowe insisted harshly.

One of the unconscious men moved. Marlowe tried not to look directly at him, caught a glimpse out of the corner of his eye. The man had his head down on the table, feigning sleep, and Marlowe saw that he had a knife in his lap.

"I posit, at least," Marlowe said, whispering even softer, "that Bartholomew's a villain. There were men in his class antechamber, and they followed me to your rooms, overheard you say we were going to the church, and set about to attack us there."

Boyle barely lifted his head.

"That old man hired Arab assassins?" he managed to say. "Not likely."

"You don't understand," Marlowe began.

Then, out of the corner of his eye, Marlowe saw the man with the knife move again.

Boyle rested his head on the table once more. "I have a much simpler explanation. Someone has seen through this ridiculous disguise you're wearing, and reported you to the local authorities, and they sent men after you."

"Those men weren't from Cambridge!"

"Here comes my food!" Boyle sat up.

Jen, smiling, was on her way with enough food for five men. Boyle's bribe had been substantial.

As she wafted past the man with the knife, she bumped his table very slightly. The man did not move or speak.

Jen danced easily the rest of the way, loudly clattering the plates and bowls onto the table in front of Boyle.

As she did, she leaned close to Marlowe's ear.

"Did you notice the gent at the table what I bumped?" she whispered quickly.

Marlowe nodded slightly.

"Did you notice he's got a dagger in his lap," she went on, "and he's only just pretending to be asleep?"

"You are a remarkable girl, Jen," Marlowe said. "I think I would kiss you this moment, if I weren't afraid."

"Afraid?" She straightened up.

"I know how to fight a man's dagger," he whispered, eyes heavy-lidded, "but there would be no defense against the taste of your mouth."

"Oh." Jenny tried to steady herself, but the girl was unused to the poetry of seduction. For a heartbeat or two, she forgot how to breathe. Still, she did her best to seem unaffected. She looked down at the table, then back up to his eyes, and finally composed her flushed face.

"Well, at least let me get out of your way before your friend starts his breakfast revelry." She managed a wink. "And you go carving up that boy over there."

Marlowe's eyes did not watch her leave. He simply looked down at the food in front of him. But under the table, in that relative darkness, his right hand found the small knife he had tucked in his boot.

Boyle attacked his food with the same ferocity that he had killed the assassins in St. Benet's Church. Marlowe's eating was only slightly more sedate. He hadn't realized how famished he was until he'd tasted the first bite of egg.

With one eye on the mystery man, and the other on his plate, Marlowe continued to puzzle out what had happened so far that morning.

"Those men who attacked us were hired killers," he said softly to Boyle, his mouth full.

"Yes." Boyle nodded and went back to his plate. His cheeks were puffed out and his face was only inches from his bowl of porridge. "Bartholomew had nothing to do with it."

"I don't know that," Marlowe snapped. "In fact, I have some reason to believe that Bartholomew would betray me."

Boyle hesitated for an instant, glancing Marlowe's way.

"You mean," Boyle whispered slowly, "that he knows your true identity."

Marlowe nodded once.

"By the way," Boyle grunted, once again resuming his bacchanalia, "have you noticed the man over there with his hand on his knife?"

"As it happens, I have," Marlowe answered. "So have you, and so has Jenny, our barmaid. That poor man may be the worst actor in this scene. I suppose I'll have to go and tell him that."

"*Actor?* God in heaven." Boyle shook his head. "You really ought to get your head out of the clouds, Marlowe. Forget the theatre. Maybe go to sea."

Ignoring Boyle, Marlowe stood and announced, "Got to piss. Don't eat my breakfast while I'm gone."

"No promises," Boyle answered.

Marlowe noticed, just as he stepped away from the table, that Boyle's left hand disappeared, though he continued to eat with his right.

Marlowe, his eye on the alleyway door, nodded to Jen, who was behind the bar. As he did, he seemed accidentally to bump the table where the bad actor was pretending to sleep.

Once again, the man didn't move a muscle.

Marlowe, louder than necessary, leaned close to the man and said, "Pardon."

The man showed no sign of life.

Marlowe shook the man's shoulder.

"Jen!" he called out in mock alarm, "I'm afraid this man might be dead!"

"Let's have a look," she called back.

With her father's club in hand, Jenny rounded the bar and headed for the table where Marlowe stood.

As if finally realizing that his opossum ploy was not working, the man roused himself, pretending to wake up, and lifted his head.

Marlowe took a sudden step back, just in case the man jabbed with his blade from under the table, but a second later, shock took over. Marlowe recognized the man. He was the third man in the trio, with Frizer and Zigor, who had assaulted him on campus, and later attacked him on the road to London. He was the man who had run off.

That man locked eyes with Marlowe, but no such recognition filled his eyes. His eyes were taken almost entirely by fear.

Marlowe was momentarily at a loss.

"So," Jenny said, coming closer, bat at the ready. "He's not dead, then?"

"Dead?" the man squeaked. "No. Just a bit in my cups, I'm afraid."

The man's accent and demeanor were clear enough: he was from Wales, and he was terrified.

Marlowe nodded to Jenny. "He's all right."

Jenny hesitated, but turned, after a moment, and went back to the bar.

"If you'll put away your knife," Marlowe said softly, "I'll sit down and tell you what's happened to Frizer."

The man's eyes bulged. "You know him?"

"He told you to meet him here," Marlowe surmised, "if anything happened."

The man nodded. He had not moved to put away his blade.

"But you haven't been in here for a while," Marlowe went on, guessing, "because you hoped you were rid of Frizer, and of his friend."

"The Spaniard"—the man nodded—"yes. He's what you would call trouble."

"But you hid from them both—from everyone, really—after you attacked the coach on the way to London." Marlowe's voice was very soft.

The man's look of fear deepened to a state of terror.

"How would you know about that?" he hissed.

"But now something's happened," Marlowe answered. "Now you need their help."

The man stared. "I just need to speak with Frizer. This was our arranged meeting place, see?"

"What's happened?"

The man looked around and only then realized that Boyle was staring at him. He leaned forward, clearly about to do something rash.

"I know you haven't yet sheathed that knife in your hand," Marlowe said calmly. "If you move another inch, I'll stick my rapier into your heart seven or eight times, and your troubles will be over."

"You've killed Frizer," the man moaned. "You're in league with that Spanish devil!"

"No. Frizer is in London. The other one, Zigor, is not Spanish. And I'm not in league with anyone, not the way you mean it, anyway."

"That's a lie. All of it."

"No," Marlowe repeated. "My only concern for the moment is finding a murderer."

The man looked up, finally, into Marlowe's eyes.

"Murderer?" he asked.

"To that end," Marlowe went on, "would your shirt or trousers happen to be missing a button?"

"What?" The man leaned back. "A button?"

Marlowe leaned closer. In the dim light of the public room it was difficult to see the buttons on the man's shirt, but slightly closer examination revealed a remarkable lack of stain, no sign of mending, and the presence of very clean wooden buttons, not brass.

"This is a new shirt," Marlowe said, straightening up.

"How would you know that?"

"How long have you had it?"

"A week. Why do you want to know about my shirt?"

"What happened to your old one?" Marlowe pressed.

"Here, now," the man grumbled, "what's all this about my shirt? Christ."

Without warning, Boyle appeared beside Marlowe.

"Hello," he said menacingly. "Put away your knife, like a nice boy, or I'll be forced to cut open your throat. Right?"

"Help!" the man cried. "Murder!"

No one moved.

The noise of the room diminished a bit, then here and there a furtive glance was the only evidence that the man's cries had been heard at all.

"We're going upstairs to my room," Marlowe said genially, loud enough for most people in the room to hear, "and see if we can't sober you up. Your wife is very angry with you. If you don't come home today, *that's* when you'll be shouting 'murder.'"

One man in the room chuckled; the rest seemed to lose interest in the proceedings altogether, and returned to their drink, or sleep.

"No," the man protested weakly.

Then he dropped his knife. It thudded onto the dirt and straw floor. Marlowe and Boyle each took one of the man's arms, weaving through tables toward the stairs. In no time they were up the stairs and into Marlowe's room.

By the time the door was closed behind them, the man seemed to have resolved himself to his fate.

They sat him on the bed frame. Marlowe pulled up a chair to sit in front of him, staring into his eyes.

"I have a number of questions to ask you," Marlowe began, "so I want you to pay attention. Believe me when I say that we have no intention to kill you."

The man looked at Boyle, then back at Marlowe. He sat back on the bed, nodding slowly.

"First things first," Marlowe continued, "tell me your name."

"Tom."

"Right, Tom, where have you been since you tried to kill those men on the coach to London?"

"After it went wrong," Tom answered, "I went back to my little farm, I did. That's enough of the rough business, I says. Needed the money, but not like that. Had my fill of that Ingram Frizer. He's a drunkard and a liar."

"Yes," Marlowe encouraged, "so why are you here today looking for him?"

"Need his help," Tom muttered, obviously disgusted with himself.

"What kind of help?"

"It's those men!" Tom snapped. "Thinks that a uniform and a dead eye gives them the right to toss up my farm, frighten the wife, kill my chickens—all because they're looking for the same men you're talking about: the doctor and his friend. The ones in the London coach."

Marlowe glanced toward Boyle.

"What were their uniforms like?" he asked.

"They was blue, deep blue," Tom said, "with great black gloves and odd headgear."

"When did you see them?"

"Yesterday, late," he answered.

"And when you purchased this new shirt?" Marlowe asked.

"It wasn't a *purchase*," the man insisted. "I come home to the farm with blood and grime on my work shirt, and the wife, she give me this one what she's made for the finer occasions. It itches like the devil. I'm not to soil it. And every time I sit down, the collar chokes me. Can't wait to get back home and take it off."

"You wore it to come to town."

"Aye."

"And does your other shirt, the soiled one, does it happen to have brass buttons?" Marlowe asked.

"Brass buttons?" he asked. "Why would my clothes have brass buttons? You think I'm a bleeding landlord? I work my ass to the bone!"

"What possible difference do his buttons make?" Boyle began.

"Right," Marlowe interrupted. "Tom, then, tell me plainly: why did you murder Walter Pygott?"

Tom's look of panic returned.

"Murder?"

"The man you killed outside of St. Benet's church, near the roses, several weeks ago."

Tom stood up quickly.

"God's my witness," he howled, "I ain't kill a man in my life! Never!"

"Marlowe," Boyle tried again.

Ignoring Boyle, Marlowe pressed.

"You say you went back to your farm after you fled the encounter with the London coach," he said to Tom.

"I did!"

Marlowe grabbed a handful of Tom's shirt and started for the door.

"Let's go verify that with your lady wife," Marlowe growled.

"Good!" Tom yelped. "Good! You ask her if I ain't been home these past weeks. I'd got to tend the spring crops!"

"What are you growing?" Marlowe demanded.

"Barley, vetches, oats, peas, and beans," Tom rattled. "God's truth!"

"Marlowe, damn it!" Boyle shouted. "Let this man go! He's a pawn. We're looking for knights."

"Or a bishop," Marlowe shot back. "But you're right, of course."

Marlowe released his grip on Tom, who stumbled backward.

"What the hell's the matter with you?" Boyle asked Marlowe under his breath.

"What's the matter with me?" Marlowe responded incredulously. "I'm accused of a murder I didn't commit, I'm mourning the death of a friend, I'm embroiled in a plot of universal proportions, and I'm in love with a woman who can't be in love with me. And this *bleeding* beard is killing me!"

Boyle nodded, and allowed Marlowe's brief but potent tirade to evaporate in silence.

Then: "You're still in love with Penelope?"

"What?" Marlowe blinked. "No. It's—it's someone else now. But, still."

"Yes," Boyle agreed, "but still, that's quite a lot to have on your mind, everything you just said."

Marlowe exhaled and felt the weight of what he'd said. "Yes. It is."

"But Tom, here, is probably not to blame."

Marlowe glanced at Tom's terrified face.

"No," Marlowe admitted. "Probably not."

"And," Boyle went on, "he might have useful information for us."

Tom took another step backward. "I don't."

"You do, in fact," Marlowe said. "About these men who came to your farm, killed your chickens."

"Those bastards," Tom swore.

"They tried to kill us this morning," Boyle said simply.

"But we killed them instead," Marlowe added.

Boyle turned to Marlowe. "You realize that the bodies have probably been found by now. There's liable to be quite an imbroglio brewing at the church, and on campus."

"I hadn't even thought of that," Marlowe admitted.

"You killed all of those men?" Tom asked, awestruck. "Just the two of you?"

"We killed five," Boyle said slowly. "How many were there at your place?"

"At least a dozen," Tom answered.

"There are more?" Boyle shouted.

"You may as well know," Marlowe told Boyle, "that Tom and his compatriots, including one Ingram Frizer, attacked a London coach in which I was traveling a few weeks ago."

Boyle nodded curtly. "I gathered."

Tom's eyes opened wide. "That was you?"

Marlowe turned to Boyle. "There. This disguise works!"

"It works for people who don't know you," Boyle admitted.

"My point is that when Tom and Frizer attacked us, I told Lopez that I couldn't believe they were the best the Pope could muster. Lopez warned me that they were only the *first*. The men who attacked us in the church were not only trained assassins, they may be a contingent of troops poised to invade our country."

"Invade our country?" Boyle asked.

Marlowe turned to Tom.

"Did they speak at all when they were at your farm?" he asked.

Tom shook his head. "They was gabbling some incoherent tongue."

"Were they Arabs?" Marlowe asked.

"Couldn't say," Tom confessed. "Never seen an Arab. But they was wild and strange."

"What better way for the Pope to keep his hands clean," Marlowe mused, "than to hire infidels as murderers? Assassins have no souls to worry about."

"I have no idea what you're on about," Tom began, "but them men was lunatics, raging. The wife and me, we hid inside. But then one of them pulls me out and starts talking in English."

"They questioned you about me and the doctor."

"Yes."

"And you told them?"

"What could I tell them? I says you was gone. You killed one, the rest wounded, I barely escaped with my life, and only wanted to be left alone."

"You told them that the coach went on to London."

"Oh." Tom looked down. "Well, yes. I did that."

"What in the hell is going on, Marlowe?" Boyle finally demanded. "There's more to this than the murder of that idiot Pygott or some girl you fancy."

"Well." Marlowe smiled.

And he began to wonder at once if lying, or at least avoiding the truth, was beginning to come a little too easily.

"Then do you mind telling me," Boyle huffed.

"I think we should go back to the church," Marlowe interrupted, almost to himself.

"Back to the church?" Boyle exploded.

"No one saw us there earlier," Marlowe said lightly. "We'd only be students, come to pray. We need to see what's going on there."

"When do I get to see Frizer?" Tom interrupted.

"You don't," Marlowe snapped. "You're coming with us. How good a farmer are you?"

"Best in all of Cambs," Tom said firmly, "if you want to know the truth."

"Then why did you throw in with Frizer?" Boyle muttered.

"Don't know much about farming, do you?" Tom answered Boyle. "It's been cold hard winters for as long as I can remember. And when the snow and ice is there, it's wind and water for sup. I told him, I told Frizer, I was out come spring. And now it's spring, so there's an end to it."

"All right." Marlowe grinned at Tom. "Could you tell if a certain patch of grass had benefited from a feeding of blood?"

Tom tilted his head. "I suppose I could. Fed the barley and oats with the blood of them dead chickens just before I come into town."

"Right, then," said Marlowe, heading for the door, "you're going to church before we take you back to your farm."

TWENTY-TWO

Outside the churchyard was quiet. Inside St. Benet's there was a riot. Dead bodies had been found. Marlowe and his two companions stole past the door, around the building to the roses, and found the strange patch of grass.

Tom nodded, knelt; pressed his nose against the earth. Sniffing like a hunting dog, he nodded again. Then he jammed an index finger into the dirt and scratched around. After a moment he examined his finger closely and snorted.

"There's been blood here all right," he confirmed. "You can smell it."

"Even though it may have been spilled here almost a month ago?" Marlowe asked skeptically.

"It's been frost most of these mornings," Tom answered. "That's kept it preserved. Then there's the flea cocoons. Fleas need blood, you see. Some clever flea family's set up stock here. It was a good bit of blood at one time."

So Pygott may well have been killed on that spot. The brass button in Marlowe's boot pocket pressed into his shin, as if insisting on finding its owner.

"Inside," Marlowe said softly to Boyle. "Tom, will you wait here?"

Tom nodded and searched for a shadowy hiding place.

Marlowe and Boyle plunged through the side door of the chapel, as if oblivious to the noise within.

As soon as they were in, all eyes looked their way.

Three clergy, two local constables, and several college ground-keepers filled the front part of the church. Of course, there were also five dead bodies.

One of the clergymen rushed toward them, eyes wide.

"No, no, no, you may not come in," he gasped. "What do you want here?"

"We've come to pray," Boyle said innocently, glancing momentarily at Marlowe. "We're students."

"What's happened here?" Marlowe asked in mock shock, gaping at the bodies.

"Someone has defiled our church once more!" the panicked clergyman cried.

"Are those men dead?" Boyle asked.

"Yes!" the man howled.

"Did you say 'once more'?" Marlowe asked. "This has happened here before?"

The man lowered his voice.

"Only several weeks ago. A student was found outside, on the ground."

"My God, what student?" Marlowe asked quickly.

"I don't know," the man answered impatiently. "Father Edmund told me that he saw the body, but it was removed before he could call the authorities. And now this!"

"How did this happen?" Boyle asked carefully.

"No one knows." The man lowered his voice considerably. "But these men, I think, are not Christians. They may well have been sent by the devil."

"They're not Christians?" Marlowe asked, trying to get a better look at any one of the dead bodies.

"Get those boys out of here!" another man shouted.

Marlowe turned toward the sound of the voice. It had come from the rector, by his costume, an older man with no hair and a face as cragged as the surface of a mountain.

Marlowe nodded and looked to Boyle, who was crossing himself and already heading for the side door.

Back outside, Marlowe whispered Tom's name, and Tom appeared from around the corner of the building. After a moment's discussion it was decided that Boyle would escort Tom back to his farm, verify his whereabouts with the wife. Marlowe had already moved on to other thoughts. Boyle agreed to meet at the Pickerel that evening.

As soon as they were gone, Marlowe strode to the hiding spot and stood as he had before. From that place he could scarcely be seen, but could see all the yard close to the door.

He dropped to his knees and searched the grass around him, hoping to find another slip of cloth, a second button—anything to help further his investigation. After nearly a half hour's examination, he found, stuck hard into the stones of the wall close to where he'd stood, three threads. They were nearly an inch long, and could have been from anything or anyone. They were wedged into a crack near a particular stone that stuck out. A shorter man might lean an elbow there and snag his sleeve, leaving a bit of thread.

Head swimming, Marlowe stepped away. A bit of red cloth, a button, and three colorless threads would never tell him who the murderer was. He suddenly felt foolish and a bit lost.

Of course he would speak with Father Edmund to confirm once and for all that Pygott had been killed on that spot where the grass grew well. Giddily Marlowe acknowledged that feeding the lawn might have been Pygott's single redeeming act.

The noise inside the church increased suddenly, and Marlowe judged it best to leave. Back to Bartholomew's office; confront the old man about the killers hiding in his anteroom.

Alas, once in the building and up the stairs to the rooms, he found that the professor had not yet arrived.

Glancing about, Marlowe walked to the old man's desk. He stared down at the mad array of papers, books, letters, odd objects, and crumbs. For a moment nothing caught his attention and he considered seeking out the professor in his lecture hall once more.

Then, out of the corner of his eye, he spotted a small golden cylinder beneath several books.

"Where have I seen you before?" he asked it out loud. "Or your cousin?"

He stared at the container. It was exactly like the one Captain de Ferro had possessed onboard his ship, the one containing a message from Walsingham.

Stifling an impulse to seize the cylinder, Marlowe instead moved to an ornately carved wooden chair close to the tall window. Stacks of books were littered around it. If he sat there he had a view of the door but his presence would be, momentarily, hidden by the dazzle of sunlight through the window. In that chair he might have a moment to think.

Too many details were unexamined. First he thought to trace the path and the meaning of the Rheims-Douai Bible. It had certainly been written by conspirators at Coughton and then given to Pygott to deliver to someone at St. Benet's. Why had it been delivered there, and not taken directly to the Catholic collaborators in London? Then, why had Frizer and his band wanted to retrieve it from the relative safety of the church? There were two significant possibilities. Someone had told Frizer to retrieve it and deliver it to Spanish agents in London, for some reason. Or Frizer, as a double agent, thought to intercept the message in the Bible and deliver it directly to Walsingham. Either way, it seemed very strange that Frizer and his lot would stumble about asking students to steal things from the church. And it was even stranger that Pygott should be killed at the exact moment he was coming out of the church with the Bible, only to be left dead in the yard with the Bible still on his person.

Marlowe began to slowly untangle the knot.

Throckmorton was in league with Catholic forces in Spain. They hoped to replace the true Queen with her Scots cousin Mary. That would restore the papist church in England. Throckmorton and John Pygott and other cohorts had a plan: assassinate the Queen, foment rebellion from within, and attack England from without. Setting all else aside for the moment, a part of that plot had been outlined in a communication hidden in the Rheims-Douai Bible. That missive had been given to Pygott, an oblivious dupe, to deliver to someone at St. Benet's in Cambridge before being taken to London. To whom? And why?

Was it possible that the Bible's message could be, in fact, a code within a code? Marlowe realized that he had found the message quite easily, as Frances had said. Others would be able to accomplish that as well. Perhaps the message had been delivered to a conspirator at St. Benet's for further coding. Who would that conspirator be? Another possibility was that the message had never been intended for London at all, that there was someone in Cambridge who would receive the information. For what purpose? A third supposition: the message was a trick, as he'd thought when he'd first translated it.

Marlowe's brain continued to roil; he hit on the most devious possibility of all: Pygott had been sent to retrieve the Bible and was killed by the same people in a deliberate attempt to have the Bible discovered, the message decoded, and the plot to kill the Queen seemingly discovered. Which would mean that the plot as outlined in the message was a decoy, a feint within a feint.

But what possible advantage could there be in making it appear as if Marlowe had murdered Pygott? Was that a part of the plan, an improvisation once Pygott was dead, a concerted effort to eliminate Marlowe from the picture entirely?

Marlowe twisted in his chair. It was too much, too confused. No mind could create such a vast and devious map of deception.

He bit his lower lip, and started over.

"What if this were my play?" he said aloud. "Why would I have written the scenes this way?"

In order to have a satisfying conclusion, he posited, a play must have tension and in order to create that tension, a certain amount of misdirection must be employed. That way the ending was a surprise, and the release of the tension was satisfying. How many of these events were misdirection, and how many were genuine intentions?

What if he were writing a play called *The Murder of Pygott and the Assassination of a Queen*? How would it go? And wouldn't there have to be a better title for it than that?

In any case, it would begin with a young student, lately come to college in Cambridge. He would be taken away by an old friend. He would travel over the seas. He would rescue a wonderful woman. He would be accused of a murder he did not commit. He would be forced to solve that murder.

Suddenly Marlowe's head snapped back.

He thought of how quickly Frances had recovered from her time in the Maltese prison, and torture at the hands of an Inquisitor. Also her subsequent behavior belied the proposition that she would ever need anyone's help, or need rescue of any sort. Perhaps that was a part of the misdirection.

If I were Kyd, Marlowe thought, I would compose the first act as a test of our young hero's mettle. Both Lopez and Frances had hinted that they were observing me during the course of the rescue from Malta. Had all of that been a ruse?

No. Frances had truly been taken by the Spanish and held in the Maltese prison. But Lopez could have gone by himself, could have gone to his cohorts on that island more easily without Marlowe. Marlowe had been taken along as an unknowing apprentice.

Marlowe supposed for a moment that he might be a pawn in a much larger and more confusing pageant. He was being tested for service to the Queen at the same time as he was being diverted from that service by opposite forces—Spanish and Catholic. If that were the case, then Lopez had been murdered to stop Marlowe from being completely initiated into Walsingham's legions, and Pygott's corpse had been laid at his feet to eliminate him from the equation entirely.

Before he could go any further with his thoughts, Marlowe heard a rustling sound close to him in the room.

Twisting in his chair, he jumped up and pulled his rapier, only to come face-to-face with a very startled Professor Bartholomew.

"Christ in heaven!" Bartholomew swore, dropping several of the books he'd had cradled in his arms.

"Ah, Professor," Marlowe said calmly. "I've been waiting for you."

He put away his sword and stood silently.

Bartholomew stared back for a moment, and then grunted.

"Help me pick up these books, then," he said, bending over with some effort.

Marlowe moved quickly, picked up most of the books, and helped the old man to his desk.

Bartholomew sat. Marlowe stood.

"First," Marlowe began before the professor could completely compose himself, "tell me who was hiding in the anteroom of your lecture hall. They were Catholic agents?"

"What?" Bartholomew rocked forward.

Marlowe glanced down at the professor's desk.

"And that cylinder there," he said, "the golden one—I've seen its like before. Explain it."

Bartholomew hesitated, not breathing, and then sat back.

"It's from Walsingham. Frances and I both told you I was acquainted with her father."

"But you did not tell me your part in all of this," Marlowe said. "It's clear to me now that you are his assign."

"Because of this cylinder?" Bartholomew did his best to voice his incredulity. "If you were in my class I would give you low marks for such a leap of cognition."

"Instinct is a great matter with me," Marlowe responded. "When I see such an obvious clue as that golden container, I fear I know all too well what it means."

Bartholomew glanced toward the container once more.

"Well," he sighed, "worldly men have such miserable, mad, mistaking eyes. I leave such simple interpretations to youth."

"That is not an answer," Marlowe told the old man, smiling.

"No. It is not."

After a moment of silence, Marlowe resumed the conversation, as it was apparent that Bartholomew would not.

"What about the men who tried to kill me in St. Benet's just now?"

The old man's face changed instantly. For the first time in Marlowe's memory, the demeanor was one of utter confusion.

†

"What are you saying?" Bartholomew stammered. "What men in St. Benet's?"

The professor had no idea what Marlowe was talking about.

So Marlowe took a few moments to relate the events at the church, omitting the more recent encounter with Tom.

"Remarkable," Bartholomew responded when Marlowe was finished. "You and Boyle stood against five? And five of that sort? Genuinely laudable."

"Thank you," Marlowe snapped dismissively, "but if you didn't have anything to do with them, who did? The men who were spying on us from the anteroom?"

"Let me address that first," Bartholomew said uncomfortably. "That was President Cole. He's taken to watching my lectures and jotting down notes. He is a Puritan, and they mean nothing but harm to our nation. That is why I spoke to you as I did. Mark my word, these men will one day attempt to overtake our government, our entire way of life. And more specifically, Cole is likely to be the ruination of this institution!"

Marlowe exhaled, and felt the ache of disappointment. What he had taken to be some significant part in a vast plot was, in fact, nothing more than academic infighting. Cole hated Bartholomew. Bartholomew hated Cole. That was as far as it went.

"I see," he said to Bartholomew. "Then neither you *nor* Cole set those men upon us in the chapel."

"You went from my classroom directly to Boyle's rooms?" Bartholomew asked. "And thence to St. Benet's?"

"Yes."

"Why?" Bartholomew asked.

"To see another student, Carier," Marlowe answered. "Boyle thought he would be there because he prays every morning."

"Carier," Bartholomew said to himself. "Yes, he hated Pygott. But if you went directly from Boyle's rooms to the church . . . not much time for assassins to hide there."

"I've been trying to puzzle it out myself," Marlowe admitted.

The old man nodded for a moment, then opened his eyes.

"Unless, of course," he said, "those men were not intended for you."

Marlowe threw his head back. "Christ!" he whispered.

"You and Boyle stumbled onto someone else's execution!"

TWENTY-THREE

Once Bartholomew made his pronouncement, it seemed ridiculously obvious.

"Those men didn't follow us to the church." Marlowe leaned against the professor's desk before he thought better of it. "They were already there—for someone else."

"The question is," Bartholomew went on, "for whom?"

"Carier?" Marlowe wondered. "Could they have had the same information that Boyle did, that he prayed there every morning at that time?"

"But why Carier?" Bartholomew asked, his brow furrowed.

Marlowe stared at the old man.

"Ah," Bartholomew said suddenly. "You think that because of his Catholic leanings, Carier might be a part of Throckmorton's plot, along with John Pygott."

"So you know about the plot."

The professor nodded, but would not say more.

"It's possible that Carier was Walter Pygott's contact, but something went wrong, and Carier killed Pygott. Before Carier could explain what had happened, someone, John Pygott for example, hired thugs to kill Carier."

"We may have underestimated Pygott's father," Bartholomew said. "He is wealthy, ignorant, and vindictive, a trio of the worst qualities in our lower nobility. But you must know that he has spared no expense in trying to capture his son's murderer and he thinks that murderer is you. It would be in keeping with his mindless rage that he might hire assassins to kill you."

"Kill me?" Marlowe shook his head. "John Pygott thought the murderer would return to the place where his son Walter was killed?"

Bartholomew leaned back. "Certain murderers revisit the sight of their evil to see if the body has been discovered, or to make certain no evidence of their crime was left behind."

"But it's been a month or more since the boy was killed!"

Bartholomew nodded. "True."

Suddenly Marlowe stiffened.

"Unless," he mumbled.

"What's that?" the old man asked.

Marlowe saw Nell the landlady in his mind, gossiping at the Pickerel about the odd new lodger in the murder room.

"It may be that word has gone around town: the killer's returned to Cambridge," Marlowe began slowly.

"I saw through your disguise immediately," the professor agreed. "Others might have."

"And there are a number of other people who know for certain that Marlowe is here. Any one of them might have betrayed me."

Bartholomew smiled. "Stop saying the name *Marlowe*, that's my advice. Although I might also avoid the name of *Greene*. He is in London. Most people of his acquaintance would realize that."

"This all adds up to folly. I was mad to come back to Cambridge."

"Truly," the old man confirmed, "but who else would solve Pygott's murder and prove your innocence?"

"No one."

"Has your time here merited anything of use?"

Marlowe smiled, deciding not to tell Bartholomew everything.

"For one thing," he answered carefully, "I know that Basque rebels are gathering in England."

"And that relates to the murder?" the old man asked.

"Not as far as I can tell," Marlowe admitted, "but it helps to eliminate several suspects. Including, incidentally, Ingram Frizer."

"You mentioned his name in this office when Frances was here," he answered. "You said he was the murderer."

"He's not."

"Ah." Bartholomew's brow furrowed. "Frances has told you something that made you to reconsider."

"Yes."

"Now you suspect Carier," the professor mused.

"Has he gone, do you know? He wasn't in the church."

"He wasn't in class either, which is unusual." Bartholomew pursed his lips. "He may have gone to Kent. That's where he was born. His father is Anthony Carier, a minister of the Church of England, though now a Puritan. Benjamin Carier came to us in February of last year. About your age, I believe."

"The father is Anglican and a Puritan, but the son's sympathies are Catholic?"

"Which is perhaps why he's gone home. He may have been summoned by an unhappy father."

Marlowe's mind was racing. Here was the conceivable scene unfolding in his imagination: Carier was the agent in Cambridge to whom the Rheims-Douai Bible was to be delivered. Pygott arrived with it, stowed it at St. Benet's for safekeeping, and it was Carier, not Frizer, who had actually encouraged Pygott to retrieve it. Then Carier killed Pygott to ensure that Pygott would not betray the plan—which he might readily have done, owing to the pea which God had given Pygott instead of a brain. But something happened. Perhaps Father Edmund stumbled on the murder scene at an inopportune moment, and Carier had been forced to flee.

But if Carier was the agent, why would he have left without taking the Bible? Was it that he had, indeed, been seen by Father Edmund, run away, and, somehow gotten a message to his coconspirators, Frizer or Zigor—told them to clean up the mess, fetch the Bible, and frame Marlowe?

The reason for such chicanery was unclear, but the scenario seemed at least minimally plausible. There was no trusting Frizer, or Zigor. They were both complicated puzzles.

If Edmund had seen the murder, why had he not come forth?

Possibly Edmund had not seen the actual deed. Carier had heard him coming, and hidden. The priest had seen the dead body and sounded an alarm. Others had come running. That's what forced Carier to abandon his task.

He contacted Frizer and Zigor immediately. They came to the churchyard and stole the body away.

But if all that were true, why didn't Edmund come forward?

Marlowe stood.

"There may be a man at St. Benet's, a priest, who witnessed the murder," he said. "I have to question that man."

"Which one?" Bartholomew asked. "I know them all."

"Father Edmund."

Bartholomew's lip curled.

"You do not care for him," Marlowe observed.

"He is not a priest by any definition I would use," the old man grumbled.

"Why do you say that?"

"Fornication!" Bartholomew blasted back. "Half the serving girls in Cambridge know him."

Marlowe tried to hide a grin. "Then half the churchmen in Christendom are not priests."

"Pah!" Bartholomew exploded. "Revolting."

"Still, I must speak with him."

"Better to disguise yourself as a maid," Bartholomew growled. "You'd have his attention then."

"I think not," Marlowe answered lightly, "at least not today."

The old man lowered his voice. "You must not stay in Cambridge. Pygott's father has scattered money all about the town. He has eyes and ears everywhere."

Marlowe cocked his head. "I thought the old man didn't care for his son."

"He did not," Bartholomew said. "He has other reasons for wanting you dead. I assume they have to do with his part in the Throckmorton plot."

✝ "I have to question this priest," Marlowe answered the professor softly, "but after that, perhaps you're right. It's time for me to leave Cambridge."

"Where will you go?" Bartholomew asked.

"No idea," Marlowe answered.

But that was a lie. He was bound the next morning for Coughton Court.

"Will you tell me what's in that missive from Walsingham?" Marlowe asked, glancing toward the golden cylinder.

Bartholomew smiled.

"That's a good trick," the professor said, "asking your question in that manner. I never said that object was from Sir Francis."

"Is it?"

"What will you ask Father Edmund?" Bartholomew asked.

"I see." Marlowe nodded, offering Bartholomew a knowing glance.

Bartholomew sat back, slumped a little in his chair.

"I have no idea what you imagine that you *see,* young man," he said, "but you must always accept the possibility that half of what you *think* is wrong."

"And with that," Marlowe said, turning away, "I take myself to church."

Once outside, Marlowe cleared his mind. There were so many unanswered questions that a man might be driven mad. Best to ignore the larger picture, perhaps, in favor of the more specific issues at hand.

First, speak with Father Edmund. Second, find out more about Carier. Third, get out of Cambridge for a while. Coughton Court was only a two-day ride.

He walked deliberately across the lawn toward the tower of St. Benet's. No students were about, and the yard was eerily quiet. A single bell was tolling, an invitation to pray for the dead.

As he came into the garden Marlowe could see the bodies piled onto a wooden death cart. They had been taken out through the side door, past the roses.

Marlowe stood at a distance for a moment, watching the last of the corpses heaped unceremoniously onto the cart. When the cart pulled away, he moved quickly. The rector was nowhere to be seen, but two priests stood close to the doorway, talking softly.

They looked up when Marlowe approached.

"I must speak with Father Edmund," he said quickly, "about a matter of grave urgency. I know who murdered those men."

They looked at each other, and then one went inside without another word. When he was gone, the remaining priest spoke.

"I am Father Edmund," he said. "What do you know about this horrid business?"

Marlowe took in a quick breath and stepped up to the priest's side.

"I know who killed those men," he repeated.

Edmund looked into Marlowe's eyes.

"And I also know about you," Marlowe continued.

Edmund's eyes widened. "Are you one of them?"

Not knowing what that meant, Marlowe decided on a bold course.

"You hid a certain Bible from Coughton Court in your room," Marlowe said sternly. "On your desk."

Marlowe wanted to see the priest's reaction.

"Pygott stole it back," Edmund railed, "before I could complete my work!"

"Your work." Marlowe spoke carefully, hoping to give the impression that he knew more than he actually did. "You were to revise the code."

"Upon my life, I do not have it!" Edmund was nearly hysterical. "I did not want to give it to him; he took it away!"

"No," Marlowe lied, "it was not on his body when he was discovered in that room at the Pickerel Inn."

"But he wasn't killed there," Edmund insisted, his eyes wild, "he was killed right here where we stand!"

"How is that possible?" Marlowe continued in his best imitation of an Inquisitor.

"I saw the murder with my own eyes! Pygott was slain here, dropped here, bled here; died here. As God is my witness!"

Marlowe put his mouth close to the terrified man's ear.

"Why have you not divulged that fact to the constabulary here in Cambridge?" he rasped.

"You well know why!" came the answer. "I do not care to be taken from this place on a death cart, all full of holes."

"Did you see who killed Pygott?"

"Yes, God help me. I did."

"Could you describe him?"

"Slight," Edmund said, "young, golden-haired."

"That doesn't sound like Christopher Marlowe, the one accused of the murder."

"I don't know," Father Edmund whimpered.

"Did you see the murderer's face?"

"No. There was a headpiece that obscured all but the eyes. He wore a cape, but underneath he had a manner of dress I might recognize."

"What manner of dress?" Marlowe's heart quickened.

Suddenly the rector appeared in the doorway of the church.

"Father Edmund," he declared loudly, "send that man away this minute!"

Edmund lowered his voice then, and his entire demeanor changed. He leaned close to Marlowe and whispered.

"Listen to me carefully," he said, close to Marlowe's ear. "For the correct number of coins, I will identify anyone you like as the murderer of Walter Pygott, regardless of dress or visage. Do you understand me?"

"Send him away!" the rector shouted, stepping into the yard.

"But this man tells me that he knows who killed the villains who invaded our sanctuary," Edmund answered quickly, pointing to the death cart.

"Indeed?" The rector hurried their way. "Tell *me*."

"I will only tell Father Edmund," Marlowe said steadily.

"Why should that be?" the rector asked, coming closer.

"Because the death of Walter Pygott is of interest to me," Marlowe answered, "and Father Edmund knows something about that."

"Walter Pygott?" the rector said, his voice rising. "That unkempt bully?"

"If you'll allow me a few more moments with Father Edmund," Marlowe began.

"No." The rector interrupted, taking Edmund by the arm. "Father Edmund is an excitable man, and has had enough turmoil today. Go inside, Father."

"But," Edmund began.

"This minute," the rector insisted. His voice sliced the air like a fish knife.

"I hope you will remember what I told you," Edmund said quickly, looking at Marlowe before he turned and went inside.

"Now then, young man," the rector said to Marlowe, "you may tell me: who killed those men in my church?"

Marlowe locked eyes with the man. "I wonder why you do not ask what men like that were doing in your church in the first place. They had not come to pray."

The rector stepped closer, his eyes burning with disdain.

"Do you imagine yourself to be a person who might speak to me in this manner?" he declared haughtily. "I will have your name, young man."

The rector was close enough by then for Marlowe to recognize the distinct smell of brandy wine. The old man was in his cups.

Marlowe examined the man for the first time. He was short, seventy, skeletal, drunk, and uncomfortable in his own loose skin. He had a slight rash at his neck, and his nose was nearly the color of the roses in the garden.

"I have learned what I can here," Marlowe said, dismissing the man in his mind.

He turned his back on the rector and moved steadily away.

"What have you learned?" the rector demanded. "Young man!"

✝   For one thing, Marlowe thought as he continued away, I have learned why the Bible needed to be stolen from the church: Father Edmund was holding it ransom, hoping for more money. That's why he chose not to come forward about Pygott's murder. Could Father Edmund have killed Pygott?

TWENTY-FOUR

The ride to Coughton Court was pleasant enough. It didn't rain. The fields were beginning to show signs of life: violet, cowslip, pale daffodil, here and there a cherry tree in bloom.

He'd left without telling anyone. Better that way. He could not think of a single person in Cambridge he trusted entirely. Obviously Frizer was a potential enemy, but he couldn't feel certain of Bartholomew, nor even Boyle. Nell and Pinch would do whatever money told them to do. If Zigor and Argi were occupied with their Basque cause, as they wanted Marlowe to believe, then they were not a part of a larger picture. And if they were Spanish agents, they were to be avoided.

He had discovered one very interesting fact, however, which seemed to make no sense. For that very reason, he deemed it significant. On his way out of town he thought to stop at the baker's for a bit of bread.

Just before he left Cambridge, Marlowe strolled into the baker's shop. The man didn't recognize him at first, owing to the fact that Marlowe had abandoned his beard and cassock in preparation for a long ride.

Marlowe bought two loaves of bread and made idle conversation until the baker's face darkened.

"I've seen you," he said suspiciously.

Marlowe lowered his voice. "I've been in before. To fight with Frizer."

The baker's head snapped back. "Christ, you can't be in my shop!"

✝

"I'm leaving," Marlowe agreed, paying the man for the bread.

Then, just as Marlowe neared the door, he had a sudden instinct to ask a foolish question.

"Frizer's not here, by any chance, is he?" Marlowe turned slowly.

The baker shook his head. "Gone. Left town."

"Ah, that's right," Marlowe said, as if he'd just remembered. "London."

"Aye," the baker confirmed, "they left yesterday."

Marlowe tried not to register any particular response.

"I thought they left the day before—wait, you might be right. He and—God in Heaven, what's the man's name, the other fellow? Jesus, why can't I remember names?"

"Benjamin Carier." The baker leaned forward sympathetically. "Another one of those students at the college. Why Frizer packs in with that lot I'll never know."

"They have their father's money," Marlowe said, grinning. "They buy the drink."

The baker laughed. "That may be the reason."

"I hope they're back soon. You know Frizer. He owes me money."

The baker shook his head.

"Frizer told me he'd be gone for a while," he confided, still smiling. "And if you was the only one in Cambridge he owed money to, well, I'd be surprised. You want that money back? You might just have to go to London to fetch it."

"London." Marlowe nodded. "Good suggestion."

An hour later, the sun on new fields, small brooks roiling with the last of winter's melted snow, Marlowe longed to speak with Lopez.

He had not given himself time to grieve the loss of his friend. It was all the more keenly felt because Marlowe knew just how few people in the world were worthy of trust. He tried, and failed, dozens of times to imagine what Lopez might advise as he rode to Coughton.

As the sun set, he was delighted to find himself nearing Northampton, where he might have food and lodging. Ale, a big meal, a good night's sleep, those were the things he needed to take him out of himself, to clear his head.

An hour later he was snug in a small, quiet public house. He'd followed the smell of food and stumbled into the place. Its low beams and flickering lamps were instantly comforting. Several men were playing cards at one table, another man sat back from his plate, his head nodding, almost asleep. The thin, sad-eyed man at the bar attended to him with a minimum of talk, and an old, slow Irish wolfhound came to Marlowe's table, blinked, and lay down at his feet in obvious contentment.

Boiled beef and onions, three large tankards of ale, and a plateful of manchet bread sated his stomach. The fire made him drowsy. The relative quiet of the place soothed the pounding in his brain, and he suddenly realized how long it had been since he'd felt safe.

Before another hour had passed, Marlowe was asleep in his room upstairs at the nameless inn, reveling in dreamless slumber.

Without warning he was awakened from his corpselike exhaustion by noises below in the public house. A table grated across the floor; someone had nudged it suddenly. Low voices exchanged urgent commands.

Marlowe rolled out of bed, taking his dagger in his hand. Footsteps came up the stairs. Marlowe tightened his grip on the dagger as he lay on the floor, the bed between himself and the door. The windowless room was small, ten by ten feet, barely room for the bed and a washbasin. Not much space for a fight.

The footsteps were closer, and he heard the rustle of clothing. There were at least three men, maybe more.

Marlowe took hold of the bedcover. He moved just enough to get his legs in a position to pounce, and held his breath.

The door burst open, and lamplight sprayed the room.

There was a moment of confusion when the men at the door saw an empty bed. Marlowe used that moment to strike. He leapt over his bed, flared the bedcover like a sail, whipped it forward, and engulfed the two men standing inside his room.

Without hesitation he drew his rapier and stabbed several times through the cover, finding flesh every time. The men cried out and did their best to rid themselves of the cover, but Marlowe moved to one side, arced his dagger in the direction of the cries, and killed one man. The lifeless body fell to the floor with a thud, taking the cover with him. The other man in the doorway was wounded, confused, and desperate. He was dressed in the same vague uniform as the men in St. Benet's Church: blue doublet, thick black gloves, desert headdress.

Turning quickly, Marlowe jumped on the dead body at his feet. It made a sickening sound, ribs cracking, dead air exploding from the lungs. The other man in the doorway heard it and gasped.

That was the second Marlowe wanted. He swung his dagger arm wide in a backhanded motion, cleanly cutting the man's throat.

Several other uniformed men were out in the hall, he couldn't tell how many. They would have a difficult time coming in, scrambling over two corpses. Marlowe jumped backward, rapier straight, dagger at the ready.

Just then a musket exploded somewhere out in the hall. Marlowe only had time to fall back against the wall before he realized that the shot had not come from his attackers.

"I've got two more muskets here," a thin, sneering voice warned, "and I'm happy to kill the next man that moves!"

The men at the door turned in the direction of the voice.

Marlowe squinted, took his dagger by the point, and threw it directly at the arm of the man holding the lamp. The blade sliced, did not stick, but forced the man to drop his lantern.

"Right!" the thin voice snapped.

Another musket blast ripped the air, and the man who'd held the lamp grunted, dropped, and began to bleed to death.

The lamp rolled over Marlowe's two dead bodies and threatened to catch them on fire. He dropped low and grabbed the candle.

"Who's out there?" Marlowe called.

"Who's asking?" was the answer.

"I am the tenant of this room," Marlowe said, a little softer.

"And I am the landlord," the voice said. "Tell your friends it's too late for visitors. This is a decent house."

Marlowe reached over to retrieve his knife, stood, and held the candle high, rapier at the ready in his other hand.

One of the two remaining men at his door turned his way, distracted by the light. Marlowe caught his eye. There was the same terrifying look he had seen in the men at St. Benet's: the aspect of a man only partly alive.

"Do you speak English?" Marlowe asked the man.

"Do you speak any sort of Arabic?" the man responded with barely a trace of any accent.

Marlowe raised his eyebrows, even proffered a slight smile.

"Well," he admitted, "not as well as you speak English. So you understood the landlord. He'd rather you were gone."

"I would imagine," the heavy-lidded man said softly, "that you feel the same way."

"I do, indeed," Marlowe told him, with a hint of reluctance, "but I would know your reason for waking me from the first sound sleep I've had in a while."

"Reason?" The man shrugged. "Money."

"Enough talking!" the landlord interrupted. "Leave or be shot! I have another loaded musket!"

The assassin in the doorway made as to leave. He might easily have killed the landlord, and then gone for Marlowe, but for some reason he and the other man chose to leave.

"Who pays you?" Marlowe asked quickly.

The man hesitated.

"Why do you want to know?" he asked.

Marlowe chose his words carefully.

"So that I can take my revenge on him after I've killed you." It was a variation of the bravado Lopez had taught him: assure your opponent that he will lose before the actual fight has begun.

The man almost smiled, but did not respond.

"If John Pygott hired you," Marlowe confirmed, "I must tell you: you're after the wrong man. I did not kill his son."

The man was already headed toward the landlord, and the stairs.

"I know nothing about that," he said. "We were paid to kill Christopher Marlowe. You are Christopher Marlowe."

Marlowe stepped over the bodies and into the hallway. He gave a single glance in the direction of the landlord, who was dressed in a brown nightshirt. A spent musket lay at his feet, and he clutched a loaded one in his trembling hands.

"How did you know I was here?" Marlowe demanded of the assassin.

The man shrugged. "We followed you. From Cambridge."

"Right." Marlowe held his breath. "Why were you and your companions at St. Benet's Church?"

He knew that the assassins were waiting for someone else in the church. But here were some of the same men at a tiny unmarked inn, trying to kill him. The question was necessary.

The man exhaled. "You ask a great many questions for a corpse."

"I'm not quite dead yet," Marlowe snapped. "Answer me."

"Another part of the job," the man intoned. "We were there to clean up loose ends."

"Your English is very good," Marlowe said mockingly.

The man shook his head. "Enough. We will meet again when you will not have luck on your side."

He turned away and began his descent down the narrow stairway, utterly ignoring the landlord.

"What about your friends, here?" Marlowe called after the assassin.

"They are not my friends," he said. "I don't even know their names, and they did not know mine. Dispose of them as you will."

But he spoke reluctantly.

"Hang on," the landlord said, emboldened by the apparent retreat of the troublemakers. "Why should we have to take out your trash?"

The assassin paused on the stairs. Marlowe tensed. The assassin turned slightly and was about to speak.

"I'll see to it," Marlowe suggested in the next breath. "They'll be bathed and shrouded, and I will offer *Salat al-Janazah* before they are buried."

The assassin looked Marlowe in the eye then, and it was not the lifeless stare that Marlowe expected.

"You assume they are Muslims," the man said slowly.

"Despite your odd uniforms," Marlowe said, "you are Bedouin, so identified by your headdress, your *kufiya*."

The man stared. "And what do you know of *salat*?"

"Nothing save what I have learned in researching a play I would write, odd as that may sound to you," Marlowe confessed. "It's about Timur, who called himself the 'sword of Islam' more than a hundred years ago."

"A play about Timur the Lame?" The assassin shook his head. "England is a strange place."

"Very," Marlowe agreed.

"And research tells you about our burial prayers?"

Marlowe nodded. "I will attend to these men if you leave quietly now."

"Why?"

"Because then you will owe me a debt," Marlowe answered.

The man looked away at last.

"My name is Fahd. If you kill me, I would like you to know it, as I know yours."

With that he and his companion left immediately.

"What the hell was all that?" the landlord demanded after he was certain the men were gone.

"They tried to kill me," Marlowe answered vaguely, already beginning to wonder how he would actually dispose of the bodies in his doorway.

"Well, I won't stand for it," the landlord raged. "You pack off. Take them corpses with you."

Marlowe sighed. "Yes. Let me get my boots on."

He turned and went back into his room. The landlord came to the doorway, trying not to look at the bodies.

✝

"And you get no refund, you see," the landlord went on, still holding his musket. "Disturbing the peace is a crime in this town."

"I didn't disturb the peace," Marlowe objected, pointing to the corpses. "They did. I was asleep. Peacefully!"

"Well." The landlord exhaled. "I see the truth of that. But you can't stay. And you have to get rid of this trash."

Marlowe sighed and pulled on his boots. He was suddenly faced with the prospect of disposing of dead bodies, and the difficulty of that project gave him a new appreciation for the plight of the men who'd labored to deal with Pygott's body.

"Is there a field nearby," he asked, "or a yard that's not too public? I mean to bury these men tonight."

The landlord's first impulse was to renew his scolding. He raised a partial fist and sucked in a breath. But Marlowe stopped him with the two words.

"I'll pay."

The landlord turned his head.

"I've got a small garden out back," he said calmly.

Marlowe stood. "Well, then. I'll lug these guts downstairs if you'll introduce me to your shovel."

After bathing his would-be killers, Marlowe said aloud the words of a prayer seeking pardon for the deceased. *Salat al-Janazah* was the collective obligation of all Muslims. If no one fulfilled it, all Muslims were accountable. After the words were spoken, he buried the dead men in the landlord's garden.

Several hours later Marlowe was on the moonlit road to Coughton Court, surprisingly well-rested, contemplating the man who called himself Fahd. He knew that Fahd would kill him if he had the opportunity, but it would be with reluctance, because they'd exchanged names. Fahd reminded him of the Jews he'd met on Malta. It was truly said that Jews and Arabs were only feuding cousins—family squabbles were the deadliest on the planet.

On a less philosophical note, Marlowe began once more to question everything about the attack at St. Benet's. Was Boyle somehow a part of that treachery? But Boyle, too, had been nearly killed by the brutes. Did Professor Bartholomew alert the killers? But the timing was nearly impossible, and the motive was absolutely opaque. Could the farmer, Tom, have been involved somehow? That man had, after all, been a part of the original band who attacked the coach to London. Marlowe's head swam with dozens more questions, and no answers.

Finally Marlowe settled once again on immediate practicalities. He began to develop a plan for his appearance at Coughton. Of course he would try to avoid Throckmorton himself, owing to the close relation with the Pygott brood. But he would have to alert Frances of his presence without being seen by very many people. His murder investigation had produced more questions than answers. He had a list of men who had not killed Pygott, and only conjecture to say who had. Maybe Frances had discovered something. It would also be important to confirm suspicions of Throckmorton's direct interaction with the Spanish ambassador, Mendoza, if the message in the Bible was the reason for Pygott's death.

The best hiding place would be with Tin and her father in the stables. Marlowe might even masquerade as an ostler. He knew horses. It might work. Yes. Assume the role of a carefree ostler for a week or two. It might even be a welcome moment of calm, even respite. As he considered it, he grew happier with the idea.

The day dawned. The road widened. Narcissus were suddenly everywhere in the clear light. Green buds filled the trees and called to his mind a line of poetry: "leaves that differed both in shape and show, like to the checkered bent of Iris' bow."

Marlowe lamented that the beauties of spring were lost on him. More urgent matters had supplanted nature's effort. It suddenly seemed to him that spring and passion ought to be all there was to life, and he ardently wished to rekindle the simpler longings of a young man in May.

But just as he thought that, his horse came to the top of a small rise in the road, and Coughton Court came into view.

Its entrance was reminiscent of the grander one at Hampton

Court, with two towers on either side, but the surrounding buildings and gardens made the place more a home than a castle. The immediate grounds stretched in every direction, more than twenty acres, and beyond them: untold miles of property.

Though it was just after dawn, working men were about. Marlowe slowed his horse, sat for a moment studying the estate. He did not dare brazen his way in for fear of being recognized as Walter Pygott's killer. He would have to find Tin and her father, which meant he would have to find the stables. To find the stables without attracting too much attention, he would have to assume another disguise.

He slid down from his horse, pulled off his doublet, turned it inside out, and put it back on again. The gray linen lining was a bit worse for wear, but once the collar was turned down and the sleeves pushed up, it could almost pass for a servant's garment.

He took off his rapier and secured it to the saddle, slightly hidden. Then he tucked his dagger away under his doublet, invisible to anyone.

Next, he looked around for a stone.

Finding a small round one, he took out the dagger.

"Sorry," he said to the horse, patting its neck, "it'll only last a moment or two."

With that he pried a small gap between the front left shoe and the horse's hoof and wedged the pebble there.

"Right," he whispered to the horse, "let's go. The sooner we get there, the quicker we'll get that out."

He put his dagger away, ran his fingers through his hair, setting it awry, and then began to walk toward a side entrance to Coughton, leading the limping horse.

As he drew near he assumed a pained gait, altering his body, appearing much older than his nineteen years. He was noticed as soon as he came within five hundred yards of the gate.

Two men looked up from pulling weeds, another stood staring, his weight on one leg.

Marlowe soured his face a little, nodded at the men once, and took in a deep, rattling breath.

"The master's horse is got a limp," he wheezed. "I'm told to see Tin's father, the stable master here. And to be quick about it. The master's up the road, impatient as ever, and looking to take it out on me."

The standing man nodded. "Tin's father, is it?"

"If you please," Marlowe said wearily, lowering his voice. "Otherwise I've got the notion the old man's riding *me* back to Northampton."

The men kneeling on the ground laughed at that.

"He's from Northampton, your master?" the standing man asked suspiciously.

"No," Marlowe answered, "he's from Cambridge."

"I see," said the man, "and what's his name, at all?"

Marlowe's eyes narrowed. "His name? It's not to be bandied about by the likes of us. Do you want me to walk this poor horse back to him and say I was turned away?"

"He knows Tin," one of the men on the ground said reasonably.

"Well," the standing man sighed.

"I thank you," Marlowe said, headed for the gate, "and the horse thanks you double."

"It's just to the right and back as you go in," one of the men on the ground called out.

"Many thanks," Marlowe answered back, his voice deliberately exhausted.

Once inside the gate, the yard and the grounds and the general appearance of the home were all remarkable. Everything was astonishingly clean and well-kept. Even the stones in the courtyard seemed scrubbed and washed.

Marlowe's nose led him to the stables. As he drew near them he had the distinct impression that they were a tiny kingdom all their own. Tin's father might be considered Yeoman of the Horse rather than a more common stable master, which would mean he was in charge of acquiring most of his own goods and services. And if that were true, he might hire Marlowe without much fuss, and Marlowe could take care of his business at Coughton more quickly.

Marlowe came to an open doorway and stood quietly, petting his horse's neck.

After a moment a voice came from within.

"What is it?" the gruff man asked.

"I'm sent," Marlowe replied with just the right degree of growl.

"Sent?"

"The master's told me to take this horse to Tin's father. It's come up lame, he says."

Out of the shadows a sleek otter of a man emerged, gray hair full and wild atop his head. He wore work clothes, but they were immaculately clean. His face was like the leather on the saddle Marlowe's horse wore: brown but smooth, aged but soft.

"Tin!" he roared.

"Sh!" a voice immediately behind Marlowe insisted.

Marlowe spun around, reaching for his dagger. He came face-to-face with Tin. No longer dressed in her gray man's costume, she wore a plain green linen dress. Marlowe found it a significant garment: the Queen's Sumptuary Laws allowed both lower and upper classes of women to wear that particular color. It meant that Tin could move as freely in the household as she could in the stables.

Marlowe tried his best to maintain a slightly contorted face. Tin stared into his eyes. After a moment she smiled.

"Let us go into the stall here, sir," she said with great amusement to Marlowe, "and see what might be done for your master's horse."

Once in, she closed the stable door.

"Father," she whispered, "this is Kit Marlowe. He's arrived at our door as Frances predicted he would."

Marlowe completely failed any attempt to mask his astonishment.

"How—but," he stammered, "the last time you saw me—I mean, I had a beard!"

"You were Robert Greene," she agreed. "Only Robert Greene was in London at the time, living with his whore, the very sister of Cutting Ball, in Shoreditch."

"Cutting Ball?" Marlowe asked, befuddled.

"A common criminal," Tin answered dismissively.

"But how did you know me?" he rasped.

Her face softened, and some of the light left her smile.

"I looked into your eyes when first we met," she answered, sighing. "You may recall that I pronounced us *doomed* when I saw the pain there. We are in love with the same thing: an elusive shadow that we can never hold."

Marlowe nodded, determined to avoid further discussion of that particular subject.

"So if you know who I am," he said quickly, "you know what I've come for."

"Only in part," she admitted.

"Would someone mind telling me who the hell this man is?" Tin's father asserted.

"I've told you," Tin shot back, exasperated as only a daughter can be with a father, "it's Kit Marlowe, the man who killed Walter Pygott!"

"Christ," the father whispered.

"No," Marlowe began.

"Let me shake your hand, if you'd not mind, sir," the father interrupted. "You did what doubtless hundreds of others wanted to do, including myself. The name's North, Geordie North."

Without waiting for further conversation, the man seized Marlowe's hand and squeezed it tightly.

Marlowe shook the man's hand and looked him firmly in the eye.

"While I will agree that many men wanted to kill him," Marlowe insisted, "I must tell you most emphatically that I am falsely accused and did *not* murder Walter Pygott. Though I will find the man who did."

Geordie stepped back, confused.

"There is a warrant about for Mr. Marlowe," Tin told her father quietly. "We must not say his name too often."

"Right," Geordie replied, tapping the side of his nose with his finger. "Then what should we call you?"

"Can't be Robert Greene," Tin warned. "He's known."

"Why not *Kit*?" he said as if he were resigning himself to an uncomfortable fate. "Frances already calls me that, though God only knows why. And it matches Tin, which is surely not your given name."

"It's Christina," Geordie said, "but she hates it. Her mother, rest her, took to calling her Tin when she was four or five. It stuck."

"God, I hope I don't get stuck with *Kit*." Marlowe sighed.

Without another word, Marlowe patted his horse on the neck, pulled up the left front leg, and popped the irritating pebble out of its place between hoof and shoe.

"Again," he whispered to the horse, "sorry."

The horse set his hoof down gingerly, tested it, and seemed to offer up a sigh of relief.

"Now," Marlowe announced, "I must speak with Frances at once."

"*At once* may be difficult to manage," Geordie said. "She's not up yet, is my guess. The rich, you see, don't have honest labor to ward off the sin of sloth."

"Frances is not lazy," Tin bristled.

"But Miss Elizabeth, her so-called friend in the house, is." He glanced at Marlowe. "Don't get up sometimes to near midmorning!"

"I see." Marlowe looked around. "So, in the meantime?"

"Ah," Geordie said, "I take your meaning. Well. Let's put up your horse, get you an apron, and pass you off as an ostler. What do you know about horses, Kit?"

"I've cured lampas and fives," he answered instantly. "I bred Barbs to good end."

"So!" Geordie seemed pleased. "You know the Arab horses, then."

"A bit," Marlowe answered.

"Then come have a look at this beauty," Geordie told him.

Marlowe spent the rest of the morning with Geordie, inspecting horses, tending to a mare going to foal, and, in general, forgetting his troubles, if only for a few hours. As midday approached, Tin re-appeared.

"I've made arrangements for you to work at the kitchen garden for the second cook's girl," she told Marlowe. "I'll take you to the station beside the kitchen door. You're meant to fetch whatever the girl tells you to, that's the job."

Marlowe shook off the haze of common contentment and got to his feet.

"I've been working certain words in my mind this morning," he told Tin, wiping his hands on his thighs. "It's another verse to a poem I've begun. Do you want to hear it, the verse?"

"No."

"I'll tell you anyway."

They walked out of the barn and into the yellow light. Marlowe blinked. Tin led him at quite a pace out of the stable yard and around the side of that portion of the house.

"It goes," he said to her, " 'A belt of straw and ivy buds, with coral clasps and amber studs; And if these pleasures may thee move, come live with me, and be my love.' "

Tin slowed, but only slightly.

"Some girl might find that fetching," she snorted, "but not Frances."

"And not you."

"Me?" She nearly spit. "I've spent most of my young years trying to escape a belt of straw and the odd amorous ruffian."

"The simple joys," Marlowe remarked, "they're not for you."

"God, no. Give me better conversation than I can find in a stable, and new music, and great theatre, and something more interesting than oats and peas to eat."

"London."

That stopped her.

"What?"

"You want London."

Tin looked down.

"I do," she whispered, a bit too fiercely for Marlowe's comfort.

"Well," he said sympathetically, "take me to the kitchen garden, and when our work here is done, who knows but you may accompany Frances and me back to that city, there to see for yourself that you've abandoned a paradise here for the dun jakes and piss streets of Hell."

Tin rolled her head, and without another word took Marlowe to a place close to the kitchen door where he was to wait for the girl to give him instructions.

TWENTY-FIVE

The kitchen garden was only four acres, but the variety there was surprising. Rosemary had survived the winter and was green and fragrant. Lettuces and radishes were abundant. Young onions had appeared. Early flowers that might flavor a cake or brighten a plate were everywhere.

The back of the house, the kitchen entrance, was equally beautiful. Ivy and climbing roses covered the gray stone walls, three stories high. On the second story there were stained glass windows and on the third, flower boxes filled with pansies.

Marlowe only had to wait several minutes before the girl appeared. She was twelve years old or so, riotously freckled, hair flame red. She blushed when she saw Marlowe, and looked down at her hands. She carried a small piece of paper, which Marlowe presumed to be a list of the items he was to fetch.

The girl inched her way to Marlowe, never once looking up, and held out the list as if it were poison.

"Thank you, miss," he said, taking the paper.

The girl sipped a breath, almost a hiccup, and looked as if she might run away.

"I'm to wait," she managed to squeak.

Marlowe unfolded the page and read it.

"Join me peeling onions," it said. "The girl will show you which door."

A note from Frances that meant she had peeled back more layers, found new information, or so Marlowe assumed.

"You're to show me a door?" he said to the girl.

She nodded once and turned immediately.

Marlowe followed her past the kitchen door and into the shadows until the girl came to a dead halt. She pointed toward a small red door that looked as if it might lead to a cellar or root storage. Then, without another word or glance, she bolted and was gone.

Marlowe headed for the door. As it creaked open, he stood aside and waited. After a moment he heard a faint whisper.

"Are you coming in or not?" it said.

"Possibly," Marlowe whispered back.

"It's Frances, idiot," she called softly. "Come in and close the door."

Without another word, he moved into the cellar. There was light from a taper somewhere in the cavernous room, but until his eyes adjusted to its scant illumination, he thought to stay by the door.

"You're waiting until you can see," Frances said softly.

"Partly," he admitted. "But several recent events encourage me to stand close to the nearest egress."

"Ah, I understand," she said sympathetically. "All present fears are less than horrible imaginings."

"Just so."

His eyes began to see the room. It was a wine cellar. All around him were two hundred or more barrels in a room perhaps thirty by sixty feet. It was quite an impressive volume of wine in an otherwise drab room of nondescript brick walls, dusty floors, and a low, cobwebbed ceiling.

"Still," Frances insisted, "you'll have to come over here. I don't want us shouting things that would best be uttered in hushed tones."

"Agreed," he answered tentatively. "Are you alone?"

"You had difficulties in Cambridge," she suggested, "that make you less inclined toward rash behavior. Good. I am, in fact, alone."

Marlowe sighed and rounded the stack of barrels that had separated him from Frances. He saw her sitting at a small table. She was wearing a deep purple cloak, the hood pulled back only slightly; her hair was ornately tied with ribbons. The taper, an open bottle, and two cups took up most of the table's surface. There was only one other chair at the table.

"I fear that my eyes have been pierced," he told her, "searching out the secret treasons of this world."

"I take it that you have discovered the identity of Pygott's murderer," she responded, "else you would not have risked coming here to Coughton."

"Alas, I have not," he told her. "I have come here because the risk at Cambridge was greater than anywhere else in England. Sir John Pygott may have hired a glut of Arab assassins to kill me."

"Arab assassins?" She sat back. "How—colorful."

"Yes," he agreed. "I would never write that into a play. No one would believe it."

Marlowe spent a few brief moments sharing the events of his encounter with the assassins at St. Benet's, Boyle's heroism, and a description of the killers.

"So you've come because you think it might be safer than Cambridge," she concluded, "and I have been planning how to leave here because it is no longer safe for me."

"Have they found you out?" he asked.

"Not yet. But Bess, my excuse for coming here at all, is nowhere to be found." She leaned forward again and took up the wine bottle, pouring both cups. "Please, have a seat."

Marlowe sat, took a cup from her hand, careful to avoid touching her fingers, and drank half the wine at once.

"I must leave for London as soon as possible," she said, sipping a bit of wine in what appeared to be an attempt to seem calmer than she actually was. "Look."

She took several papers from a hidden fold in her cloak and set them on the table in front of Marlowe.

He looked into her eyes. In them he saw a world of opposites: fear and resolve, passion and control, tension and grace.

"The first is a letter to Throckmorton from Mendoza in Mendoza's own hand unequivocally verifying what we suspected. The second, written by Throckmorton, is a detailed explication of their plan, most especially William Allen's part in fomenting revolt in London, as we suspected. Allen is shortly to be made a Catholic Cardinal, a reward for his part in this treachery. There are details: dates, times, places. And finally there is a document which I know must be important, which I believe may contain the particulars of our Queen's assassination, but I cannot decipher its coded words. I found them all in Throckmorton's hidden letter box."

Marlowe's eyes widened. "You've been busy."

"Yes, and I was hoping I might say the same to you."

"Well, let me see." He finished his cup of wine. "I've discovered that Pygott had allies at St. Benet's, and I saw the exact spot where he was murdered, which was most certainly not my room at the Pickerel. He was killed in the churchyard by the roses."

"We already knew that," she said uncertainly, "from the man, Zigor."

"We suspected," Marlowe corrected. "Now I have spoken with a priest who witnessed the murder, and it was indeed outside the chapel, but the entire truth is still elusive. Firstly, despite your assurances, I do not believe Ingram Frizer can be trusted. Additionally, I have reason to doubt Zigor and his lot altogether as I have uncovered an enclave of Basque separatists scheming in Cambridge. But you are in danger. I was an idiot to come here. We must leave for London immediately."

"Agreed," she told him. "Your brain seems a muddle."

"More that the events of the past several weeks are a muddle, and my brain is swimming through them, trying to make any kind of sense."

"And have you had success in that regard?" But the sound of her voice had changed suddenly. She seemed almost to be interrogating him.

"Ah, well," he answered, ordering his mind to focus on anything but the blush in her cheek. "I have found several small pieces of evidence. I spoke with this man, the priest I mentioned, who saw the murder. Alas, I was interrupted in my questioning of him. Oh, and

I fear that I no longer trust Professor Bartholomew. Neither should you."

"Very curious," Frances began.

"I have not yet told you my most significant conclusion," Marlowe interrupted, realizing that his logic had been jumbled. "I *do* know the identity of Pygott's murderer."

"Well." Frances sat up.

"Benjamin Carier. He is a known Catholic sympathizer, though his father is a Puritan parson, or so it has been said. If I can but match the priest who witnessed the murder with this Benjamin Carier, I'll have solved the crime."

Frances took a brief moment to assess the information Marlowe had offered, primly finishing her wine.

"What makes you suspect Carier, other than his possible sympathies?" she asked.

"Carier disappeared from school very shortly after I arrived there. It is presumed by some that he's returned to his home in Kent. I know that is not the case."

"Oh?"

"He went to London," Marlowe said slowly, as if revealing a winning hand of cards, "with Ingram Frizer."

Involuntarily, Frances covered her mouth with her hand.

"The man who murdered Pygott went to London with Frizer?" she whispered.

"So I was told," he answered.

"Then why have you come here?" She hesitated. "Why haven't you pursued the killer to London?"

It was a fair question, and Marlowe had several answers. The truest was that he found it impossible to stay away from Frances. He eschewed that explanation in favor of the more practical reasons.

"You and I must go to London together."

"Yes, I see," she mused, putting the pieces together quickly. "Alone each of us might encounter difficulties or delays."

"Yes," Marlowe said hastily, "for instance, you might assure stray

London constabulary that I am to be remanded to Lord Walsingham instead of to the Tower."

"In that I am his daughter."

Marlowe smiled. "And what army could stand against the two
of us combined?"

"Right, then," she said, patting the tabletop impatiently. "I must
arrange for a plausible reason to leave Coughton and return to
London. But you must hide. You can't be seen in the house."

He smiled. "I'm quite comfortable in the stables."

"The stables?" She thought for a moment. "Ah. Tin."

"Yes. She recognized me at once, in spite of the fact that I looked
so different when last we met. She told her father who I was. He has
allowed me to stay in his kingdom on the other side of the fence."

Frances looked down. "Tin is a remarkable person."

"But I want to show you," Marlowe said, "the scant items of evidence I have procured. I believe that you may have insights which
I do not."

Marlowe reached into the slim pocket of his boot and produced
the red ribbon, pieces of thread, and the brass button he had hidden there. He set them on the table.

"I believe that the ribbon is from Pygott's codpiece," Marlowe
began, "and the threads and button are from the murderer's doublet
or cloak. The ribbon was found in the yard at St. Benet's, pressed
into the ground, as was this button. I believe that if I can find Carier
in London I will be able to match this button to his clothing. You
can see that the design of the button is quite distinctive."

"Let me think," she said softly, staring at the miniscule items on
the table.

Marlowe picked up the third letter that Frances had set in front
of him and took a moment to examine it. His eyes widened; he
glanced up at Frances. She was staring at the button.

"These scant toys are not enough evidence for a legal proceeding,"
she demurred.

"No," Marlowe agreed, holding out the coded paper, "but combined with what is on this document, and what we know from Cambridge, we shall expose Carier and he will be forced to confess."

"To Pygott's murder?" Frances asked.

"Yes," Marlowe answered confidently, "and to his part in the attempted murder of our Queen."

Frances tilted her head. "What is in that document?"

"This document," Marlowe said excitedly, "is written in the code similar to the one in the Rheims-Douai Bible. It indicates that Carier and an unnamed lady-in-waiting to the Queen will poison Her Majesty in her own chambers before the end of this week!"

"God in heaven." Frances stood then. "That means—do you realize what that means?"

"Among other things?" Marlowe stood too. "It means that the person who murdered Walter Pygott is the same one trying to kill our Queen."

Frances leaned over the table, her voice greatly lowered. "This document does not say which lady is the cohort?"

"No," Marlowe answered, "but it's not obvious? The conspirator is Bess Throckmorton, your companion in the Queen's chambers."

"No." Frances closed her eyes. "I can't believe it. She is like a sister to me, and the Queen's favorite, despite the betrayal of her kinsman."

"And yet she is not here," Marlowe said.

Frances nodded. "I cannot force myself to think her a murderess. Why could it not be Carier himself?"

"He may be the man in charge of the treachery," Marlowe answered, "but how would he gain access to the Queen's inner chambers?"

"And not Frizer himself, for the same reason," she said absently. "Bess is the logical suspect."

"Yes," Marlowe agreed, "but you understand now why Frizer is not to be trusted."

"He's taken Carier to London."

"And," Marlowe added, "I'd be very much surprised if Frizer has done as he was told."

"You mean the letters we found in your room." She shook her head. "He has not delivered the Mendoza letters to my father."

"I believe not."

"We must leave for London immediately," she said. "We cannot wait. I'll make some excuse to get away. Perhaps a ride about the estate. I'll request a groomsman from the stables as an escort. Geordie will assign you."

"And Tin," Marlowe mumbled. "She'll go with us."

Frances stopped. "What?"

"She longs for London," Marlowe told her. "We had a talk."

Frances was about to respond to Marlowe when a sudden noise behind one of the barrel racks startled them both.

Marlowe's rapier was in his hand instantly, and Frances held a long dagger low and close to her thigh.

Without a word, Marlowe moved to his right; Frances to her left.

For a moment there was a complete absence of sound, then a small scrape betrayed the location of the intruder.

Out of the corner of his eye Marlowe saw Frances move to the edge of the barrel rack. Marlowe countered, around the other side. The rack nearly touched the ceiling of the cellar, and was ten feet long, big enough for nine large, stacked barrels of wine.

As if reading each other's minds, Marlowe and Frances stood as one. Then, prompted by some invisible clue, both leapt, boxing in the intruder.

A squeal of terror broke the silence, and Marlowe stood face-to-face with the redheaded girl who had led him to the cellar. She was quaking and gasping.

Marlowe took a step closer to her. She squealed again and turned, only to find Frances and a dagger in her way.

"What are you doing here?" Frances snapped.

The girl burst into tears.

Remembering himself, Marlowe returned his sword to its scabbard and came to stand beside the girl.

"This wasn't your idea," he began in soothing tones. "Someone told you to come into the cellar and—and see what we were saying."

The girl nodded, but would not stop crying.

"Who told you to spy on me?" Frances demanded.

The girl was unable to answer. Shivering wracked her body and she was having difficulty breathing.

Marlowe knelt.

"I hate secrets," he said to the girl. "I don't like to have them in my head. You're probably the same. No one will harm you if you tell the truth."

The girl nodded, doing her best to stop crying.

"The truth shall make you free," the girl whispered, "Our Lord Jesus said."

Marlowe could not hold back a slight smile. "He did indeed."

The girl looked down.

"Tin says I was to listen," the girl murmured.

Marlowe looked up at Frances. "Tin?"

"Did she tell you why she wanted you to do it?" Frances asked the girl.

The girl shook her head.

"And what did you hear?" Marlowe asked cautiously.

"I don't know," she confessed, "couldn't make sense of it. Something about letters and documents and the Queen. And—and you're leaving for London."

Marlowe stood.

"Now what?" he asked Frances.

"Is everyone on the planet suspect?" she answered, mostly to herself.

"Yes," Marlowe affirmed. "You should go. Make your excuses, ask for your groomsman; prepare to return to London. I'll go back to the stables with—what is your name, child?"

"Rebec," she responded at once.

Marlowe looked down at her. "For Rebecca?"

"No," she answered, barely above a whisper, "for the musical instrument. It has strings. My father was a musician here."

"I—very well," Marlowe said, "Rebec and I shall repair to the stables, there to confront young Tin with regard to—listen. I do not wish to be indelicate, but Tin is—Tin has certain feelings for you that—is it possible—"

"Yes," Frances said curtly, not looking at Marlowe. "That is the most likely reason this girl was sent to spy on us. Tin knows that I do not share her affections. And that I bear a certain—attachment to you. Kit."

He smiled at that. Then he realized that his heart had quickened to hear her say it.

"I've told you not to call me that," he said softly. "And you do realize, of course, that I—that the reason I came to Coughton, the actual reason—"

"We must hurry," Frances interrupted. "I concur with your plan: I'll make excuses for London, you settle things with Tin."

Without another word Frances headed for the door.

"You understand," Marlowe called after her, "that mine is by far the more difficult task."

The only response she offered was the closing of the cellar door.

TWENTY-SIX

The stables smelled of new hay and old leather. Rebec took Marlowe's hand and walked in silence toward the farthest stall, where someone was raising a racket.

When they came to the stall Marlowe saw that Tin was whirling madly, blindfolded, skirts hiked to her waist, rapier in hand. She stabbed rhythmically at certain intervals, and managed to hit the exact spot at every rotation. Then, as if sensing Marlowe's presence, she stopped turning and thrust her rapier, freezing its point only inches from Marlowe's face. Rebec shrieked.

Tin tore off her blindfold and stepped back. Marlowe had not moved. Rebec was cowering behind him, sobbing again.

"You should never have sent my friend Rebec to spy on me," Marlowe said, petting the little girl's head. "It frightened her. And now you've tried to kill her. Honestly, Tin, if you want to know what I'm up to, you have only to ask. As I've explained to the girl, I hate secrets."

Momentarily made speechless by Marlowe's words, Tin stood frozen until she remembered that her skirts were not remotely covering her bare legs, and had in all probability revealed that she wore no undergarment. Her face flushed, she loosened her belt and her skirt fell to her ankles.

"Am I your friend?" Rebec whispered to Marlowe.

He looked down at her. "Of course you are. We've met twice in one day, once in a garden and once in a hidden place. In some parts of England, that would make us betrothed."

The girl blushed and giggled once.

Tin lowered her rapier.

"That's better," Marlowe told her. "Now, what would you like to know?"

"I—I wanted to know," Tin began, but seemed unable to continue her thought and, instead, sighed as if she had just learned some terrible news.

Marlowe smiled at Rebec. "Would you like to leave now?"

"Yes, please," she piped.

Marlowe nodded once, and the girl ran, gone from the stables in a matter of seconds.

"What would you like to know?" he said again, more softly.

She shook her head. "I already know it."

"Your affection for Frances has not abated."

"Has yours?" she shot back accusingly.

"Alas," was his only answer.

"That's why you came here," Tin went on, here face hot and her eyes wet. "You came for her."

Marlowe wondered how much he should tell her and how much he should hide, a difficult thought considering that he had just been so vehement about hating secrets.

"I came because it's time for us to go back to London and finish things," he said, his voice soft and steady, "to solve a murder and save a queen."

Tin blinked.

"You came to save your skin and win a maid," she countered.

"I hope you will think better of me," he responded patiently, "when I tell you that it occurs to me that you might come with us."

Tin could not believe her ears.

"To London?" she managed to say, her voice weaker than the little girl's.

"I have no idea why I suggested it to Frances," Marlowe confessed. "But, yes, let us discuss it with your father and see what he says."

"He'll say I can't go," she answered immediately. "He says that every time I want to leave his stables."

Her voice was forlorn, the sound of someone defeated before the battle had begun.

"And yet you came to Cambridge," Marlowe said.

Tin twitched and her eyes grew wide for a moment, and then she exhaled. "Yes. I did."

"You left without telling your father."

"I left without telling him the truth," she admitted. "I said I was going to Northampton. For a special mare physic."

Marlowe nodded, but he wasn't certain he believed her.

"What will you tell him this time?" he asked.

"Why are you—why have you asked me to go?"

Marlowe looked away, out the open stable doors, into the sunlight on the stones. He was surprised, once more, at his response.

"I am in pursuit of the man who killed Walter Pygott. He is named Carier and he's gone to London with Ingram Frizer to aid in the murder of our Queen. If I find him and stop him, all justice will be satisfied. I was once accused of being very young. It was a crime of which I was guilty, until experience rewrote the indictment. You paint yourself with that same brush of youth. Life is not always about the maiden one loves, or the wine one gets, or even the friend one loses. Sometimes there is a higher purpose, one beyond the boundaries of appetite and longing."

Tin would not look at Marlowe.

"A fine speech," she whispered bitterly, "but those are the words of a man. What do women have in this world but passion—and regret? What higher purpose can there be than love? Love spins the globe. Love built our religion. Our Lord's message was clear and concise: love everyone and do no harm—a task too difficult for most men, but the secret virtue of every woman on the planet."

"Spoken," Marlowe sighed, "like a very young person."

It only took a moment for Marlowe to realize that those were essentially the words Lopez had said to him.

"I am not so young as you might imagine," Tin snapped, not realizing Marlowe's sudden melancholy. "I have done things beyond my years."

"As have I," Marlowe said, cutting her off impatiently. "Do you want to go to London with us or not? Frances will be safer, you'll have a chance at the life you want, and I'll have help with my task."

Tin only thought for a moment. "I do know Frizer by sight, of course," she mused. "And I am not the worst with a rapier. I practice daily."

"So I observed," Marlowe agreed, beginning to smile.

"And you know who killed Pygott, but you'll need help with that."

"Yes."

"London." Tin said the word with a mixture of longing and wonder. "I might even find a young man there, one who would not mind my forward nature. If Frances can do it, so can I."

"I believe you could," Marlowe responded, unable to hide a grin.

"I'm still not certain why you've asked me to come with you," she said, eyeing Marlowe suspiciously.

"Nor am I," Marlowe admitted, "but of late I have come to rely on my instinct as much as my intellect."

Tin looked Marlowe in the eye, and smiled back at last.

"A very feminine attribute," she told him.

"If you seek to insult me," he warned her, laughing, "you'll have to do better than that. I cannot count the number of feminine attributes I admire."

"Nor can I," Tin answered. "How strangely alike we are."

"In many ways," Marlowe agreed. "So. Shall we go to London and save the world now, or would you rather eat something first?"

She considered before suggesting, "I could murder a boiled egg."

Before they had taken two steps they heard Rebec's voice call out in a very theatrical manner.

"Good morning, sir," she sang out, "what a wonderful surprise to see you here in our stables so early!"

One of the men grumbled something and the girl fell silent.

"Throckmorton," Tin whispered.

She pointed to an empty stall and hid her rapier behind several bales of hay. Marlowe moved silently and hid himself just as Tin stepped into the open area of the stables.

"Sir Francis," she said deferentially, "and Sir John. Shall I ready horses?"

A whining, effete voice complained, "There are quite a number of girls in your employ, Sir Francis."

"Pardon, my lord," Tin went on. "I am only the stable master's daughter. Shall I fetch my father?"

"At once!" the other, more commanding voice insisted.

Tin scurried away.

Marlowe peered between slats in the stall, and saw the two men. One was an older, fatter version of Walter Pygott: chinless, slack-jawed, and balding. The other, Throckmorton, was stiff as a rail, tall but weak-chested. Pygott was dressed for travel: buttoned cloaks and thick gloves.

"You make too much of the feminine presence here," Throckmorton said to Pygott in a low voice. "The one you fear is but my daughter's companion."

"I will not stay and be discovered here by Walsingham's daughter!" Pygott objected. "We must assume that she reports everything to the father."

"She's a *girl,*" Throckmorton chastened.

"And girls chatter," Pygott countered. "I daren't be gossip fodder."

Throckmorton considered the thought and sipped a breath. "Perhaps you're right. The better valor lies in safety. The plan proceeds apace. The bitch Queen will be dead within the week."

Pygott smiled. "It's a brilliant gambit, tricking the Queen's most trusted girl."

"Silence," Throckmorton commanded. "How many times must I tell you not to speak of these things aloud?"

Pygott laughed, looking about. "Are you afraid that one of your horses will give us away?"

"I am afraid that your idiot son has already done that!"

"My idiot son is dead," Pygott yawned, "and his demise served us well."

✝

"I don't see why you and Mendoza place so much emphasis on this student Marlowe. Why pursue him for your son's murder?"

"Because Walsingham has been watching him, and the Jew trained him," Pygott snapped. "He is an unknown commodity and a risk we cannot afford. He must be eliminated precisely because we don't know what he can do."

"Well," Throckmorton answered with a toss of his head, "Mendoza has seen to it, and that is that. Now listen to me carefully."

But before he could go on, Geordie interrupted, barreling into the stables.

"Pardon, sire," he announced, "I've made ready the two best, the black Arab and the sable—"

"Just Sir John's horse," Throckmorton interrupted.

And without further ado, he strode out of the stables, followed by the other two.

Marlowe let go a breath. These two men weren't capable of taking a piss without help. He'd come face-to-face with devils only to discover they were fools instead. Mendoza was the puppet master. He, not Pygott, was responsible for the Arab assassins, and for Walter Pygott's death.

By early afternoon Marlowe, Frances, Tin, Rebec, and Geordie were gathered in the most remote stall of the stables. Rebec was shaking with excitement, unable to control her joy at being included in such adult adventures. She had worked most of the morning as a go-between for Frances and Marlowe. She had reconciled with Tin; Geordie had let Rebec feed three horses by herself. It was the best day of her life.

She stood in the stall silently, looking up at everyone as they whispered.

"My host believes I will be gone for the morning riding," Frances said to Geordie, "and that I've taken a groomsman with me for protection. It was a nice touch. The men in the house thought it was an appealing bit of weakness from a woman they had come to think of as too masculine, I suppose."

"And of course the groomsman is Marlowe"—Geordie nodded—"so that no one will think anything of it when they see the two of you riding together."

"And I have let it be known," Tin said, "thanks to Rebec, that I am bound for Northampton once again. I was going there anyway, on an errand of trade with an eye toward our breeding program."

"So that no one will suspect when they see you with Frances's kit," Geordie said. "They'll take it for equipment and trade items."

"I'll return the kit to Frances on the road closer to Northampton," Tin added.

"But what happens when you don't return from your ride?" Geordie asked Frances. "Night comes on, you're not here; my new groomsman is missing. It won't take long for that lot up in the manse to realize something's not right."

Marlowe smiled. "Rebec's thought of something."

He looked down at her and nodded, encouraging her to speak.

"Well," she began breathlessly, "what if I was to say that I saw Mistress Frances and—and a man, a stranger. They would think—everyone would say that she had a sweetheart, you see, and that she and this sweetheart had gone away together."

"The beauty of that particular story," Marlowe acknowledged, "is that Rebec would only be telling the truth, allowing wagging tongues to do the rest."

"There are several young men who might be suspected," Frances said. "There is no dearth of ridiculous suitors at Coughton."

"And by the time all those fine young men are accounted for and greater suspicions have grown," Tin concluded, "you'll be in London, putting an end to this Throckmorton plot."

Geordie looked down. He kicked the straw at his feet, sniffed, and nodded after a moment.

"Right, then," he said. "It might do."

"You're in no danger, father," Tin said gently. "No one will suspect you had anything to do with this."

"It's not me I'm worried about," he said softly, still staring at his feet.

Before he could elucidate, the stable dog, which Geordie had stationed in the open courtyard, began to bark.

Everyone moved. Marlowe stepped into the next stall and began to dress the pair of horses there. Frances stood close by, squinting impatiently, as if to scold her servant. Tin headed for her tiny bedchamber behind her father's rooms where Frances's kit had been hidden. Geordie and Rebec went to quiet the dog who had, as it turned out, been barking at crows.

Within a quarter of an hour, Frances and Marlowe had gone off toward the west at a leisurely pace, Frances leading, her *groomsman* dutifully behind. Tin had loaded a pack mule with Frances's things and disguised them with blankets, heading in the direction of Northampton.

Geordie was in the stables, inspecting the right front shoe of a horse near the front entrance. And Rebec was sitting on the ground outside, petting the dog.

After a moment she glanced into the darkened stables because she heard what might be the sound of someone crying. She stood, brushed her hands on the front of her dirty dress, and tiptoed in.

She found Geordie in the first stall patting the horse and brushing tears from his eyes.

"What's the matter?" Rebec asked, wide-eyed.

"It's Tin," he rasped.

"What about her?"

"I'll never see her again."

"What?"

"She's gone to London," he lamented, "and she'll never come back."

"London?" Rebec said. "No. She's going to Northampton."

"That's what she said, all right," Geordie sighed, "but I know better. I saw that mule. She packed all of her things along with Miss Frances's kit. She's gone. My little girl is gone. I've lost my only daughter."

He struggled mightily against an impulse to sob.

Rebec came into the stall and took his hand.

"Well," she began tentatively, "my father is dead, and your girl is gone. Maybe we could come to some sort of an arrangement, you and me?"

Geordie looked down at the sad, expectant face. The dog wandered in and sat, the only audience to the scene. There was no further dialogue in that particular play, and eventually the dog wandered away in search of a warm place to nap.

TWENTY-SEVEN

Once again Marlowe found himself standing in a small room in the Palace of Whitehall. Unlike the others in which he'd met Walsingham, there were several chairs and a table, but no desk. This room was bigger, and all four walls were covered with matching tapestries, each depicting a larger-than-life-size musician playing an instrument. Represented were the sackbut, a lone viol, a small crumhorn, and a tilted virginal—an odd quartet.

It was impossible to tell how big the room was. Anything, or anyone, might be hidden behind those hangings.

Without warning Walsingham stormed into the room from behind the sackbut player. He had a sheaf of papers under one arm and a monstrously distracted scowl on his face. He stood behind the desk, staring down at something on its surface.

"So," he boomed unceremoniously, not bothering to look at Marlowe, "you've found Pygott's killer."

"Not exactly," Marlowe began.

"Carier is a pestilence," Walsingham interrupted.

"Yes," Marlowe agreed hastily, "but I haven't found him yet."

Walsingham looked up.

"He is in London," Marlowe continued, "with Ingram Frizer, who is, I am convinced, primarily in the employ of the Spanish king. He may even be the Pope's man. He is certainly not your double agent."

"Frizer is only a distraction," Walsingham growled. "Carier is the game."

"Yes," Marlowe said, and took a breath.

But even his breath was interrupted.

"You've done well," Walsingham said absently, looking down once more. "You solved your murder, and in doing so you've also discovered Throckmorton's instrument of assassination."

"Lord Walsingham," Marlowe snapped impatiently, "I have done neither."

Walsingham looked up once more. He set down the papers he'd been carrying. He sat.

"What are you saying?" he asked quietly.

"I am saying that I have suspicions, I have very few pieces of evidence, some gossip, and several dozen questions. That is, at the moment, the extent of my investigation."

"But Frances has told me," Walsingham snorted.

"I do beg your pardon," Marlowe interjected, this time his turn to interrupt, "but I have not told Frances everything."

The scowl on Walsingham's face became a threat.

Marlowe hastened to explain. "It must be obvious to you that I have a great affection for your daughter, Lord Walsingham—too great, in fact," he said quickly, with as great an air of deference as he could muster, "and I would do anything to protect her from harm."

Marlowe stood very still, letting what he'd said fill the air.

"What could you not tell her?" Walsingham asked.

Marlowe drew in a slow breath. He felt his face flush. A tingle of uncertainty edged the back of his neck.

"I could not tell her that you were the one who betrayed her to Throckmorton," Marlowe said steadily, "and had her imprisoned in Malta."

Walsingham glared, his eyes ablaze. It was an expression that might have murdered other men. But he did not disagree with Marlowe's bold statement.

"Of course you had no direct contact with Throckmorton," Marlowe went on, staring firmly back at Walsingham's burning gaze. "You somehow had the idea planted in Walter Pygott's mind, so that he would believe he had discovered a spy. I knew something was amiss the moment I heard that. Walter Pygott possessed the observational skills of a dead vole. He couldn't discover the balls in his own codpiece."

Walsingham sat back. His expression changed slowly. It was an oddly familiar one. It took Marlowe a moment to realize that the Queen's spymaster looked, at least a little, like Professor Bartholomew. It was the mien of a Socratic instructor.

"And why, in heaven's name, would I do such a thing as betray my own daughter?" Walsingham asked slowly.

"I can think of a dozen reasons." Marlowe leaned forward imperceptibly. "You might do it to test her, though it would be a harsh father who could condemn a daughter to the place I saw on that island. It was more likely a feint to confuse Throckmorton, to make him believe that he'd discovered a spy, to allow him a false sense of safety. You had no idea that Frances would be taken to Malta. That's why you were in such a panic to rescue her that you turned to Dr. Lopez and his strange student friend at Cambridge."

"Mr. Marlowe," Walsingham sighed.

But Marlowe would not relent. His voice gained strength. "I suppose it's possible that you were testing the Pygott family, assessing their loyalties. It may even be that you sought to expose Frizer for the traitor he is. Oh, and by the by, I have suspicions about Bartholomew as well. You may have had them, too, which might have somehow figured into your bizarre shadow play."

Walsingham stared at Marlowe for what seemed an hour.

"And you've come to these conclusions," the old man said slowly, his voice thin, "based upon what evidence?"

"Pygott was not capable of lacing his shirt, as I say," Marlowe railed, "let alone discovering a spy as cunning as your daughter! Also there is entirely too much fuss about Pygott's death. No one liked him. The warrant for my arrest is flimsy even by rural standards. His own father, as I have learned, doesn't actually care that he's dead, though someone is trying to make me believe he's hired a small army of assassins to kill me. Instead, these assassins work for a larger purpose, on the side of the Spanish. That they keep me from discovering Pygott's murderer is, to them, unimportant."

Marlowe glared at Walsingham, daring him to disagree with anything he'd said.

"Please, do not fall silent now." Walsingham nodded, encouraging Marlowe to go on.

"It has been brought to my attention by several people," Marlowe continued more tentatively, "that you might be testing me."

Walsingham sat still, as frozen as the musician on the tapestry behind him.

So Marlowe forged ahead. "For example, I do not know why you would choose me to save your daughter. No one seems to know. I can only assume that a great many of the things that have happened to me since Lopez fetched me from Cambridge and delivered me to you have been tests. The other possibility is that I was a pawn easily lost in the greater game. Who would miss an upstart student and the son of a boot-maker? You gambled with my life, and with the life of my friend Rodrigo Lopez. It was a devil's gambit that lost you Her Majesty's best physician."

"I see." Walsingham closed his eyes.

Marlowe opened his mouth to go on, thought better of it, and bit his lower lip. Instead, he paused and waited. Walsingham would speak eventually, and something would be revealed.

"You are *half* right about *some* things," Walsingham confessed, wearily emphasizing the qualifying syllables.

"It is true to some minor extent," Walsingham went on after a moment, "that we wanted to discover who killed Pygott, and that investigation also provided us with an opportunity to further test your capabilities, as you put it. And you did discover that the same man who would kill our Queen is the murderer you seek, which is very convenient."

"And was it convenient as well that Dr. Lopez lost his life in the theatre of your testing?"

Marlowe knew, even as the words flew from his mouth, that he should not have spoken them.

Oddly, Walsingham seemed not to hear the question at all.

"But we must put all of this aside for the moment," the spymaster said crisply, "and set to more important work immediately. If your intelligence is correct, this assassin, Carier, will attempt to murder Her Majesty within the next twenty-four hours, before she leaves Hampton Court. You will find him and stop him. You will attempt to report him to the authorities, without reference to the offices of the Queen if possible, simply as the true murderer of Walter Pygott. You have, I am told, evidence to that effect."

"I—no, I—I have a button."

Walsingham nodded once. "The fate of the nation has depended, many times, on less."

"I have a *button*."

"Use it to obtain a confession." Walsingham said it as if it were simple, obvious.

Marlowe's mind drifted slightly. "I may also have an eyewitness, a priest in Cambridge."

"Employ whatever methods you think best," Walsingham snapped impatiently. "Here."

He shoved several papers toward Marlowe.

"It's been arranged," the old man went on, "that you will ally yourself with William Allen, the man in charge of the College of Douai at Rheims."

"Allen? Yes." Marlowe nodded, forcing himself to focus. "Carier will be with Allen, and the rest who would foment revolt from within our own country after they've killed the Queen."

Walsingham nodded, his impatience growing. "Allen is here in London and has been told of your father's affiliation with the Catholic Church. He believes that you would work in the Catholic cause. We've arranged to have you meet with him tonight."

Marlowe's head was swimming. "This is all—everything is happening quite quickly."

"These events are in motion now." Walsingham stood. "You have no time to digest the meal I've just forced down your gullet. You must be off without delay. These papers instruct you. They will tell you where to meet Allen, assure your safe passage to the man, and offer him evidence of your fealty to his cause."

"Frances?"

Walsingham turned away, and a guard, who had been hidden all along, pulled back a tapestry revealing the door through which Marlowe had entered.

"My daughter has suspicions of her own," Walsingham mumbled, striding toward the door, "things she has not told you. She is approaching Allen's main cohort, the Jesuit priest Robert Parsons, with a mad plan of her own design."

With that, the old man was gone.

Marlowe stood alone in the room, and was suddenly cold.

The eastern wall of Fulham Palace blocked out the stars. Frances Walsingham leaned against it, smiling. She could hear voices inside through the open window next to her. She took a moment to adjust the dagger hidden in her boot and then rounded the corner toward the guarded door.

"Who's that?" one of the guards called out, jittery.

"I have a message for Robert Parsons," Frances whispered loudly. She moved toward the door with a display of subservience.

"What's the message?" the other guard asked.

"Pardon," Frances squeaked, "I am to give it only to Robert Parsons."

A voice from inside snapped, "What's all that, Groot?"

The first guard answered, "Some girl. Says she's got a message for you."

"Send her away!" the voice commanded.

"It's from Bess Throckmorton, sir," Frances called out. "Most urgent, she says."

A moment of silence was followed by the sudden appearance of a cleric in the doorway.

"Keep your voice down!" he commanded. "Get inside."

He stepped back and Frances entered. Down a short hall and to her right she found the man in a small dining room. Seven or eight men, two of them sitting at the large oak table, turned to look at her as she came in. The room was ablaze with candles, bright as day. Despite the soft spring night, there was a fire in the hearth. A stack of paper, a pen and inkwell, and a dozen or more muskets adorned the tabletop.

The man Frances had followed sat down at the head of the table and stared at her.

"Well?" he said, irritated.

"Are you Robert Parsons?" she asked, managing to sound frightened.

"Yes. God. What is your message?"

"I'm to say that Bess has been called back to Coughton by her father," Frances began with a deliberately tentative air, "and that I am to take her place in the—in the business at hand."

Every eye looked her way.

"Why has her father summoned her?"

"She told me that he feared for her safety in this enterprise, but she also apprised me of her mission. I stand ready to carry it out."

Parsons licked his lips. "I see."

One of the other men at the table leaned close to Parsons's ear and whispered. Parsons smiled.

Without a word his eyes flicked to the man nearest Frances. He took her by her arm and tugged hard.

"And I stand ready as well, Frances Walsingham," Parsons sneered. "Your captivity shall provide further safety for our endeavor. Have a seat. You will compose a note to your father."

With that Frances stomped her boot heel down and the man who held her howled in pain. Before he even let go of her arm, Frances had pulled her dagger and stabbed the man three times.

Ducking to the floor as the man fell, she slid under that table and threw her knife toward the head of the table, but Parsons had already shoved himself aside and stood.

Frances grabbed the foot of one of the other men at the table and pulled hard, toppling the man with a thud. She reached out and kicked him, turned him, and freed his rapier from its sheath.

Rolling, she emerged from the table just in time to stab at a man who held a pistol. The pistol went off, but only damaged the table.

She got to her feet and turned. Parsons and two others faced her from the other side of the table, each holding a musket.

"I don't want to kill you yet," Parsons allowed, "because you're too useful to me alive. For the moment. So put down that rapier and pick up the pen. You're going to write a letter to your father."

Frances turned her eyes to the man who had whispered to Parsons.

"This would have worked if you hadn't given me away," she said to him.

"You are not a modest young woman," the anonymous man responded, his accent vaguely French. "Anyone who has ever been to court would know you."

"But not anyone at court would betray our Queen," she said. "All it will mean to you tonight is that you'll be the first to die."

With that she tossed the rapier backhanded and it flew through the air into the man's heart.

As she did it, she dropped once more to the floor, but not quickly enough to escape the musket blast that tore through her lovely blue dress.

Marlowe stood outside St. Etheldreda's Church, one of the oldest places of worship in the city. Publicly, of course, it was Church of England, but everyone knew that Catholic masses were offered there in secret nearly every week. Only a few years earlier it had been leased to Sir Christopher Hatton, said to be one of the Queen's bed partners. The rent was £10, ten loads of hay, and one red rose per year—a fee so little that it only increased the gossip about Her Majesty and Sir Christopher. It didn't help matters that Hatton used the crypt as a tavern. It was in that tavern that Marlowe was to meet William Allen.

The sky was dark and the moon was dim. It was only nine o'clock, but the air had midnight in it. Marlowe felt for the dagger hidden at his side, and the second one in his boot. The rapier was deliberately obvious.

Despite hard weeks, little food, and less sleep, Marlowe felt the intense thrill of being alive. He knew that he was perched on the precipice of history, and that he would soon be the Queen's salvation. Or he would be dead.

The street outside the crypt tavern was narrow and strangely curved. While the moon's light illuminated the stones around him, though barely, Marlowe could not see the moon itself. He took a moment to consider what sort of metaphor that might be—that he could only see the effect of the light, not the source—but that poetical exercise was interrupted. Someone came at him silently and held a blade at his back.

"If you turn around," the man behind Marlowe rasped, "I'll stick this through your ribs. It's a long blade. It'll come out the other side."

"Fair enough," Marlowe answered amiably, "and what will you do if I don't turn around?"

"I'll ask you several questions," the man replied.

Marlowe nodded. "I like a good game, but let's make it more interesting. For every question I answer correctly, I get to cut off one of your fingers. We'll keep the stakes small, I'll start with the littlest."

"What?" the man snapped.

Without warning Marlowe grabbed the hilt of his rapier and tipped it, neatly forcing the man to stumble backward. That done Marlowe twirled, almost dancing, and in a flash the point of his own rapier was touching the other man's gullet.

"Now then," Marlowe said lazily, "ask your first question."

The man gaped, still holding his dagger, mouth open, eyes wide.

"I'll tell you what," Marlowe continued, "I'll give you the first question for free—but the bet still stands."

The man licked his lips, trying not to move too much. The point of Marlowe's rapier tickled a small nick of blood from his Adam's apple.

"Ask," Marlowe demanded.

The man sucked in a breath. His face was obscured by a cowl. Perhaps he was a monk, impossible to tell. He wore a plain black robe under an unadorned black cape attached to the cowl. The knife was interesting. It was made of silver, more a work of art than a weapon.

The man managed his first words in full voice, despite obvious trepidation: "The moon shines bright in such a night as this, does it not?"

It was one of the questions that Walsingham's notes had told him to expect. He offered the countersign.

"In such a night did Thisbe fearfully trip the dew," Marlowe answered.

The man nodded, relieved, and went on. "In such a night stood Dido with a willow in her hand."

Marlowe smiled. "And in such a night Media gathered the enchanted herbs, are we done?"

"I heartily beg your pardon," the man said, swallowing. "You understand I have orders."

"But do you understand that these words we've just spoken are an allusion to the Easter Mass, only thinly veiled?"

The man blinked. "They are?"

"What manner of Catholic are you," Marlowe growled, "that you don't recognize that? The moonlight, the suggestion of music, the repeated use of the phrase 'in such a night'?"

"Please," the man coughed, "let's just go in."

Marlowe hesitated, but sheathed his rapier. The man, as an afterthought, put away his knife and moved past Marlowe, headed for a small alleyway.

"I detest these stupid codes," Marlowe complained. "Some idiot half as clever as he thinks has devised a secret language twice as complicated as it needs to be."

"I don't know what it means," the man answered. "I just say the words."

"Spoken like a true Catholic," Marlowe mumbled.

✝

"What's that?" the man said, cupping his ear but not bothering to turn around.

"I hope there's ale," Marlowe answered loudly.

"Aye," the man said, granting himself a single chuckle. "Where there's men of God, I always find good drink."

The man turned into an open doorway, waved to someone, and stood aside.

Marlowe stepped in. He found himself at the top of a short staircase staring into an ancient burial arena. Torches did their best to illuminate the place, but a palpable air of gloom and decay could not be so easily overcome. The gray stones seemed to absorb sound rather than echo it, and it was quiet as the grave.

The crypt had been left as it had always been, without an iota of adornment. Only tables and chairs had been added. It seemed an appropriate place for a meeting between men who might, at any moment, be dead.

"That's him," the man told Marlowe, nodding in the direction of a man in inky blue robes.

The first thing Marlowe noticed about William Allen was that his beard was divided. Beginning at his chin, it grew in two separate and distinct directions. Though Allen had the eyes of a doe, he had the beard of a satyr.

That assessment made Marlowe smile as he descended the stairs into the dank tavern.

Several men sat around tables. There were no women in the place so far as Marlowe could tell. A plank set on several up-ended barrels served as a bar. Tall barrel racks made walls against the darker inner reaches of the crypt. No one looked at Marlowe as he strode toward Allen, not even Allen himself. But out of the corner of his eye Marlowe observed several shadows behind one of the barrel racks, and one of the men at one of the tables had a cocked pistol on his lap.

Marlowe came to Allen's table and sat without being asked. He took hold of the jug next to Allen's cup and pulled it toward him.

Eyes on Allen, who had still not looked up, Marlowe raised the jug to his lips and drank.

"Claret," Marlowe remarked, setting down the jug. "French wine. That's interesting."

"The French," Allen said softly, "see wine when they look at any grape."

"And they see the Pope," Marlowe countered, "when they look at any church."

"Yes." Allen looked up at last.

"You knew my father, once," Marlowe guessed.

It was a good guess: unimportant if it were not true, significant if it were.

"He was of some small service to our cause in Canterbury," Allen agreed. "But that was long ago."

"And you wonder if time has altered his sympathies."

"No," Allen said, eyes now locked on Marlowe's. "I wonder if you share them."

"I wonder if you know me at all, sir."

"I know that you have been missing from your Cambridge classes for some time. I know that you are wanted for murder. I know that the man you murdered was in our service."

"Would you happen to know," Marlowe interrupted, "how I'll fare on my year-end examinations? I'm a bit apprehensive about them, having missed so much instruction, and you seem to know everything else."

"I know that you are a degenerate poet," Allen went on as if Marlowe had not spoken, "and I know that you have no honor."

"Ah," Marlowe interrupted again, "there's the one false note. You had the tone almost right, but you insisted on going a single step too far. Too clever by half."

Allen took in a breath as if to speak again, but remained silent, staring at Marlowe.

"I understand that you mean to provoke me by saying that I have no honor," Marlowe continued, "because you have heard that I am

261

easily provoked. I was a boy six weeks ago, and might have leapt to my feet then, dagger drawn. But I've lived a strange life since then, and I better understand the odd things men do in order to manipulate the weak of mind. If I may say it: I possess the strongest mind you will ever meet in this life."

Marlowe set his elbows on the table and leaned forward, a slight smile in his lips. He produced one of the pages given him by Walsingham and slid it slowly across the tabletop. It was a note of safe conduct from Mendoza.

Allen's eyes flashed for a second, and Marlowe heard a slight clicking sound behind him, a pistol being uncocked slowly.

"Well," Allen said with a tilt of his head, "I won't kill you just yet."

"Nor I you," Marlowe answered, "for the moment."

Allen sneered. "If you kill me you'll be dead the next instant."

"But that won't bring you back to life," Marlowe said lightly. "And it's all one to me. I'm ready to explore what lies out there beyond this life, the undiscovered country. Are you?"

"Maybe tomorrow." Allen sighed. "I have work to do today."

"Then may we get on with it," Marlowe snapped impatiently, "and have done with all this bandy?"

"You want me to believe you'll help us?"

"I've already helped you," Marlowe answered. "I've killed that idiot Pygott and rid you of a weakness in your scheme."

Allen sat back. He tried to hide the look of surprise on his face, but it was too late. Marlowe had seen it.

"What's more," Marlowe pressed on, "I have friends in your contingent of Basque troops."

Allen's face betrayed him once more, telling Marlowe that he had been correct in such a wild postulation.

"Those men, the Basque men, have gone missing." Allen steadied himself. "Perhaps you can tell me where they have got to."

"They are men of strange conscience," Marlowe answered. "Separatists. They may simply have gone home."

"And you admit your responsibility for Pygott." Allen sighed again. "Well."

One of the figures that had been hiding behind the huge wine barrel racks rounded the dark corner into the flickering torchlight.

"So you did kill that sack of bones after all," said Ingram Frizer, walking toward the table. "You almost had me believing you was innocent."

"I had no idea whose side you were on," Marlowe said to Frizer, though he kept his eyes locked on Allen's. "Best not to reveal too much to a double agent."

Allen's eyes shot toward Frizer's approaching saunter.

"It's all right," Frizer assured Allen. "The girl, *Lady* Walsingham, she most likely told him that. The trouble is, you see, Mr. Marlowe, once a thing is bent, it's difficult to tell which way it's pointing."

"Yes." Allen smiled. "Well, that particular person is no longer— Frances Walsingham—she is no longer a problem."

Marlowe tensed before he could stop himself. Hoping no one had noticed, he quickly leaned forward and glared at Allen.

"You sent this man Frizer to enlist me in a cause," Marlowe snapped, "to which I was already affixed."

"*Affixed*?" Allen's head tilted. "What an odd way to put it. I had been told you were better with words than that. It was a clumsy turn of phrase."

"It was a clumsy thing to do," Marlowe countered, "sending Frizer, trying to force me into St. Benet's to retrieve your Bible. When, exactly, did you realize that Walter Pygott didn't have the brains or the guts to do your work?"

There was a commotion at the door to the tavern, and the man who had accosted Marlowe in the streets came rushing in.

"Queen's guard," he muttered, heading toward the inner recesses of the crypt. "Something's happening!"

Everyone in the tavern stood and moved at once.

"This way," Allen whispered to Marlowe.

Without further ado, the men in the crypt raced almost silently to the hallways behind the barrel racks, and into darkness.

TWENTY-EIGHT

Past ancient dead bodies, into a sewer, up stone stairs, Marlowe, Allen, and Frizer came out into the moonlight, near the river. The others had gone separate ways. The night was dark and the wind was high; clouds ran past the moon.

Allen's face betrayed a troubled mind. He was still trying to decide about Marlowe's true affiliation. So as he walked along the river's edge with Frizer and Allen, Marlowe chose to shove matters forward.

"I can't afford to be seen with you two," Marlowe whispered, "especially not by the Queen's guard. I'll go my own way, and we'll meet again before dawn with Robert Parsons in Fulham."

Without waiting for a reply, Marlowe headed in an easterly direction.

"Parsons?" Frizer called.

Allen immediately grabbed Frizer's arm, urging him to be silent. Marlowe spun around.

"I hope he hasn't killed the Walsingham girl yet," Marlowe rasped. "Frizer can tell you that she had a fondness for me. I might be able to eke a bit of useful intelligence from her if she yet lives."

Marlowe held his breath.

"The girl did seem to like him," Frizer said.

"You're an idiot," Allen whispered. "Be silent!"

Marlowe's conclusions were equal parts deduction and gambling. Frances had gone to Fulham to meet with Parsons, according to Walsingham. Allen had just said that Frances was no longer a problem. That meant Frances had been captured or killed by Parsons.

If she was dead, Marlowe's path was simple: kill them all—Parsons, Allen, Frizer, Carier; anyone else who had played a part in her death.

If she was alive, the way was equally clear: secure her rescue.

Careful, Marlowe thought. His heart was pounding, and if the moon had been clearer, the other two men would have seen the flush in his face.

"Incidentally," Marlowe said suddenly, willing the sound of his voice to be languid, "you wouldn't happen to know where Benjamin Carier is at the moment, would you? I need to speak with him."

"Carier?" Frizer's face contorted.

"You brought him with you to London."

"Not really," Ingram went on, still confused. "We did come together, but his father hired me as his road companion."

"His protection, you mean." Marlowe nodded. "I know that he's a part of this. His sympathies are well known."

"They are," Allen answered. "And he is of some use to us. At the moment."

It was impossible for Marlowe to tell if they were lying. The same lack of moonlight that had obscured his own feelings worked to conceal their faces as well.

"He's asleep in his uncle's home, most like," Frizer complained. "Why do you want to know?"

"A trivial matter. He may have been at classes more recently than I have, and my year-end examinations are at hand. Have I already mentioned that? I don't like to waste my father's money. I thought Carier might tell me what I've missed."

"College," Frizer said, as if it were a curse word.

Allen was less dismissive. "This way, Mr. Marlowe. We'll meet Parsons, but not at Fulham."

Without another word he led the way and Marlowe could only follow. Around several corners and through a foul-smelling alley, they moved quickly to a small storehouse behind several taller buildings.

Inside, the room was small and entirely bare, no rugs, no wall hangings, only bare cold stones. It was, however, quite bright, filled with ten or more wall torches.

Marlowe's skin felt like sand and his spine was burning. He ground his teeth. Every muscle in his face stung from the effort of maintaining an appearance of composure. And no matter what he said out loud, the only prayer in his mind was "God, let her be alive" over and over again.

Allen sat on a small stool. Frizer tumbled into a corner of the room on the floor and began snoring almost at once. Marlowe stood by the door.

They were waiting, Allen had explained, for Robert Parsons. But Marlowe suspected that other work was at hand: someone was checking on Marlowe's story, his background; his father's affiliations. Walsingham was a genius at establishing false facts, but Marlowe recalled words his father had often repeated: "There's always someone cleverer than you."

These men had mobilized a Spanish army at the border, Basque rebels in England, hidden Catholics in London, old families with ties to the Queen, and an innocent young girl, a lady-in-waiting, who would be the instrument of her monarch's death. They were not to be underestimated.

Without warning the door burst open. Marlowe's hand flew to grasp the hilt of his dagger.

Allen glanced at Marlowe and held up his hand.

"Robert," Allen said.

The Jesuit took in the room at a glance. He wore a black cassock wrapped around his body and tied with a cincture, a black biretta atop his head, and a floor-length cape tied around his neck. It was a deliberately uncomfortable costume.

The priest stared at Marlowe.

"This is the student?" he asked softly.

"I am, sir," Marlowe answered before Allen could, "a student at Corpus Christi Cambridge, and an admirer of your brotherhood."

"Indeed." It was not a question. "What is it that you know about the Company of Jesus?"

"The Jesuits?" Marlowe's eyes narrowed. "I know that it is a company but fifty years old, founded by Ignacio Lopez de Loyola, a Basque, in a crypt beneath the church of Saint Denis near Paris. I know that his guiding principle was 'For the greater glory of God,' which glory is to be achieved by being *perinde ac cadavere*—well-disciplined like a corpse. Possibly a dictum borne of your society's original meeting place."

Parsons exhaled slowly. "Do you mean to mock my brotherhood?"

"Do you mean to challenge my intellect with elementary questions?" Marlowe answered calmly.

Parsons turned to Allen.

"You were right," Parsons said. "This man is a dangerous weapon. One may never know which way he cuts."

"A fair observation, your grace," Marlowe began, "or is 'your grace' the proper address? Among conspirators would 'Robert' do?"

Parsons clasped his gloved hands behind his back. "Why do you seek to insult me?"

"I was just about to ask you the same question," Marlowe told him.

"Were you." Again, it was not a question.

"Before the coming day is done, Queen Elizabeth will be dead and we'll all be in a different county than this one." Marlowe looked around the room. "And yet you waste our time."

He wondered, himself, why he was being so aggressive. He heard the sentences as they came out of his mouth, heard the sound of his voice. No forethought prevented or encouraged a single syllable. He was comprised almost entirely of instinct. Like a mystic. Or an animal.

"Is it a waste of time to ferret out a traitor?" Parsons asked.

"You've already heard from Zigor that I am not a traitor," Marlowe snapped. "You know that I have been in contact with your Basque legions. You know that I killed Pygott for you. So I am forced to wonder why you hesitate with me now. Do we not find that oddly suspicious, Mr. Allen?"

Allen watched the two men from his seat, trying to follow what was happening.

Marlowe's hand was still on the hilt of the dagger at his waist. Throwing Zigor's name into the room, and emphasizing the Basque involvement in the plot, might reassure the Jesuit. But there was no telling what the Basque men were actually up to.

"In fact we have not yet heard from brother Zigor," Parsons said at last, "but you are correct in your assessment of our urgency. Our work is nearly finished. And even if you are not the man we think you are, it will scarcely matter. There is nothing you can do to stop the death of the Queen."

"Fine." Marlowe shrugged. "Then let me go back to Cambridge. I have my year-end examinations to consider, as I've told these other men. Direct me to Benjamin Carier and we'll travel together. I have need of his aid. I've missed too many classes."

"Benjamin Carier is not going back to Cambridge," Parsons said calmly. "Not tonight. He has work to do. And you're not going anywhere, Mr. Marlowe."

"You amaze me, Robert," Marlowe said. "If I am a weapon, even one that cuts both ways, you have but few choices: kill me, use me, or put me back in my sheath."

"Your sheath being Cambridge," Parsons allowed.

"He could be of use to Carier this morning," Allen suggested.

Parsons's eyes shot to Allen, but just as he was about to speak, there was a soft knock on the door. Without waiting for an answer, a small dark man entered. Marlowe recognized him as the man who had held the cocked pistol in the crypt tavern where he'd met Allen. The man moved quickly to Parsons without looking at anyone in the room. He whispered several sentences, turned, and flew away.

"There, I am assured of your sympathies," Parsons said, his voice greatly changed. "Mr. Marlowe, you will forgive my reservations. I am about to take over a country and alter the course of history. I may be permitted a bit of caution."

"By *caution* you mean *discourtesy*," Marlowe answered with a flourish of his hand as he let go of the hilt of his dagger, "but no matter. Let us get on about our business."

"Right you are," Allen snapped crisply. "Mr. Marlowe, I think you will go to Fulham Palace; Frizer will take you there and give you details along the way. You'll meet Carier there and you, instead of Frizer, will escort him to Whitehall, owing to your relationships with Walsingham and his daughter. Carier must deliver the packet to our lady-in-waiting because he is the one she knows. After that, you and Carier will return to Cambridge, schoolboys returned from London to sit for examinations. Clear?"

"More than clear," Marlowe said, making the effort to smile. "And by the by, did you pick Benjamin for this task *only* because you were to use him as a carrier?"

"Good-bye, Mr. Marlowe," Allen said, smiling. "We shall not meet again."

"You won't see our business to its fruition?" Marlowe asked as casually as he could manage to.

"I'm away with the tide," Allen said absently.

Before Marlowe could pursue that notion, Frizer rumbled to a more-or-less standing position and stumbled toward the door.

"Come on," he mumbled, not looking at anyone.

Frizer took Marlowe's arm and dragged him from the room.

Down stairs and out into the night, Marlowe pulled his cloak around him. The night had turned cold and the moon had hidden once more.

As they walked toward the home of the Bishops of London, Frizer explained the basics of the plan to Marlowe. Frizer showed Marlowe a small packet, which he referred to as "an unction of a mountebank," the poison which was to kill the Queen. They were to give it to Carier, who would deliver it to the Palace. Carier, a bookish, pasty boy, was in need of an escort, a protector. It was supposed to have been Frizer; now it was to be Marlowe. Carier would deliver the poison to a certain lady-in-waiting, who would take it to the Queen's private chambers and slip it into her wine that very morning. Marlowe and Carier would be gone by then, on the road to

Cambridge. But Marlowe realized, as he listened to the plan, why Carier had been chosen. He would absorb blame if anything went wrong, keeping Parsons and Allen one step removed.

That realization did nothing to assuage Marlowe's primary fear: that Frances was dead.

When they arrived at a hidden garden path in Fulham Palace, Frizer went silent. He paused under the shadow of an arbor. Marlowe stared at his profile, almost impossible to see in the dark of the moon. Who was he? He was Walsingham's man, but he'd brought Carier to London. He worked for both sides. Where were his true loyalties?

Marlowe decided that he was a man without moral principles, owing his allegiance more to money than to any cause. Good. That made him easier to deal with.

Frizer gave out five short whistles, the nesting call of a mourning dove.

Immediately it was answered back.

It was a good signal. Dawn was coming on. Soon there would be real doves in the garden—and mourning in the air, if Marlowe did not succeed in preventing the death of his Queen. Fate had been kind in a single regard; it had made Pygott's true murderer a part of the conspirators' plan. Marlowe would save England and his own skin with one simple action: bring Carier to justice.

Carier appeared. His skin was so white that it reflected every bit of starlight it could find in the wind. The veins in his face pulsed blue, and Marlowe had a sudden urge to cut those veins, force a confession, and take revenge for Frances's death. His hands were shaking with the effort of holding himself back.

Carier was dressed, foolishly, in silver and pale blue, a good costume for court, but one that prohibited any secrecy.

Frizer handed Carier the small packet wrapped in a bright scarf, tied with a bow. Carier took it but his eyes were on Marlowe. His jaw was slack, giving his face the distinct aspect of a village idiot.

"Is—is that Christopher Marlowe?" Carier stammered.

Marlowe remained silent.

"He's to take you to Court now," Frizer whispered. "He's been—*affiliated* with Lady Frances Walsingham."

Frizer had managed to make the word *affiliated* imply so many things that Marlowe was at once impressed with the dexterity of nuance and enraged by the suggestion.

"I see," was all that Carier would say.

Marlowe's mind traveled like lightning from thought to thought. He could kill Frizer then and there, and turn Carier in to the authorities. But that would scatter the conspirators. Many would get away, including Bess Throckmorton. Best, at the moment, to continue the game, though his hand still twitched in the direction of his dagger.

"I'll leave you to it, then," Frizer went on. "Just head on past the watch house, through the yard. That'll put you on the way to Whitehall without being seen."

Then he took Marlowe by the arm and put his lips close to Marlowe's ear.

"This idiot," Frizer said, inclining his head slightly in the direction of Carier, "he don't know what's what. He thinks he's taking a gift to Bess, from her father. He has no idea what's in it, nor does he know the rest of that lot at Fulham. He's a bit of a sacrificial lamb, you might say. You can use that to your advantage if you get into trouble."

With that, Frizer slipped off into the last of night.

Marlowe smiled at the confirmation of his suspicions, even as he found it cold as winter: if Carier was captured, he would continue to play the idiot because it was the only part he knew. He could give nothing away. He didn't realize that he would be caught; he was unaware that Frances was dead. Marlowe had a momentary sensation of pity for the boy. It passed almost immediately.

"You know Frances Walsingham?" Carier said, failing to keep his voice down. "I met her once at a party, at Coughton Hall. I don't know her well, but she's very charming, don't you agree?"

Marlowe put an index finger to his lips. Carier nodded.

"It is less than an hour before dawn," Marlowe whispered. "We should go."

"Oh, absolutely," Carier agreed sheepishly.

Past a hedge of roses and around a bend in the path, they neared the watch house, lit with torches. It was a small stone building, not attached to any other. There were open windows and a single door, and smoke drifting upward from the chimney. Several men talking, one laughing. Marlowe and Carier would have to be silent as they passed.

Then, as if struck by an arrow, Marlowe heard her voice.

"I'm thirsty," Frances moaned.

Marlowe's blood stopped pumping. His entire body felt numb. He tried to think, but his brain stopped working.

"Wait here," Marlowe commanded Carier.

Without any further consideration, Marlowe drew his rapier and his dagger. Abandoning all subtlety or stealth, he raced forward, kicked in the door of the small stone building, and found five men sitting around a table, drinking and playing at cards. Frances sat in a corner, bound to a wooden chair, blindfolded.

Before any of the men could stand, Marlowe jumped onto the tabletop. He thrust his rapier at the youngest man first but a musket went off like thunder. The ball grazed Marlowe's calf. The pain brought his mind into complete focus.

He whirled in the direction of the blast, flailing with his rapier. It caught the barrel of the gun and knocked it to the floor. Then he leapt, kicking the underside of another man's chin as he went, sending that man flying backward.

Marlowe winced but managed to land on his good leg right next to Frances. With a single flick of his dagger he cut loose her bonds. Her hands flew to the blindfold and tore it away. She stared into Marlowe's eyes.

"If I have to keep rescuing you over and over again," he said to her, "I'll never finish college."

He handed her his rapier and turned immediately to face the

men in the room. Frances was on her feet in the next instant, rapier leading her forward.

The young man Marlowe had stabbed was lying on the floor moaning; the one he had kicked was unconscious in a corner. That left three: the man who'd fired the musket, an older man with rapier and dagger, and a tough with two knives. The musketeer had already retrieved his weapon and was fumbling, trying to reload it. The older man guarded him, knowing that once the musket was reloaded the intruder and the woman would be easier to subdue. The tough, heedless of the greater situation, jumped like a rabbit directly at Frances, daggers out.

Marlowe slashed the tough's arm from elbow to wrist and Frances stabbed the boy's side as she moved out of the path of his blades. The boy fell to the floor, bleeding and gasping.

"How's your rapier arm?" Marlowe asked Frances, breathing hard.

"What?" she asked, staring the older man in the eye.

"You've been tied up," Marlowe explained loudly, "and I want to know if you're able to kill that man by yourself or if you need help."

Reading Marlowe's mind, Frances smiled.

"I'd like very much to kill him myself," she said. "He was rude to me."

With that Marlowe cocked his arm, held his breath, and threw his dagger. It cut the air as it flew directly across the musketeer's hand and stuck there. The man screamed, dropped his weapon, and stumbled toward the door, hoping for escape.

"Go ahead then," Marlowe encouraged Frances. "Kill him. We have things to do."

Not waiting for a response, Marlowe slid around the table and launched himself after the musketeer, who had just achieved the doorway.

Frances sighed and lunged forward, rapier point first.

The older man batted the rapier to one side with a single flourish.

"Get help," he said steadily to the musketeer.

Before the man could obey, Marlowe grabbed his hair, pulled him backward, and retrieved his dagger.

Frances had already pivoted to her right and had the older man off guard. He was solid, wary, and possibly more dangerous than anticipated.

He was dressed in a simple guard's uniform, but his face displayed a calm intelligence that belied a position as a late-night guard at the bishop's palace. He was someone else's man.

Holding his knife at the musketeer's throat, drawing the merest trickle of blood, Marlowe urged Frances.

"Are you going to kill him or not?" he asked her.

Frances smiled. "I want to play with him first."

"We don't have time," Marlowe insisted.

In a flash Frances dropped to her knees, sliding forward across the stone floor, her silken dress tearing. At the same time, she jabbed. The point of the rapier caught the older man's midsection, near the stomach. She leaned into it, and the sword moved upward, farther into the man's body.

The man gasped, eyes wide. He was still looking at the place in the room where Frances was supposed to have been. He thought she'd disappeared.

Rolling to her left side, Frances withdrew the rapier, and with a second roll she came to her feet, bent low, and prepared to strike again.

The older man was still at a loss. Frances danced forward with a wide, sweeping flourish of her blade, and disarmed the man. He sat down at the table, nodding.

"I'm killed," he said softly. "By a woman."

Frances put the point of the rapier into the man's ear and leaned forward, chin out.

"You're killed by Frances Walsingham," she said as if she were spitting. "Now I'm going to run this blade through your brains and hang a sign around your corpse that says, 'killed by a girl of sixteen.'"

"Frances," Marlowe cautioned.

She was still staring at the man, her face nearly violet.

"He was *rude* to me," she repeated, pushing the blade ever-so-slightly into the man's ear.

"Have you learned your lesson, sir?" Marlowe called out.

The man blinked.

Marlowe let go of the musketeer, pushed him forward, and bashed him in the back of the head with the hilt of his dagger.

"All right," he said, "I want my rapier back."

Frances glared at the older man. His eyes were unfocused. Blood soaked his uniform.

"Frances," Marlowe said sweetly, "let him be."

The fire in her eyes abated, and with a single motion she took the point of the rapier away from the man's ear and tossed the weapon to Marlowe, hilt first. The older man slumped forward, his head gently knocking the top of the table. It was impossible to tell whether or not he was dead.

"We really have to go," Marlowe said. "I've got Benjamin Carier in the garden, and he has the poison that would kill our sovereign. He wants to deliver it this morning."

Frances smiled and headed for the door.

"Carier. You found him? You're getting good at this business."

"Providence more than I prevailed," Marlowe said, sheathing his blades.

They both moved crisply out of the guardhouse and into the darkness.

"And I don't really have him," Marlowe continued. "We have to get him to the palace so that he can deliver the poison to Bess Throckmorton."

"Why not just turn Carier in now with the poison, save the Queen, and have done with it?" Frances whispered as they neared the all-too-obvious figure of Carier, fidgeting in the pale moonlight that had suddenly appeared.

"We want to catch Bess in the act, as the assassin," Marlowe answered softly, "and for that we must have Carier deliver his package directly to her. When he does we'll have them both. I'll use that circumstance and Carier will confess to Pygott's murder in front of witnesses."

"Confess so easily?" she asked, realizing that Marlowe had something up his sleeve.

"Carier is a dupe in this greater treachery," Marlowe told her. "He has no idea what's in the packet. When he finds out that he's being charged with attempting to murder the Queen, I'll convince him that he might save himself by admitting to Pygott's murder. He'll do it because it's the lesser of two crimes. He may even convince a judge that he killed Pygott in order to stop the plot. That would be his best hope. I don't really care as long it proves *my* innocence."

They stopped talking when Carier saw them. He smiled.

"Lady Walsingham," he said too loudly.

"Please be quiet," she answered, "I have just escaped the guardhouse."

"Escaped?" Carier asked, gaping.

"We must hurry," Marlowe snapped. "We are pursued."

Carier looked about wildly, eyes popping. Marlowe took his arm and Frances fell in on his other side.

They began to run, slowly at first, then picking up speed.

By the time dawn touched the eastern spires of the city, they were nearing the Palace of Whitehall.

TWENTY-NINE

The new Palace of Whitehall, redesigned by Elizabeth's father, sprawled over twenty-three acres or so. Henry VIII delighted in his indoor tennis court, his bowling green, cockfighting pit, and a large yard for jousting. He had married Elizabeth's mother, Anne Boleyn, in the palace, before he sent her to the Tower Green and had her head chopped off. The king himself died in that palace, in bed.

The front gate was formidable, rarely approached on foot. Frances guided Marlowe and Carier to a shaded side entrance guarded by two men. Both wore pistols, and were dressed in the dark blue uniform emblazoned with the Walsingham Family crest. They bowed to Frances, acknowledged Marlowe with a slight nod, and glared at Carier.

"He's on the Queen's business," Frances said softly.

Carier was actually shaking. He held out the package he was supposed to deliver, showing it to the guards, another indication that he had no idea what was in it.

"I'm delivering this to one of Her Majesty's ladies," he managed to say.

One of the guards locked eyes with Frances, read her thoughts, and opened the door behind him.

Frances plunged ahead, Carier was next, and Marlowe followed the poor man in.

"First things first," Frances said, gliding down the dimly lit hallway. "Get that package delivered."

If Carier was beginning to wonder what he'd gotten himself into, he did not find words to express his misgivings. Marlowe kept behind him, hand on his dagger's hilt. Frances moved quickly. Down several corridors and suddenly out into an anteroom, the unlikely trio found themselves the object of surprise by the rest of the courtiers there. Many of these men, and several women, had arisen before dawn to prepare for a day at court. There were twelve in the small room, all standing still with a deliberate air of nonchalance. Each had dressed in finest array, ready to speak with Her Majesty or, more likely, just to stand in the room in her presence, smiling, doting; being seen. One man in a raging purple doublet and ridiculously elaborate collar looked down his nose at the three strangers bustling into the room. Then he affected a yawn to show that he disapproved of what he saw. Frances was dirty and disheveled from her evening's adventures. Marlowe was significantly unkempt, here and there a spot of blood. Carier had the look of a terrified rabbit.

Frances moved briskly past the courtiers. Without hesitation she pushed through the inner door of the room, ahead of everyone.

A collective gasp arose from the company, and the man who had yawned began to sputter, "See here!"

Carier and Marlowe followed Frances into the next room. It was small. Two more guards stood on either side of another door, but these were different. They were of the Queen's guard, weapons drawn. Frances nodded, they relaxed, but the swords remained out.

Frances turned and stood in the open doorway through which she had just barged, addressing the dozen or so sycophants.

"I am Lady Frances Walsingham," she announced harshly, "I speak for the Queen. She will receive no one today. You must all leave at once."

With that she slammed the door and smiled at the guards.

Their weapons disappeared, and they stood aside.

"Thank you both," she told them.

They did not speak as they opened the door to a larger hall. Early morning sunlight streamed in through high openings in the stone walls, but the evening torches were still lit. The walls were hung with simple tapestries, and the floor was mostly bare. At one end there was an ornate chair, not quite a throne, on an elaborate red rug. It was the only place in the room to sit, and belonged to the Queen. Several women stood about, but fell silent when Frances and the two men entered.

Frances looked about the room, found the person she wanted, grabbed Carier by the arm, and strode deliberately toward Bess Throckmorton.

Bess stood motionless in a pale blue gown, her hair tied and looped in a remarkable, balance-defying coif that seemed impossible to maintain. She turned her head very slowly in the direction of the oncoming juggernaut.

"Hello, Bess," Frances said bitterly, "I believe this man has a present for you."

Carier began to drag his feet, and pulled his arm away from Frances's grip.

"What are you doing?" he demanded.

"Helping you to deliver your package," Frances told him, staring at Bess.

Marlowe's hand was still on his dagger's handle. Several guards in the room had already drawn their weapons, and one was moving quickly toward the commotion.

"No," Carier moaned, "you're not!"

"Go on," Marlowe said, coming to stand behind Carier. "Give her your package."

"No!" Carier cried. "It's not for her!"

Frances spun around in the direction of the oncoming guard.

"Please be so kind as to detain this man and Lady Throckmorton," she commanded. "Fetch my father and let us examine the small bundle that has been brought into the palace for Bess to use against Her Majesty's life."

"What?" Bess gasped.

Carier's face whitened and he looked around the room as if he were drowning.

†

"Take this man," Frances continued to the guard, "and hold him with this package until my father can examine both. I will accompany Bess into an outer chamber."

"Hang on," Marlowe said softly.

He had stepped away from Carier and was staring at Bess Throckmorton.

"What is it?" Frances demanded.

"Hang on a moment," Marlowe repeated, his eyes boring into Bess's.

He read the truth in her eyes as if it were a book, and was certain of its contents. He turned to Carier, whose quaking threatened to shake loose his bones.

"This package, Benjamin," Marlowe said quietly, "is not for Bess, is it?"

Carier could only shake his head, clearly not comprehending anything that was happening.

Frances's head snapped back. "You were not delivering this to Bess Throckmorton?"

"N-no," Carier stammered, his silver clothing beginning to show signs of dank sweat.

Frances stepped closer to him, her face nearly touching his.

"To whom, then," she began very deliberately, "does this package belong?"

"Lady Devereux," he rasped, "Penelope Devereux. Like the other two."

"The other two?" Marlowe's eyes flashed to meet Frances's.

"To Penelope Devereux?" Frances confirmed.

Carier nodded. "Yesterday, and the day before."

Frances looked wildly about the room, and then back at Marlowe.

"She's not here," she said.

"I know," he responded at once. "Where would Her Majesty be at this moment?"

Frances grabbed the nearby guard by his sword arm. "Take him! Take him now!"

The guard looked confused, but only for an instant. He sucked in a breath and shot in the direction of a small door close to the chair.

"Go!" Frances said to Marlowe. "Follow him! I'll hold Carier here!"

Marlowe dashed after the guard just as Carier dropped to the floor and fainted dead away.

Through two short hallways, another dark passage, and into a circular room painted white, Marlowe followed the Queen's guard.

In the white, windowless room there were two doors, the one through which they entered, and the one opposite, where the guard stood, tapping gently at the door.

"Your Majesty?"

There was no answer.

"Go in!" Marlowe barked.

The guard turned to Marlowe.

"It's a bit delicate," he mumbled. "If the Queen is not answering this door at this particular time of day, she is doubtless in a second chamber—you see—attending to the royal morning—shite. Sometimes the half of an hour."

"She's in there alone?" Marlowe asked tentatively.

"Lady Penelope was in earlier," he said. "Now it's just the new chambermaid."

"New chambermaid?" Marlowe drew his rapier.

"Started today, hang on," the guard said hesitantly, suddenly realizing the problem.

"We must go in immediately!"

"No," the guard said, startled, "that's not permitted!"

"Your Majesty!" Marlowe sang out. "You are in grave danger! I'm coming in!"

With that he charged the door, knocking the guard aside. The guard plummeted to the floor, cracking his skull on the hard stones.

Plunging into the royal room, Marlowe was confronted with a stunning array of mirrors and windows, and was momentarily blinded. It was obviously a dressing room, blazing with candles in addition to the morning sunlight. A table laden with makeup was the centerpiece.

A lone figure stood at an inner door, the royal chamber-pot closet. The sudden light made it impossible for Marlowe to see clearly.

But the voice was familiar.

"Mr. Marlowe?" Tin said.

Marlowe's eyes adjusted to the light, and there stood Tin, dressed in a dull brown frock, hair tied tightly behind her head, holding towels and napkins.

"Tin?" Marlowe kept his rapier point in front of him.

"What are you doing?" Tin stood her ground.

"I might ask you the same question."

"I'm attending to the Queen," she said firmly. "Frances placed me here, said I was the only one she trusted."

Marlowe stood, assessing the situation. On the one hand it was a good plan since all other chambermaids and ladies-in-waiting were suspect. On the other hand, Tin might be a Throckmorton ally, trained at his home to kill the most powerful monarch on the planet. Because *everyone* was suspect.

"Step away from that door," Marlowe said carefully.

Tin shook her head. "No. I have a dagger under these towels."

"I wouldn't like to kill you, Tin," Marlowe said, beginning to move toward her slowly.

"And I wouldn't like to die," she answered steadily, "but if I must, in service to the Queen, I will, protecting her with my last breath."

Marlowe stopped.

"You think you're protecting the Queen from me?" he asked.

"I know about your dubious loyalties." Tin tossed several of the towels to the floor, exposing the dagger she had in her hand. "Your sympathies are Catholic."

Marlowe lowered his rapier a bit, reassessing the situation.

"Someone will attempt to poison Her Majesty this morning," he said, failing to keep the urgency from his voice. "Frances sent me here to prevent that from happening. If you would save the Queen and serve our Lady Walsingham, tell Her Majesty what is afoot, and get her to safety. Now."

Tin stood, trying to decide what to do.

Before any decision was reached, the guard Marlowe had disabled outside rushed into the room, sword drawn.

He glared at the two others, trying to make sense of the scene.

Tin sucked in a breath.

"Is the Queen always in this chamber at this time of day?" Marlowe asked the guard.

Still confused, the guard nodded. "Every morning of the year. She sits in here for an hour or more, attended by at least one maid or lady. She has a single cup of wine to start the day, and then is off to break her fast."

Marlowe glanced toward the table. His eyes having adjusted to the light, he could see a golden goblet of wine where the royal right hand could find it easily.

"This is it, then." Marlowe nodded. "That wine. This is where the villain will strike."

"No one gets in here," the guard objected.

"Except for maids and ladies-in-waiting," Marlowe corrected, "as you've just said."

"Well, yes," he admitted.

"*That* is why I believe the deed will be attempted here, and soon," Marlowe explained. "Is there a close exit other than this door?"

The guard nodded. "Other side. Blind hallway."

"Then go," Marlowe told the guard urgently, "meet us at that exit, secure that hall!"

And the guard was gone.

"Go to Her Majesty now!" Marlowe told Tin.

"Once we're gone you should hide in this closet," she answered, "better to catch the assassin. There's a peephole. Do you know who is coming here to do this? The poison?"

"Yes." But he would not say more.

He'd been wrong about Bess Throckmorton, but it was impossible

283

for him to believe that Penelope Devereux would be the assassin. The most beautiful face in England could not be a mask.

Tin disappeared into the closet. Seconds later she tapped from the inside.

"It's clear," she whispered.

There was a rustle and a click and then silence.

Marlowe opened the door and stepped inside, trying not to think about where he was. There was, indeed, a peephole. Marlowe held his rapier at the ready, blinking through the small hole that looked like a knot in the wood. He did not have to wait long.

He heard the door to the Queen's chamber open, watched it swing in slowly. But what he saw stopped his heart; froze his blood.

There was a flash of red and the flourish of a crimson cloak.

THIRTY

Rodrigo Lopez went immediately to the Queen's dressing table, leaned over, and examined the goblet of wine. He sniffed at the rim, then reached into some inner pocket and produced a small leather bladder. He opened it, let slip several drops into the Queen's wine, and stepped back.

Marlowe's thoughts were racing, and his heart began to beat again. Buried doubts about Lopez erupted into his consciousness once more. Lopez had orchestrated the murder of Pygott to get Marlowe out of the way. Every thought of Lopez as a friend and hero seemed to be met by an equally believable fear that Lopez was a spy and a traitor.

Frizer had said as much: "Lopez is a double agent."

That might be discounted, owing to Frizer's dubious allegiance, but what had Argi said? "Dr. Lopez was not the man you thought he was. His entire life was a secret, a lie."

It had certainly been a lie that Lopez was dead.

Marlowe stilled such thoughts. He needed every nuance of his abilities to survive a deadly encounter with Lopez. Ignoring the certainty that Lopez could not be killed, Marlowe held his breath and shoved open the door to the closet.

Lopez dropped the drinking pouch, drew his dagger and rapier, and danced backward in a single elegant move.

He paused when he saw that his assailant was Marlowe.

"Chris," he said hesitantly.

Marlowe knew that Lopez would attempt to win the battle before it started, win it with words. He mustn't let Lopez speak. He knew Lopez's methods, and most of his gambits. That realization gave him heart, and some small advantage.

Without another thought, Marlowe lunged.

The tip of Marlowe's rapier actually touched Lopez's doublet before Lopez slapped it away with a gloved hand. Lopez lunged and thrust his own rapier directly for Marlowe's right shoulder.

Marlowe easily parried and launched a blinding riposte, nearly nicking Lopez's dagger hand.

For a few heartbeats their blades snapped and clicked, dazzling faster than the eye could see. That exchange ended with Marlowe moving the tip of his blade under Lopez's, twirling it to slip underneath Lopez's weapon.

The ploy worked, and Marlowe struck Lopez in the side, the left of his rib cage.

Lopez smiled.

"I had almost forgotten how good you are," he said to Marlowe.

"Your second-best student," Marlowe answered.

"Ah." Lopez nodded. "You mean Frances. Yes. She's the best."

Another ploy, Marlowe realized. Undermine confidence.

Willing himself not to think, Marlowe jumped. He flew forward without warning and crashed into Lopez. It was a wild and unpredictable move that shoved Lopez backward into the stone wall next to the outer door. The thud knocked the breath out of Lopez and Marlowe bashed the side of Lopez's head with the hilt of his dagger.

Lopez crumpled, but Marlowe did not press the advantage, wary of the move he had learned from Frances. If Lopez was on the floor, he intended to use the surrender motif, and strike Marlowe unaware.

Lopez seemed dazed, but Marlowe knew better. Keeping his distance, he moved slowly to Lopez's wounded side, just out of reach of the rapier point.

Lopez did not move his head, but his eyes followed Marlowe.

"You won't survive," Lopez said softly.

"You've come back from the dead," Marlowe answered, smiling. "Maybe I can learn that trick from you, the way I have all your others."

Lopez pushed himself up, using the wall at his back.

"You haven't learned all of my tricks," he said.

In the next instant Marlowe saw Lopez's dagger flying directly toward his face. At the same time, Lopez careened forward, rapier lunging at Marlowe's heart. It was as if two men were attacking at the same time.

Marlowe moved his head just enough to avoid the dagger. He was not so fortunate with the rapier. He parried wildly, but only managed to spoil the aim, not the thrust. The point of Lopez's sword sank into Marlowe's flesh, tearing through his side just below the rib cage.

Pain once more brought the moment into crystal focus. Marlowe watched as Lopez withdrew his blade, took a single step backward, and prepared to strike again.

Marlowe's rapier was all the way down, tip touching the floor. Lopez would deliver the death blow before his rapier could rally.

Marlowe blinked, without expectation, without emotion. He was exactly as the point of the rapier: at the instant between life and death.

Feeling his hand floating, as if coming up from under water, Marlowe grabbed his dagger. Gripping it low on the hilt he aimed not for Lopez but for the point of Lopez's rapier. He watched, in detached appreciation, when the point of the rapier passed through the filigreed hilt of his dagger, like catching a bird in a trap.

Normal time engaged once more, and Marlowe flung his dagger wide, whipping the sword out of Lopez's hand, caught in Marlowe's hilt.

Lopez only had time to gasp before Marlowe thrust the tip of his own rapier into Lopez's dagger hand, piercing it through and through.

Lopez's dagger clattered to the floor; his rapier bounced against the wall next to the Queen's dressing table. Marlowe put the point of his rapier under Lopez's chin, ready to thrust upward into the traitor's brain.

Lopez stood frozen.

"That's new," he said after a single breath, "that trick with the hilt."

"You chastised me in Cambridge for having such a visible weapon."

"Did I?" Lopez answered. "I don't remember."

Marlowe stepped forward slightly. It gave the illusion that he was pressing his rapier forward, though he was not. Lopez did not flinch.

"You may have some questions for me," Lopez said steadily. "And I for you."

"I'm not interested in speaking with a corpse." Marlowe laughed.

"I'm not quite dead yet," Lopez argued.

"I may not kill you now," Marlowe answered. "You'll be just as dead when this final betrayal is reported to Walsingham."

That, of all things, seemed to puzzle Lopez.

"What will you report?" he asked. "To whom?"

"What will I report?" Marlowe repeated incredulously. "That you attempted to poison the Queen! And Walsingham will report that *to the Queen*."

"Ah," Lopez sighed. "Let us begin to unravel the fabric of your confusion."

"I am not in the slightest confused."

"You left me on the beach. You were subsequently told I died. I did not."

"So I see."

"Don't interrupt," Lopez chided gently. "After you left, Argi and I were set upon by the strangest of assailants: Moorish *hashishim*. We would surely have been lost but for Captain de Ferro. He and his men were close at hand. They were able to kill most of the attackers, and bind our wounds. We sailed at once with five hundred of Her Majesty's troops, including the contingent of Basque separatists you encountered in Cambridge—they told me about you.

Together we upended the Spanish invasion in secret. Of course, we had to do that without alerting Parsons. Am I correct in assuming that he still thinks his plan is in place?"

Marlowe swallowed.

"I thought as much," Lopez continued. "Without going into great detail, we were able to prevent the Duke of Guise from mustering his Spanish legions. That part of the Throckmorton plot has been dismantled."

Marlowe knew better than to believe Lopez. A man at the point of a rapier would say almost anything to escape it.

"I saw you put the poison into the Queen's cup," Marlowe accused. "There's a peephole in that closet."

Lopez closed his eyes. "That's not poison, Chris."

"I don't believe you."

"Hand me that pouch and I'll prove it."

Marlowe's eyes flashed to the small leather pouch that Lopez had dropped on the floor. That proved to be a mistake. The instant Marlowe's eyes were averted, Lopez moved his head half an inch backward and swatted Marlowe's rapier away.

Marlowe recovered, but it was too late. Lopez sank to the floor, rolled, and retrieved his own weapon. When he was standing once again, he was also holding the leather pouch.

"Now," he said.

Without hesitation he drank from the pouch.

Marlowe gaped.

Lopez's face contorted.

A second later, he said, "It tastes terrible. But it's not poison. Quite the opposite, in fact. Will you put your sword away?"

Marlowe continued to stare.

"Well, at least do you mind if I put mine away?" Lopez sheathed his rapier while he was asking the question.

"What is in that pouch?" Marlowe managed to ask, lowering his blade.

"Something I concocted," Lopez answered, "to detect the presence of poisons in food or drink. It has proved quite useful to Her

Majesty and, incidentally, saved the lives of several of the royal food tasters."

"It's not poison," Marlowe said slowly.

"It *detects* poison," Lopez told him.

Marlowe looked to the Queen's goblet. "And?"

"Oh, that wine has definitely been poisoned. Have a look. It's turned a lovely shade of green."

Warily Marlowe moved to the Queen's table and stared down into the goblet. The liquid there was, indeed, the color of light jade.

"Someone has already poisoned this wine," Marlowe said slowly.

"Yes."

"But how did you know Her Majesty was to be poisoned this way? I only learned—"

"I've been testing everything the Queen eats or drinks for some time now," was all Lopez would say. "Who else was in this room when you came in? One of the ladies?"

"No, only the—it was—Christ!"

Marlowe would not believe it, but some voice in his brain forced him to say it: Tin *had* attempted to poison the Queen.

"Through here!" Marlowe shouted. "Her majesty's with a chambermaid and a single guard."

He tore into the closet, through the room, and out the opposite door. He could hear Lopez behind him. They burst into an outer hallway. It stretched fifty feet in either direction.

Lopez brushed by Marlowe.

"This way," he whispered. "The guard would take them to an eastern gallery. Lots of light."

Not quite knowing what that meant, Marlowe dashed after Lopez. Down several more long corridors, their boots echoed against the bare stone walls. A final turn presented them with an open gallery crowned with high windows. Light was everywhere. The walls were covered with blazing tapestries, images of fire and phoenix, and the floors were softened by large rugs of Arabian design. There was no furniture, nothing else in the room.

The Queen was not immediately in evidence, but the guard who'd been standing outside her dressing chamber was at the door, sword drawn. And next to him was a young man in gray costume. Its headpiece obscured all but the eyes.

Marlowe knew Tin at once, and stopped short.

Tin was armed, rapier and dagger. She threw her head back and the cowl fell away, revealing her face, and the fire in her eyes.

"I couldn't maneuver in that damned dress," she complained.

The guard shrugged. "I have no idea what this is all about, but this person and I stand alone guarding Her Majesty."

Lopez moved into the room, sheathed his rapier, and went to the tapestry of a phoenix warring with a dragon. There was a grating of stone and wood, and then silence.

Marlowe stared at Tin. She met his gaze with equal strength. He was utterly unable to read anything in her eyes. His eyes widened, and he opened his mouth to say something, but was interrupted by a chaos of noise coming down the outer corridor. Marlowe turned immediately and stepped in between the guard and Tin, ready to defend the entrance to the room with his life.

Frances appeared from around the corner, dragging Carier in one hand and Penelope Devereux in the other. They were both complaining, but unable to extract themselves from Frances's iron grip. Behind that trio were several guards, Walsingham's personal men.

As Frances drew closer, she saw Tin, and slowed.

"You must stand aside," she said to the guard, not looking at Marlowe or Tin. "I would see the Queen."

Marlowe was the first to sheath his weapons.

From behind he heard the grating of wood and stone once more, and then the booming voice of Lopez.

"Her Majesty is unharmed," he announced rather formally, "and it is her wish, Lady Walsingham, that you should enter this room with the baggage you have in tow."

The guard stood aside. Marlowe acknowledged with a flourish of his right hand that Frances and her prey must precede him into the room. Tin, weapons still drawn, stood amazed.

As Frances strode through the room, pulling her captives with her, the guard who had followed her came to Tin. She realized then that she must put away her weapons.

Clearly at a loss, she began to speak, but Marlowe ignored her, following Frances into the room beyond the tapestry. The guards escorted Tin behind him.

Instead of the Queen, Lord Walsingham emerged from behind a heavy wooden table. He was dressed in a long flowing deep blue robe held at the neck by a crisp white frilly collar and crowned with a black skullcap. His beard seemed carved from black and gray stone.

Not waiting for her father to speak, Frances took several steps toward him, face flushed, voice thick.

"It was not Bess Throckmorton," she growled. "I told you it wasn't. It was Penelope."

With that she thrust Penelope Devereux forward, keeping a tight grip on Carier.

Penelope nearly tumbled, caught herself, and sucked in a breath. It was obvious that she had been crying, and was only composed at that moment through great effort.

"Is this true?" Walsingham asked simply. "Did you pour poison into Her Majesty's cup?"

"No!" Penelope wailed. "It was a purgative! Tell them, Benjamin. I wanted—my desire was to induce an illness in Her Majesty and then come to her with the cure. It was all planned. This man, Benjamin Carier, he was helping me—along with a churchman, a bishop."

"The Jesuit Robert Parsons," Walsingham said.

"Yes!"

"Why did you wish to attack our Queen in such a manner?" Walsingham asked, staring Penelope in the eye.

"You know why," she snapped bitterly.

"Do I?" he asked.

"I love Philip, you know that!" she wailed, letting loose her well of tears. "And she forced me to marry Robert Rich! She ended my life!"

"The Countess of Huntingdon proposed your marriage to Robert Rich," Walsingham responded. "Not Her Majesty."

"No!" Penelope was verging on hysteria, an odd, uncomfortable display in a courtly room. "The Queen did it. She did it because my mother married Robert Dudley and the Queen wanted Robert Dudley for her own! She did it to punish my mother!"

"I hardly see how your marriage to the first Earl of Warwick, a very wealthy man, is a punishment. The Tower is a punishment. Torture is a punishment. Slow death is—but what exactly was your plan, Lady Rich?"

Penelope was visibly stung by the use of that title, and she collapsed to her knees, her gown around her like a sea in which she was drowning.

"The Queen would be sick," Penelope said weakly, "and I would cure her. She would be grateful. As she has been to Dr. Lopez under similar circumstances. She would release me from my prison, my Rich prison."

"Ridiculous puppet!" Walsingham exploded.

Everyone in the room was taken aback by the force of that voice.

"You have been duped by our enemies," he continued. "You poured poison into Her Majesty's cup, deadly poison!"

"Poison?" She raised her head, barely able to comprehend what Walsingham had said.

Carier shook his head violently.

"No," he protested, "no. It wasn't poison. I know it wasn't. Robert Parsons told me what it was: a mild purgative, something to disrupt the Queen's digestion."

"Robert Parsons is a traitorous monster," Walsingham said calmly, "and my men will have him soon. He has made you his ignorant accomplices in a vile plot to kill the Queen and take the country."

"Penelope is also responsible for betraying me at Coughton,"

Frances interjected. "Walter Pygott did not find me out—she did. She told Pygott."

Walsingham's face grew dark with barely controlled rage. "Take her."

Two guards flew into the room; each took an arm, and Penelope Devereux was dragged away. She could not form coherent words, only soft sobbing sounds.

Marlowe watched her as she went, stupefied. It was only by chance that he happened to catch the look in Tin's eye. It was a look of abject horror.

Just as Marlowe began piecing together what that look meant, Walsingham forged ahead.

"And now for you, sir," Walsingham said, bringing his eyes to focus on Carier.

"This man," Frances trumpeted, shoving Carier to the floor, "is a traitor to his country and the murderer of Walter Pygott."

Carier yelped like a small dog.

"Wait," Marlowe interrupted, "I believe I have been in error concerning Benjamin Carier. He did not, in fact, murder Walter Pygott."

Frances turned to Marlowe, brow furrowed.

"The mistake was entirely mine," Marlowe went on. "Carier is almost certainly an innocent dupe in this entire affair. He is a secret Catholic. That much is true. But he had no idea what was in the packages he delivered to Penelope Devereux, no more than Penelope did. They were both manipulated by William Allen, whom, I fear, may already have left London."

Everyone in the room stared at Marlowe. Frances was the first to find her voice.

"Carier did not kill Pygott?" she asked.

"No." Marlowe sighed.

"Do you know who did?" Walsingham demanded.

"You're not going to like it," Marlowe answered. "It's someone we all know."

No one in the room moved.

"Well?" Walsingham boomed.

"Walter Pygott was murdered by Ingram Frizer." Marlowe nodded once. "He is a double agent, but not for us. He works with Allen and Parsons. He killed Pygott with the intention of blaming me for the crime, which he did, thus eliminating me from the picture. I failed to cooperate. Frizer is here in London, and should be easy to find. I saw him in the garden at Fulham less than an hour ago. He can't have gone far."

"Ingram Frizer killed Walter Pygott," Walsingham confirmed slowly. "Is that what you would have me believe?"

"Yes." Marlowe stood very still.

"And you are certain that Frizer has turned against us?"

"Completely."

"Well." Walsingham sniffed. "Then we shall have to fetch him. Now then, Benjamin Carier, you are detained."

Without further utterance from the Queen's spymaster, guards dragged Carier away.

"No," he wailed as he left, "I can't be detained. I have my year-end examinations!"

When the room was silent once more, Walsingham spoke again.

"Dr. Lopez, Mr. Marlowe," he began, "you have done a great service to England. I give you leave to refresh yourselves and tend to your wounds."

"They are of little consequence," Lopez assured him.

"Then you are to meet in my official rooms. Shall we say an hour? I would discuss these events; one or two small items must be clarified. And I will also present a more significant demonstration of Her Majesty's gratitude."

He turned at once—a strange, sudden move—and vanished behind a dragon tapestry. Guards went with him.

Frances, Lopez, Tin, and Marlowe were left to themselves. The air was filled with a palpable tension. Only the eyes moved.

"Ingram Frizer did not kill Walter Pygott," Frances whispered finally.

"No," Marlowe admitted. "He did not."

"But he is a double agent for the Spanish," Lopez suggested.

"Perhaps." Marlowe shrugged. "Hard to tell."

"Are you going to tell me who did kill Pygott?" Frances demanded.

In answer, Marlowe bent over and retrieved something from the small pocket inside his boot. He stood up and turned to Tin.

"I happened to notice that you had a button missing from that silver jacket of yours," he told Tin calmly.

He held out his hand and produced the dull brass button, a perfect match for the others on Tin's jacket.

Frances could not stifle a sudden breath.

"Wait." Tin was careful not to move. "That's been missing for weeks."

"Yes. But I only noticed it missing from your jacket a few moments ago."

"Where did you get it?" Tin's blush was deepening.

"It was pressed into the ground in the garden outside of St. Benet's. In Cambridge."

Tin closed her eyes.

"It was pressed into the ground by the weight of a dead body," Marlowe went on. "Walter Pygott's dead body."

Tin's breathing was noticeably louder.

"Tin?" Frances stared.

Tin looked away.

"I also see that your jacket is frayed at the elbow," Marlowe went on softly. "I believe I found the place in St. Benet's wall where you left some of the missing threads."

"I thought that Walter Pygott had betrayed Frances." Tin's voice was barely audible, her eyes were still closed. "And I heard the vile things he said about you every day at Coughton. When I discovered—thought I discovered—his treachery, I followed him to Cambridge. He didn't know who I was. He was a remarkably ignorant boy."

"You fought," Marlowe prompted.

"He denied knowing that Frances was *Richard*"— Tin nodded— "but he had more odious things to say about Frances. I drew my sword. He drew his. It didn't take long. He was dead before I knew it. Dead on the grounds of a church, beside some roses."

Marlowe looked at Frances, whose face was drained of all color.

"I love you, Frances," Tin murmured, opening her eyes at last. "When you were taken, I could not bear it. When I learned that you were so far away, in Malta, I lost my mind. You must believe me this: I was as much a prisoner in that place as you. My heart and my brain and my fevered dreams were all with you on that island, in that cell. Can you understand that? I love you."

Tin's eyes were filled with tears.

"That," Marlowe said softly, "is why I could not reveal that she's the one who murdered Pygott."

"Yes," Frances rasped, "but why on earth did you tell my father that Frizer was the murderer?"

Marlowe drew in a slow breath.

"Difficult to say." He looked at the floor. "Tin did what she did for you. I can understand that better than anyone else on the planet. The instant I knew that she had done it, I couldn't let her die for it. But I needed someone to be guilty. Frizer's a traitor. Hardly innocent. Now the authorities will forget about me. And Walter Pygott is just as dead either way."

"I killed Walter Pygott." Tin sobbed once, as if she had only then realized her crime. Unable to control herself, she sank to the floor.

Frances rushed to her, knelt beside her, cradling her head. She looked up at Marlowe.

"This may be the best thing you've done in your life," she said, her eyes filled with a terrible gratitude, "saving this girl."

"Although I'm not certain that lying to your father was the *wisest* thing I've ever done," Marlowe answered.

"About that," Lopez said, breaking his silence. "You and I must go now and prepare to meet with Lord Walsingham. We have much to discuss beforehand, and I am in dire need of wine and food."

Marlowe turned to Lopez.

"I'm *famished*," he told the doctor.

"Then come with me," Lopez told him, heading for the door.

Marlowe followed, not looking back. He was, however, haunted by the sound of sobbing, and soft whispered comfort, even as the door closed behind him.

THIRTY-ONE

Lopez hurried down the corridor toward the smell of baking bread.

"You were lucky," he said softly to Marlowe.

"In what regard?" Marlowe asked, distracted by the prospect of food.

"A button is a very tiny thing upon which to hang a murder," Lopez told him.

Marlowe took a moment to examine the side of Lopez's face. The man looked ten years older than the last time Marlowe had seen him. And there was a barely healed cut across his jaw, the kind a dagger would make.

"Well," Marlowe allowed, "the possibility of Tin's being the killer had been building in my mind for some time. First, I systematically eliminated all other suspects."

"By which you mean you guessed incorrectly several times."

"Yes," Marlowe plunged ahead, "but one of the suspects, Father Edmund, was a witness to the murder, as it turns out, and offered a few salient observations about the murderer."

"To wit?"

"He saw an oddly dressed hooded figure with yellow hair."

"Hardly a perfect portrait."

"Yes," Marlowe agreed, "but Tin's manner of dress, when she's parading as a boy, is singular—all that gray."

"Possibly."

"And there is the observation, also from Edmund, that the attack on Pygott was particularly vicious. A simple murder for elimination would require stealth and speed, not ire."

Lopez nodded slowly.

"*And* the killer did not take the Rheims-Douai Bible, which was the prize. It contained a coded message outlining certain parts of this Throckmorton plot. Pygott was not killed for it."

They rounded a corner. The smell of bread was almost overwhelming.

"Then you found the button."

"Yes," Marlowe said dismissively, walking faster toward what he assumed would be a kitchen, "but *clues* were not as important as my instinct."

Lopez slowed. "What?"

Marlowe took Lopez by the arm, urging him forward.

"Instinct," Marlowe repeated. "Tin would have done anything for Frances. That was obvious. When we locked eyes, Tin and I, an understanding passed between us. In later contemplation I realized that I would kill anyone who tried to harm Frances, so Tin would do the same."

Lopez shook his head. "I wouldn't put too much stock in that sort of thing."

"It produced a confession," Marlowe snapped. "Walk faster. I'm famished."

Within the hour, Lopez and Marlowe had eaten, washed their faces, smoothed ruffled clothing, and presented themselves to Lord Walsingham. Absent all guards, the three men stood in a large room bereft of tapestries or hiding places. There was a blinding array of candles, and several windows high above them let in the morning light. An enormous rug designed like a forest floor covered the stones beneath their feet. Several tables lined the walls.

Walsingham had changed his clothing for some reason. He wore a grand dark purple robe, fit for important courtly business, and a small but crisp ruffled collar. The skullcap had been replaced by a ceremonial miter.

"Christopher Marlowe," Walsingham announced formally, "the Queen, in gratitude for your service to her person and to our country, hereby wishes to award you the rank of commander in the Royal Navy, with a salary of two hundred pounds per annum."

Marlowe swallowed, trying to find the perfect words to reject such an offer.

"Don't worry, my friend," Lopez said, smiling, "I have already informed Lord Walsingham of your discomfort with the water. There will be very little actual sailing involved in this. It is a figurative appointment."

"You will, of course, continue your study at Cambridge," Walsingham added.

"But," Marlowe began, at a loss.

"You have acquitted yourself most admirably over the course of the past several weeks," Walsingham said quickly.

"As I said you would," Lopez interjected.

"Yes," Walsingham continued, "and to that end, you must know the true meaning of my offer."

Marlowe took a moment, but it was not to think. He had the dizzy feeling that he was in some odd play, the jest of an unfathomable God.

Lopez mistook Marlowe's silence for hesitation.

"You are to be Lord Walsingham's chief investigator in London," he explained. "When certain affairs of state present themselves—"

"By which he means to say," Walsingham interrupted impatiently, "murders that have any sort of affiliation with the Queen's business—"

"You will be charged with finding the murderer," Lopez concluded, "and rectifying the situation."

Marlowe nodded. "I have no idea what either of you is saying. I have to return to Cambridge. I have year-end examinations."

Walsingham tossed his hand grandly. "You've already passed those, Mr. Marlowe. You're on to your next year of study. You have a bit of free time now to reflect, and to gather your strength for your coming duties."

"I passed my—how is that—Bartholomew," Marlowe said, nearly to himself. "He *is* your man. He saw to this."

Walsingham raised his eyebrows, but did not comment further.

"Well, Chris?" Lopez prompted.

"I'm to be a royal—what was it? A royal investigator?" he answered weakly.

"*The* royal investigator," Walsingham corrected.

"With an annual salary," Marlowe continued.

"Not to mention," Walsingham added, "the usual allowance for necessities: food, better clothing, several residences, of course."

"Of course," Marlowe agreed.

"You will play the part, here in London, of a carousing poet and playwright," Lopez told him.

"Of course," Marlowe repeated. "What else? The best actors play what they know."

"Exactly," Lopez concluded, unable to stifle a grin.

Marlowe shifted his weight, and looked around the room.

"This would, I suppose, offer me the opportunity to see more of Frances," he ventured.

"No," Walsingham answered immediately. "You are to have no further contact with my daughter. The risk is too great."

Before Marlowe could prevail upon Walsingham to explain the meaning of that risk, a guard entered and strode quickly to Walsingham, handing him a note.

"Ah," Walsingham sighed, reading the note. "We have Frizer."

Marlowe looked down at the rug, as if studying its pattern, to avoid eye contact with anyone.

"We have informed the authorities in Cambridge, and here in London, of his guilt in the matter of Walter Pygott's death," Walsingham told Marlowe briskly.

Marlowe nodded. "Good. What will happen to him?"

"To Frizer?" Walsingham asked. "We'll find something for him. He's been a good double for us, and will be again."

"He's not to be tried for the murder?"

"As he did not actually kill Pygott, I feel that would be unjust," Walsingham said, not looking at Marlowe. "Would you agree?"

"I—how did you—but—sir," Marlowe stammered.

"Well, then," Walsingham said, "there's an end to it."

The guard moved to escort Marlowe and Lopez from the room.

"Sir," Marlowe began.

"Dr. Lopez will continue his good instruction in these matters, young man," Walsingham said absently. "He has already agreed."

With that, Walsingham headed for one of the tables in the corner of the room, on to other matters of state.

Marlowe and Lopez were outside, strolling along the edges of the bowling green, before they spoke again. The morning air was soft, filled, at last, with the assurance of spring. The sunlight slanted hard and golden, impossible to look at directly.

"Does he know that Tin murdered Pygott?" Marlowe whispered.

Lopez shrugged. "Frances told him, wouldn't you think?"

Marlowe nodded slowly. "You know, for a brief moment, I suspected that you killed Pygott. Another test of my abilities."

Lopez avoided looking at Marlowe. "That would have been very clever of me."

Marlowe studied his friend's face, but nothing was given away.

"What do you suppose will happen to Tin?" Marlowe asked at length.

"Again," Lopez said, a little impatiently, "Frances will take care of that."

"Frances," Marlowe moaned softly. "How am I going to manage without her?"

"Manage?" Lopez glared at Marlowe. "What do you mean?"

"I love her, Rodrigo."

"Frances Walsingham?" Lopez shook his head. "I thought you loved Penelope."

Marlowe stopped walking. "Well, it's difficult *not* to love Penelope, despite what she's done. I mean, you've seen her."

"Ah." Lopez smiled and resumed his stroll.

"No, but I," Marlowe began, catching up, "I'm confused."

Lopez looked him up and down. "Confused in love? The perpetual state of the modern young man."

"What would you know about love?" he chided. "You're dead."

Lopez held up his hand. "Listen, my friend, there is a great advantage in being dead for a while. I've done it several times before. You should consider it if ever your arrangement with Walsingham gets out of hand."

"Don't be ridiculous," Marlowe countered. "What could possibly go wrong? It's an agreement with the Queen!"

Lopez looked away. "I have several agreements with Her Majesty. They all trouble me."

"Well, this won't trouble me," Marlowe answered lightly.

"You'll be trying to find the most clever murderers and assassins on the planet, Chris," Lopez warned. "I think you'll find that you need every trick there is."

"Speaking of which," Marlowe answered, careless of Lopez's warning, "it was very clever of you to use Argi and his men to attack Allen's Spanish forces. I was completely fooled: I mistook them for Basque separatists. That's the way Allen was fooled."

"Oh, you were not mistaken," Lopez said. "Not entirely. They are very much agents for their own cause. But they were *also* useful to us. The best lies are the ones that are also true."

"Wait," Marlowe said, slowing again, trying to absorb what Lopez had said. "They were working for you *and* for the Basque cause?"

Lopez only nodded, but a sudden idea sparked in Marlowe's brain.

"Wait a moment," Marlowe said slowly. "You were nearly killed by Moorish fighters, men whom you called *hashishim*."

"Yes, I wondered when you would ask me about them. Some of them were the men who tried to kill you and Boyle, I'm certain of that. They were Spanish assigns."

"Spanish," Marlowe muttered to himself, shaking his head.

"Do you have any idea how long the Moors ruled Spain?" Lopez began.

"They were not sent from Pygott's father?" Marlowe snapped.

"They allowed John Pygott to think so, and to pay them," Lopez answered, "but they were primarily agents of Spain."

"The Basque working for England, the Bedouin working for Spain—it's madness!"

"Yes, but consider your forged identity in this business with Walsingham. You are to play the part of a quarrelsome, headstrong poet. The fact that you *are* a quarrelsome, headstrong poet makes it entirely believable. You make the truth look like a lie, when in fact the lie is true."

Marlowe stopped altogether.

"I'll never be able to do this," he said.

Lopez kept walking. "You already do it. When you tell a girl to come with you and be your love, do you actually intend to live with her, singing and dancing all May? Or is that just something you've written to entice her into your bed?"

The distance between Lopez and Marlowe widened.

"You've read my poem," Marlowe called out.

"Everyone's read your poem, Chris," Lopez answered, still walking. "That's why this will work."

"But I actually do mean it," Marlowe said, "when I write it. It's true when I say I am in love."

"The best lies," Lopez repeated, "are the ones that are also true."

Marlowe watched Lopez walk away until the doctor disappeared behind a stand of trees.

Then, without any warning whatsoever, Marlowe had the sensation that everything he'd ever done, would ever do, was nothing more than the insubstantial creation of God's pen. He knew he was not a passionate shepherd, and would never live with any girl, and be her love.

He knew, in that moment, that he was an agent for the Queen. It would be his life, a role written for him by a laughing God on pages of sunlight, with ink of darkest night.

THIRTY-TWO

Christopher Marlowe stared across the lawn from beneath the tower of St. Benet's Church. The summer was warm; the roses in the graveyard were still blooming. He sat on a small stone bench, composing a letter.

Dear Father,

I write in answer to your most recent queries. I am in good health, I acquitted myself quite well in my year-end examinations, and I remain in Cambridge to get an early start on my second year, for reasons too elaborate to discuss in this short note.

Gossip travels faster than my letter ever could, so you may already know much of what this missive will tell you. The barest facts are these. Throckmorton is to be executed. Incriminating documents—communications between Catholic villains on the continent, Mary so-called *Queen* of Scots, and the Spanish ambassador Bernardino de Mendoza—were found in Throckmorton's house. And after sufficient torture on the rack, he confessed. Mendoza has been expelled from England, and we are to have no more Spanish ambassadors in our country, thank God. Mary is under permanent confinement at Chartley Hall in Staffordshire.

Though I am not at liberty to tell you the full extent of my adventures with Dr. Lopez, I will say that he has proved to be, as you said he would, my great teacher and true friend. Partly owing to his hand in stopping the invasion led by the Duke of Guise, he has at last been awarded the position he so rightly deserves. He is the Queen's First Physician.

As to my part in these matters, I will only say that it is a story best told in person, which I will do when I come home for Christmas. Except that I must ask you a strange question. Are you somehow acquainted with Lord Walsingham or, more specifically, his daughter, Frances? I ask because she undertook to call me "Kit" on several occasions. As you are the progenitor of that appellation, and the only other person who has ever used it, I wonder if you two have met. Something else to discuss at Christmas.

Until then I remain your devoted and loving son,

Kit

P.S. I have included in this envelope the poem I have been working on. It's not finished. They never are. I hope it amuses you:

THE PASSIONATE SHEPHERD

Come live with me and be my love,
And we will all the pleasures prove
That hills and valleys, dales and fields,
Woods, or steepy mountain yields.

And we will sit upon the rocks,
Seeing the shepherds feed their flocks
By shallow rivers, to whose falls
Melodious birds sing madrigals.

And I will make thee beds of roses
And a thousand fragrant posies;
A cap of flowers, and a kirtle
Embroidered all with leaves of myrtle;

A gown made of the finest wool
Which from our pretty lambs we pull;
Fair-lined slippers for the cold,
With buckles of the purest gold;

A belt of straw and ivy-buds,
With coral clasps and amber-studs:
And if these pleasures may thee move,
Come live with me, and be my love.

The shepherd-swains shall dance and sing
For thy delight each May-morning:
If these delights thy mind may move,
Then live with me and be my love.

A FEW OF THE HISTORICAL PERSONAGES

1. Christopher Marlowe (1564–1593) was arguably the foremost playwright of his day. He was certainly a great influence on Shakespeare, who only came to prominence after Marlowe's suspicious death at a public house in Deptford.
2. Sir Francis Walsingham (1532–1590) was Queen Elizabeth's first secretary from 1573 until his death, and is the man for whom the term *spymaster* was invented.
3. Frances Walsingham, Countess of Essex and Countess of Clanricarde (1567–1633), was the daughter of Francis Walsingham. She became the wife of poet Philip Sidney when she turned sixteen. Her second husband was Robert Devereux, 2nd Earl of Essex, one of Queen Elizabeth's favorites. After Devereux's execution in 1601 Frances married Richard Burke, 4th Earl of Clanricarde. She died in Ireland.
4. Sir Francis Throckmorton (1554–1584) was a conspirator against Queen Elizabeth. Educated in Oxford, he traveled to the continent often, meeting with Catholic expatriates from England, mostly in Spain and France. Sometime between 1580 and 1583, in Paris, he met Charles Paget and Thomas Morgan, agents of Mary, Queen of Scots, and the Throckmorton Plot began.
5. Elizabeth Throckmorton, Lady Raleigh (1565–1647), the conspirator's cousin, became Sir Walter Raleigh's wife in a hidden ceremony in 1591. She had been a Lady of the Privy Chamber to the Queen, but the secret marriage resulted in great enmity between the Queen and Raleigh for many years.

6. Dr. Rodrigo Lopez (1525–1594) was a Portuguese physician who served Queen Elizabeth. He was the likely inspiration for Marlowe's play *The Jew of Malta,* and Shakespeare's Shylock. At the beginning of 1593, Lopez was a wealthy and respected royal physician. Toward the end of that year Robert Devereux accused Lopez of conspiring with Spanish Catholics to poison the Queen. Lopez was convicted in February of 1594, and subsequently hanged, drawn, and quartered.

7. Richard Boyle, 1st Earl of Cork (1566–1643) was Lord Treasurer of the Kingdom of Ireland. He was born in Canterbury and went to The King's School with Marlowe and then Corpus Christi College, Cambridge, England, in 1583. Eventually on the Privy Council and a Member of Parliament, Boyle has been called the first colonial millionaire.

8. Ingram Frizer (exact dates unknown) is primarily known as the man who killed Christopher Marlowe. Marlowe, Frizer, and several others were at a public house owned by Eleanor Bull. There was an argument about who would pay the bill, and Frizer stabbed Marlowe in the eye with Marlowe's own knife. The circumstances of that event, however, remain so greatly suspect (the dead man's face was too bloody to identify; Frizer was never indicted for the crime) that conspiracy theories abound. A favorite insists that Marlowe faked his own death, possibly in service to the Privy Council or even the Queen. It has even been suggested that after this "death" Marlowe began to supply a little-known London newcomer with plays, beginning with *Romeo and Juliet, A Midsummer Night's Dream,* and *The Merchant of Venice.*